Beginning the World Again

Also by Roberta Silman

The Dream Dredger (novel)
Boundaries (novel)
Blood Relations (stories)
Somebody Else's Child (for children)

Beginning the

Roberta Silman

· ·

World Again

Viking

VIKING
Published by the Penguin Group
Viking Penguin, a division of Penguin Books USA Inc.,
375 Hudson Street, New York, New York 10014, U.S.A.
Penguin Books Ltd, 27 Wrights Lane, London W8 5TZ, England
Penguin Books Australia Ltd, Ringwood, Victoria, Australia
Penguin Books Canada Ltd, 2801 John Street, Markham, Ontario, Canada L3R 1B4
Penguin Books (N.Z.) Ltd, 182–190 Wairau Road, Auckland 10, New Zealand

Penguin Books Ltd, Registered Offices: Harmondsworth, Middlesex, England

First published in 1990 by Viking Penguin, a division of Penguin Books USA Inc.

10 9 8 7 6 5 4 3 2 1

Grateful acknowledgment is made for permission to reprint excerpts from the
following copyrighted works:
    Letters and Papers from Prison, Revised and Enlarged Edition, by Dietrich
Bonhoeffer. Reprinted with permission of Macmillan Publishing Company and SCM
Press Ltd. Copyright © 1971 SCM Press Ltd. Translation copyright ©
SCM Press, 1953, 1967, 1971.
    Robert Oppenheimer, Letters and Recollections, edited by Alice Kimball Smith
and Charles Weiner, Harvard University Press, 1980.

LIBRARY OF CONGRESS CATALOGING IN PUBLICATION DATA
Silman, Roberta.
    Beginning the world again / Roberta Silman.
       p.   cm.
    ISBN 0-670-83062-3
    1. Manhattan Project (U.S.)—History—Fiction.   2. Wives—New
Mexico—Los Alamos—History—Fiction.   3. Los Alamos (N.M.)—
History—Fiction.   I. Title.
PS3569.I45B44   1990
813'.54—dc20   90-50053

Printed in the United States of America
Set in Sabon

For Bob

Author's Note
• • • ∎

This is a work of fiction. Because many of the events in this novel are historical ones, however, a word of explanation is necessary. Several of the minor characters—like Robert Oppenheimer and General Leslie Groves and Enrico Fermi—are real people and are referred to by their real names even when they are occasionally found in invented situations. Other than these historical figures, the characters of this novel, except one, are invented, and are not intended to portray any real people, although there may be some similarities between them and one or more real people who were at Los Alamos during those historic years. The exception is Erik Traugott; there is a clear and deliberate resemblance between him and the great scientist and humanist Niels Bohr.

By its very nature a novel like this is dependent on many historical works. Among the ones that meant the most to me were *The Making of the Atomic Bomb* by Richard Rhodes, *Brighter Than a Thousand Suns* by Robert Jungk, *Day One* by Peter Wyden, *Dietrich Bonhoeffer* by Eberhard Bethge, *Alsos* by Samuel Goudsmit, and *Robert Oppenheimer, Letters and Recollections,* edited by Alice Kimball Smith and Charles Weiner.

In order to get the background I needed to create the characters in this novel, I met with several people who had been at Los Alamos in the early 1940s. They were extraordinarily helpful and kind. Because the views expressed in this book are mine alone, however, I feel it would be inappropriate to thank them by name. But I do want them to know how grateful I am for their time and energy.

I would also like to thank the John Simon Guggenheim Memorial Foundation and the National Endowment for the Arts for their support during the early years of my research for this novel; my husband, Robert Silman, to whom the book is dedicated and without whom I could never have written it; our children, Miriam, Joshua, and Ruth, for their understanding and encouragement; my sister, Victoria Fisher, for being there; my agent, Philippa Brophy, for her unflagging faith in this novel and my ability to write it; my editor, Pamela Dorman, for her intelligence, patience, and thorough understanding of what I wanted to do; and Katherine Griggs, my copyeditor, for her painstaking attention to detail.

The ultimate question for a responsible man to ask is not how he is to extricate himself heroically from the affair, but how the coming generation is to live.

—Dietrich Bonhoeffer

Though in many of its aspects this visible world seems formed in love, the invisible spheres were formed in fright.

Who aint a slave? Tell me that.

—Ishmael, in
Herman Melville's
Moby Dick

February 1982

1

There were so many things I didn't know when we were at Los Alamos: that memory cannot be controlled and has a will of its own; that a chain of events has continuous consequences; and that fame, even limited or dubious fame, is a second skin. Unlike a piece of clothing that can be shrugged off or folded and put away for a time, fame becomes part of you; it hugs and imprisons you and can never be shed—not even years and years after the fact.

So far Peter and I have been lucky in this Vermont village. That's one of the reasons we return each year. For here Peter is as anonymous as the next man.

Another reason we come back is the landscape. When we were at Los Alamos, people insisted that the Southwest was the most beautiful place on earth. Probably because of the light and the sky and the sense of space.

Yet that Southwest landscape had a strange, almost frightening severity. Everything was on such a grand scale that you felt as if you were living not in the world but at the edge of the universe. Whereas here in northern Vermont we feel as if we've come home.

Soon the cross-country ski trail winds through a stand of hemlocks; with no sun to soften it, the surface has slicked to a streak of ice. My muscles tense. I hate to ski on ice, I've always hated it, and now it's not so easy to sit down and tumble into a fall. Yet I used to do that with no trouble at all—when the children were small and flying past me, their skis like sleds beneath their supple bodies, their eyes daring danger.

"Come on, Lily, let's not fight the ice," Peter suddenly urges, then extends his arm and pulls me off the trail. Here in the woods are more than two feet of old, caked snow.

"Are you planning to murder me?"

He laughs. "Hardly. Just keep moving and you'll be fine. Up ahead someone's broken a trail. We can follow that." Before long the narrow woods trail dips and bends, and we are skiing from one glade of sunlight to another. The soughing of the wind is broken by distant ripples of laughter or an occasional shout. I open my jacket, grateful for the breeze. Peter zigzags in and out of sight, never breaking stride. Sometimes, after he has taught for a whole week, he looks his age, but here, still slim and graceful as he skis, he has shed years.

Now I am in a cul-de-sac that the wind cannot invade, so quiet I can hear myself breathe. Tatters of blue sky fly above trees that look like giant soldiers at attention, outlandish, skinny soldiers with pine-needled heads. Then I hear, "Lily?" I hurry from the thicket of pines. "Over here," he calls, and I see her.

"I got separated from my family, and your husband was kind enough to let me ski with him," she apologizes. She has large brown eyes and beautiful teeth and curly brown hair. Tiny droplets of perspiration glisten on her firm young neck. She reminds me of our daughter, Anne. "I hope you don't mind."

"No, of course not. Peter's the best bushwhacker you'll ever meet," I tell her, and the three of us begin to ski again. Soon we can see the marked trail. Peter skis down to it.

"It's not nearly as icy here," he reports as the young woman and I pick our way down the slope. As I concentrate to get a rhythm going, I see she's not an experienced skier, and now she's asking Peter to show her how to stop.

"The trick is to start slowly and not let yourself get going too fast." Then Peter shows her how to hold her arms and knees. He's delighted; he loves nothing more than to teach, and she is a willing student. At the end of the trail her face is glowing with pleasure.

"You saved my life, you've taught me how to stop, and I don't even know your names," she says.

"Lily, Peter," Peter replies. No last names on skiing and hiking trails. His old rule.

"Hope. Hope Eliason."

Peter nods abruptly, one of the few hangovers from his European upbringing, and we part. But something tells me we haven't seen the last of her.

That evening, while we are consulting our menus, Hope Eliason appears at Peter's elbow, this time with her husband, Ted. She looks even lovelier than she did this afternoon, and Peter's eyes take in her pretty red blouse and milky skin. Her husband looks at us with a question in his eyes, and I can feel myself growing wary. Do they know who we are? I wonder as Peter carries the conversation, then I think about what they see:

A tall, thin man, perhaps touching seventy, white-haired, balding, with strong features, a largish nose and bad teeth, which nonetheless have never prevented him from smiling broadly when he's pleased. And large, expressive hands that often gesture when he speaks. But most outstanding are his vibrant, purplish-blue eyes that refuse to age and that shine with his extraordinary intelligence. Blue eyes that can go strangely flat when he's uncomfortable or bored or angry, but that have countless layers when he's interested or when he's enjoying himself, as he is now.

And me? A small gray-haired woman in her early sixties, who

refuses as stubbornly as a teenager to give up her hair and wears it in a topknot that is never as neat as it should be. A face that is worn, though not nearly as worn as the faces of many of her contemporaries, so that when she's not with her husband she's taken for younger than she is. A still-trim woman more conscious than she ever dreamed she would be of the onset of age, who chooses her clothes carefully and has begun to wear makeup to bring out her eyes that were once as large as this girl's eyes. Eyes that have grown, oddly, darker with the years. Onyx eyes, Peter calls them.

But now Ted Eliason has stopped staring and is saying, "We're going to a meeting nearby, a meeting about nuclear arms."

Finally I let my glance hold Peter's, warn him, and in that swift exchange Hope asks her husband, "Shall I take a guess?"

Peter's eyes dart from my face to hers and then to Ted's, and I think they are going to dull with anger, but I'm wrong. He is still the elderly attractive man; imperturbable, amused, he stares at Hope's reddening face.

"You're Peter and Lily Fialka." Her voice is breathy, earnest. Peter nods. "I knew it. I told you it was them when I came off the trail," she tells her husband.

"Hope's a physics teacher," Ted explains. "In our local high school, and also once a week at NYU. She's also an antinuke activist." He sounds so serious.

"I've seen pictures of you," Hope adds.

"Oh, Hope has a fabulous memory. If she sees something once, she never forgets it," Ted goes on. Hope blushes but doesn't deny it. Peter and I exchange glances.

Then Hope says, "Why don't you join us?" She searches our puzzled faces.

"No, no. Impossible. Never go to meetings unless I'm running them," Peter says. "Besides, I'm deep in the middle of Thomas Mann. *Doktor Faustus.* Wonderful book. An old man's book where he can say what he pleases without worrying what anyone will think." He waves his hand dismissively.

Hope retreats, humiliated. Suddenly I'm sorry for her. She's stepped onto a hornet's nest, but how is she to know that since September Peter has been hounded by letters, phone calls, advance copies of books—all about the dangers of nuclear war? As if all the intellectuals in the country, having had ten years to recover from Vietnam, had finally awakened.

You're not being fair, my eyes tell Peter. He gives a slight shrug, then looks at her.

"Please come," she urges. "When I called to find out about the meeting, the woman in charge said they were having a well-known speaker, someone very knowledgeable, a surprise."

Peter shakes his head. "They all have surprise speakers." Yet as the Eliasons leave us to our dinner, I feel my heart sink. I long for the Trapp Family Lodge, which burned down last year: the large library where we would read before the dying fire, the background trill and hum of voices assuring us we had company if we wanted it. Our room in the motel unit near the old lodge is dismal, lonely. Besides, Peter will be engrossed in the progress of Adrian Leverkühn's syphilitic existence, and although I was looking forward to reading Ibsen, *Hedda Gabler* seems flat compared to the idea of attending a community meeting.

If we were back in Boston, we wouldn't consider it, but we should do this sort of thing once in a while, I hear myself saying, and what better place than Vermont?

Hope returns while we are dawdling over coffee. I can see she expects a no. Impulsively I ask how they are getting there.

"Oh, Ted will drive, he's a wonderful driver, and we have a four-wheel-drive car." Peter's face softens. His eyes shine with that peculiar tender light they get when he knows I will be pleased. As we stand up, I have the strangest feeling: that we are walking to the brink of something. It's a feeling I haven't had in years and years.

• • •

Sitting next to Peter in the backseat of a car on a cold winter's night takes me back to the days when Tony and Anne were teenagers and they would chauffeur us. I don't know why I'm stricken with such a yearning for the past. Perhaps it's because of the lodge that is now real only in our memory. Or perhaps it's the appearance of this young couple who take themselves so seriously, who honestly believe that each action they take has tremendous importance. How easy it is to think that at their age. But how easy it also is to make mistakes, to believe one knows the whole story, or what is best, when only an infinitesimal part of any story can be known to one person.

Peter takes my hand, and we lean back into the luxurious upholstery. My eyes drink in the darkness of the country night: so black, so encompassing, so unremittingly harsh, broken only by the flash of headlights on the beards of blue ice that have slowly formed on the rocky sides of the road since winter began. I am lulled into a sweet, dreamless doze until the car jolts to a stop.

Valentine decorations festoon this school cafeteria, brightening its two-tone walls, its heavy furniture, its dark wood floor. At the back, behind the neat rows of chairs, are long tables covered with red cloths, a coffee urn, large platters of home-baked goods. The audience is mostly young; I recognize a few ski instructors from the Trapp Lodge who are constantly knitting hats and mittens for sale at the shop. The small, double-pointed knitting needles arranged in squares on their fingers look like odd appendages, like the hands of creatures from another planet.

Hope's cheeks are flushed with excitement. Could she be so foolish as to introduce Peter during the discussion period? Her deep brown eyes rove through the crowd, and as I watch them I decide that her kind of enthusiasm can lead to almost anything. I touch her forearm and whisper, "Peter would prefer no one know who he is."

She nods and tucks her arm into mine. She's a few inches taller than I, and as we walk to our seats, sidestepping cartons of books piled along the edge of the room, I know that people could take us for mother and daughter. It makes me miss Anne.

The leader of the meeting glances toward the doorway of the cafeteria and finally confesses that their speaker is late. One woman reports on the progress of the SALT talks; a man discusses the still-embryonic plans for a huge disarmament march in the late spring, probably in New York City; another woman gives a synopsis of the article in *The New York Times Magazine* last November about the feelings on disarmament in West Germany. She holds up the cover, which has hovered at the back of my mind since I saw it: a woman with a chalked face wearing the sign *Wir Wollen Kein Euroshima*.

"She looks like something out of a Brecht play," Peter said when he saw it.

Then the noise of cartons being slit open, and I see that the boxes contain copies of *The Fate of the Earth* by Jonathan Schell. The publisher sent galleys to Peter, and we both read them before Christmas. Without looking, I know that the muscles at the back of Peter's neck are tight.

Oh, why did we come? When will I learn to stay home, where I belong? Soon a man with flowing gray hair begins to read Schell's description of Hiroshima after the bomb struck.

Silence.

He waits. Then, " 'If it were possible (as it would not be) for someone to stand at Fifth Avenue and Seventy-second Street (about two miles from Ground Zero) without being instantly killed, he would see the following sequence of events. A dazzling white light from the fireball would illuminate the scene, continuing for perhaps thirty seconds. Simultaneously, searing heat would ignite everything flammable and start to melt windows, cars, buses, lampposts, everything made of metal or glass. People in the street would immediately catch fire and would shortly be reduced to heavily charred corpses. About five seconds after the light disappeared, the blast wave would strike, laden with the debris of a now non-existent midtown. Some buildings might be crushed, as though a giant fist had squeezed them on all sides . . .' "

My fingers and toes begin to tingle, as they always do when I feel threatened. When I read the book, I had to keep going back, because no mind, however brilliant, can comprehend what Schell is trying to describe in one reading. I remembered feeling that way years ago when I read John Hersey's *Hiroshima,* but we dismissed that as fiction because we couldn't bring ourselves to believe its truth.

Now it isn't so easy to evade the truth.

Peter's face is stone, his eyes dull. I put my hand under his elbow. I want him to know I'm here, as I was then, when we were so young, so naive, so convinced we were saving the world.

What we should do is leave. But how can we? We have no car. Besides, these people aren't country bumpkins; there are no country bumpkins anymore, especially in Vermont. More than one of them might recognize Peter, which would be even worse.

Like an empty museum, the cafeteria is utterly still; not a footfall, not an echo breaks the silence. A smart man, the speaker reads only enough to make them want more, then ends with a passage Peter starred: " 'But when it comes to judging the consequences of a nuclear holocaust there can be no experimentation. . . . We cannot run experiments with the earth, because we have only one earth . . . we are not in possession of any spare earths . . .' "

The tautness in the air is as painful as that in a hospital room after the doctor has told a patient who entered for routine tests that, instead of going home, he must stay.

In the lull I observe the elaborately decorated valentines—modern versions of the ones that lie, frayed and faded, in a box in our attic marked CHILDREN.

Cash clutched in their hands, people line up to buy Schell's book. Peter and I stay in our seats. Suddenly there is a flurry at the door, and someone says, in a relieved shout, "Ah, here he is!" When I turn my head, our son, Tony, is walking through the doorway.

"It's Anthony Fain," a woman says. Peter and I stiffen, each wondering how Tony, who lives in Maine, is here. But why shouldn't he be here? He's a well-known antinuke person in New England who travels and gives speeches whenever he can. When we spoke on the telephone a week ago, he never said anything about coming to Vermont, but neither did we.

I can still see the pain in Peter's face, the slate flatness of his eyes, when Tony told us he was changing his name. It was during Christmas vacation of his senior year at Yale. We were finishing dinner with Anne and her boyfriend and Peter's sister, Margot, and her husband.

"It isn't that I don't like it; it's a good Russian name, I'm proud of it and Grandpa and you," he told Peter, "but it doesn't let me be me. Everyone I meet asks if I'm related to you." Then Tony studied the floor, the giveaway that the last was a lie.

Margot was the first to collect herself. "But it was such a respected name in Kiev. All those Fialka doctors," she reminded Tony, her tone wistful.

"And there are still Fialkas from the other side of the family, bankers and lawyers, in Odessa," I added stupidly. What the hell did a kid of twenty-one care about distant relatives on the Black Sea? When Peter caught my eye, his glance urged me to stop. But I didn't want to stop. I wanted to shout, "You're our only son, and this is our name, and that is, in the end, the only thing that will absolutely connect you and your children to us."

Then I wanted to remind our son that every year on our anniversary—wherever we were—Peter somehow found a cyclamen because *fialka* in Russian means wild violet or cyclamen. "It's such a beautiful name," my father had said when we told him we wanted to marry. "Those wild violets cropping up with minds of their own in woodland bogs and swamps." He'd paused. "Lily Fialka, it suits you," he'd added, as if, suddenly, the name were the most important thing, as if he had not loved Peter for years.

But now Tony was telling us he didn't want the name of that free-spirited Russian flower. I could feel the blood drain from my face as Peter came to sit next to me, putting his hand over mine.

Tony ran his hand through his straight, dark, almost Indianlike hair, and began again. "I don't deny that there are wonderful brainy people named Fialka. Believe me, I don't know another person whose father has won the Nobel Prize. But the truth is, I'm tired of being Peter Fialka's son." Well, that wasn't a lie.

Maybe we were wrong to have dragged the children to Stockholm. They were fifteen and twelve, and we thought it would be exciting for them, but maybe that elaborate ritual, ending when the king of Sweden placed the award into Peter's hands as if it were a piece of Baccarat, turned them off. Still, Tony always seemed proud of Peter when he was growing up, and he had no interest in physics. What he adored was history.

How naive I was even then! In my early forties, but still I didn't realize that atomic physics was history. It was exactly Tony's love of history that led him into the antinuke movement. And perhaps it had all begun more than twenty years before, when Tony saw the blinding silvery flash that was the Trinity test. I wonder now, in this Vermont school cafeteria, if any of Tony's friends even suspect that he was the youngest person to have witnessed Trinity.

Layer upon layer of the past melds together, and like a glassblower with his torch, we mold it into what we wish rather than what is true. Still, I know now and knew even then that Tony wasn't asking our permission to change his name; he was changing it. After his graduation, Anton Fialka had become Anthony Fain. A. Fain, c/o Fialka, was how his mail was addressed.

"At least he waited until he graduated," Margot tried to console us. "In view of all the crazy things kids are doing these days, this isn't the worst thing that could happen."

No, it wasn't. After all, it was the end of the sixties. But I never suspected how much it would hurt. And now, sitting in a town meeting, I flinch as our firstborn, our only son, stands before us, and we are not even connected by our name.

Tony speaks well and has charisma. Part of it has to do with his leanness, his sticklike black hair and golden skin. When he was an infant, we thought he would have coal-black eyes. I think I wanted him to have eyes that were his very own, this child who had come like a gift when I needed him most. But nature is filled with surprises, and Tony's eyes are a combination of Peter's and mine: a brown flecked with aquamarine so astonishing that strangers actually step backward when they see him. I wonder if he knows how extraordinary his eyes are. There are so many things I wonder about him and Anne.

I glance at Peter. He looks bored. Tony's zeal has always bored him; zeal in general bores him. He would respect Tony more if he stayed home and taught his students as much history as they could retain. Last year, when Tony gave up teaching to become principal, Peter was wild. And he has no sympathy with Tony's antinuke activities.

"It's a colossal waste of time, all the running around he does," Peter said. Then, "Total disarmament is a wonderful idea because it's naive. All wonderful ideas are naive. Opposing nuclear energy is unrealistic. What we need are well-trained, intelligent people to run the plants, what we must have are people who care."

Whenever they spoke about it, Tony would retort, "Impossible, impractical," and Peter's face would close on his son.

Tony knows that since we left New Mexico in the fall of 1945 Peter has refused to have anything to do with defense or the American military establishment, but he never acknowledges that when he and Peter argue. And Peter would never remind him, or anyone else, of his convictions. It has been enough for Peter to teach physics at MIT and to pursue his research on subatomic particles and particle theory. Whatever government work he does has to do with the peaceful uses of nuclear energy. Peter has wrestled with nuclear problems for more than a generation, more than the span of Tony's life, and he knows—we both know—that the answers are infinitely harder than the questions.

Still, when the audience breaks into applause, stomping on the old floor so enthusiastically that we can begin to feel it vibrate into a rhythmic pulse beneath our feet, I see pride in Peter's eyes. He respects excellence in anything, even speech-making.

Peter says to Hope and Ted, "A wonderful speaker, I respect him enormously, but what else would you expect from a father?"

Ted Eliason's eyes race from Peter to Tony, and back to us. Hope pales, swallows hard. "I can't believe it. I read that your son was dead."

Peter laughs heartily. "Thank God that's not true," then makes his way toward the steaming mugs of coffee.

Hope and Ted look embarrassed. I shrug, and Hope takes that as a signal to say, "He's a terrific speaker, you must be proud of him." I nod. Her eyes are thoughtful as she looks at me. Then she says quickly, as if it were a secret, "I've always wondered about the women of Los Alamos."

Speechless, I stare. The women of Los Alamos. I've never heard that before. She makes us sound like a band of pioneers, a tribe led by Elizabeth Cady Stanton or Susan B. Anthony.

"You make them sound like a union," Peter chuckles. He has returned with a cup of coffee for me. Our eyes meet. But the Eliasons don't know he's teasing them and retreat quickly.

Now I turn and watch Tony talking to a group of admirers. His wide gestures, so open, so friendly, remind me of Peter's when we were first married. But Tony looks older than when we last saw him; deeper lines are etched around his mouth and eyes. I try to catch those amber eyes, but my son's glance slides over me.

Suddenly I am in New York in the fifties, going to see *The Power and the Glory*. We hadn't told a soul we were coming to New York. As we entered the theater from a pelting snow, I noticed a couple who looked familiar from the back, but I couldn't think about them until I was warmer, drier, able to wipe my eyes. Of course they were my parents. I couldn't believe I hadn't recognized them instantly, and I made such a fuss about meeting them that my mother finally said, "Lily darling, enough. This isn't the Eighth Wonder."

It took me seconds. It's taking Tony longer, but after about a minute and a half, he shouts, "Dad!" and they hurry toward each other with the same loping stride and hug. Then I am encircled by my son's lanky arms, feeling as relieved as I did when I kissed my parents in that theater lobby.

But my pleasure is cut short when I hear, "Isn't that Peter Fialka?" I don't turn around. I don't want to see who's speaking. Then, "It sure looks like him, but why would he be here? No, it couldn't be, not Peter Fialka with his arm around Anthony Fain. Fain and Fialka are coming from opposite ends of the earth."

● ● ●

After I wheedle an extra bed from the desk clerk, I listen to Peter and Tony talk. It's been so long since we've been alone; the last time was four years ago in Boston. We usually see Tony with his wife and children at family holidays or when we visit them in Maine. But it's just the three of us now, so in this flimsy, ill-furnished room I was sure I detested, I suddenly feel at home. The Bonnard print I criticized before has a comforting golden glow. And Tony looks younger, a child once more.

But very thin. Under the pretext of wanting tea, I pull on my jacket. The searing cold shoots through my forehead as I walk to the dining room, but I feel more surefooted than usual. That's what I hate most about getting older: I never used to think about where to put my feet; now sometimes that's all I think about.

A girl is serving drinks to a few diehards. She's so tired it isn't hard to convince her to let me make some sandwiches and a thermos of tea. I also take a few bottles of Schlitz for Tony.

After he has finished one sandwich and is eyeing the other, he says, "How do you know Faith?"

"Hope," I say.

"Hope, then. All those names are the same."

"We don't. Your father picked her up on the trail and gave her a skiing lesson."

"I didn't pick her up. She was lost."

"Very pretty girl," Tony says. "Reminds me of Anne."

Peter shakes his head. "Not as much Anne as your mother." Tony stares at me. I blush.

"It's the high color, that's all," I murmur.

"Very, very pretty. Are you sure you met her just today? She seemed to know you—she was so protective of you, Mother."

"She recognized us. She's a high school physics teacher," Peter says, "but she's a little mixed up. She thought you were dead, for one thing." Tony and Peter laugh.

"Peter, you're not being fair. You know that an awful lot of nonsense was written about all of you, about all of us. She happened to read some. And you can't exactly blame her," I say and turn to Tony. "Oppie encouraged any publicity—after 1945 he seemed to live on it, need it like food or air, so naturally a lot of stuff was dashed off. Don't be so quick to blame her." Peter has averted his eyes; he seldom has anything to say when Oppenheimer's name is mentioned.

I begin to make Tony's bed while the two of them talk about other things—Proposition 2½ mostly. Tony's eyes follow my every gesture. I check my waist to make sure my shirt isn't creeping out of my slacks. Do I look fatter?

Finally, when his close scrutiny has brought me almost to the point of asking what's the matter, Tony says, "Mom, you look terrific—better than ever. How do you stay so young?" I breathe a sigh of relief. How easy it is to assuage a woman's fears. Then we talk about his family—his wife, Jo, and his three children.

When they sleep, their breaths mingle into an arrhythmic whisper. I lie awake, remembering how we used to sleep in one room on vacation when the kids were small. A cocoon of contentment we were, Peter and I sleeping as soundly as the children. How simple I thought it would be.

But the past doesn't die easily. What was it Faulkner said? "The past isn't dead, it isn't even past." Meeting that girl has awakened emotions in me I could have sworn were buried. Or maybe it was hearing Schell's book read aloud, or seeing Tony's anger and frustration when he spoke. Yes, anger, at both of us. Still, what does he expect us to do? What can we do?

The best line in Schell's book the speaker didn't read. "If scientists are unable to predict their discoveries, neither can they cancel them once they have been made."

Yet who knew that then? Who knows that when you're young and the future stretches far in front of you like an endless line?

Suddenly, it is March 1943, and I am in my childhood bedroom and Peter and I are looking at each other, triumphant that we have finished packing. Abruptly there is a knock, and here is my father in his bathrobe, his brown eyes deeper than usual because he has put away his glasses for the night, the frown lines between his thick gray eyebrows deeper, too, because he's worried. Too worried to apologize for catching me in my slip and Peter with his shirt off. His voice is solemn: "Are you two absolutely sure you know what you're doing?"

We stare. Is there a choice? our eyes ask. Then he adds in a whisper, "You know, no one is forcing you to do this."

But we don't agree, and after an hour of thrashing it out, he rises, his eyes as glazed as a pudding that has sat too long, his back stooped with resignation. He cups our faces in his hands and kisses us. I sigh with relief that his questions are over, yet as he turns the knob of the door, he asks, "But what will you do with the whirlwind?" He is so exhausted he does something rare: He says, "Hosea," and is gone.

Too tired to let our lips form another word, Peter and I fall into bed. But later, at Los Alamos, and for a long time afterward, I would recall my father's face that night. He knew that once you begin something, you are caught and must see it through.

Yet to have refused to go was unthinkable. We were Jews, Peter a refugee from Hitler. Now that this destructive weapon seemed a real possibility after Hahn's discovery of fission, it was imperative that the United States have it first. The nuclear physicists still in Germany—Hahn and Heisenberg and Weizsächer and the rest—could make a bomb, so of course Peter had to help, of course we had to go. It could not fall into Hitler's hands.

Besides, how wonderful the prospect was! Finally to be part of the war effort, to share in that intensity, that brilliance. We were so exhilarated by it that the setting and the other characters became more important than the plot.

After the war when my mother learned where we were, she said, "All those brains in one place, it must have been nothing less than a miracle." Reporters still call it "a unique time in American history." How could we have chosen to miss it? The question was too absurd to ask.

Except to my father.

I throw off the covers and tiptoe through the room. Tony and Peter are fast asleep in exactly the same position on their left sides. In the moonlight the snow-covered mountains shine like tin roofs. So fixed, so still, it is a canvas. Then I hear Hope saying, "I've always wondered about the women of Los Alamos," and suddenly, standing before me are the women I loved—Steffi and History and

Pamela and Bess and Kate and Thea—and others who
such close friends, but whom I also love because we sh;
crucial time. I hear their voices, the same voices they h
for although faces and figures change, voices rarely do.
of Furies talking and laughing at her presumptuous phr;

The women of Los Alamos. Ours was such a compl
filled not with details about Leslie Groves's precious b
more with the knots and loops of our personal lives—liv
and loyalty and innocence, and anger and temptation an
edge. And questions, some of the hardest questions we w
face.

Oh, how complicated it was! Slowly the tangle begins t
and I feel light-headed, as if back on that high mesa
sometimes felt so strange we might have been walking t
landscape of our dreams.

I grip the windowsill and look out into the clear, sta
Vermont night, but the more I look the less substantial it
Now a photograph materializes before my eyes: The
tonwood is leafless as it thrusts itself from the pink ea:
Ildefonso; behind it is the Black Mesa, to the left the k;
sky cumulus clouds are racing to get out of there, as if t
even then, what was coming; and everything is tinge(
lilac light that seeped from the heavens at dusk, when
would be pricked by the sharp air and you could almc
cottonwood's stubbornness stretching into the lonely n

Jacob Wunderlich took that photograph and gave it t
after I went to work as his secretary. As he handed it
said, "We will need the strength and determination of
and his luminous gaze seemed to rest on my face like ;

1943

2

Where do stories begin? In different places and at different times. The last five years had been filled with random, seemingly unconnected incidents that later became part of the complete story.

On the day before Christmas, 1938, Lise Meitner, a brilliant physicist who was the second woman to be awarded a Ph.D. from the University of Vienna, found herself in a country inn ten miles north of Göteborg, Sweden. She was a small, vigorous woman, with almost alarmingly black, penetrating eyes. She had been beautiful when young, yet her utter lack of vanity had made her age more quickly than her years. Now she was sixty, and for the first time in her life desperately lonely. An Austrian with Jewish blood, Meitner had become subject to Hitler's racial laws after the *Anschluss* and was forced to leave the Kaiser Wilhelm Institute for Chemistry in Dahlem, where she had worked with the famous chemist Otto Hahn since 1909; now she was living alone in Stockholm and working at the Academy of Physical Sciences.

Today, though, would be different. For today, through the kindness of some Swedish friends, she would meet her nephew, Otto

Frisch, who was also a physicist and lived in Copenhagen. His mother, Lise's sister, was still in Vienna, and his father had been taken to Dachau. But Lise was determined not to spoil this holiday visit with worry. While she waited for her nephew, Otto, she turned the beautiful diamond ring on her finger that had been a gift from the other Otto—Otto Hahn. He had thrust it into her hand just before they parted; it was his mother's and more lavish than anything she would have chosen, but she cherished it, for she knew that it signified not only his affection for her, but also his hope that if she found herself in trouble, she would be provided for. In her mind it had become her lucky ring.

But here was Otto. As she rose to kiss her nephew, she turned the diamond to the inside of her finger; she would explain about it later.

After she and Otto had breakfast, Lise took out a letter she had received from Otto Hahn. Back in Dahlem he and Fritz Strassmann were bombarding uranium to see what would happen, he wrote. Uranium was the heaviest stable element in nature, and they were bombarding it with slow neutrons expecting to knock a neutron out and come up with an element just below uranium in the periodic table. Like radium. Instead they were getting barium, which is only half the weight of uranium.

"It's not possible," Otto said; both he and his aunt knew that heavy nuclei could not be split in two.

Yet Otto Hahn was too good a chemist to have made a mistake or to fail to allow for impurities. What could be happening? they asked each other. Then they decided to get some air; while Otto plowed ahead on his cross-country skis, Lise walked quickly to keep up with him and thought about Hahn's puzzling result. The uranium nucleus was not a solid that could be cut or broken in two; it didn't behave like that; indeed, it had once been likened to a liquid drop.

Suddenly Lise stopped and sat on a log and pulled a piece of paper from her pocket. She let the sun play with the diamond on her finger, her eyes followed the darting rays of light, and then she turned her face upward to feel the sun's warmth. She knew she looked terrible, with dark circles under her eyes; as soon as he saw her, Otto's face had fallen with dismay, which he then tried to cover up. Perhaps if she got a little sun, she would look better.

As she looked up at the sun, she squinted, and her eyes teared. A tear was a liquid drop, she thought.

And if you thought of the uranium nucleus as a drop of water that becomes unstable and starts to wobble and forms a waist and finally splits into smaller nuclei of barium and krypton, then Hahn's finding might be right. But with such an action there would be a strange release of energy.

Quickly she and Otto made some calculations and realized that Hahn and Strassmann had split the uranium atom.

When Frisch returned to his lab in Copenhagen, he asked an American friend who was a biologist what the term is in biology when one bacterium divides into two. "Binary fission," was the answer.

"Can you call it 'fission'?" Frisch asked. His friend nodded.

Hahn's discovery was described hereafter as fission. Within weeks after they realized what had happened, Lise Meitner and Otto Frisch interpreted Hahn's findings in the British journal *Nature*; Frisch's father was released from Dachau and Lise's sister and brother-in-law came to live with her in Stockholm. Happily surrounded by her German-speaking family, Lise Meitner now had a new worry: like her colleagues around the world she was asking herself if this release of energy could be harnessed to make a nuclear weapon.

And worse, would this become part of Adolf Hitler's master plan?

In June of 1939 Jacob and Stephania Wunderlich were living in New York; Jacob had taken a year off from Cornell because he and Steffi needed to live in a city. Now he was on a research grant at Columbia.

It had been an unusually warm spring, and tonight they were sitting at the drop-leaf table in their tiny living room, wearing loose summer clothes and sandals. Steffi was very pregnant and very hot, but they were happy, for sitting with them, as if he had been there forever, was Dietrich Bonhoeffer.

A brilliant theologian, Dietrich was becoming known in Germany for his refusal to accept the edicts of National Socialism in the Protestant Church. His ideas had been noticed not only by other theologians, like Reinhold Niebuhr in America and Bishop George Bell in England, but by the SS as well.

Steffi had just received a letter from Dietrich's twin sister, Sabine, who, though older than Steffi, was one of her dearest friends. Sabine had married Gerhard Liebholz, a Jew, and now they were living in England. Sabine was worried, and she hoped Dietrich would accept work in the United States. If he returned to Germany, she was afraid his outspokenness would put him in grave danger.

Tall, stocky Dietrich, whose fine flaxen hair seemed spun of sunlight; lovable Dietrich who brightened every room he ever entered. It seemed a miracle to Steffi that he was actually here; in her excitement, it took her a while to realize that he was not nearly as happy as she was.

"What's the matter, Dietrich?" she finally asked, no longer able to ignore the frown that kept returning to his features. Why was he turning so nervously the ring he always wore? He should have been elated to be here where his colleagues in the Protestant Church had arranged for him to have a job helping the Christian refugees who were fleeing Hitler. Everyone agreed that it was exactly the job for Dietrich.

Except Dietrich.

"I don't know, Steffi. I feel like a fool. After you and Jacob have welcomed me, and everyone else has gone to all this trouble to find work for me here—meaningful work—I don't know if I can stay," Dietrich replied. His lower lip jutted out as he spoke; always so stubborn, even when he was a boy. How well Steffi knew that lip, but the voice was new. So solemn and so serious, heavy almost. His preaching voice instead of the rapid conversational voice she knew. She sat up straighter and looked quickly at Jacob. His eyes were wary, worried, as they fixed on Dietrich's face.

"I know everyone thinks I should stay. I know Sabine has written to you. Here I am out of danger, and here what I say can't be held against me. But how can I stay here when my heart and soul are in Germany?"

"But here you are safe," Steffi said. "And here you can do good work, important work." But Dietrich was shaking his head.

"Physical safety isn't everything, Steffi," he said quietly. "Everything I care about is in Germany. I know there are Germans who hate Hitler, who don't believe in his ideas, who still believe in God. How can I abandon them? I would feel like a traitor." He paused and shook his head.

"It was a mistake to think I could leave. I'm a German, not an American, and I must stay and help my country. I know it sounds pompous, but it's the truth. If I don't live through this terrible time in Germany, I will have no right to take part in the reconstruction that will occur after this madman is defeated. So I must be there now."

As always, Dietrich was utterly clear. And incredibly optimistic. No doubt of Hitler's ultimate defeat. No confusion, no questions. His courage was unmistakable. Yet now Steffi wondered: Is this courage or idiocy? People thought that if Dietrich returned, he would never be safe. Besides, Dietrich was not only a thinker; he was a doer. And if he returned to Germany, he would surely become involved in the resistance against Hitler that was growing in Berlin, especially. That was what worried Sabine so much.

Steffi leaned forward and searched Dietrich's vibrant blue eyes. Not a trace of fear. Perhaps a little resigned. And a lot tired. But not afraid. Never afraid. Then he continued, as if he were preaching, "Germany and I are bound for life. Her fate is mine." Done. Finished.

He used to be so easygoing, careless almost. Didn't even go to church that regularly when he was young. But now he was different. Well, the world had changed, Steffi thought, then sighed. But she knew there was no way to persuade him to stay. Behind that sweet, benign expression was a stubborn, steely intelligence; all the Bonhoeffers had it, which was why she had loved Dietrich and Sabine, idolized them, really, from the time she was a girl. They always stuck by what they believed.

Steffi sat there watching Dietrich and Jacob talk, thinking about a dream she had had only a few nights ago. There were people who said dreams were portents of the future, and now she realized that she must have known this was coming. In her dream her unborn baby was floating in a rowboat, helpless, bundled in blankets, and the boat floated farther and farther from her while she screamed for help that did not, could not come. She had awakened screaming, and Jacob's arms enfolded her and he murmured into her mussed hair, then lulled her to sleep with a Brahms lullaby. She woke up calm. But now the panic was surfacing again.

"I have no choice," Dietrich was explaining to Jacob, who kept shaking his head, not so much in disagreement, but because he also knew there was nothing he could do. How disappointed Sabine would be! Steffi felt like a failure because she and Jacob had been unable to convince Dietrich to stay.

So the evening, which had begun so happily, ended in tears and the first of several good-byes. For all three of them knew that Dietrich would return to Germany. Despite what anyone else thought.

After Dietrich left, Steffi was filled with sadness for him, for Germany, for all those who were still there. She begged Jacob to promise that whatever happened, he would not participate in war work that would harm Dietrich and his family and all the other friends they loved who were still living in the hell that Germany had become.

Jacob shook his head. "I can't, Steffi. It's too much to ask. Besides, no one knows what will be. Maybe there won't be a war," he told her. But that night Steffi dreamed the rowboat dream again: this time Dietrich and the baby were together and Dietrich saw her and heard her cries, but he would not take up the oars and row back toward her. She tried to yell to them, but nothing would come from her throat. And when she woke up, she wasn't screaming as she had been the other night. No, the room was as silent as a tomb, and Jacob was sleeping peacefully beside her. Steffi lay there in a heavy sweat, paralyzed with a helplessness that was the most frightening feeling she had ever known.

It was achingly cold, even for Chicago—below zero. December 2, 1942. "Colder than a witch's tit," Tom Schweren muttered to Enrico Fermi, who stared, puzzled, sure he had heard the English words wrong. Schweren laughed, embarrassed. Had he offended Fermi, the famous physicist who was also a spectacular engineer, the man who had suspected the atom could be split back in 1934? He couldn't tell, but there was no time to worry about it. They had too much to do.

For now fission was a fact. Hahn and Strassmann had done the experiment, and Meitner and Frisch confirmed that it was possible to break up the atomic nucleus of U-235 by bombarding it with neutrons. The nucleus of U-235 would then split into two parts that would fly away with incredible speed; in addition a few secondary neutrons would break off and fly away, too. The release of those few extra neutrons would cause other atoms to split also, and that, in turn, would give rise to more neutrons, which would again bombard other atoms. The whole process had been likened to the spreading of a fire, but in fission there was a release of energy 100 million times larger than the energy that came from ordinary burning. The idea was to collect the energy and to produce a bomb, which would then release that lethal energy.

There were manifold problems, not the least of which was that ordinary uranium is a mixture of two substances, called isotopes. The abundant one was U-238. The rare one, which occurred only in 0.7 percent of ordinary uranium, was U-235; this was the isotope needed for a chain reaction. It was therefore far more likely that the free neutrons would collide ineffectively with another atom of U-238. But if you could slow down the neutrons, they would have a better chance of finding the U-235. This was accomplished by imbedding ordinary uranium in a substance that could slow down the neutrons; the best substance was deuterium, or heavy water. Another possibility was carbon. Fermi had coined the name given to the slowing-down moderator—a uranium "pile."

Now Fermi had been given the responsibility of figuring out how this pile of graphite (carbon) bricks and uranium rods could produce a self-sustained release of energy from the atom, which would also be controlled. For only if you could produce a chain reaction could you then figure out how to make a weapon. The figures were something like 770,000 pounds of graphite, 80,000 pounds of uranium oxide, and 13,000 pounds of uranium metal. To the tune of a million dollars. Its only moving parts were cadmium control rods, one of which Tom Schweren was to move by hand today on orders from Fermi. This would prevent the pile from getting out of control and, according to the pessimists, possibly destroying the city of Chicago.

Everything in this squash court under the west stands of Stagg Field was tinged with black: two weeks of working with the graphite, building the pile by hand, had made them look like chimney sweeps. A scrim of black dust covered their faces, their lab coats, the cloth balloon that encircled the pile. And so cold, the kind of dense blue cold that went for the marrow of your bones. Which was why Tom said what he did.

But suddenly he felt foolish. Fermi was staring at him oddly.

Then Tom realized that the older man was simply rolling the words "colder than a witch's tit" around in his head, thinking.

Finally Fermi said, "That's one I've not heard before, but it's very descriptive. Sounds as if it could come from Shakespeare. As if it *should* come from Shakespeare," he added, then he and Tom looked at each other and laughed, and all at once Tom knew that everything would be all right, that what was going on here today would succeed, that Stagg Field and the university would not be destroyed, that the "suicide squad" would not have to throw their cadmium solution on the pile to dampen it. For the pile would not go out of control.

It was a vision as strong as reality, and it reached into Tom Schweren's brain and bones. Finally his teeth stopped their faint, persistent chatter, and he began to whistle a theme from the Verdi Requiem. Fermi looked up, startled. And smiled.

Like Tom Schweren, the others watching Fermi were in total awe at his calm. He behaved as if this were an ordinary day. As if the almost forty people who were gathered here were about to watch some athletic event. As if the guards so carefully placed at the exits and wearing raccoon coats someone had found in the locker room were ticket takers for a football game that would soon take place in this field named for the great Chicago football coach. Indeed, as if the crucial counting now under way were the counting of yards for a first down.

As the cadmium control rods were withdrawn, the clicking of the neutron counter registered what was happening inside the pile. This continued until the interval between the clicks merged, and the counting of the neutrons switched to the silent mechanism of a pen recorder on a graph that Fermi had designed. People watched in silence as the pen showed higher and higher neutron intensities. Then Fermi announced that the self-sustaining chain reaction had begun. "The pile has gone critical," he said. The next four and a half minutes seemed like hours. No one stirred, and suddenly nothing mattered in the entire world but the movement of the pen on the graph. Just when the anxiety seemed overwhelming, when the fear that this chain reaction might go out of control, Fermi called, "ZIP in." ZIP was the control rod designed to stop the chain reaction; Tom pushed it back and the clicking stopped.

It was 3:53 P.M., and there had been a controlled release of atomic energy at one-half watt for more than four minutes. Dulled by exhaustion, Tom realized that it was over.

"But he never doubted that it would work," someone said later. "That's Fermi. Look"—and then the speaker stopped for emphasis—"it was really Fermi who split the uranium atom back in 1934. Fermi and Segrè. Years before Hahn and Strassmann. But the powers that be said the uranium atom couldn't be split, so they didn't realize it until later. But he never looks back. He's amazing. Unbelievable confidence. You saw it here today. An Italian friend of a friend once told me that they called him 'Iron Man' when he was young."

In the house of Dan and Sophie Schweren on Mitchell Street in Ithaca, the lights were on in the kitchen until two o'clock in the morning. It was the first anniversary of Pearl Harbor, December 7, 1942.

The first reports of the concentration camps were reaching the United States. According to the news accounts, two million Jews were dead and several million more were in acute danger. It was too much for the mind to grasp; people protested that the numbers weren't true, couldn't be true. Another six months would have to pass before the truth of those numbers—and more—was irrevocably, horribly, established. And still the fighting went on, and the Germans were holding strong. As Rommel's forces recovered from Eisenhower's surprise attack on Algeria and Morocco, military strategists tried to predict their next move. In the Pacific the control of Guadalcanal in the Solomon Islands seesawed constantly between the Americans and the Japanese in some of the bitterest battles of the entire war. Japanese-American citizens were beginning to be interned in camps in California. It had been a dismal month.

But the news Dan Schweren had might be the worst of all, he told his wife, Sophie. She stared at him in disbelief. What could be worse than news of the killing of the Jews? But then Dan's eyes filled with tears, and Sophie knew better than to ask any more questions, and she listened to her husband's anguished voice tell her that his cousin, Tom, had called this afternoon to report that Enrico Fermi, the Italian physicist, had produced a controlled chain reaction in a uranium pile under Stagg Field at the University of Chicago a few days ago. Tom was beside himself with joy, which only made it worse. For the first time since these two cousins had decided to become physicists, they were in total disagreement.

Schweren was twenty-four years old, a brilliant student of Hans Bethe. His cousin, Tom, his father's brother's son, who was trained at Columbia and was now working in Chicago, was thirty. Now Dan drew picture after picture for his artist-wife, Sophie—pictures of uranium atoms and neutrons and the inside of a pile. "Fermi has proved experimentally that a chain reaction can be controlled." Sophie frowned. "That we can make a bomb," Dan added in a whisper, for the walls were paper-thin. "That we will make a bomb." His voice was grim.

Then Sophie rose and made a pot of coffee. Between them they drank almost two quarts of the thick inky liquid. Sophie could feel it scorching her throat, but she seemed to need to punish her body to make her brain absorb what Dan was telling her.

He was like a demon when he was determined. And he was determined now to make her understand that under no circumstances could he join the effort that would surely be made to create a weapon of destruction. "A horrible weapon, darling, worse than anything the world has ever known," he kept saying.

When they fell into each other's arms, breathless with fatigue and despair, Sophie warned, "You know that you will be a pariah."

Though he was almost too exhausted to answer, Dan replied firmly, "That's not the worst thing that can happen to a man." As a Jew studying nuclear physics, he was a pariah in Vienna. The Nazis called nuclear physics "Jewish physics."

Being scorned was hardly new to Dan. He would survive. At least here he had the freedom to choose; at least here there was no Hitler. Yet as he answered Sophie, he saw Tom's disappointed face floating above his now-closed eyes. He could hear Tom trying to convince him to work for his new country. Dan knew he could not, but he also knew that Tom would never forgive him.

About three months later, thousands of miles away, Robert Oppenheimer visited the small, modest home of a woman named Pamela Bye in Otowi, a few miles from the new city that was being built on the Pajarito Plateau and that would be named Los Alamos after the boys' school that had been there. Oppenheimer had met Miss Bye several years before, when he stopped at her tearoom for her famous chocolate cake. Though they spoke only briefly, Oppenheimer never forgot the calm in her eyes and suspected that if he asked her to do the work he had in mind, she wouldn't refuse.

No one seemed to know very much about her. Some said that she had had tuberculosis and had come here and found a cure. Or that she had had a nervous breakdown and was sent to a sanatorium in Santa Fe, where she became well. That she had asthma and needed the dry climate. That she was very rich, the daughter of a cousin of J. P. Morgan. That she was very poor, but well educated, a graduate of Bryn Mawr College, where her father was a professor. That she came from a coal-mining family in Kentucky. Sometimes, when she thought about those rumors, not even Pamela could sort them out.

The truth belonged to her alone. No one needed to know why she had come almost twenty years ago, or why she seemed compelled to stay.

What was known was this: From the time of her arrival Pamela Bye had led an uncertain existence, going wherever she could get a job: as a secretary, as a hostess in a restaurant, and as a cook. Then she got a most unlikely offer—as a kind of watchman at the Otowi crossing for the freight railway of the Denver & Rio Grande Railroad that unloaded mail and supplies for the Los Alamos School. By the time Oppenheimer first met her toward the end of the 1930s, she had rebuilt the house at Otowi with the help of the Indians at San Ildefonso, and she lived in it with an Indian named Estevan. Since the closing of the railroad in 1941, she had expanded her general store and gas station to a tearoom.

Once Pamela Bye tried to explain her past to someone in the Southwest, a man from Chicago who fancied himself a writer and wanted to know her story. "It sounds like 'The Woman Who Rode Away.' You know, the Lawrence tale," he said when she finished. She didn't know. But she went to the library and read Lawrence's strange tale of that obsessed, blue-eyed woman who left her husband and sons and rode into the wilderness out of a capricious mixture of boredom and curiosity. But instead of becoming a goddess to the Indians who so fatally attracted her, she became a holy sacrifice. No, Pamela thought, only a fool would compare her to "The Woman Who Rode Away." So after that she never spoke about her past, and her long, careful silence fed the rumors.

But she didn't care. She was too happy to care.

For when she arrived in New Mexico, Pamela sensed that perhaps—after all—she could continue to live, that here she might find a place for her beleaguered soul. During the twenty-odd years she had been here, she had developed such a strong kinship with this place that she often felt her soul had left her body to mingle with the sacred earth of this windswept desert. A wild, eerie sensation, which she cherished whenever it came. And Pamela never did leave, not even for a visit, not even when her parents died. It was as if she were afraid she would expire if she couldn't breathe this transparent, sun-drenched air or if she couldn't see the Black Mesa that loomed like a talisman over her life.

On the day in 1943 that he knocked on her door, Pamela remembered Robert Oppenheimer. How could she forget him? He had the most delicate build she had ever seen on a man, and a stance that reminded her uncannily of her brother.

When he arrived that sunny morning in February, she knew, from the stubborn determination that flowed from his sharp blue eyes, that he had a mission. Without any introduction, he told her that many brilliant scientists would be gathered in the city the Army was building at Los Alamos, "and the work will be tense and pressured and urgent. They will need a place to relax, a place where they can forget their work and bring their wives to eat a proper, well-cooked, nourishing meal. Will you expand your tearoom into a restaurant and serve dinners to my scientists?" Oppenheimer asked her.

She was so startled that for a moment she couldn't even speak, and Oppenheimer stared at her with a worried frown. Then she recovered her composure and invited him into the tearoom. He refused. There wasn't time. But he wanted an answer.

"Of course," Pamela replied.

Here, at last, was the war work she had been aching to do. After they spoke for a few more minutes, she watched Oppenheimer mount his horse; he handled the animal gently, and somehow that reassured her. A man who handled a horse like that was not interested in violence. And she liked the way he called them "my scientists." Exhausted from the excitement, Pamela sat down on the wooden steps in front of her house. As Oppenheimer's slim frame receded into the distance, she felt an unfamiliar catch in her heart—as if she were young again.

On Lake Erie, at the edge of the city of Cleveland, was a machine shop known for its unusual attention to detail. The foreman and owner was Lenny Unwin, whose father was a professor at Oberlin, and who, everyone had thought, would become a teacher like his dad. But Lenny was happiest working with his hands, and when he got polio, in 1937, at twenty-one and almost died, he decided that if he lived, he would do exactly as he pleased. No matter what anyone else said or thought.

So he started a machine shop, and worked for the railroads and the steel mills. Whenever anyone needed anything special, they were sent to Lenny Unwin, for whom nothing was too hard. Happy-go-lucky was how people described him, despite his marked and uncomfortable limp. He had married his high school sweetheart, Kate Hendrickson, they had three children in four years and now she was pregnant again.

As a matter of fact, on the day Enrico Fermi appeared at Lenny Unwin's machine shop, Kate had just left, and as she walked toward the Cleveland Arcade, she noticed a somewhat thickly built man gesturing to his companion as he passed her. He had an accent that sounded Italian to Kate's ears, and she had a funny feeling he was heading for Lenny's shop. So Kate wasn't surprised when Lenny came home that evening, his eyes glowing, and told her he had had a visit from a well-known physicist.

"There's a secret project starting out in New Mexico, and they need good machinists," Lenny said. Later Kate realized that she had thought more about the climate than about the project. She sometimes wondered what they would have decided if Fermi had come in spring or summer. But now the thought of escaping the Cleveland winter was uppermost in her mind, and she didn't ask as many questions as Lenny expected. In turn, he told her as little as he could about the project. But he did tell her that Fermi, who was living in Chicago, knew all about him and his shop. Lenny was flattered. He admitted it. And proud. As he should be, Kate assured him.

They had to go. She knew that. For how could she deny her

crippled husband, whom she loved more than life itself, what he wanted most in the world? Now Lenny Unwin would be part of the war effort. This is manna from heaven, Kate decided, as Lenny took her into his arms, after they had finally finished talking, after the children had been checked and were, at last, fast asleep.

3

... ■

Early in 1943 people began to make arrangements to board the train to Lamy, New Mexico. Some reported that the railroad agent in the Princeton station tried to urge those who inquired about a ticket to Lamy not to go there. "Several others have gone, and they haven't come back," the distraught stationmaster explained. As if they were embarking on some fantasy, like John Unger in "The Diamond as Big as the Ritz," I thought when I heard it. And the story of the stationmaster always got a laugh when it was told at Los Alamos.

Our story—Peter's and mine—started just before the beginning of that year, at the skating rink at Rockefeller Center in New York City, my home town. Now no one thinks of New York as anyone's home town, but in the twenties and thirties you could call it that. Once I discussed it with Oppenheimer, who had grown up near me on Riverside Drive, and he agreed with me.

What was always most vivid was the sound of the city: the rhythmic hissing of the cars and swoosh of the buses punctuated by an occasional horn, the wind moaning through the trees on the Drive, and in winter the muffled snowy stillness draping itself over the ordinary sounds, lending them an aching mysteriousness. When we talked, Oppie said, "It's the low tinnitus of New York that I associate with my childhood." Leave it to Oppie to use a word I never heard, but when I looked it up, I saw that he, too, had remembered the sounds.

We had come to New York from Ithaca where Peter was doing research and teaching in the physics department at Cornell, and where I was working in the English department while I finished my thesis for my master's degree. On the day after Christmas 1942, we were sitting at my parents' dining room table, stuffing ourselves on my mother's famous brunch. A white-capped Hudson glinted in the bold midday sun. Suddenly my father chuckled and announced, "Why Lily and Peter are a half."

I stared. "Think, Lily, think." He tapped his forehead. It took me only a few seconds to realize that this was our six months' wedding anniversary.

"A half," Peter repeated. "Leave it to Joe to think of it. We'll have to remember that one, Lily." He turned to me as if I had a file in my head for all the things we were to do for our children.

Then my father leaned across the table and pressed a fifty-dollar bill into Peter's hand. Which is how we, a young married couple on a physics instructor's salary, found ourselves at Rockefeller Center that afternoon. Our plan was to skate, then have dinner in the French or English restaurant; we couldn't decide which and spent the trip downtown on the bus discussing it.

New York was blindingly bright and cold; the streets and buildings and buses and cars glittered with tinsel-like iridescence. As if to compensate for the shocked and doleful Christmas after Pearl Harbor the year before, the department stores had wonderful windows this year—"brave windows," my mother said.

Yet as we rode I became conscious of something new; all the khaki or blue uniforms. Sometimes in groups, but more often just one pressed against the body of a girl: two bodies as close to each other as decency would permit, almost visibly needing to memorize the outlines of the other. The sight sent my heart to my throat. I groped for Peter's hand and held it tightly. He raised his eyebrows, but when I tilted my head and looked out the window, he saw and understood. What right had we to have each other when those couples were thinking of only one thing: when they must part? And what was going to happen to all those young men? Would they ever walk with their girls up Fifth Avenue again? For the Allies were being defeated at every turn.

Suddenly a voice pierced the air. "You too good for the war, young fella?" A red face and several days' beard leaned over our seat. "Or are ya afraid to fight? Scared, are ya?"

Peter's mouth whitened as he pressed his lips together. He had learned—we had both learned—that if he tried to defend himself he would simply make matters worse. Every accent since Pearl Harbor seemed to be taken for German.

"My husband's doing research in physics, at a famous university," I blurted. Quickly we rose, heading for the door. Abruptly the man's manner changed; contrite and more than a little drunk, we now realized, he said, "Oh, I'm sorry, miss, didn't mean to offend ya. Not everyone in this war wears a uniform. I know there are people working in science—I'm not stupid, ya know." Remorse and awe oozed from the man's eyes. He lurched into the seat across from us.

"Now, sit down, no need to go off half-cocked." He smiled. "I had a son once, would have been just about your age, young fella, but he was hit by a bicycle when he was just a lad, thrown against a brick wall in the Bronx on his way to school, and by the time the wife and I got there he was dead. Stone cold dead. As much life in 'm as that wall." I stared straight ahead, but Peter made a clucking sound. "Couldn't even live to die for his country," the man shouted, rambunctious again. Gratefully, we stepped off the bus into the stinging cold.

By now I didn't care where we ate, or if we ate. Still, we were here, and I didn't want to spoil the day. I took a deep breath while Peter waited, and after a few minutes he began to put on his skates, then helped me lace mine. Soon I was gliding in deep sharp curves across the rink, letting Peter's strong arms guide me.

I couldn't remember a time when I didn't know about the Fialkas. They were cousins of cousins of my mother's family in Odessa, and from the time I was small I knew of the courageous rescue by a Fialka of my mother and my aunts from a fire in the nursery of a Crimean resort. The hero turned out to be Peter's grandfather, and Peter's aunt was in the same nursery they were.

Like most of the men in their family, Peter's father and grandfather were doctors, and it was assumed that Peter would go into medicine, too. But Peter was far more interested in mathematics, and later physics, so when the Fialkas left Russia in the late twenties, Peter attended the Kaiser Wilhelm Institute in Berlin. When he finished, he was invited to the prestigious University of Göttingen for his doctoral work, but right after his arrival was relieved of his status as a lab instructor because he was a Jew. The Fialkas left Germany late in 1935.

My parents, Joseph and Natalia Sparr, met them at the pier. I was fifteen and it was my job to entertain Peter for about two weeks—until he went off to Cornell, where he would continue his studies. Actually, the first thing we ever did together was skate, on the lake in Central Park.

I was about to remind him of that when he stopped short and

drew me closer and turned up a corner of my hat and whispered, "Now, Lily, you and I are going to dance." The music had changed from a benign fox-trot to a Strauss waltz. At the sound of the Austrian melody, some people standing at the railing began to boo, but the music went on, heedlessly, mechanically, in a kind of dogged defiance.

"I can't. Listen to them." I could feel myself straining, listening for the drunk from the bus. Besides, the rink was emptying. You could feel the purplish New York dusk slowly snaking its way along the edges of the buildings. My favorite time of day—anywhere.

"Of course you can. A Strauss waltz is beautiful and has nothing to do with Hitler. Just relax." Peter gathered me into his arms so deftly that I had no choice but to follow, breathless with fear that I would land on my face and give those now booing voices something real to jeer at.

"Come on, Lily, don't listen to them, try to relax," he urged and of course he was absolutely right, as usual; once I stopped caring so much, the steps came easily. Soon we were glissading, whirling, aware of nothing but our bodies moving in tandem, never knowing until the music had stopped that we were the only couple left on the ice. Suddenly there was applause. Peter grinned at me and was about to lead me from the ice when a voice called, "Bravo, brava, Peter, Lily!"

Our pluming breath misted our vision as we turned toward the familiar voice I couldn't quite place. And there, standing in front of the French café, was Peter's physics professor, Jacob Wunderlich.

"Jacob!" Peter shouted. "What are you doing here?"

"The same thing you're doing, but you do it so much better," the older man said, and of course we didn't have to talk anymore about where to eat. We followed Jacob to the table where his wife was sitting with another couple; in no time at all the waiters brought two more chairs and we were seated around the table with them.

I was so relaxed after skating that I forgot to be afraid of Jacob Wunderlich. He was a brilliant German whom Peter adored, who loved games and puns and was impatient with anyone who wasn't as quick as he was. He wasn't tall, but gave the appearance of tallness because he was so elegantly built; "well-made," someone once called him later. He had a beautifully shaped head with thin, almost aquiline features, and graying hair, though he was only in his late thirties. He made it clear that he thought the only way to try to make sense of the world was through the study of mathematics and physics; he also thought the only sport worth playing was tennis.

Since I was too literal and earnest to be good at puns, and since I didn't care about tennis and did care, passionately, about American literature, I had rarely done more than linger on the periphery of any conversation with Jacob. I wasn't even sure he knew my first name or what I did.

Yet as they began to talk that December evening, I realized that Jacob and his wife, Stephania, whom everyone called Steffi, knew quite a lot about me. Why? I wondered. I would have to ask Peter later, but now it was time to celebrate, and soon I could feel myself melting into the chair. How pleasant it was to eat a meal I hadn't cooked. My biggest problem since my marriage had been getting the whole meal onto the table at the same time.

"And here no one can attack us," I murmured to Peter. Steffi raised her eyebrows and we told her what had happened on the bus. Jacob seemed about to say something, then thought better of it.

The other couple were Mark and Bess Chanin. They were in their late twenties and from Boston, where Mark taught at MIT.

Bess looked exactly what she was: a descendant of Puritans who had arrived on the *Mayflower,* and a native of Nantucket, where her family had lived for generations. The all-American girl with straight strawberry-blond hair and innocent blue eyes—just what I had always wanted to be. How she had married Mark Chanin, who had a thick Eastern European accent, must be an interesting story, I thought. Yet Bess seemed entirely comfortable with Mark and the rest of them, and I loved watching the nostrils of her perfectly American pug nose widen when she laughed, which she did often.

I had guessed Steffi Wunderlich to be about Peter's age, and I was right. Her twenty-eighth birthday was only three days away, and they were here in the café to celebrate, too. They had left their little boy, Sam, with Steffi's mother.

Everyone on the Cornell campus knew Steffi, for she was a tall, athletic woman who was a fabulous tennis player. As soon as the weather got decent, you would see her and Jacob and occasionally other men playing on the court near Sage Hall. Now I wondered if Steffi and Peter had ever played tennis together, for Peter loved tennis, too.

Then Steffi turned to me, and when I leaned forward she said, "What's your thesis on, Lily?"

"Melville."

"Why Melville?" Jacob asked.

"Why not Melville?" Steffi replied, and I could feel myself stiffen. I was in no mood to justify my thesis to anyone. But I didn't have to say a word, because Jacob had already begun to answer his own question.

"Because he had a real understanding of the loneliness of the human condition and wrote the most effectively symbolic book of his time, either in America or Europe; because he stubbornly believed in himself and didn't care that he wrote books that were, as he put it, 'destined to fail'; and because he was unappreciated in his time and began to be read only because people became interested in the South Seas in the twenties.''

I looked around, bewildered and a bit repelled. I'd thought all Jacob Wunderlich read was physics and math journals, and maybe a little Goethe or Thomas Mann. And then to recite all that information; he reminded me of an actor playing a new part, trying it out, gauging its effect. Still, his flamboyance was magnetic, and I think that for a moment I must have looked like a stagestruck kid. Then I tried to catch Peter's eye, but he was staring at Jacob, as amazed as I was. So were the others, including Steffi.

"Now it's your turn, Lily," Jacob coaxed softly.

"I've been interested in him since I was in high school because he was a native New Yorker and knew New York as well as he did the sea. And 'Bartleby' is the saddest story I've ever read." My voice dwindled lamely. Why did I find this so embarrassing? I could see that they were taking me seriously, and Bess was nodding. She knew Melville; all Nantucketers did.

Still, Jacob's eyes were also slightly mocking as he listened to me. How charming and earnest she is in defense of her writer, they seemed to say. I hated to be looked at like that; friends of my father used to look at me like that when I was an adolescent. So before I knew it, I said, annoyed, "To turn your question around, Professor Wunderlich, why math, or physics?"

"Ah," Jacob said in a sort of protracted sigh. "My dear girl, that would take hours, days, maybe a lifetime. But I admire your passion for Melville—he's a difficult writer; not many pretty young women would undertake such a task."

At that moment I despised him and could feel my throat clogging with anger as Steffi said sharply, "Honestly, Jacob, why must you be so condescending? Sometimes you act as if you were a hundred, and the rest of us were about to be born." And then, thank God, the appetizers came.

Who was Jacob Wunderlich? I wondered. I was angry, and my face was flushed, I knew, my cheeks two circles of red that made me look feverish. My typical reaction to someone like Jacob. As soon as she saw me after I had been embarrassed, my mother always knew. "You must try to mask your feelings as you get older, Lily," she would say gently, then sigh and shake her head. But it was no use, and we both knew it. Those red circles were a physical reaction that I had no hope of controlling. Besides, I had every right to be angry at Jacob's treatment of me. He *was* condescending. Almost as if he were testing me, I thought, then dismissed it. Why would someone as powerful as Jacob Wunderlich be testing me? The very idea was ridiculous.

The more I mulled over the incident, though, the more I felt guilty. My head buzzed with confusion and remorse. Why couldn't I keep my mouth shut? Jacob was Peter's teacher. If Peter had behaved that way with one of my teachers, I would be furious. But Peter seemed quite calm. Every now and then he smiled encouragingly at me. As if to say, don't worry about Jacob. And Jacob had provoked me. So why was I so ashamed of myself for reacting?

I couldn't sort it out, and for the rest of the meal I played it very safe, talking to Mark and Bess about the differences between Ithaca and Boston. Only in the lull before dessert did I realize that Jacob had been talking steadily in a low voice to Peter. When I concentrated I could catch "very isolated lab," "Oppenheimer's pet," "knew him at Göttingen," "chain reaction in Chicago," "high plateau," "everyone to wear uniforms," and then some names: "Fermi, Bethe, Lawrence."

But as soon as dessert was served, Peter was explaining to everyone how he had learned to skate so well. Then he and Jacob and Mark and Steffi were comparing notes on their long-ago childhood holidays in Europe. Bess and I listened, and later, while the men were toting up the bill, Bess murmured, "Makes

you a little envious, doesn't it, the way they talk about their childhoods?"

Steffi stared, her beautiful, thick eyebrows raised.

"You have all lived so intensely, your memories are so vivid— that our lives seem pale by comparison," Bess explained.

A shadow flitted across Steffi's features. Her voice was grim, steely. "We had to remember everything, I guess, because we knew they were going to take it away from us."

Once again I was unnerved. The Fialkas always presented their coming to America as something positive; they had gotten out together, they were alive and in good health. None of them ever talked very much about what they had left behind. But here, in the fierceness of Steffi Wunderlich's voice, in her now rueful eyes and the distracted way her long fingers twisted and untwisted her napkin, I sensed something very different.

I looked at her, wondering what to say. Nothing seemed right. We hardly knew each other. I caught Bess Chanin's eye, and we shrugged helplessly while Steffi averted her eyes, then pretended to be searching for something in her pocketbook.

• • •

Before we boarded the train to Lamy, my mother asked, one last time, "Are you absolutely sure you have enough warm clothes?"

"Of course, we're sure." My voice was brusque, and immediately I hated myself for the hurt, defeated look in her eyes. But damn it, I was grown—a fact they seemed to forget a lot of the time. By then I was twenty-two, Peter and I had been married almost a year, and I had spent more than five years in all kinds of wretched weather near Lake Cayuga. I knew very well how to dress for the bleakest climate. Besides, now it was April; crocuses were blooming in window boxes in Greenwich

Village and Harlem, and our destination was one of the most glorious spots in all of the Southwest. In my mind the Pajarito Plateau, where Los Alamos was situated, was a radiant, resplendent world.

When we stepped off the train, we couldn't see the Lamy station. A thick fog swirled between us and the few ramshackle buildings that were the town. Drab gray mist blurred the road as our taxi crawled to Santa Fe. There hail rattled on the sidewalk of the Plaza. Against the walls of the portico that surrounded the square were Indians huddled behind their wares. Never had I seen such stolid faces; in the raw cold their features seemed to be congealing before our eyes. I buttoned the jacket of my navy wool suit and pulled my new felt hat down over my ears; then Peter and I hurried to the office of Army Engineers at 109 Palace Avenue. As we walked, I kept seeing my mother's worried face.

In the warm cluttered room that was supposedly an Army office was a tall woman with a beautiful mane of long, almost black hair braided around her head, and a face with the shiniest apple cheeks I had ever seen. Her name was Thea MacFadden, and she introduced us to another couple whose names were Herb and History Lerner. We were all in the same boat; our apartments weren't ready.

"You'll have to spend a few days with some friends of mine near San Ildefonso," Thea explained. "You do know about San Ildefonso, the Tewa town where Maria Martinez lives? It's near the Black Mesa." Surely you know about that? her eyes added.

The four of us shook our heads, too tired to be ashamed of ourselves. Exhausted. So exhausted that History Lerner kept rubbing her right eye with the heel of her left hand, almost as if to push the tears that were in her throat from rising into her eyes. She was a pale blonde with oddly deep, greenish-hazel eyes, very small and fragile-looking; now she looked more fright-

ened than I felt, and reminded me of myself when I had arrived
for my first summer at camp only to discover that my trunk
had been lost by Railway Express. That's exactly what the
two of us must have looked like to Thea: two little girls who
were terrified at being sent away from home for the first time.
If only Steffi and Jacob would materialize, or the Chanins, whom
we had met at Christmas and who were supposed to be here
already. But when I asked about them, all Thea would say was
that they were settled on The Hill and we would see them in a
few days.

A young Indian was assigned to take us to Thea's friends. Our
trunks and the rest of our baggage would remain in a storeroom
not far away. Our furniture had been sent from Ithaca several
weeks ago, but so far no one had any record of its arrival.

"Don't worry." Thea patted my shoulder. "Things will
straighten out—they have for everyone else." Then she smiled and
looked thoughtfully at us. "And you won't need that hat, Lily—
it's a dead giveaway that you're from the East." I pulled it off and
crumpled it into my fist.

We climbed into the dented station wagon that was to take us
to the Windoms, Thea's friends, and I heard Thea instruct the
Indian to stop somewhere first. "Otowi." I had no idea what that
was, and I was suddenly miserable at having been dragged more
than halfway across this vast country where the weather was foul,
my new hat an eyesore, and where God knew how many more
unknowns lay in wait for us.

Then I remembered the faces of my friends in New York and
Ithaca whose only connection to their lovers or husbands was the
occasional letter or the maps of Europe and the Pacific and Africa
that they had memorized as carefully as cartographers. No, I
wouldn't want to trade places with them, even if they could stay
in their homes or go back to their parents for the duration of the
war. Now, as we sat back in the cracked leather seats of the old

car, I knew that as long as Peter and I could be together, we would manage.

Otowi was a small house nestled on the west bank of the Rio Grande. A thin woman who could have been forty or fifty came out into the hushed, falling snow.

"I'm Pamela Bye," she said, then ushered us inside where the most delicious smell of baking bread and warm chocolate filled the air.

"I feel like Hansel and Gretel," I murmured to Peter. History heard me and smiled in agreement. Then Miss Bye gestured the four of us to a table that had benches on either side, and soon we were drinking hot tea and eating huge pieces of the best chocolate cake I had ever tasted. In the center of the large room a fragrant piñon fire glowed. Around the adobe chimney were shelves filled with glistening, beautifully shaped and etched pottery bowls. Over the backs of the chairs were Indian blankets, draped as gracefully as shawls. As soon as she had entered the cottage, Miss Bye had changed her heavy boots for moccasins, so her steps were soundless as she moved from one task to another.

While we ate she asked us where we were from, where we had grown up and gone to college. She wasn't prying but simply trying to make us feel at ease, and we didn't hesitate to answer her questions. After all, hadn't Thea sent us here? Then she moved to the stove and removed some bread and shaped more dough into smooth, oval loaves.

Melville was right. You cannot hide the soul. Here, before our eyes, was a purity, a calm I had never seen before. Each gesture, each phrase had a completeness about it that made you pay attention to what Pamela was doing or saying. As I watched her, I wondered who she was and how she had come to live here.

After a few minutes an Indian entered. His name was Estevan.

He wasn't young or old; his features were ageless, and his face had a striking mobility. He smiled and spoke with an easy assurance. Quietly he deposited an armload of juniper twigs near the fireplace, then sat down and removed his leather boots. Miss Bye offered him some tea, but he shook his head and disappeared into another part of the house. I would have loved to ask who he was, but I didn't dare; even the most innocent question might disturb the tranquillity of this place that was like something from a fairy tale.

Besides, it was time to go. Our driver looked relieved when we rose, and we left quickly, not realizing that we should have paid for the cake and tea, that this place was really a little tearoom, but of course Miss Bye didn't say a word. She merely invited us to come back again, smiled a quick, bright good-bye.

Later, when we related the events of that day, people could not believe we had stopped at Pamela Bye's. "That's a treat only the big boys are able to get at a moment's notice," we were told.

"Or a couple of homesick kids," I would reply, part of me chagrined that History and I had been such obvious babies, and part of me grateful that Thea had taken pity on us and sent us to Otowi. In the end I was more thankful than abashed, for it was that first meeting, I was convinced, that allowed History and me to become Pamela's friends.

• • •

"Where did you get an odd name like History?" Mrs. Windom asked when we were finishing dinner: beef stew, corn muffins, salad, squash, rice, and fresh fruit for dessert. "Charles can't take those enchiladas and refried beans—you won't get anything like that in this house," she had announced before the meal.

"My mother liked unusual names, lots of people in Maine have them: Charity, Learned, Persis," History said.

Mrs. Windom nodded. She knew all about Maine. She knew all about everything. And now as my eyes tried to take in all the spotless knickknacks and objects that crowded the room, I still couldn't believe that this elderly couple were Thea's friends. Mrs. Windom was such a charmless know-it-all, and her husband was so dour. That trip to Pamela Bye's seemed a dream, and now I was right back where I had been when we arrived: exhausted and depressed. I looked around, trying to get my mind off myself. Many of the pieces here were similar to the ones at Otowi, but there were too many of them, and they looked tawdry. The place reminded me of one of those tourist shops near Times Square.

And now that we had finished dinner and the table was cleared, Mrs. Windom was bringing out a hideous arrangement of porcelain fruit that she placed in the center of the table. From the way she handled it, you knew it was a prized piece that she expected us to admire. But I couldn't. Not even after she had fed us so well. History caught my eye and we both swallowed in the silence. Mrs. Windom shrugged, then went into the kitchen and came back with a box of fancy chocolates. While she took her time unwrapping it and her husband filled his pipe, she said, "We know a man who gets everything through the black market in Albuquerque. When Thea called, I told Charles to find something to cheer you up."

Of course we couldn't resist. We were simply too tired. Once more today I savored the thick rich taste on my tongue. I hadn't had a piece of chocolate for months—and now twice in one day. It seemed positively decadent. Then I glanced furtively at my watch. How soon can we excuse ourselves and still not be thought rude? I was wondering when Mrs. Windom turned to History and asked, "Have you any brothers and sisters?"

History nodded. "A sister named Memory and a brother named Justice."

Finally Mrs. Windom was speechless. Silence filled the room as she sat there, rolling a piece of chocolate around in her mouth, defeated. "Did you hear that, Charles?" she whispered. Then we knew she had given up and put all four of us into the category where we belonged: as part of the wave of craziness that was invading Santa Fe, a wave that could be stopped no more easily than a blizzard or a tornado, and that included the Army with its noisy trucks and all the men, in uniforms and in civilian clothes, who were wandering around somehow convinced they could build a whole new city that no one was supposed to know about.

"They're all fit for nothing but the loony bin," Mr. Windom finally began. "They had just enough water up there for that boys' school with the pond, but that's not nearly enough for a city. When you girls get there"—he looked sternly at us—"you keep a big bucket of water in your kitchen for emergencies, and be sure to get yourselves some decent fire extinguishers. Otherwise, God help you." He was a retired sanitary engineer, he now told us, and had met Thea years ago when she first came to Santa Fe and was building an adobe house on the outskirts of town. "I was working on a new sewer line then," he said.

Why the Windoms had volunteered to put us up, I still couldn't figure out. Especially when Mrs. Windom looked at me slyly and said, "We know all there is to know about Thea, and Pamela Bye, too."

"God, have you ever met anyone so awful?" I asked Peter when we were finally alone.

"She's putting us up and feeding us, Lily—she can't be that bad." He was asleep before I could think of a reply.

On our fourth and last day Mrs. Windom said, "We're leaving. We came here thirty years ago for the climate and the peace, but now there'll never be any peace here. We have no intention of waiting till they blow up this part of New Mexico." At last Peter and Herb Lerner reacted to something she said. She noticed their startled glances and gave them a smug little smile.

"Oh, we know it's top secret, no one's supposed to know what's going on up there, and Thea would have my head if she heard me shooting my mouth off, but plenty of our Indian friends are working up there, and they're not as stupid as those Army people think. Neither are we. You'd have to be deaf, dumb, and blind not to notice all the machinery they're carting up there. It's a wonder the trucks don't topple off that miserable old road and kill someone. One of these days they'll have the accident they deserve—" She stopped for breath. "They're developing some new kind of hand grenade up there that—" She straightened her thin shoulders and moistened her lips. I steeled myself for some more, but Mr. Windom spelled her.

"That's what all those scientists are doing here. The bigger the machines and the more men involved, the smaller the end product. You don't have to be born yesterday to figure that out." He paused. "But we won't be here. As soon as someone makes a decent offer for this house, we'll be hightailing it out of here and starting fresh in Florida." He let his glance wander hopefully around the room as if he would be happy to sweep everything from sight.

"Of course we're planning to take the valuable things— Maria's bowls and those pieces from Frijoles Canyon and Puma and some of the other pieces," Mrs. Windom reminded her husband. "You never know what'll turn out to have some value," she added, looking severely at History and me in case we had any ideas.

For months after we left the Windoms, History and Herb and Peter and I laughed about them, mimicked them—"You never know what'll turn out to have some value" became a catch phrase among us—and then realized that Thea MacFadden had known exactly what she was doing. We learned later that Mrs. Windom was well-known in Santa Fe—for her tongue, and her penchant for gossip.

But we all felt better after our short stay with the Windoms. While Peter and Herb began working in the Theoretical Division, History and I had time to read about the Pueblo Indians and D. H. Lawrence and Kit Carson and Bishop Lamy. In the afternoons, while Mrs. Windom did her shopping, the two of us would walk around Santa Fe as leisurely as tourists. Though we were careful to dress in casual skirts and blouses and cardigan sweaters, I'm sure we didn't fool anyone. And when we came back to the Windoms' we could read or nap until dinner, because while we were staying in her home Mrs. Windom wouldn't have dreamed of letting us dry a dish. She vacuumed every day, said she had to because of all the trucks that went up on the nearby road to Los Alamos. But she had always vacuumed every day. That's what she thought a woman like her was supposed to do. And although she got on our nerves, Mrs. Windom gave us an opportunity to get the rest we badly needed to make the adjustment to this high place.

When we reported back to Thea at the end of our stay at the Windoms', History and I no longer looked or acted like frightened adolescents. "Lily, good news, your furniture has arrived," Thea greeted us, then handed me a slip of paper that would get me into the warehouse where I could authorize it to be sent to The Hill. "But you'll have to do with Army gear for a while longer, History," she added. The best news was that the Lerners and we were in the same row of apartments, each with one bedroom.

"The families with children get larger quarters, single people live in the dorms," Thea told us, then added, "Don't worry about food for the first few days—you can get good meals at Fuller Lodge, near Bathtub Row." This time she didn't stop to explain. You'll figure it out, her confident glance told us. "You made out all right at the Windoms'?" she added, but didn't wait for an answer. Now she had to concentrate on the new arrivals, who reminded me of myself five days ago. For a second I wanted to interrupt Thea and assure these new people they would be all right, but I didn't dare. Thea had it all in hand.

Besides, we were curious to get going. We hurried out in the direction of the warehouse. On our way past the Plaza, History put her hand on my arm.

"Oh, my God, Lily," she said in a worried voice. But she always reacted strongly even to little things. "Lily, do you realize that we forgot to thank Thea for sending us to Pamela's?" she asked.

"I'm sure we can call her when we get settled," I replied cheerfully, not yet aware that there were very few phones on The Hill, and the chance of our having one was almost nil.

4

I see glowing tawny light that has bathed the Rio Grande Pueblo lands since time began. And the dry, flinty earth, so dense and packed, has been there since long before Abraham or Christ, for at least ten thousand years, according to archaeologists. The Pueblos are the most peaceful, most self-contained Indians in North America—with a strength of character, a stubborn belief in nature, and a need for beauty and quiet that surpasses all the other instincts, even the so-called instincts for survival. That is why they are such a puzzle to the white man.

They are descended from the Mogollon and the Anasazi, who were hunters and gatherers. Then, about five thousand years ago, they began to grow corn, which they called maize, and beans and squash. After they became more agricultural, they settled into villages and built elaborately constructed apartmentlike homes and large ceremonial structures called kivas. For irrigation they used flood-farming techniques, as well as canals and ditches whose source of water was the Rio Grande and its tributaries.

By the beginning of the fourteenth century, at a time when their culture is believed to have reached the height of sophistication, certain of the Pueblo tribes simply left; all that remains are their tools and their cities on the highest mesas: Tsirege, Tsankewi, Navawi, Puye, Shupinna, Tyuonyi. Were they attacked? Or was it drought that forced them to seek homes lower down? No one knows. Around the end of the fourteenth century they were joined by nomads who were the ancestors of the Navahos and Apaches. Though they were more competitive and warlike than the Pueblos, these wanderers lived peacefully with the remaining Pueblo tribes.

All that changed by the 1530s when Francisco Vásquez de Coronado came with several hundred troops and five Franciscan missionaries and established the brutal rule that was to characterize the Spanish oppression of the Rio Grande Pueblos from that time onward. Coronado forbade them to practice their religion and changed their lives for the next 150 years. But in 1680, several Pueblo tribes revolted. After that, the oppressive measures were relaxed and the Pueblos were permitted to return to their religious ceremonies.

With the coming of the Anglo-American missionaries at the end of the eighteenth century, Indian language and customs were again suppressed. But instead of eradicating Indian tradition, these zealots merely pushed the Pueblos underground. In their kivas they sought the solace of their ceremonies. They became angrier and more secretive until, at last, in the 1920s, religious tolerance prevailed.

"They are still wary," Pamela tells us when History and I visit her at Otowi, "but they are an amazing people who have achieved a rare bond with this beautiful wilderness."

How confident she is; every word, every gesture—even the way she pushes back her grayish-blond hair from her temples—reflects her happiness.

Her eyes dart quickly as they follow the birds while we sit in the little spot below Otowi called Posahcongay—literally translated as "the place where the river makes a noise"—and watch the thick, lumbering line of water that is the Rio Grande make its way through the arroyo and out into the mesa below. For here the river slows down, encumbered by silt it has gathered on its way through Colorado and northern New Mexico, and the red sandstone and yellow clay that it has picked up from the Chama River that joins it from the west. Hardly the sparkling, cascading river they call the Rio Grande hundreds of miles north.

"But I like the river this way. Neither of us is rushing to get anywhere, " Pamela confides, then rises, for now it is time to go in and prepare another one of the dinners she makes almost every night for the more important men and women from The Hill.

How brilliant of Oppie to arrange those dinners at Pamela's for "the big boys." In Pamela's home the intensity of all our lives seems to diminish; after an evening there you can return to The Hill a little less pressured, a little less anxious. And perhaps that is why we're all so curious about her.

Yet I wonder what all this feverish activity has done to her life. Before we leave, I screw up my courage and ask, and her answer astonishes History and me. We expected her to talk about the peacefulness of this ancient land, and how science has no place here.

Instead she says, simply, "I am happy to be useful. Now I feel as if I am helping in the war effort."

"We're all the same," History says as we make our way back to the road where we'll hitch a ride with one of the Army trucks as it goes from Santa Fe up to The Hill. "No one, not even Pamela, can escape this war." Then she shakes her head and stops for a moment to stare up at the huge expanse of sky. It is bathed in such dazzling May sunlight that my eyes tear. But History's stare is clear-eyed; without a trace of timidity she regards the sky as if it were an immense crystal ball from which she could learn the future.

• • •

You could hardly call Leslie R. Groves a villain, or a Coronado, and of all of us the Indians seemed to accept him most placidly. Perhaps because he was just another in a long line of white men who had intruded on their land and their way of life.

But to many of the people at Los Alamos he was a son-of-a-bitch. Oddly, Groves didn't bother me. I never did entirely understand why. Maybe it was because he had chosen Oppenheimer to direct Site Y.

Oppie wasn't an easy man, and he had alienated more than one scientist here. But I liked him on sight, and Peter respected him, and as time passed, he proved to be an inspired choice. Los Alamos seemed to bring out everything that was fine and generous in Oppenheimer's personality, and to suppress all the snobbery and aloofness and even brutality that had characterized him when he was younger.

To most of us at Los Alamos Oppie was the important one. Groves was merely a general who had to keep the Manhattan Project going, and although it was really an enormous job, I never thought of it as being as momentous as Oppie's task.

Like the war itself, the Manhattan Project could be thought of as an octopus whose tentacles reached from Washington all across the United States. We knew about Hanford and Oak Ridge and Chicago, but work on the Manhattan Project was done in dozens of small labs scattered all over the country in places we had never heard of by people who often had no idea what they were working on. That was because of Groves's almost pathological need for secrecy, but, after all, he was the one who had to coordinate the whole.

When he set up all his rules for Los Alamos, Groves had had the idea that each person would work in his own compartment and never communicate what he was doing to anyone else. How that would work he never found out because Oppie convinced him that it was impossible, that they must have a weekly colloquium. We heard that Groves called it the weekly gabfest. It sounded too much like him not to be true.

An engineer by training, Groves never really understood what physics was about. "It looks too much like talking, it's worse than philosophy," he once muttered after he met with some of the younger men. And for a man like Groves talking was never work.

But what wonderful talk. "The beauty of physics," Peter had told me before we ever came to this place, "is its openness. Everyone knows what everyone else is doing. And because the very study of physics is a world of possibilities, its knowledge is cumulative. Everyone builds on what has been done before."

At first General Groves seemed unreasonable. Even bitter. We had heard that he was disappointed not to have been assigned to active duty. He was forty-six years old when he got this assignment, and because he was a true soldier, war meant combat, not another administrative job. But either his disappointment was short-lived, or he learned to mask it very well. After a few months as director, General Groves had convinced himself that he was crucial to the victory of the Allies, perhaps its most influential element.

I had had a few glimpses of him here and there on The Hill, but our first official contact with Groves was a meeting for all the Los Alamos wives in the main room at Fuller Lodge, in the middle of May. History and I filed in with the others—there were more than a hundred—like obedient schoolchildren, and I saw many familiar faces—Steffi Wunderlich and Bess Chanin and Thea MacFadden and many others, like Kitty Oppenheimer, whom I knew only by sight. At the front were Oppie and Groves.

What a pair. Fat, lumpy, stolid Groves and skinny, loose-limbed, nervous Oppie. As they greeted us, they resembled Jack Sprat and his wife. History murmured in a surprised voice, "They look like Laurel and Hardy," and there was a suppressed trickle of laughter down our row.

It was soon clear, though, that this was serious business, and we had better pay attention. Oppenheimer introduced Groves and then let the general do most of the talking. Groves's voice was somber and resonant. We had heard that he had no use for women, just as we had heard he had no use for the scientists, but he needed them, and because we were married to them, he needed us as well.

Still, standing there that day between History Lerner and Bess Chanin, I didn't feel that Groves disliked us; more that he was incapable of understanding us. He didn't understand women's talk any more than he understood the talk of the theoretical physicists. But Groves had given in on the weekly meetings of the scientists, the Colloquia, and now, probably because Oppie suggested it, he was welcoming us.

He talked about the commissary, the laundry, the library, the school, health care, the hospital, the ways to deal with the Indian help, the need to have whoever was childless and healthy work. As he spoke he apologized for nothing, and if he had had to tell us that we were each getting washboards and had to wash our clothes in Ashley Pond, he would have used the same tone of voice. When one woman tried to complain about the Black Beauties, which was what we called the stoves they had given us, he gave her a blank look, as if to say, This is the way it is. You're in the Army now, the country is at war, make do.

He reminded me of the headmaster of a boys' school that has

just decided to take girls. He shifted his ample body a little as he spoke, clearly ill at ease to be in the company of so many women. Yet we knew he had a wife and two children—a boy and a girl— back East, whom he visited from time to time on his journeys around the country. Suddenly I wondered who took such good care of him. He always looked so neat and clean and pressed in his full uniform. Such a contrast to Oppie, who was usually dressed in a rumpled blue work shirt and jeans. How strange that the man with the wife looked almost unkempt and the man without so well taken care of.

Then, in a pause, another question. This time it was Steffi. "Is it really necessary to have these fences and all these guards? We feel as if we're living in a cage." It was more accusation than question.

But Groves didn't flinch or budge. He simply launched into a speech about his pet subject: the need for secrecy. "This is more than an Army base," he told us. "This is a scientific laboratory. As all of you know, the work being done here must remain secret, even from you, who are so close to those who are doing it. But let me assure you, it is of tremendous importance to this war effort, and I know all of you will cooperate with the need for such careful security. We must have fences to see who comes in and who goes out, and guards to check your security passes."

General Groves was not asking us for our cooperation; he was telling us he expected it. Which is why some of the women resented him. Groves's demands defined the limits of our lives. They left nothing to the imagination. And therein lay their virtue.

Moreover, Groves was prepared for the consequences. History was the one who articulated it first. "We're lucky we have Groves as a scapegoat—so there's someone to blame when we're disappointed or tired." She was right, and I think Groves knew exactly what he was doing, if not consciously, then perhaps unconsciously. He had lived long enough in the Army to know there was bound to be griping in this confined, isolated place. So he was willing to deal with it, and let Oppie concentrate on the science.

What Groves didn't really understand was that, in addition to the scientists and the machinists and the Army personnel, he was in charge of a group of young women who were more unpredictable and assertive than he had ever anticipated. And any deviation from his plan seemed to unsettle him.

Even Arlene Feynman's tuberculosis. Every Friday the indefatigable, cheerful Richard Feynman would hitchhike from Los Alamos to see his beloved young wife in the hospital in Albuquerque. But Groves found it difficult to cope with Arlene's tragic disease, or the young couple's love for each other, or Richard's great good humor, which made each trip to Albuquerque a gay jaunt out into the world.

Or our desire to have families. Groves wasn't a fool; he knew many of us were newly married and very much in love; he should have foreseen what he always called, contemptuously, "the baby boom" at Los Alamos. But when the pregnancies began, he was truly appalled, and when they multiplied in what seemed a geometric progression, he regarded us as mischief-makers conspiring against him.

• • •

History and I are sitting on some crates in the Lerners' apartment while we unpack others. The GIs have finally hauled away the tables and beds and straight chairs History and Herb were forced to use, and now they will be able to live among their own things. Only two months have passed, but already we are learning how to live like Army wives. The chamisa on the hillsides has changed from a dull purplish-gray to a luminous, sometimes iridescent bluish-green. Each day the sun grows stronger as it rises behind the cottonwoods that give Los Alamos its name. And that endless sky, that infinite blueness that Willa Cather described so unforgettably, is beginning to be a part of our daily lives.

"Elsewhere the sky is the roof of the world, but here the earth was the floor of the sky," I reread a few nights ago in *Death Comes for the Archbishop*. Last winter in Ithaca I had no idea what Cather was talking about; I didn't even realize that the bishop in her book was based on Lamy, the nineteenth-century missionary who gave his name to the small town south of Sante Fe.

The thinness of the air here at 7200 feet makes us all a little strange. "High-strung," Steffi says, though I'm not sure that's exactly the right word. Every activity, even unpacking these crates, seems to be charged with a tremendous importance. I say so to History.

She pushes her straight blond hair back from her forehead and frowns. Her greenish eyes shine like opals in her pale face. "Do you really think it's the altitude, Lily? Can air and altitude have so much influence over our lives?" History shakes her head before I can answer. "No, I think it has to do with what's happening here."

When History uses the words "what's happening here," I become uneasy. We've made oblique references to a weapon of destruction, but I don't know how much History knows and History doesn't know how much I know because Peter and Herb aren't supposed to discuss anything outside the lab. There is no way we can sit down over a meal or a cup of coffee and talk about the progress of the gadget.

Really a ridiculous word for it. It reminds me of that utterly meaningless catch-all word my brothers have begun to use: gizmo. Leave it to Oppie to figure out a word with so many ironies. Calling this weapon a gadget is almost as bizarre as the

Windoms' conviction that the end product will be a super-duper hand grenade.

Actually, Peter and I talked more about the making of a weapon when we were deciding whether to come. Now that we're here, talk about what is happening seems useless. And the talk has an unreal, even surreal quality. Everything is euphemized: a weapon is a "gadget," a dangerous lab is "hot," the water shortage is "a dry spell." Like some children's game, a colossal hide-and-seek with all the ritualized chanting of "You're hot, you're cold."

The problem, though, is not to find the treasure, but to invent it. That gives the whole business a dimension no one has ever experienced before and is probably the cause of this intensity we all feel so acutely. History is right. It's not the altitude that's making me sleep badly and feel more vulnerable than I've ever felt before.

Besides, the world has been turned topsy-turvy. No one is where he or she belongs. If there had been no war, these physicists would be scattered all over Europe and the United States, meeting for an occasional conference, quietly teaching their students the theories of Planck and Einstein and Rutherford and Bohr.

Or would they? Peter insists that nothing would have stayed the same after the discovery of nuclear fission. "As soon as they realized you could produce fission by bombarding uranium, the world changed. There was no going back. That was the beginning, Lily, and this"—he gestured out the window toward the ugliness stretching as far as the eye could see—"is merely an extension of that."

"But what if there had been no war, no Hitler?" I persisted.

Peter shrugged. He has never been interested in "what ifs." I suppose he's right; "what ifs" are useless, and there is Hitler and there is a war, and no one knows that better than Peter and Jacob and the rest of them who were hounded out of Europe and who have suddenly found themselves in this isolated desert where all they are supposed to do is talk, think, breathe atomic physics.

"This is a race," I overheard Jacob say recently. "A race with two of the most powerful forces in the world: Germany and Japan. A race we cannot afford to lose." His voice was solemn, harsh.

So of course they are obsessed. How could they not be obsessed? And so are we wives.

Now I feel History watching me, and there's a warning look in her eyes; some people believe that the apartments are bugged, so I shrug, then sigh, as History reminds me, gently, that even the women who don't know as much as we do—like Bess Chanin— seem to be feeling the effects of the altitude. And then she adds, "What good does it do to try to identify it, dissect it, Lily? That's a dead end. The only practical thing is to adjust." Her smile is rueful. "You'll adjust," has become a joke among the women on The Hill.

She begins to pry open another crate. "How can the same Army that packed this crate so well run such a lousy commissary?" she asks.

It's the bed frame and mattress. When we finally get it apart, History empties the straw packing and I round up items that belong to what Housing calls "the borrowing basket." Silverware, cooking utensils, towels, soap, pots, dishes. History won't need her basket now that she has her own things, and it will be passed on to another newcomer, who will then pass it on to the next. It's a rite of passage here, how we wives know we're settled in. My borrowing basket came from Bess Chanin and was passed on to a couple with two children who are waiting for their things to come from Chicago.

Now we drag the mattress over to the frame. "My mother's gift to us—this queen-sized bed. No child of hers could possibly sleep in just a double bed," History says with a smile.

At the mention of her mother I say, impulsively, "Why did your mother give you such odd names?" Then I look warily at her, to make sure I haven't said the wrong thing. But she is still smiling as she speaks.

"She's pretentious, doesn't think much of people, doesn't trust anyone's intelligence. A snob. She once told me she did it so we would know we were special, that certain things were expected of us. But you can teach kids that without giving them odd names, can't you?" I nod.

"She didn't do it maliciously. Actually, she's very limited, for all her pretensions. She would have died if she had had to clean all the soot on the walls when we arrived, and she would starve before using Black Beauty." She tilts her head toward the black stove that sits in every kitchen like a mourning Sicilian woman, a doleful reminder that we're in the Army now. History and I had been alternately horrified and fascinated by it, but like everyone else, we have learned to cook on it with either oil or wood. Only the other night Peter complimented me on dinner— me, who couldn't get a decent meal together in Ithaca on a Chambers stove that was practically new compared to this monstrosity.

"What would she have done for meals?"

"Dragged my father to Fuller Lodge every night, then wondered why they were broke. She can never do anything the way everyone else does. If she were here, the first thing she would have done would be to finagle Housing into giving her a place on Bathtub Row." I smile. Bathtub Row is the street of log houses that once belonged to the Los Alamos School, as Fuller Lodge once did. Those houses have bathtubs, but only the bigwigs live there: Oppie, Groves, the Bethes, the Wunderlichs, and other top administrators. I shake my head.

"No one finagles Rose Bethe into anything at Housing, Steffi says. And she ought to know."

"My mother would have figured out a way. Developed a fatal allergy to coal heat, or broken her ankle in the mud caked around the apartments, or become catatonic in her fear of fire. Something dramatic and irresistible."

"How lucky for me that you're not your mother." Then we place the bed in the center of the room. Morning sunshine floods the room. The wind is blowing from the north, and now the fragrant scent of pine off the high horned peak, Truchas, fills the air. History flings open the other window, and we sit for a moment.

"Still, my mother would be complaining even on Bathtub Row." We start to pry open the next crate. "Probably about the Jews," History adds. Startled, my head shoots up. Why do I hate the expression "the Jews"? But when I look at History, her eyes are benign, amused.

"When I told my mother I was marrying Herb, she didn't say a word about my age—I was twenty—or about Herb's work, but simply inquired as to whether I was prepared to lose my inheritance since she would have no choice but to cut me out of the will if my father died before she did. 'You know I have a problem with Jews,' she said as casually as someone might announce they can't eat lamb."

"And what did you say?"

"The truth. That I was planning to marry Herb because I loved him and I had no worries about my inheritance. It has never been mentioned since. My dad liked Herb, and by the time the wedding took place Mom had come around. I knew she would."

"You mean you did it all yourself—the wedding, I mean, the preparations . . ." My voice dwindled; suddenly I felt so stupid, remembering how my mother had done so much for me.

History nodded, then said, "We were married in Chicago, a very small wedding, not that much to do, really. I converted because it was important to Herb, and we were married by a rabbi. The Fermis came—of course that impressed her; I guess she doesn't know that Laura Fermi is Jewish. Or maybe by then she didn't care, because she never said a word about my conversion and had a wonderful time at the wedding. She loves parties." As she speaks, History becomes sturdier, and I realize how different she is from the person we met in Thea's office, or even the woman I knew at the Windoms'. Then all I could see was her slight figure and her wan blond looks, which can be drab when she's tired. But here is a woman who is very sure of herself and not at all timid, because she has had to cope with so much more than I have.

Friendship wasn't easy at first. Years after we were at Los Alamos, many of the women claimed that it was the happiest time of their lives. It was the most exciting time of my life, but it wasn't as easy as some of those women would have us believe.

Perhaps it had to do with the deadening sameness of the buildings or the disorganized way they were slapped together: a maze of gray and green meandering haphazardly around the white cruciform that was the hospital. Or those hateful barbed-wire fences. Or the way life at Los Alamos was propelled and regulated by an endless series of bells—for wake-up, for work, lunch, back to work, quitting time. Or with that undertow of security, like a pulse creating mistrust and suspicion or else slowing up everything—going through the gate or making a long-distance telephone call or sending a telegram or arranging an appointment with the dentist in Santa Fe, which I had to do quite often, since Peter was having trouble with his teeth, as usual.

Or perhaps friendship is never as easy as some people would like to make it.

But these are speculations one can make only later, after the fact. On the day that I am helping History, all I can think is how lucky we are to have met that first day because we would never have met through our work. I am Jacob Wunderlich's secretary in the Technical area, and History works in the hospital. We're together this morning because Jacob is away for the day and History got some time off to unpack. Tonight, after Herb and Peter come home, we have all been invited to the Wunderlichs' for dinner, but now we have the whole day to do what young married women have done for generations: talk about their families as they unpack the belongings they have acquired to make a home. Yet as I review all the things History has told me today, I'm horrified.

I say so, but she just laughs that tinkly laugh of hers and shrugs in a gesture that is part defiance, part acceptance. "It wasn't so bad having her as a mother. Actually, she spent hours quizzing us for our tests and sewing our clothes and baking gorgeous desserts. We always had the most spectacular birthday parties. Besides, if you have a name like History you know by the time you're six that your mother is strange. So you accept her." She makes everything sound so simple, so logical.

"I can see that, but I don't know how you can forgive her for saying that about the Jews. Herb is Jewish, and now that you've converted so are you." And so am I. No wonder I sound so angry.

"That's because you don't know any Gentiles from Maine. She didn't mean anything terrible by it. It was simply a fact of her life. Besides, now that I've lived away from home for several years, I feel more sorry for her than angry at her. Think about her life, Lily. She never lived anywhere but Maine, on vacations they went to the Rangeley Lakes or the White Mountains or the Greens. She was always rich by Maine standards, and she has never felt the exhilaration I feel now that I have my own things again. Or the pride of getting through those first few weeks here. Remember, all I knew was Maine and Chicago."

"I know. All I knew was New York and Ithaca."

"My mother didn't even understand why we had to leave Chicago. This war isn't very real to her. Her life hasn't changed very much, after all, except that she can't do as much baking as she likes. My father's too old to go, and my brother, Jus, is too young. She has no idea what Herb does or why it might be important. She's never had to stretch herself."

Then I think of my mother sitting at her desk in her bedroom, making up shopping lists and cleaning lists and laundry lists: all those compelling lists that are the calling cards of comfortable housewives everywhere, and I wonder if I will ever be able to make my mother understand what has happened to me in these last weeks. What it feels like to live on this mesa, so high that you feel as if your little piece of the universe has been snagged on an invisible thread in the sky and you're hanging up here, destined to look down on the world for who knows how long.

Such a primitive place, this Pajarito Plateau. Surrounded by the deep, narrow canyons that were cut into the rock thousands of years ago, we could be living in some strange ancient castle protected by a huge impassable moat. Daily I hear the mothers complain about the still-inadequate school, the holes in the fences that surround us, and the nagging temptation of the—oddly—unfenced pond. Or the general discontent with the arbitrary system of apportioning the Indian help that comes each day from Santa Clara and San Ildefonso. Or, most important, the chronic, disturbing shortage of water that Charles Windom had warned us about. Still, none of it seems to matter.

Each morning when I open our closet, I smile at the sight of the hatbox and my two correct suits. What on earth was I thinking of? There is no room for correctness on this plateau. We wear full casual skirts, pants, cotton blouses, flat shoes or sneakers, and socks. In the midst of those barren hillsides which seem to compete with each other to support the least amount of vegetation, I feel freer, more reckless, than I've ever felt in my life. One day I came upon a neighbor crying because some of her crystal had arrived smashed to bits; I could hardly comfort her. Who can worry about such things here? Who would want to?

Even the children are wild. Exhausted by the hot sun and thin air, they seem bold, overexcited, sometimes feverish. They remind me of my mother's stories of her brother and sisters and cousins running helter-skelter on the old gated estates, through the high, spindly wildflowers of that last Russian summer before the First World War, that last summer of childhood, before their world changed forever.

By now we have unpacked several small crates. Together we pull a mattress pad taut across the double bed. "This will be a nice change from those single army cots," History admits shyly, then pushes back a few loose strands of hair from her forehead.

"We've been trying to have a baby for three years," she says so softly that I have to stop pulling at the sheet in order to hear her. "I'm almost twenty-six and Herb is thirty, and no go in Chicago. Every month, like clockwork, there it was. But now I think I'm pregnant." She mouths the words as if afraid to say them aloud. My heart sinks. It could be the altitude; lots of women have complained that the altitude has affected their periods. When History sees my face, she laughs.

"Oh, Lily, you're such a worry wart. It's not just the change. I've missed two periods and had a test," she says, then walks to the southeast corner of the bedroom that is drenched with yellow light. "And here's where we'll put the crib."

I can almost taste my relief. Finally there is an explanation for those dark rings under History's eyes, her glassy skin. Or why she looked so relieved when I offered to get the day off to help her unpack.

For the rest of the day, while we eat, then unpack a few more crates, and finally push the cheerful chintz-covered furniture around until we hit upon the best arrangement, I feel awed by History's body, by the knowledge of what she carries within it. Peter and I don't want children yet, but living here among these families with their suntanned, free-wheeling kids, I have found myself wondering what it would be like to have a family.

At last it is all in place. The bell for the end of work hasn't rung yet, so we are ahead of ourselves. History looks happy but tired. Well, she has every right to be tired. "Can I tell Peter?" I ask.

History nods, then hesitates. "But promise not to tell another soul. I hate to admit it, and Herb won't, of course, but we're both . . . the fact is we're both a little superstitious."

"So am I. So is anyone with a brain in his head." I kiss History and tuck the borrowing basket under my arm. I will drop it off at Housing tomorrow, but now it's time to go home and get dressed for the Wunderlichs' party.

5

When Peter arrived in the United States at the age of almost twenty-two, he had known exactly what he had to do: finish his doctorate, continue to do research in physics, and teach. But six years later, after Pearl Harbor, Peter was suddenly faced with the question: Am I of use? And although his research on the evolution of stars was important, and he had a perfectly legitimate deferment from the draft, Peter had struggled with the temptation to leave Cornell and enlist.

That struggle ended when we heard about the work Fermi was doing in Chicago: finally physics was not merely theoretical and arcane; now it would have a practical value. How great a value no one could predict, but the possibilities were enormous. I had known that when I saw Jacob Wunderlich's face at Rockefeller Center.

At Los Alamos, surrounded by the rituals of secrecy and security that characterized Site Y—and that could have been invented by Hollywood—Peter felt more American than he had ever believed he could. He had been summoned, and he had come.

Although there were a few scientists, like our friend Dan

Schweren, who chose not to come, and although some of the older, more sophisticated women who came to Los Alamos might have wished to say, like Bartleby, "I would prefer not," we were all committed to help in whatever way we could to complete the immense task that had been set for our husbands.

I knew about fission, about Fermi's Chicago pile—why, any fool who was here knew about them, and those women who claimed, so innocently, not to know "what was happening here" were ostriches who chose to bury their heads in the desert sands.

For suddenly science had a new place in world affairs, physics a specially favored one. But what would the outcome be? To make a weapon of destruction based on Hahn's prewar discovery of nuclear fission was evil. Had any scientist the right to go that far? Yet what if the German scientists made the weapon first? That was a real possibility, for the Germans had started uranium research two years before the Americans and could be as much as two years ahead of us.

So many unknowns in this equation. Peter was right. No use in speculating. One step at a time, people said, one day at a time, catch phrases like that rueful, ironic "Live and learn."

● ● ●

Charles Windom had called The Hill an anthill, but in an anthill all the frenetic activity is visible on the surface. As spring stretched into the long mesa summer, Los Alamos was like a live volcano, as if the very recesses of the Pajarito Plateau were being churned up and turned inside out.

Five million years ago this plateau, the Plateau of the Little Bird, had been created by a series of volcanic eruptions, which came from the mountains to the west like huge clouds of flame, then spread deposits of sand and incandescent ash a thousand feet deep over an area of four hundred miles. The erosion of water and wind had formed, over the millennia, the canyons and high mesas of this exotic desert landscape—an unearthly place in which there was the deepest silence I had ever known.

Though I couldn't hope to fathom the depths of that silence, I knew that whatever disturbed it was harmful and dangerous. And yet it couldn't be helped. So, with the rest of the inhabitants of Los Alamos, and Pamela and the Indians of San Ildefonso, I watched helplessly as a new means of erosion, the monstrous Army bulldozer, single-mindedly rearranged the earth for badly needed housing, labs, and offices.

Once the heat came in earnest, the mud dried. In a few days the roads were hard, baked, and our throats and nostrils parched to sandpaper. The churning of the machinery had been less violent, less offensive when the earth was waterlogged and muddy; now each ram of the shovel into the caked reddish clay reverberated through the sunlit air like a thunderclap.

Seeing that machinery attack the landscape, hearing its unremitting whine, I understood why the Pueblos build their adobe homes with the flat of their palms in the spring, when the earth is doughy and pliant. Some days my anger at what was being done to this mesa spread through my body until I felt almost sick.

By early June it had gotten especially bad, since they were building more housing near our row, yet while History and I had been together it had been blessedly quiet. After I left History, I looked forward to a peaceful hour before Peter arrived home. But when I stepped from the shower and heard the machines, I was furious. That meant a weekend of noise.

"There's no choice," Peter said later. He was knotting his tie and combing his hair. I was sitting in the corner of our bedroom while Truchas turned bloody in the sunset. Two Truchases really: the real double-peaked mountain outside the window and its reflection in the mirror. When Peter turned around to look at me, he was frowning.

"I hate it, too, the noise, the flimsiness of whatever they build, all of it. But that can't be helped, darling. We wouldn't mind it so much if we weren't here, if they had done it before we arrived. But they didn't." He stared out the window for a moment, then turned toward me again.

"They didn't know what they needed. Oppie thought thirty scientists would do it, never even thought about the machinists and technicians and the Army. So they have to do it now. No use moaning. We're damned lucky Groves is giving us what we want."

A long speech, for Peter. Be thankful you have a roof over your head, his eyes added. Some of the newcomers, even those with children, had been set up in tents in Bandelier Park. Peter's flat, clinical tone reminded me of the one he had used several months ago when we talked about coming here. But today there was a trace of annoyance, probably apparent only to me.

You should be married to one of the real complainers, I wanted to retort. But what was the point? I merely shook my head and concentrated on the feathery motes of dust that filmed the dresser and desktops. I tried to keep after the dust—we all did—but it was impossible. Even Bess, our Puritan, as we fondly called her, and the most compulsive housekeeper among us, had given up.

"Mark sometimes writes his formulas in the dust," she'd confessed recently. "He says it's perfect, saves paper and conforms to the secrecy regulations because all he does when he's figured something out is wipe it away. Not even a carbon to burn," she'd added airily, but no one had laughed.

Now Peter stood over me and raised my chin with his forefinger. He smiled his "don't brood, Lily" smile and pulled me up from the wicker chair that had been a hand-me-down from my grandmother. When he drew me closer, rubbing my left temple with his freshly shaved cheek, I wished we could let our party clothes drift from our bodies and we could lie down and make love, as we sometimes did at just this time, enveloped by a vermilion sunset.

But we had to leave. "The Lerners are waiting, we can't be late,"

Peter reminded me. That was true. Word had it that Steffi Wunderlich had no patience with latecomers who might spoil her carefully prepared meal.

At the Lerners' Peter admired all that History and I had accomplished. Still, as his glance skimmed the sofa, chairs, tables, and lamps that History loved so much, I could see he wasn't really interested. Peter had no feel for material things; I could never remember him admiring a room or a rug or a piece of silver or porcelain or glass. Standing there, realizing this essential fact about my husband, I also remembered that I hadn't told him History was pregnant.

Why hadn't I told him? Could I be jealous? Was that why I'd been so out of sorts before? Come on, Lily, be truthful. But no, it couldn't be. Peter and I were still getting used to each other, I was only twenty-two, we had time to think about children.

No, I hadn't told Peter because of the noise and the dust. That combination was enough to put the most even-tempered person into a foul mood. It was nothing more than that. I'll tell him later, I decided as we were walking to the Wunderlich party, when we are sleepy and naked and in each other's arms, and the sharp, cool mountain darkness has dampened the echo of the machines and the dust has dissolved, if only temporarily, into the thick black Pajarito night.

I'd had no idea that the top brass would be at the Wunderlichs' party. But here were Oppie and his wife, and General Groves, alone as usual, and several of the men in charge of the other divisions. Clearly we were here to usher Oppenheimer in as head of Site Y—the Los Alamos part of the Manhattan Project.

How elegant, how chic the women looked! Now I was glad I had persisted, despite Peter's gentle mocking, in dragging out my long apricot chiffon dress and pressing it, then holding it above my ankles on the walk over so it wouldn't be grimed with dust.

Steffi was in a strapless silvery-green dress with a stole; the color made her eyes blacker and her chestnut hair richer than usual. Thea MacFadden wore a red off-the-shoulder gown that showed off her splendid figure and made me realize she was much younger than History and I had guessed. And Bess was so healthy looking in a sleeveless white sheath that made her golden skin look deeper than usual. Watching the three of them talk, I felt that old envy of tall women I have had since childhood. Not even the knowledge that the Lerners thought Bess horsey looking, with her pug nose and wide nostrils that flared when she laughed, could assuage my envy. But Bess must not have felt as confident as she looked, for on her arm was one of those absurd lighthouse baskets from Nantucket that the women who are born there get when they reach adolescence. "A rite of passage on the island," she had once told me, "that I wear when I feel in need of a little luck."

I could certainly understand that. This was the first time we women were seeing Teller and Oppenheimer and Lawrence and Allison close up; of course the younger wives felt shy. Sensing my discomfort, Peter stayed close to me, and soon I began to relax as we slowly threaded our way through the crowd.

While Peter was introducing me, I felt a strange new sensation. The last few Sundays we had hiked in the hot sun to the summit of several nearby mountains—Tsi'como, Caballo, Pajarito, Cerro Grande—and now Peter was more tanned than I had ever seen him, handsomer than I could remember. His pale skin, so chalky at the end of an Ithaca winter, was a deep bronze that made his eyes sparks of bluish light. It was astonishing, Peter's sturdy, plain features being lit up, transformed by those eyes. Since our arrival I had noticed several of the Indians start a little, almost frightened at first, but as soon as he spoke and they heard his soft, easygoing voice, they had warmed up. Yet tonight those eyes gave him a magnetism that you could feel, and soon my shyness was replaced by a self-confidence I had never known so powerfully before. It was as exciting as the familiar knowledge that I was married to a very promising young theoretical physicist. Suddenly, that night, I realized I was also married to a very attractive man.

He walked beside me, his fingers cradling my elbow, pressing my skin through the thin chiffon, his jawbone sometimes grazing the top of my hair, and all I could think was: He's mine. I have washed and ironed his clothes, I have made countless appointments with the dentist to take care of his terrible teeth, I have seen his expression quickened by hunger and anger and, yes, lust, and I have also seen it flattened by confusion and misery and boredom. I know things about him that no one else here can possibly know, and I also know that when we leave this party and are back in our small apartment, we will slowly undress and gossip and laugh a little about these very dignitaries we are now so respectfully greeting, and when we have had enough of that and are pleasantly sleepy and talked out, we will turn to each other and make love. And then all the questions, all the uncertainties will drift, miraculously, away. A powerful escape, lovemaking, and in this new warm climate it had a more compelling place in our lives than it had ever had before.

Suddenly I heard, "Lily, how lovely you look, what a pretty dress!" It was Jacob, coming up behind us, then shaking Peter's hand and looking at me. "Only someone with your high coloring could wear that shade. Let me see the back again," he urged, and I turned around, tempted to pirouette for him as I used to after my mother and I had shopped all day and I would have to summon one more ounce of strength to show my father my new clothes. But I controlled myself and looked around while Jacob and Peter went to get the drinks.

Although Steffi and I had talked several times in line at the commissary, I had never been here before, and now I searched my memory for an image of the Wunderlichs' Ithaca apartment. But I couldn't recall anything like this. For Steffi—who always seemed to have perfect taste and who was wearing the prettiest dress I had ever seen, here, in this out-of-the-way place that wasn't even supposed to exist in June of 1943—had filled this lovely desert home with an unbelievable amount of clutter.

We all knew that Jacob had insisted on bringing his grand piano to Box 1663, our mysterious address; Thea had personally overseen its precarious journey up the winding rutted thirty-five-mile road from Sante Fe. Jacob was a wonderful pianist, something I hadn't known until we came to Los Alamos. Peter and I often heard him playing when we took a walk in the evening. When General Groves had practically roared with frustration at Jacob's request, Jacob was rumored to have replied, "It's the only piano I have, and I'm not about to buy another one." At Los Alamos he played every morning before coming to work.

But why all the rest of this junk? It reminded me of the apartments of all the spinsters my parents knew who had arrived from Europe in the thirties. "They need those knickknacks," my mother once explained, "because they have nothing else."

Yet Steffi had Jacob and their son, Samuel, and their friends. I sipped my drink, trying to make some sense of the clutter, but who could explain the Dresden figures, delicate porcelain cups and saucers displayed on wooden braces, gilt-edged plates and ornate trays and vases of Venetian glass, even some carved wood Chinese statues, all along shelves that had been clearly made to hold books. It was a miracle that they were all intact.

I had never been very good at concealing my thoughts, yet since our arrival here I had promised myself to be more discreet; this place where secrecy was so highly valued seemed an excellent one in which to teach myself tact. But Jacob had learned a lot about me in the weeks I had been working for him. Although he was talking to Peter and a large, bearish man named Noel Jenkins, he was also observing me. So I wasn't exactly surprised when he found an opportunity to refill my drink and we meandered onto the porch.

"I saw you looking before at all those knickknacks," he said. "It's embarrassing to have to explain getting them here."

"You don't have to explain."

He smiled. "As you didn't have to justify your work on Melville?" I gave him a startled glance. He had never referred to that meeting in New York, and I'd been sure he had forgotten it.

"I loved your spunk that day, Lily. I knew then that I would ask Peter to come here and that, if I could, I would get you to work for me. I knew that you would be able to cope with all this if you consented to come."

"Was there a choice? About coming, I mean?"

"I didn't think so, I still don't, but Steffi does. She didn't want to come. And when she finally agreed, she seemed to need to drag all this stuff with her. About half of it isn't even ours—it belongs to her mother and maiden aunts."

I merely raised an eyebrow, giving him an opportunity to stop. I knew Steffi was a pacifist. In Ithaca I had heard that she didn't think the Germans were doing anything about an atomic weapon, that she still had many friends in Berlin, that she was very close to the Bonhoeffers. But he went on. "Steffi talks about Fritz Haber and Hahn and how they were deluded into thinking their work on poison gas in World War I would save lives and end the war sooner. She thinks we're deluding ourselves here, that we're in exile. She doesn't want to do anything that might help Groves or the Army, so she's going to teach part-time at the elementary school." I was surprised at that. Most of the women with children didn't work.

"She says if she doesn't work she'll think too much about what's going on and make us both totally miserable." He shook his head, as if amazed at how the words were tumbling out of him. "I never thought I'd be married to a *bei unser. Bei uns* means 'at our house,' and the expression means . . ."

I put my hand on Jacob's arm. "I know what it means. My mother was born in St. Petersburg, and some of her family settled in Berlin before they came here. Several of them were *bei unsers.*" People who thought everything was better in Europe, especially those acquisitive spinsters, I now realized. People who never could get used to leaving their homes.

That's something you can never predict—who will be able to make a new home and who will not. I was trying to find something comforting to say, when he said in an amazed voice, "You, why, you look as American as apple pie. I could have sworn you were from Yankee stock, German Jews who came here at the end of the nineteenth century, especially when I heard about your passion for American literature."

I smiled when he called me a Yankee. Hardly what History's mother in Maine or Bess's family in Nantucket would think. Yet finally I had the courage to confront him. "And how do you know so much about Melville? I could hardly believe it last winter."

Jacob shrugged. "I once had a colleague who was writing a book on him. I read the proofs of her book."

"You mean you've never read him?"

"No, of course not. When would I have had time to plow through *Moby Dick*? I never read fiction, except for Thomas Mann, occasionally."

I stood there, stunned. I had consented to work for him because of that conversation. How bad could someone be who knew that much about Melville? I had asked myself. Now I felt as humiliated, as angry at Jacob as if he had made a pass at me. I felt like slapping him. Tact, tact, control, I urged myself, and looked away. But Jacob knew.

"I'm sorry, Lily. I guess you think me an awful fraud. But look, maybe your beloved American writers are what Steffi and I need. Especially here. Isn't this Willa Cather country? I'll suggest it to her and maybe you can give us a book list." Again he sounded desperate, and my heart softened when I watched him observing his wife. I had never seen him look so miserable; woebegone, almost. Then he touched my elbow, and leaning toward me, let his lips graze my forehead in an almost-kiss. "Thank you," he said.

For what? I wanted to ask. But he was gone.

Jacob had risked a lot talking to me so frankly in the midst of this crowd. But perhaps it was safer here than in the office; some of the men were convinced that the offices were bugged, though Jacob said absolutely not.

Yet now several things were clear: why Steffi worked while most of the women with children didn't, why she was so often distracted and once or twice looked as if she had been crying, and why she was so insistent that all her discomfort had to do with the altitude. Most of all, why Jacob sometimes looked so weary, despite his neat, pressed clothes, when he came to work.

But now as I stood there at this first official party, I found myself thinking about Fritz Haber's wife, Clara Immerwahr, a chemist herself, who had begged her husband to stop his work on the poison gases. When he refused, she killed herself.

There wasn't a single woman at this party who didn't know about Clara Immerwahr; she was one of the legends of the physics community. Whenever her name came up, the men said: "She was depressed, it wasn't a good marriage, Haber never paid any attention to her, people don't kill themselves over big impersonal issues." I had heard it all. But I wasn't so sure.

I looked around the room for Peter. He was talking to Noel Jenkins, the Englishman who had recently arrived at Los Alamos. Noel had lived in Berlin and had known Steffi since they were teenagers. For now he was staying with the Wunderlichs, instead of living in the singles' dorm. Someone said he was part of the English delegation that was rumored to be coming in a few months; others said he was a lone wolf, so incredibly talented that he had been given a special invitation to come here.

Now my eyes were drawn to Jacob and Steffi moving comfortably from one cluster of people to another. Jacob looked like the perfect diplomat, so well proportioned that his slender body seemed to fit together much more tidily than other men's, and his handsome, thin face was exactly the type my mother meant when she described someone as "European-looking." Slightly formal and distinguished in an old-fashioned way. That was why I'd been so surprised when he'd spoken so openly before. And why he looked doubly bad when he was preoccupied; it seemed out of character.

But finally I also understood the frown that lingered around his eyes for days on end and that I had assumed had to do with an order from Bethe or my inadequate typing. I also understood why, once he saw me wondering about all these extraneous knickknacks, he had told me about Steffi. Here, plunked in the midst of this sea of possessions, I could grasp Jacob's situation more easily, and then, perhaps, forgive him his moods.

Nothing was what it seemed. To look at Steffi tonight, you would have thought her the happiest woman in the world. Her long iridescent gown shot through the crowd like an exquisite stray thread in a piece of silk as she urged the Pueblo waitresses to fill the glasses with more and more of the excellent wine that, we were told, had been a gift from the Oppenheimers. Her face shone with pleasure, and while I was eating the delicious beef goulash and sourdough biscuits and salad with Steffi's tarragon dressing, I knew that this party would become a legend not only for its intensity, but also for this wonderful food.

Here we were, a group of people at a party, some of us so young-looking we were mistaken for college kids by the natives of Santa Fe—most of us were barely thirty and Oppie was the "old man" at forty—and yet we were confident that what the Army had summoned us here to do would be accomplished, would somehow work out all right.

I felt myself beginning to float above the scene, which always happened to me when I'd had a little too much to drink. I saw History's fair skin become flushed with excitement and wine, Thea's pride that she had gotten us and our belongings here, Bess clutching the handle of her Nantucket basket for dear life, and in that brief moment I had some intimation of what it had cost those

women to be here tonight. Yet, at the same time, it seemed absolutely natural, in fact inevitable, that we should all be in this
place at this time.

I wondered if soldiers felt that way when they were finally about
to confront the enemy: this sense of destiny that a particular battle
could never take place without them. Our husbands' conviction
that they would be able to make this atomic bomb—yes, that was
what it was going to be, and I could finally say it, if only to myself—
had been absorbed by us wives, and as I observed the other women
I saw in their faces a radiance, a sense of astonished anticipation,
I had never before seen.

The only thing that came close to it were my mother's stories
of how people looked on the boat coming to America. Finally I
knew what it meant not to be able to take your eyes off someone.
That night I couldn't take my eyes off those women who had come
dressed so bravely and so beautifully to the Wunderlichs' party.

Soon no one could drink another drop or swallow another mor-
sel. This was the point at which the men usually wandered off
into a corner to talk shop while the women would clear the dishes
and tidy up the kitchen. But talking shop was forbidden, and there
were Indian waitresses to clear the plates and do the dishes. Still,
we couldn't leave; it was much too early. But if someone didn't
do something soon, we would all be collapsed on the furniture,
dozing, a modern Daumier.

I straightened my shoulders and made an effort to say something
intelligent to Mark Chanin, who was sitting on the other side of me.
Peter was talking to Thea and Oppie. Mark seemed to be making
the same kind of effort as I was, and after a few moments we smiled
at each other, giving up, then let ourselves sink into the pillows and
sat there in a companionable silence. When I glanced across the room,
I noticed History rubbing her eye with the heel of her hand.

Then a rustling behind us, and when we turned around, Jacob
was leafing through some music in a basket near the piano, and
a few people were moving their chairs so he could sit down.

He spread his oddly thick hands, which didn't seem to go with the rest of his body, over the keyboard and played a beautiful rendering of Chopin's Nocturne in E flat. At the end Peter's hand pressed mine and his eyes flitted frantically across my face. I stared at him stupidly, wondering why he looked so agitated, until I realized that tears were dribbling down my cheeks. He handed me his handkerchief and nodded; he had heard my mother play that piece. Why shouldn't you be homesick? his eyes reassured me.

Next a Brahms waltz. That was better, and at least I didn't embarrass myself. I couldn't believe I had started to cry. But now I gave Peter a bright smile. While the final chord of the Brahms still lingered in the air, Jacob played a Schubert scherzo, a melodious joke that broke the tension; a few people giggled when it was over. Then he opened a worn book and began to play the somber beginning of "Ol' Man River." Cautiously people looked at each other, then three or four began to sing, and soon others were joining in. I was amazed to see General Groves's eyes brimming as his lips started to move with the rest.

After that "Smoke Gets in Your Eyes," "Bill," "Make Believe." Jacob wiped his palms with a handkerchief, loosened his tie, and looked around. Someone called "Embraceable You," sang a few bars, and he picked it up and played it, adding a few cadences of his own. Then, in a beautifully clear and strong voice, Bess gave him the beginning of "Someone to Watch Over Me."

We must have sung twenty or more songs that evening as people stood by the piano. " 'S Wonderful," "Of Thee I Sing," "Anything Goes," "Begin the Beguine," "You're the Top," "I've Got You Under My Skin," "Nobody Knows the Trouble I've Seen"—oh, all those wonderful, elegant, sad songs from my childhood, almost jagged-sounding now in that mixture of accents from all over America and Europe, yet somehow fresher, more touching because of them.

Jacob was tireless that night, the center of a wheel that refuses to stop, giving us more and more music, our faces glowing in the lamplight. Even Steffi had stopped playing hostess and sat in the long curve of Noel Jenkins's arm, as mesmerized as the rest of us. She seemed entirely happy with her old friend's arm around her, watching her husband do what he loved to do. But if you took the time to look way back into her eyes, you could see not only love but misery as well. Masked, but there, and seeing it, I suddenly felt completely alone; for the first time in my life I understood that strange yet marvelously graphic word Melville had coined: *isolato*.

And what, I wondered in the midst of this gorgeous rush of music, was really going to happen to us?

6

. . . ■

Each day when I walked to work I would hear Steffi ask Groves, "Is it necessary to have these fences?"

What we didn't understand until we arrived was that Los Alamos was an Army camp. A barbed-wire fence surrounded the settlement of Los Alamos and another barbed-wire fence separated the technical area from the rest of The Hill. Fences within fences. Not wooden civilian fences, or even the all-American picket fences made higher, but degrading barbed wire, especially offensive to the women who had come from Europe.

And soldiers at the gates, smiling, courteous, helpful soldiers, but essentially Military Police who never forgot their job: to secure this place. No one was exempt. Why, even when Oppenheimer had once forgotten his pass on his way out of Los Alamos, he was stopped and had to go home to get it before he could leave.

There was no real escape. Oh, sure, we could go on hikes or ride horses into the Jemez and Sangre de Cristo mountains, we could go to Pamela's or Santa Fe for dinner or even for the night, or we could wander around the Indian settlements. But there were no furloughs for us, and no one routinely left to go East or visit friends elsewhere. Only illness or some pressing event back home could release you from this voluntary prison where your driver's license carried no name, where your address was Box 1663, Santa Fe, New Mexico, and where your identity was required to submerge itself into what Groves hoped was an anonymous whole. I think it was harder for the women with children. They were home all day and had more time to think. For those of us who worked there was no time to chafe under the Army's restrictions.

My shorthand had gotten me the job as Jacob's secretary. I expected Jacob to be brusque, easily angered, commanding, impatient, awesomely witty. Exactly the sort of person not to work for. Instead, he was gentle with my mistakes (which were legion in the beginning, for I had taken no college math or physics), kind, straightforward, and fair. He did have a temper, though. I saw him lose it with Groves, whom he loved to mock, and very occasionally with Edward Teller, the thick-browed, talented Hungarian physicist who had come here from Chicago.

And once, to my astonishment, with me. It was after one of the first Colloquia, those meetings Oppie had convinced Groves were necessary to move the work forward at Los Alamos. For some still unexplained reason, no one had been present to take notes. Yet they needed a record of it. So Jacob had hurried into the office and dictated what he remembered. When he finished, he told me he wanted several copies. It was almost five o'clock on Friday afternoon, but I knew there was no way I could postpone this until Monday.

I put together the paper and the carbons and began to type. But I was tired and soon discovered that I had put in the carbons backwards. There was no way to cover up what had happened; Jacob was practically standing behind me while I worked, and when I realized what I had done, he looked at me disgustedly and said, "Damn it, Lily, I needed those in a hurry."

My hands trembled as I reassembled the carbons and paper, but nothing would soften him today. His face was stone. We had lost only about fifteen minutes, yet he seemed unable to forgive me. It was as if I had failed some kind of test under stress. I went home furious at him. I even considered quitting. I couldn't imagine working indefinitely for someone who could be so moody and unforgiving.

But on Monday morning he apologized. "I was upset about something else," he confessed, though he didn't tell me what. I didn't really care. I only cared that he had apologized. Anger had never frightened me; it was the inability to forgive that made me so uncomfortable.

The hardest thing about working for Jacob was how helpless I felt in the face of his sometimes inescapable sadness. When I got to know him better, he would shrug and say, "It's *Weltschmerz*, Lily, ordinary *Weltschmerz*, part of the human condition. The world is filled with grown-up Werthers."

"I hate it when you say that. You make everything sound predestined," I would reply.

"Isn't it?"

• • •

My office was a tiny cubbyhole in an alcove off Jacob's. What redeemed its size was the window next to my desk. As I typed I could feel a welcome breeze cooling my temples. Though the temperatures often climbed into the nineties that first summer, the air was not the oppressive shroud that could blanket New York or Ithaca for days on end. This was a dry mountain heat, moved constantly by a shifting wind, the evenings and nights often deliciously cool.

We awoke to a tender turquoise sky, and as the day grew hot the sky became bluer and the colors sharpened. Both of us were early risers, Peter even earlier than I, and when I opened my eyes I usually found him reading beside me. He had to be at the lab by eight, but I didn't have to report until nine, so I had time after breakfast to tidy our apartment and prepare lunch. We both came home for lunch, then returned to work until late afternoon. The long dusk, what the Russians call *soomerki,* my grandmother's favorite word, was the part of the day I loved best. Then, as the cobalt brilliance faded into the coppery tones of sunset, we would drift home, sometimes doing errands on the way, often dazed by the late afternoon heat.

Sometimes we made love after work. I knew how History felt when she had welcomed the arrival of their double bed. Only in our bed did Peter and I feel completely safe, away from all the pressures of this strange, surreal place. Safe to whisper secrets—what we felt, what he was working on, what I knew from some of the things that had crossed my desk. Our bed became a refuge, an escape, for our minds as well as our bodies.

Perhaps that was possible only because our lovemaking was different here. We sought each other with a hunger new to us, a hunger that may have been in part due to the altitude or the heat, or to the intensity of our lives, or perhaps to that ephemeral sense of freedom that History and I had tried so hard to define. Or maybe it had to do with the simple fact of time. We had been married for more than a year and were less timid with each other about giving and taking pleasure.

Other afternoons we would sink into the cozy easy chairs and sip the weakest possible Tom Collinses, then talk in a mixture of phrases that vaguely resembled my somewhat fractured shorthand and that became more and more like code as the months passed. For the first time in my life I had some inkling of what it might be like to be a spy. Eventually, though, we would sigh, "If only we could have a swim!"

But here was only that dishwater Ashley Pond—so different from the incredibly cold and refreshing lakes of upstate New York, or that endless expanse of Atlantic Ocean I had known so well as a child. "I never realized how much I would miss water," I confessed again and again to Peter.

"Especially the sea," he agreed wistfully. Some of our happiest times together had been at the beach near my grandmother's home in Atlantic Beach. I had spent at least part of every summer of my childhood at my Grandma Julia's, my mother's mother. She and my grandfather had bought the shingled cottage years before I was born, not long after they came here from Russia, and after she was widowed, my grandmother moved from Manhattan and lived there all year round. It was on the ocean side, near one of the big hotels, probably once part of the hotel, not on the bay, as all the other houses were. During the summers the small house would be filled to bursting as guests came and went.

How well I remembered falling asleep to the sound of the waves lapping the moonlit shore. "If you can go to sleep to that sound," my grandmother used to say, "you can't possibly be unhappy." How extravagant that seemed to my teenage ears, yet when I was grown, I realized she was right. She believed that the sea was the closest one could get to the center of the earth. She and Melville, I realized that first summer at Los Alamos.

I remembered helping my grandmother in a garden ringed with ruby hydrangeas; I remembered trying, in vain, to swim laps in that rough and scary sea, and reading under an amber circle of light on the porch, sometimes half the night. But most of all, I remembered the constant sound of the waves, "the heartbeat of the world," she called it.

My grandmother's life revolved around her visitors, her garden, and the library, where her grandchildren went almost daily to gather armfuls of books. In collusion with the sparkling-eyed librarian, my grandmother slowly educated me. Before I went to college, I had read a lot of American writers, from Mark Twain to Thomas Wolfe; I had even read Hervey Allen's long biography of Poe. Then, when I was older, Jane Austen, the Brontës, Dickens.

"Why only American and English writers?" Jacob asked.

"I guess it was a case of 'We are in America, you read English now.'"

"But surely she must have read other things."

"Of course. Tolstoy and Turgenev and Chekhov, and she was crazy about the new playwright, Eugene O'Neill, but she said he and those Russians were too dark, too sad for a young girl."

"And *Wuthering Heights* isn't dark and sad?" Jacob's eyes danced. "But she was probably right, you know. She certainly didn't want you to fall in love with some lout like Vronsky and throw yourself under the nearest railroad train." He loved nothing better than to tease me, and he had gotten very good at it. I could feel myself begin to blush. "She'd be turning in her grave if she knew you were in love with depressing old Melville."

I didn't answer. Although I loved to talk about my grandmother's books, I didn't like to talk about *her*. It had not occurred to me until I went to college how unusual she was. And I still couldn't believe she wasn't pruning her roses, staking the cosmos, cutting those flamboyant hydrangeas, searching the phlox for white spot. She had died peacefully at eighty-six, and though I knew hers was a long and lucky life, I hadn't yet forgiven her. At our wedding I kept looking for her, and even now, in my mind, she was standing in her garden, inhaling the salt air, or staring at the ocean, her gray hair in wisps around her face, a smile of contentment playing about her lips.

"It's not at all what I knew as a child or young woman. We went to the Crimea for holidays, and the Black Sea is nothing like this," she used to tell us. "Still, when I hear the sound of the sea, I'm not so homesick. . . ." Then she would shake her head impatiently. "No, not homesick, homeless." Now, at last, I understood her obsession with the sea—now that Peter and I were stranded in this land-locked desert retreat.

● ● ●

On March thirty-first, a few weeks after we had arrived at Los Alamos, the large Bonhoeffer family had a seventy-fifth birthday party for their beloved and revered father, Karl Bonhoeffer, who was professor of psychiatry and neurology at the University of Berlin. Their hospitable and beautifully furnished home on the fashionable Marienburger Allee rang with the sounds of music— the children and grandchildren of this energetic family had prepared the cantata *Lobe den Herren* by the blind German organist, Walcha, for the celebration. Only Sabine and Gerhard Leibholz and their two daughters were missing. Still, they had been able to send birthday greetings via a Swiss friend.

Yet beneath the joy of the birthday celebration ran an undercurrent of frustration and fear, apparent only to members of the family, for it was not in the Bonhoeffer tradition to reveal feelings in a crisis. In the past weeks two attempts at a putsch and assassination of Hitler had failed, and several members of the Bonhoeffer family had been involved in the aborted efforts of the resistance.

Less than a week later, on April fifth, Dietrich Bonhoeffer, who lived with his parents and was, with his twin, Sabine, the second youngest in this family of eight children, called his sister Christine von Dohnanyi. A strange man's voice answered the telephone. Dietrich realized that the von Dohnanyis' house was being searched. He quickly left the Bonhoeffer home and went next door to the home of another sister, Ursula Schleicher. He asked her to make him a meal, which he ate with his usual aplomb, then went back to his home and checked his desk and returned to Ursula's. At four o'clock that Monday afternoon, his father called to say that two men were at the house looking for him. Karl Bonhoeffer knew what was happening, and so did his wife. They approved of their children's activities in the resistance and were calm and resigned but hopeful when Dietrich returned to the house and was arrested. On that same day his sister Christine and her husband, Hans, were also arrested.

Since his return to Germany from the United States in 1939,

Dietrich Bonhoeffer had been working actively in the resistance movement to overthrow Hitler. There were many men and women, mostly in Berlin and mostly from old aristocratic families, who were also part of the resistance; there were even generals in the military who participated. Dietrich and his brother-in-law, Hans von Dohnanyi, had done most of their work under the cover of the Abwehr, which was the military intelligence organization of the Third Reich. After the two failed attempts of the resistance, the SS had decided it was time to arrest Bonhoeffer and his sister and brother-in-law. Christine von Dohnanyi was soon released, but the two men went to prison—Dietrich to Tegel in Berlin, and Hans to the Wehrmacht prison for those of officer rank. Neither was afraid. They were careful conspirators and had covered their tracks very well. They were sure that the Nazis had no firm evidence against them.

Jacob and Steffi learned about Dietrich Bonhoeffer's arrest in June, not long after the party. That was partly why Jacob lost his temper at me. But he refused to make excuses for himself, and I actually learned about Bonhoeffer from Steffi herself.

We had begun the reading project that Jacob suggested in July. Nothing formal, like a club. Just Jacob and me. For though I typed all sorts of memos and letters and specifications and charts for Jacob, we couldn't discuss what anything meant. I wasn't supposed to understand it, just type it. Of course I understood more than I let on. I was married to another nuclear physicist, after all, and there were times when a question about something would lead, naturally and unthinkingly, to an explanation from Jacob. But we had little of that give-and-take between a secretary and her boss. Whatever I typed during the day had to be locked away each afternoon in the safe that was part of every office. My last task was to burn the carbon paper I had used. So the books gave us something we could discuss freely.

We started with Willa Cather. What I didn't know was that

Steffi was also reading. After *My Ántonia* we read *The Professor's House,* and one evening Steffi appeared at the door to our apartment with a huge bunch of zinnias. She had the nearest thing to a New England garden in front of her home; everything she touched bloomed lavishly, and though Jacob often divided his flowers with me, this was the first time I had been honored with a bouquet of my own.

"Thank you for that marvelous book," she said, as I invited her in. Peter wasn't home yet from the lab.

I smiled, pleased.

"It reminded me of *Buddenbrooks,*" she said, but I looked blank. I had not yet read that.

Suddenly she began to talk about some of the similarities and differences between the German and American families in both books, and before I knew it, she said flatly, "We just had news that Dietrich Bonhoeffer was arrested," then told me, in memorized detail, everything that a letter from England had described.

She spoke as if in a daze, as if she needed to hear the words out loud in order to believe them. She hadn't planned to tell me, I knew from the way she was talking. I could have been anyone. Yet, except for tears that she kept brushing away, she was in total control, her voice utterly matter-of-fact, except at the end, when she said, "I can't imagine the Nazis in the Bonhoeffer house. It was a magical house, the most beautiful house in the world, the most beautiful people in the world. There is no one else like them."

Then she said in an angry voice, "I never thought Dietrich would take part in the resistance. He's a thinker, not a partisan."

Almost reflexively I replied, "Maybe he'll be released. His sister was released—maybe they won't be able to find anything on him."

She stared at me as if to say, What do you know about this? I dropped my gaze, abashed. She was right. I knew nothing at all.

Then she sat down, exhausted, and said, "If the Allies had given the resistance help, Hitler would have been overthrown years ago. But Churchill and Eden want this war."

I simply stared at her, dumbstruck. How could the English, who had already suffered so much, want this war? It was crazy even to think it, and to say it—why, it seemed obscene.

I didn't want her here. Not if she could say that. But before I could answer, she was gone, as unpredictably as always. And the next time she saw me, she gave me the most casual, cursory of greetings—as if she had never come to see me. I was bewildered, maybe even hurt.

I told History about it, for by that time there had been a small item about Bonhoeffer's arrest in the papers. The English news service seemed to think the imprisonment would be temporary; the tone was hopeful, so Steffi's dismissal of me seemed especially cruel.

But for once History was brusque, her voice impatient. "It's not your job to understand Steffi, Lily. Don't you see it's a dead end? Something is going on that we don't know about, and you can rack your brains from now till doomsday, but you won't be able to figure it out. Besides, why is it so important to you?"

I had no answer.

• • •

After they became an established custom, the weekly Colloquia occurred on Tuesday nights in one of the classrooms of the original Los Alamos school. Oppie's cruelty in the classroom was legendary. "He's a master at putting other people down," people said, and more than a few of the scientists he had recruited to come here could recall moments when they had detested him.

But something mysterious and wonderful had happened to Robert Oppenheimer at Los Alamos. Now a more compassionate man faced his "students"—one open to the suggestions of others and not so quick to judge.

Oppie assigned his former student, Robert Serber, the job of presenting the problems that faced them. In a series of lectures later called "The Los Alamos Primer," Serber confirmed that their goal was to produce a practical military weapon in which energy is released by a fast neutron chain reaction in one or more of the materials capable of nuclear fission. This could be achieved by discovering the precise point at which two nuclear masses could be joined to produce the chain reaction needed; that precise point was what the scientists called "criticality." The problem was how to make the nuclear masses coincide in such a way as to release the enormous amounts of energy possible for destruction without predetonating, or dissolving prematurely, in a shower of radioactive neutrons. The first idea for the gadget was based on the principle of a gun: to shoot one nuclear mass into another at terrific speed. It was thought that the two masses would be U-235 or Plutonium 239, the two metals known to be capable of fission. They would be the core, and tamped or wrapped to avoid predetonation, with ordinary uranium, U-238.

Tonight there was an expert from the ordnance division on The Hill to discuss the Primer. But the expert wasn't happy with the word *explosion* to describe the gun method of firing the two masses together. He said it was really a kind of "implosion" and went on to discuss the various problems of expansion that might occur in the core and thus affect the tamper. As he spoke, a former student of Oppie's, Seth Neddermeyer, raised his hand.

"You know how you sense at a particular moment that something really important is happening?" Peter said to me later. I nodded. "Well, that's how I felt when Neddermeyer started to speak."

"But if you see this as a gun, you can compress the core from only one dimension," Neddermeyer began. "Instead, how about packing a layer of high explosives around an assembly of tamper and a hollow but thick-walled spherical core? By detonating the explosives you would then get a shock wave that would squeeze the tamper from at least two sides and possibly three; and the tamper would then squeeze the core, which would change from a hollow shell into a solid ball. This multidimensional squeeze would truly be implosion."

"And that's what we call it," Peter added.

Nobody liked the idea. People asked, "What will prevent the tamper and core from squirting out in all directions—the way a balloon does when squeezed between cupped hands?"

But Oppie was interested. Neddermeyer was a good student. Oppie told the younger man to look into it. Soon after the meeting Neddermeyer went to Bruceton, Pennsylvania, where there was a U.S. Bureau of Mines Laboratory for experimentation on high explosives. When he returned, Neddermeyer set up a research station on the South Mesa across the Los Alamos canyon.

He ran tests on our first July Fourth in New Mexico. He used iron pipe set in cans packed with TNT, cylinders instead of spheres and a limited amount of explosive because he wanted to be able to recover remnants and assess the results. Admittedly, a primitive way to start, but a start.

"People are so quick to criticize," Peter told me that night, shaking his head. "Feynman thinks it stinks, and Parsons, the ordnance man, callls it the Beer Can experiment. But the fact is, the pipes became solid bars, just as he predicted. The problem is that the squeeze isn't uniform; the pipes that were retrieved were twisted every which way."

Peter frowned. "But I still think he's got something. And I have a hunch Oppie does, too."

• • •

Many of the women didn't like Steffi. Was it because she was so close to perfection, so capable? With her tall stately figure, she was as imposing as something from Mount Olympus. A terrific cook, gardener, tennis player, and now teacher as well. Since she had left Housing, she taught second grade, and the children adored her.

Yet she wasn't what my mother called "a sword in a jeweled

scabbard." If anything, Steffi was reticent, almost diffident, and finally I realized that she tyrannized others with her forbidding silence. Make me happy, she seemed to say as we walked up a mountain or had coffee after an evening at the Wunderlichs' when Peter would bring his violin, Herb his cello, and Bess her flute to join Jacob for some chamber music. As if either breathtaking scenery or lovely melodies were not enough.

As the summer went on, History and Bess and I rose to her bait, searching for anecdotes to amuse her, but after a while it became tiring.

"Not tiring, tiresome," History announced one day. "Steffi is like Queen Elizabeth. Petulant, unpredictable, hungry for attention." History had been a Renaissance scholar at Chicago.

I stared. Those were hard words. Especially from History, who was usually so mild and obviously so happy these days. As her small body swelled, her skin took on a rosy bloom; she was full of energy and goodwill as she plowed through exhausting days at the hospital where she was the assistant to the administrator-doctor.

"Aren't you being a little hard on her?" I asked. Stubbornly, History shook her head.

Then Bess broke into a hearty laugh. "That's wonderful, History. Steffi Wunderlich, the Virgin Queen. I love it."

I didn't. But instead of getting into an argument that none of us wanted, I turned the conversation to the drama club that was just being started.

"Not to act, not me, anyway," History warned, "but I'd love to do costumes or sets."

Later, alone, I grudgingly admitted to myself that History's assessment of Steffi wasn't far off. There was something oddly sexless about Steffi these days. Part of her seemed to have closed in on herself, like those desert flowers that refuse to bloom unless the conditions are perfect.

Peter didn't agree with me. "She's never seemed very much at home in the world, but why should she be? Her family was well off when they lived in Germany, but most of the money was tied up in real estate, so they left with very little, and her parents were sick when they came here. Her father was a well-known chemist, but the only job he could find was in a perfume factory. Then he had a heart attack, and her mother had to work at some job in an office—for a jeweler, I think. Her father died two years later. Steffi took it very hard, and her mother's health has been frail ever since."

His tone was flat, clinical, his "don't ask me any more questions, Lily" tone. I could see that it pained him to be talking about Steffi and Jacob, almost as if he were betraying them. Betraying what? I wondered, but didn't ask. Living here had taught me that there were some things you didn't ask, couldn't ask. Even of Peter.

I turned away, perplexed that my husband was treating me like a stranger. Since we had come here, he sometimes seemed so remote, so involved with his work. That fascinating, enervating work. It drained him, leaving nothing for me. Though I didn't want to admit it, it made me angry. But I didn't let him see my anger. I couldn't. It wouldn't have been fair.

But now he saw my discomfort, and his voice was softer, gentler as he said, "As far as I can see she's always been this way. Her eyes remind me of a scared cat's." Just as he didn't seem to see furniture and other household objects, Peter was oblivious to Steffi's extraordinary beauty.

"But if she was like that, why did Jacob marry her?"

"He loved her, and still does. Why else?" A tinge of disdain crept into Peter's voice. We had moved from the level of moral inquiry to the verge of gossip, and he had no taste for gossip. Besides, I could hear him say, if I pressed him, you don't refuse to marry someone because she's scared or discouraged. If you love her, you will somehow figure it out. I sighed. This was how Peter always operated—empirically, practically, unemotionally. Just find the cause and you can understand the effect. I wasn't so sure.

The more I mulled, the more complicated things seemed to get.

Later, as we were going to bed, he said, "Don't worry, Lily. Steffi and Jacob will work things out. They always have. And now that Noel's here, Steffi will feel better. They're old friends, you know."

I nodded. I had seen them together twice. Once at Pamela's, so engrossed in conversation they didn't see me. And later in the Plaza at Santa Fe. Both times Steffi had been smiling. She and Noel had known each other forever, she once said, and she looked like a different person when she was with Noel, more at home in the world, more comfortable with him than with anyone else, even Jacob.

7

General Groves loved candy, especially chocolate. Perhaps it was his consolation for not being given active combat duty. Or it made up for the absence of his wife and two children in Washington. Maybe it was a sex substitute. "Just try imagining what he might be without it," someone once ventured.

Everyone had a theory.

Whatever the reason, he ate and hoarded chocolate as greedily as a malnourished child. At first glance, Groves looked too correct for all that extra weight; surely he must have been unhappy about it and might even have heard people tease about it. One woman remarked that when Groves walked into a room, his stomach announced him.

"But, really, it isn't fair," Kate Unwin defended him. "Anyone a little bit stocky would look fat next to Oppenheimer." And we hardly ever saw Groves without Oppie.

Whenever Kate made fudge for her children, she always made a little extra for General Groves and dropped it off personally at his office. Groves seemed to like Kate better than the rest of us, probably because she was married to an honest workingman, not one of his prima donna scientists. In Groves's code it followed that if you were married to a prima donna, you were a prima donna, so he gave us all a wide berth. Except Kate. He had a soft spot for big, easygoing Kate, who had more energy than ten men.

Today, though, Kate wasn't feeling very generous. And she didn't have any fudge in the neat package tucked under her arm. Today she was angry. For the fourth time in two weeks the hamburger in the commissary was bad. It smelled rancid, sour. She had once marched herself into the office of the CO for supplies, a Colonel Tyler, and thrown the meat on his desk. What resulted was a screaming match, or as much of a screaming match as Tyler would allow himself. But today she was too angry to bother with Tyler; today she was on her way to see Groves.

When the general saw her, he smiled, expecting her to produce her famous fudge. Instead, she placed the neatly wrapped package on his desk. "I'd like you to open that, General," she said softly.

He stared at it. Kate would never bring him a gift so small. But he was caught. He had let her into his office; now he had no choice. When he looked at her guarded eyes, he must have suspected what was in the package.

Slowly he opened it. The ugly smell filled his office. He wrinkled his nose, looked at Kate, then wrapped it up again. "I'll try to see that this doesn't happen again," he said in his most even voice. Then, "I really will, Kate," he added, using her first name for the first time.

"When he called me Kate, I knew he was taking me seriously," Kate reported. "He's not as bad as everyone thinks. And he knows that the last thing this place needs is an epidemic of food poisoning."

Most people rewrote the story with a much sterner, angrier Groves. As History had said, they needed a scapegoat. The third time I heard it, Groves and Kate were yelling at each other. But I knew Groves was too smart for that, too much of a well-disciplined soldier.

Groves *had* to improve the commissary. Shopping there was the closest thing to a crapshoot. You could never be sure of getting anything but huge cans of vegetables that were clearly packed for institutions. Yet each woman cooked for her own family.

A week later Groves appeared at the meeting of the Town Council, a body established by Oppenheimer to administer the civilian needs of The Hill. His presence made everyone sit up straighter; even Tyler was more understanding. They listened to our complaints and made a careful list. After that, there was more variety and smaller cans in the commissary, and soon even fresh vegetables arrived from local farmers. When Peter and I had chicken with rice and fresh green beans a few weeks later, we felt like royalty. As more and more produce appeared— broccoli and beans and squash—and the meat improved dramatically, people would stop Kate as she walked through the commissary to thank her. But she merely brushed away their compliments.

The Army wanted to cut down the cottonwoods and pine trees in a new spot and put up yet another dark green row of apartments. As soon as the bulldozers appeared, a group of women had gathered. "You can't cut down trees that are hundreds of years old," they said calmly. The foreman, a young sergeant who had never been rude to a woman in his life, didn't know what to do.

"But, ma'am, I have my orders," he said, then reached into his pocket and opened the sheet for them to see. The women stared right back at him. They made him so nervous he told them he would see his superiors and come back in a little while.

When he returned, the women were sitting in a circle around a stand of trees they wanted to save. Sitting in canvas camp chairs and knitting.

"We are prepared to stay here just like this until your superior officers retract their orders," the leader said. She was no bigger than the sergeant's younger sister in Louisville, Kentucky, and she

had a foreign accent, but she spoke slowly, so he understood every word.

After about an hour several officers appeared. "I think a colonel was among them," the women reported later, but no one knew him by name. There was some discussion, and quietly, patiently, the women made a sketch, then showed it to the colonel. It included a playground surrounded by some houses placed in a circle instead of a grid.

A few days later the bulldozers returned. The women watched with wary faces. But before long there were cries of triumph. The concrete slabs were poured in a circle, and within a few weeks the women had their playground, too.

At first letters came in and out of Los Alamos without being censored. Then some Army zealot got the brilliant idea that we were all potential spies, so soon a group of Army personnel read everything we wrote to our families and everything they wrote back. But the Army hadn't counted on Richard and Arlene Feynman. Both were extraordinarily bright and both loved games and practical jokes. Arlene was always having something sent to Richard that she had found in a mail-order catalog. Once he got a huge cardboard figure of a curvy female to keep him company in bed. Instead, Richard had Lenny Unwin make a revolving stand for it and put it in a corner of the post office. If a certain velocity in the air was achieved, the figure would wheel around and face you. Richard loved the shrieks of unnerved customers that resulted. And when they wrote to each other, the Feynmans made up codes—loony, unique, enigmatic codes.

Feynman was called into the censor's office. "We have to have the key to this code," the censor, named Nelson, said sternly, and pointed to the letter on his desk.

"There is no key," Feynman replied with a grin.

"What do you mean, no key? There has to be a key. That's the whole point of a code."

"Not our codes. The whole point is to discover the key as you decipher the code."

Nelson stared.

"It's a game," Feynman explained. "Each letter has its own code, each letter is a game."

"But that's impossible. If there's no key, you'd be at this thing all day."

"That's the point. My wife has all day. Every day," Feynman said with an uncharacteristic trace of sadness in his voice.

Finally Nelson nodded. What the hell. There was no way a bedridden, tubercular patient could be a spy. And if anyone raised the possibility that she was passing on information to someone, he would take the responsibility.

When his colleagues confronted Nelson with the next ominously complex letter, he merely said, "Leave Feynman alone. These games distract them."

"Who? What?" they asked, but if they were too stupid to figure it out, Nelson wasn't going to explain. There were more important things in life than security. For once in his life, Nelson thought: Screw General Groves. Whatever the Feynmans could do to take their minds off Arlene's illness was fine with him. They were so in love. Not just ordinary young love. No, this was special. He could feel his spine tingle when he remembered the letters he had read before they started this code business.

It was a constant, frustrating battle. But, as the older women often reminded the younger ones, our husbands could have been fighting. Lots of women all over the United States were far worse off. We were some of the lucky ones.

● ● ●

One Friday afternoon Jacob asked me to come into his office. Outside, the landscape was tinged with a faint apricot glow, which softened its burnt, tufted, beaten-up look. The summer was here with a vengeance. After I sat down, he said, "Steffi is upset that the rest of you are angry at her."

Instead of answering I watched the coppery streaks of sunset stretch across the sky.

"Are you?"

"No."

"Then why don't you talk to her anymore?"

"I do, that's not so."

"Out of politeness, not much more."

"Are you asking, or Steffi?"

"Steffi, mostly. But I am, too. She was upset that day she came to see you, she felt badly about that, but she couldn't bring herself to apologize. So I'm apologizing now." I stared at him. I didn't know any other husband here who would have done that. "But it's more than that. Everyone is avoiding her." Jacob shifted from one foot to the other when I looked at him. But his eyes looked straight into mine.

"She makes me feel awkward, put upon, as if whatever I say will never really please her," I began hesitantly. "Or worse, might be the wrong thing." I stopped. "No, that's not right. Steffi makes me feel as if I'm in your living room, and that if I'm not careful I will break one of her priceless knickknacks."

He winced, and now I was sorry I hadn't followed Peter's advice. I had done so well these last several weeks. I had even managed to rehearse with Steffi every single night for the last few weeks in *Our Town*, which the drama club was putting on in September. Why did I have to spoil it now?

A deep frown was etching itself across Jacob's forehead, shadowing his elegant brows. Suddenly I was filled with an irrepressible desire to reach over and smooth that frown away with the pad of my forefinger. But I clenched my fists and waited.

"I understand what you mean," Jacob said. "Sometimes I wonder if I wouldn't be doing all of us a favor if I asked one of those sweet women from San Ildefonso to pack up those knickknacks so we could start all over again, with the house bare." But we both knew it wouldn't solve the problem.

I began to gather some papers, hoping that perhaps we were finished. But Jacob went on. "I told you she didn't want to come here, but there's more to it."

"There always is. Look, Jacob, I'm not sure you should be telling me this."

"You mean you're not sure that you want to hear it. But I want to say it, Lily." I sat back.

"You know that Steffi's family and Noel's were friends, and that the connection was Dietrich Bonhoeffer?" he began.

I nodded. One evening earlier in the summer there had been a heated discussion about Bonhoeffer at Pamela's. I had learned then that Noel's father was an Anglican minister who knew Bonhoeffer's father. What interested me that night more than Bonhoeffer was Noel's education: he had been trained as a doctor before he went into physics; his specialty was obstetrics and gynecology. He was such a big, rough-looking man and always looked a little dirty to me. The last person I could imagine in a delivery room. Since that evening I had wondered often why Noel was no longer a doctor, what drew him into physics, and how he had come to be at Los Alamos. But Jacob was in no mood to be interrupted.

"Four years ago, in the summer of 1939, Dietrich came back to New York with the idea of staying here. He had studied theology in the States, and he thought he might immigrate here. But after a month or so he realized that he couldn't live in exile. Before he went back to Germany, we saw him, and Dietrich managed to convince Steffi that the Nazis wouldn't do many of the things we fear, that they certainly wouldn't make a weapon using Hahn's discovery of fission.

"I don't know how he conveyed that to her because I don't think he believed it. This news of his arrest proves that he is as frightened of what the Nazis will do as we are. But Steffi has always thought of Dietrich as a saint, and because he kept talking about the good Germans who were still there, she got this wild idea that maybe if all the right people went back, if enough educated Jews went back, things would right themselves, and Hitler would somehow fade into the background." Jacob paused and shrugged.

"There was no way Hitler was going to fade into the background. Why, even in the early thirties when I was at Göttingen, there were people falling in love with Hitler—maybe not the racial laws, but everything else. Weizsächer, the physicist, for one. And maybe Heisenberg. But you must know that—Peter was at Göttingen, wasn't he?"

"He was supposed to start, but he was relieved of his post right after he arrived," I replied.

Jacob nodded, then continued. "And as far back as 1920, there was a meeting at Berlin Philharmonic Hall of the Anti-Einstein League. When Einstein showed up, they attacked his scientific views, and kept the swastikas in view and continued to sell anti-Semitic booklets in the lobby."

I could feel my eyes widen, and I asked, "Are you sure, Jacob?"

"Of course I'm sure. It was a national scandal, a disgrace, and proof that there was Nazism present in Germany even without Hitler. And if the Nazis develop a fission weapon . . ." Jacob hesitated and stared out the window, then shook his head.

"That's why we're here, for God's sake. But Steffi seems incapable of understanding that. She insists that decent people like Weizsächer and Heisenberg must have changed their minds." Now Jacob looked at me quizzically, but I had no answers. I had never even heard of the Anti-Einstein League.

He went on. "We had a terrible winter, but after we talked to several people—Peter among them, by the way—she realized she was being irrational. Besides, by then the war had started. But when I finally got her to see the light, I did something I never should have done. I virtually promised her that I wouldn't participate actively in the war effort. That was about a year and a half before Oppie approached me."

Sometime in the middle of this explanation Jacob had begun to pace, and now he stopped and sat down at his desk. He looked years older than he had this morning. His shoulders slumped, and his skin had the sickly translucence of milk glass, utterly pale against the bright yellow and rusts of the marigolds bunched in a jar on his desk.

"It was insane of me to make such a promise, as insane as Steffi's wish to return to Germany. And when Oppie came to talk to me, I felt as compelled to come here as Dietrich did to return to Germany. Now I wasn't helpless, now I knew what I had to do."

That I could understand; it was how Peter felt. I nodded.

"You see, you understand exactly what I'm saying, Lily. But Steffi doesn't. She can't bring herself to understand because if she does that, she will have to deal with the reality of Germany now, not some fantasy Germany in her memory, and that's something she won't do, can't seem to do. . . ." His voice trailed off, and he stared at something over my head.

"It caused a terrible rift between us, and we considered having Steffi stay with Sam in Ithaca. At first I thought maybe her mother or her aunts would come from New York, and that I would come here only as a consultant, but then her mother had a heart attack, and her aunts had to take care of her. We thought maybe Noel would stay with her and Sam. He had left England by then, and they're like brother and sister. Besides, no one would take it amiss—Noel is a homosexual. You did know that, didn't you?"

I was beginning to have trouble breathing. I didn't want to know any of this, and I didn't care about Noel's sexual preferences. But I simply shook my head.

"Well, he is. Common knowledge," Jacob said impatiently, as if I had failed to do my homework. "But then, when Noel found out what was going on here, he surprised everyone and decided to come, too. He comes from a long line of conscientious objectors, but I guess the excitement of the research was too much for him. After that, Steffi saw there was no way out of it, so she came. I was hoping that when she got here and saw how beautiful it is she would understand . . ." Again he stopped, exhausted now.

I stared at Jacob, amazed. Sophisticated, brilliant Jacob had expected this vast sweeping sky and this intense clarity of light to give Steffi the required breadth of vision to see what she was totally incapable of seeing, now or ever. He was more trustingly naive than she was.

"But she can't, Jacob, and to think she can is naive," I said softly. A glimmer of recognition flickered in Jacob's eyes. At that moment I felt as close to him as if we had touched.

"Why can you understand when she can't?"

"She doesn't want to. Maybe she's right. You have to admire those convictions, Jacob."

"But those convictions don't apply anymore. We have seen what this man plans to do, we know that Dietrich is in jail because he was part of an early plot to kill Hitler, and we know *for a fact* that Hitler and his cronies have begun to use Zyklon B to gas the Jews and Poles. Do we have to wait until he gets here and starts on the Jews and the Indians and the Negroes and everyone who doesn't have blond hair and blue eyes?" His voice boomed; rage distorted his fine features, darkening his usually steady gray eyes. It frightened me. I rose. All I wanted was to get out of here.

"No, of course not. But you don't have to scream at me."

"Oh, Lily, I'm sorry. This has nothing to do with you—you know that, don't you?" He stared out the window at the deepening dusk. "If only I could convince Steffi to relax a little, to enjoy this change of scenery, to take pleasure in watching Sam grow. If only she wouldn't think so constantly about why we're here."

He was so sincere I could only feel sorry for him. So intelligent, so convinced he was right, yet so unaware that emotions cannot be turned on and off. Before we came here, I had seen this deep conviction of rightness in Peter and had thought it was unique to him.

But Peter had a natural humility, almost a shyness about him. The very thing that had made it possible for him to conceal his feelings about me for those first few years. Some of these other men made you feel as if physics had endowed them with the only possible view of the world. Their belief was unshakable, as fervid as religious faith. Perhaps it was because they dealt with facts, theories that could be tested, if only they could bring their intelligence to bear upon them.

My literature professors had taught us it was possible to read a book many different ways. Science didn't allow another point of view. Things followed naturally from one step to another. That was what made it so compelling. There were answers. And if your job was to find the answers, you couldn't afford to be sidetracked. And Jacob felt Steffi's doubt and questions were sidetracking him.

Now, as I sat in Jacob's office, I could sympathize with Steffi. It was harder for some people to compartmentalize their lives, and the men I knew seemed to do it so much more easily than the women. Besides, how could Jacob expect her not to think about the work here, how could you not think about what was happening here? You could feel a sense of urgency everywhere, and the tension was growing steadily as the days and weeks and months passed.

But there was nothing to say. What I finally offered was no more than a sop. "Maybe, with time, she'll come around, Jacob."

Jacob nodded unhappily and glanced at his watch. The end-of-work bell had long since rung, yet neither of us had made a move. Jacob's fingers skimmed the papers on his desk nervously.

"If you were home you'd be playing the piano, wouldn't you?" My voice broke the silence. He smiled in assent.

"What?" I asked.

"Schubert. He's the best one when I'm feeling low. And then some Chopin mazurkas."

Now it was my chance to nod. I had heard some of those floating from his home one evening not long ago.

"Do you play? If you do, you know you're more than welcome to use the piano." His voice was harder-edged now, more the boss offering his secretary a privilege. He was embarrassed that he had told me so much, annoyed at himself for being so vulnerable. And a little relieved, I think, when I told him I wasn't a pianist.

Quickly and efficiently, we closed the office, performed our end-of-the-day ritual, then walked in silence down the hall, our footsteps clacking in a kind of odd offbeat.

Soon we came to the place where he went one way and I another. I wanted to say something more, something that would reassure him that he could trust me, but I hesitated too long. Now I couldn't call to him or even say good-bye. Voices, especially my high, clear voice, carried so easily in this thin Los Alamos air; we had all heard things that we didn't want to hear as we went about our daily chores.

But as I stood there watching him, I felt uneasy, oddly anxious, as if I, not he, had been the one to reveal too much, as if I needed to set things right. Not too different from that day in Rockefeller Center, which now seemed so long ago. Why did he have that effect on me? Yet I wasn't angry today. Just puzzled.

Suddenly he stopped and turned around and waved. "Good-bye, Lily, and have a good weekend," he called gaily. Then he added, for anyone to hear, "And thanks for listening."

Briskly I walked toward the flimsy green structure that was our home. As I made my way along the dusty path, something suddenly pulled me back to a day at a textile factory my father had taken me to when I was probably no more than seven or eight years old. A rare day when my mother was sick and we were on vacation from school, so my father had taken the three of us with him to work. We played in his office all morning and then he took us for lunch at Schrafft's, which he hated but knew we loved for its ice cream sodas. Then he announced, "And now we are going on an expedition." We went to a factory in the West Twenties. My father wanted its owners to copy certain fabrics he imported.

All around us were huge machines weaving threads from what seemed like a million spools, twisting and turning the threads into intricate patterns that somehow created the lush damasks and brocades that were tumbling in deep folds around our feet. A sea of color spreading around us, forcing us to stand still. Never had I seen such gorgeous, shimmering shades. I remember staring at the spools and wondering how those fine taut lines of thread could become the radiant, heavy fabrics that were falling so casually to the floor.

It seemed a miracle.

At that moment I imagined staying there forever, trying to fathom the mystery of it all. But no one could stay in that place for very long; the noise was deafening. And then I noticed that the women—only women worked here—all wore earmuffs.

Finally my father had seen enough; he motioned to us to follow him up a flight of stairs to an empty loft, where he showed the owners how the mammoth machines could be arranged most efficiently in this large open space. I remember watching his animated face describe the special gadget he had designed to catch the cloth and fold it automatically so that it wouldn't fall to the floor.

But it was all taking too long. I tried to catch my father's eye. He wasn't interested. We would have to amuse ourselves until he was finished.

I motioned to my brothers, and we began a series of walking races along the length of the empty loft. As we walked, we could feel the vibrations from the machines on the floor below. Shuttling vibrations that never stopped beneath our moving feet; endless vibrations needed to create those splendid colors; angry, noisy vibrations, more eerie now that they were out of sight.

Years and years later I could feel that same kind of tense energy I felt that afternoon. Expectantly I flung open the door to our apartment. It took me only seconds to realize that, once again,

Peter must be working late. My heart sank. How I wanted to sit at the smooth pine kitchen table and have a cup of tea with him; how I wanted to feel his arm around me as we talked in the thickening twilight.

But nothing. Nothing but hollow emptiness. Sometimes I hated this place, this all-absorbing work. Living in Los Alamos, I suddenly thought, is like standing on that shuddering, pulsating factory floor.

8

There were all kinds of activities on The Hill—a chorus, chamber music groups, a square dance club, a club that knit caps and socks for soldiers at the front, the drama club. Most of my friends and I gravitated toward the drama club. So did Thea, which is how she changed from official, helpful Thea in Santa Fe to one of our dearest friends. Kate Unwin was elected president. She was indomitable, and just watching her was an education for some of us.

To Kate the gadget was something remote and distant, having nothing to do with her, and the last thing she wanted to think about. Lenny, her husband, was here because he was a magician with machines. He was married to his machine shop in the canyon, as he had been married to his shop on Lake Erie. Yet Kate adored her husband and never seemed to want more from him than he could give. Her job was to take care of her four children—one just an infant—and keep herself sane. The drama club and her other activities were how she managed to do that.

Within days the casting was accomplished for our first play, *Our Town*. Noel Jenkins was the Stage Manager—big, floppy Noel, with his precise English accent, hardly seemed the choice for a wry, sparely built Yankee, but after a few rehearsals, I saw that Kate had been inspired when she gave him the part. His loose-limbed body seemed to give it amplitude, and an appealing magnanimity.

He was such an anomaly—an outspoken pacifist trained as an obstetrician, yet a key scientist here. "I didn't even like physics when I was younger," Noel confessed when I knew him better. "But when I decided I couldn't keep my homosexuality a secret, I realized that I couldn't keep on doing gynecology and obstetrics. I had never felt comfortable in medicine—it was my parents' idea. Everyone will always have babies, you know, the old saw, and they liked the idea of having a son who was a doctor. The next thing to being a minister, I guess." Noel looked at me quizzically, as if I might have the answer. But I was speechless at his frankness.

He went on. "When I finally admitted my sexual preferences publicly, I had to change careers. I applied for a fellowship in physics at the Cavendish, on a lark really, and got it and then fell in love with it. How I lived through my twenties without physics, I don't really know."

His openness was so unexpected. Even I, who had no trouble asking questions, was a little taken aback by it, for he always gave you more information than you had actually asked for. Years, even decades ahead of his time. And so different from Steffi, who was becoming, despite Jacob's hopes, more and more close-mouthed. Morose, almost, although more relaxed at our rehearsals than anywhere else.

Herb Lerner was the only man among our close friends in the play. The rest of the men were from some of the canyon labs that were working on plutonium and uranium—dry, exacting work, we were all told—and the relief of coming to the rehearsals seemed just what they needed, one wife confided. The only one I knew was Tom Schweren, the handsome experimental physicist who had been with Fermi at Stagg Field and whom Peter called "a whiz."

We met in the all-purpose room of the school at eight o'clock in the evening. Thea was the director. She had once been an actress—"in my other lifetime," she said with a twinkle in her eye—but that was all. She was so different from Noel, so much more reserved, yet how well she and Noel and Kate worked together.

Besides the actors were others, like History, who came to help Kate with costumes and sets. Kate was happiest when working on those. She was an excellent seamstress and could visualize the entire look of a play as no one else could. I've never seen anyone so good with her hands. She could sew like lightning, and her prowess in carpentry became legendary. But it was her energy and thoughtfulness that were most remarkable. During each rehearsal she somehow found a few minutes to make a bow for Arlene Feynman, who liked to wear them in her hair. Soon we were all saving scraps of fabric for Arlene's bows, which Kate would deliver to Richard each week before he took off for the hospital in Albuquerque.

You could plot the days of the week watching Richard. On Sunday when he returned, he would relate some wild adventure from the weekend—who had given him a ride, or how he had been mistaken for a doctor by some of the patients on Arlene's floor, or how they had played "Begin the Beguine" on Arlene's record player and tangoed through the halls. But by Monday morning he walked with his head down; another five days before he could go to Albuquerque. As the days passed, his head would rise, and by Friday his step was gay, exhilarated. But even when he was low, he never wanted pity. Arlene's illness was simply a fact; when he could he went to see her. And when he was stuck at Los Alamos, he plunged himself into the work like a diver doing tricks off the high diving board, with a magical intelligence that stood out even on this mesa populated with geniuses.

● ● ●

While Richard visited Arlene on the weekends, we climbed the surrounding mountains. Only when we were standing on a mountain like Tsi'como, which is 12,000 feet, almost 5,000 feet higher than Los Alamos, did I understand that the five mesas and surrounding canyons of the Pajarito Plateau are part of a caldera that is the high valley between the Sangre de Cristo Mountains on the east and the Jemez Mountains on the west. You were so high at Los Alamos that although you knew the mountains surrounding you were higher, you didn't really *know* it until you were there.

We always went on foot, but some of the others rode their horses up the rough trails. The one we saw most often was Tom Schweren, who kept a horse in Espanola and rode almost every weekend. He was easy to spot—with the sun glinting off his light hair, he would wave when he saw us, then smile shyly and canter off.

"Isn't he afraid of going so fast on these trails?" I once asked.

"Not Tom. Tom isn't afraid of anything," Peter replied.

This weekend Peter had gotten part of Friday and Saturday off. So Jacob gave me the day off, too, and we started in midafternoon walking slowly up and down hills covered with the mariposa tulips Pamela loved so much. Bright, flamboyant flowers that couldn't be real, you would exclaim, until you got up close and could feel their pliant, silky petals between your fingers. And acres and acres of what the Indians called moradilla, a starlike flower that was a breathtaking shade of purplish-pink.

Dreamily we trudged through the vibrant colors—orange and yellow and pink—shielding our eyes from the dazzling sun. The first night we were so grateful for the cool dark that we slept in the open, then started again at dawn.

The second day was less tiring, although we hiked twice as far, perhaps because the reward was the top of Tsi'como or perhaps because we weren't so dazed by the light. When we finished making camp, twilight was creeping in, giving the tilted sides of the caldera a lurid, bloodstained look.

Tsi'como is regarded by the Tewas as a sacred mountain that seems to stand guard over Puye, the ruins that were mysteriously abandoned early in the fourteenth century. For some of the Tewas, Tsi'como is "the center of it all," and there is a famous shrine on it—an ellipse with several trenches leading toward the pueblos from a hollow marked with prayer sticks. It is to this hollow that the Indians still bring their precious cornmeal to offer prayers and affirm their faith. Near the shrine is an eyed boulder similar to the one on the Black Mesa, which other Tewas consider the center of the earth.

Although I didn't know it then, these few days would be our only vacation in the two and a half years we were at Los Alamos. We had told no one where we were going. "Let's do this one alone, darling," Peter had said when we planned it, and when we arrived at the top, after almost two days of hiking, I knew that we had done the right thing. All my doubts, which had been building since my conversation with Jacob about Steffi, seemed to drift into the increasingly thin air. I stood, wonderfully content, my eyes scanning this beautiful flinty earth on which humans had lived for centuries. It seemed to represent everything that was good in the world, everything that Peter and Jacob and the rest of them on The Hill were working so hard to save.

We ate our dinner in silence, savoring each mouthful, watching the stars slowly prick through the darkness, grateful that the proverbial rain clouds of Tsi'como hadn't formed tonight. And later, as we talked for hours in front of the mesquite fire, I kept looking at Peter's face, as if seeing him for the first time. His eyes appeared to have gathered all the blue from that brilliant daylight sky and now shimmered a deep purple. And his body had a new sense of authority. I had glimpsed it the night of the Wunderlich party, but tonight I was struck even more sharply by its strength and confidence; I could hardly take my eyes from his taut, tanned forearms and his long, tapering fingers as he tended the fire. Where was that awkward, plain-featured young man who had stepped off the boat eight years ago? "The brilliant Fialka boy," my parents had called him, who had cupped his hand around his ear, like a deaf old man, when I talked to him in the tumult of his family's arrival in New York. Whose odd, formal mannerisms had made my brothers and me laugh when we first met him. He had been gone for years, but not until now had I realized what a commanding person he had become.

Commanding and tender. I don't know if Peter's tenderness would have been revealed to me so early in our marriage if we hadn't come to Los Alamos. Tenderness, at least the kind I am talking about, seems to develop as the years pass within a marriage—with the coming of children, with disappointments and setbacks, with the recognition of limitations. But for us that tenderness surfaced more quickly because of the intensity of our lives, particularly Peter's. That night, during which we barely slept, we talked for the first time about how tense Peter's life really was. About the personalities, about the doubts, about the terrific strain of completing the experiments under such an extreme time pressure. For the first time since we got off the train at Lamy, we were totally alone, under the stars, away from everything. No one could be listening. We were even safer here than we were in our wide double bed. Still we whispered, from habit.

"It's like a maze, but there's no way out except success. Most of us have never worked under such pressure for success, Lily. Science, especially physics, doesn't really work that way. It doesn't feel natural, yet we have no choice. When people say we have a time bomb ticking behind us, they're right. We do." He stared at me, then leaned toward me. We were stretched out, facing each other near the fire. Slowly Peter traced the right side of my hairline with his forefinger. That small gesture, so innocent, so childlike, almost, made me want to gather him into my arms, kiss his mouth shut. But I knew that it was more important that he talk.

"You have to have nerves made of steel, and if you don't have them you develop them," he said. Then, as if he were admonishing himself, he added, "And you can't take little slights seriously. Otherwise you'd be dead."

He was, in his blunt way, articulating all the things that had eluded History and me because we were not in those labs and discussion rooms. For the men lived with the stress that came from the sheer application of brains to this complex but soluble problem, and there was no respite from it. Except maybe here.

As I listened I remembered hearing that at least one of the bigwigs working on the Manhattan Project, Arthur Compton, had requested clearance for his wife because he knew he had to share his work with her. If Peter were one of the big boys, would he have had to make the same request? The thought pleased me, and I smiled.

"Oh, Lily, when you smile like that nothing seems so overwhelming to me. Not even the gadget," he finally murmured and took me into his arms. Slowly, we took off each other's clothes and covered ourselves with blankets, then smoothed another blanket over the earth and lay down. Such things as a bed, sheets, pillows seemed irrelevant that night. All that mattered was the touch of Peter's hands and mouth on my skin, the tender light in his eyes as they caught the reflection of the fire, the slow languor of our bodies as we opened ourselves to each other.

That night we made love as we never had before. That night on the top of Tsi'como, in starlight as bright as lamplight, we moved as if in slow motion, as if in a dream, our pleasure intensified as we both came, again and again, astonished.

People had talked about the sex that was in the air here at Los Alamos, the way people craved sex as the only escape from the pressure, but this was not merely sex, though it had everything to do with sex. Perhaps that is what true lovemaking is. I don't know. But later I realized that this was something special. Here, in this hallowed place, we had both experienced an overwhelming physical passion. It was our gift to each other that first summer: a gift that became a precious memory that sustained us and kept us going through the times that lay ahead.

———

Peter was such an easy man to love. But it had not always been that way. For years he had been a bone in my throat. Until one day at the end of 1940.

It is almost Christmas Eve, and though we don't celebrate Christmas, my mother always invites family and close friends that evening for dinner. A kind of second Thanksgiving, and the Fialkas are always included. I am dreading it. I cannot bear to be in the same room as Peter.

And now, as I enter the foyer after having my hair cut, I am greeted by my mother and Peter.

"Thank God you came right home, Lily." My mother's voice is high, frantic. "Mr. Thompson, our janitor, collects stamps, and I found a special magnifying lamp for him for Christmas on Canal Street, but the store was out of it, and they just called and they have it now. Won't you be a darling and go and get it for me, Lily? It would be wonderful if I could give it to him today, before the holiday," she says, then her glance takes in Peter, who, she explains, has been sent over by his mother with some dessert for dinner.

Although she has no trouble getting on the New York subway herself, and never thinks twice about my brothers, Ernie and Danny, or my father taking it, my mother always hesitates about sending me. "Maybe Peter would like to go with you?" she adds.

I glare at her, but she ignores me and asks Peter some innocuous question about his research in physics. As I listen to them talk, I get angrier and angrier. Why won't my parents understand that Peter has been awful to me, that never once in the two and a half years I have been at Cornell has he invited me for even a cup of coffee at the Straight? I have told them about it more than once, yet they just ignore me.

When he sees me on campus, he says, "Hi, Lily," and nods, as if I were some mediocre student in one of his introductory physics classes. And after his parents and my parents made such a point of telling me that if I ever needed anything I could always call on Peter. What a joke!

At first I was hurt, then I was annoyed, and by the time I am standing in the foyer that winter morning, I am so furious I can hardly look at him. Furious at Peter, and furious with myself when I remember all the times I went skating or swimming with him during those first few years after he came to America. Always because my parents said, "It would be nice." But the truth was I never needed Peter, and I've made my way at Cornell very well without him.

And I certainly don't need him today.

I turn and am practically out the door when he announces, "I'm coming with you," then gives my mother his flashiest smile. She's so charmed she loses all her reserve and says, in the same tone that she uses with my brothers, "Oh, Peter, while you're out, don't you think you'd better get those shoes shined? They're a mess, aren't they?" Peter glances down, chagrined.

So I say, impatiently, because, after all, fair is fair, "It's impossible to keep shoes shined in Ithaca during the winter. The salt is terrible."

We barely speak on our way downtown. We get separated on the crowded subway, and for one blissful moment I have the fantasy that Peter will simply disappear. But he doesn't, and when we arrive at the tiny, hole-in-the-wall lamp store, the lamp is not assembled, and the man who owns the place has no idea what to do with all the parts spread out on a table. He's desperate, for my efficient mother has asked specifically whether the lamp would be put together, and he has assured her it would. As the man explains this to me, Peter edges over to the table and looks at the instructions. After he reads them, he glances inquiringly at the man, who nods, and quietly and quickly Peter assembles the lamp. I stand there watching his hands.

Can you fall in love with someone's hands? As I watch Peter's long, bony fingers with their finely shaped nails find each part and put it in its proper place, I am wondering how those capable hands would feel on my body—on my hair, my shoulders, my collarbone, my breasts. It is eerie and troubling, and I am blushing when Peter looks at me, triumphantly, as soon as the lamp is assembled. But when our eyes meet, I know that he has felt me watching him, and I suspect he knows what I was thinking. Probably because he was thinking it, too.

Suddenly, in the dim light of that small store where the owner is getting ready to close for the holiday, Peter's eyes are clearer, more limpid than I have ever seen them. Gone is that film of aloofness that has irritated me so. In its place is the relief of being able, at last, to show me what he has been feeling for so long.

"You see, you were too young, Lily. Only fifteen, and I was already twenty-one. Six years is too long"—he hesitates but doesn't take the time to correct himself—"much too long when you're only fifteen, so the best thing to do when you came to Cornell almost two years later was to avoid you, ignore you, pretend you didn't exist."

He is talking to me as he sits in the shoeshine chair in the subway station; the shoeshine man humming "Ol' Man River" as he shines Peter's shoes must think Peter is crazy, bending toward me so earnestly, gesturing so broadly, trying to make me understand that he fell in love with me the day he first saw me—the very same day I remember so vividly, when I was smothering a smile as he cupped his hand around his ear in an attempt to hear me in the hurried bustle of the pier. Peter's voice is patient as he explains how it took all his self-control not to touch me when we skated and swam and went to concerts during those first few years when I was still in high school. But at last his eyes glow with love—the love that he no longer has to hide.

It still makes me smile to remember Peter sitting in the Canal Street station explaining, apologizing, then proposing to me in his socks—for by then the shoe-shine man had decided that his beat-up Ithaca shoes needed a new pair of laces. The ridiculousness of it made us double up with laughter. I was still laughing when I told my mother what had happened. Her eyes glittered with amusement and happiness, then she told me that the only person who hadn't known Peter was in love with me was me. "But of course you were too young, so we all had to be patient and hope that you would finally see the light."

As I walked down from Tsi'como two and a half years later, I knew I hadn't been wrong in that little store so long ago. The passion he had suppressed for so long was as powerful as I had suspected. It was the source of everything that was good in our marriage, just as it is in most marriages. And it made me feel proud to be the object of such passion. After that, Tsi'como became a code word between us; whenever anyone mentioned it, Peter would smile a secret little smile that gave me joy, then the pain of unspeakable guilt, then, finally, joy once more.

But that was later.

• • •

During that first summer and fall, after the trip to Tsi'como, Peter and I had to content ourselves with shorter hikes on Sundays: day trips to San Ildefonso, to Santa Clara and San Juan, to the Black Mesa, also called Tunyopin. On Tunyopin there is another eyed boulder, very like the one at Tsi'como, but this one is surrounded by a rock circle and belongs to the Indians of San Ildefonso, for whom it is a sacred site.

The eyed boulder on Tunyopin was a favorite place for Pamela Bye. "My resting place," she called it when she first took History and me to see it. It was several weeks after History told me she was pregnant, on a Sunday, when Peter and Herb had some unexpected work to do. We spent the morning gathering the particular strain of mariposas that Pamela loved so much—the pink

sagebrush mariposas that looked, as they were named, like but-
terflies just alighting on their stems.

Pamela had made lunch, and we ate the cheese sandwiches and
the crisp salad slowly, not needing to talk, content only to chew
the delicious food and breathe the velvety air. As we were drinking
the strong, dark, never bitter coffee that had made Pamela's tearoom famous, Pamela looked around.

"Rain. But not for at least an hour."

"Then we have time for a nap?" History said with a mischievous
smile. It wasn't easy to get Pamela to take a few hours off like
this, and we were determined that she should have some rest. Those
marvelous dinners she prepared at Oppie's behest at times seemed
endless, she had confessed, one round of shopping and cooking
after another, with never time to catch up.

Off in the distance we heard a roll of thunder, but Pamela
assured us we weren't in any danger, so we closed our eyes and
slept, never doubting Pamela's instincts. She knew this earth and
climate as well as her own body.

The smell of the wild plum filled our nostrils, and a bridal veil of
mist had settled over the deep green leaves of the cottonwoods. I
could hear a faint rustling and gradually had a vague sense of other
people nearby; when I propped myself on my elbow, I saw that
History and Pamela were up, too, and had turned to look behind
us. Following their gaze, I saw two figures, and it took me only a
few moments to realize that they were Jacob and Steffi, talking
earnestly to each other. You could see from the way their bodies
tilted toward each other that whatever they were discussing absorbed them completely.

"They're arguing," Pamela said softly. "You can tell from the
angles their bodies make. Angles fighting angles. Nervous edges."

I stared at the two figures and saw, in amazement, that she was
right. They looked as stiff as stick figures, and their movements
had a skittish awkwardness.

"They have a long way to go, those two," Pamela mused, as if she were talking to herself.

"Why do you say that?" I asked, almost accusingly.

But Pamela merely smiled. "I don't know why. I only know what I see. And if you see so many sharp angles when two people are married, you know there are problems. When people are really in love, you see more curves than angles, as if the air between them had softened the edges. It seems to need years to happen, and you can see it best in old marriages." Pamela's voice was patient and utterly sure of itself. "But you can also see it in younger people, and it usually means the marriage will last." She sighed. "It's mysterious, but so is everything about marriage, especially on The Hill, where people are so intense, so incredibly intelligent."

History and I glanced at each other, but there seemed nothing to say. Even Pamela could not help observing us, commenting on us, maybe judging us. The Army, the New Mexicans, people like the Windoms, and now Pamela. It seemed a betrayal, though I knew it was the last thing she intended. For Jacob and Steffi and the Lerners and Peter and I were her friends. But we seemed to live in a fishbowl, where everything we did was seen and discussed.

I would have liked to ask Pamela more about what she saw, but I stopped myself, and there was a clumsy silence. We could have broken it by calling to Jacob and Steffi, but none of us did. And they were so involved with each other they never even knew we were there.

We stood there, waiting, I hardly knew for what. And then it came. A cry as thin as the cry of an animal in pain. But unmistakably human. My head shot up, and now I could hear Steffi saying, "How can I not think about it? It's with me all the time, even when I sleep! I dream about it almost every night. Him lying in that cell, or reading, or trying to think, waiting for God knows what. And now this. Their bodies became flame, the papers said, a human flame—" Then they turned, and the wind blew their words away.

The three of us couldn't even look at each other. So we stood there, motionless, for a few seconds. Soon Pamela was staring up at the sky with a worried frown. The rain was coming. We hurried down Tunyopin, arriving at Otowi only minutes before the quick slash of wind and rain. On the way I saw that History had unbuttoned the top few buttons of her skirt. Of course, Pamela noticed. When she caught us looking at her, History gave us a shy shrug, and as soon as we were sitting safe and dry in Pamela's house, she said to Pamela, "I'm pregnant."

Pamela nodded. "So I noticed." And then she smiled, and we all burst into laughter. It felt good, to laugh so hard. It kept us from thinking about Jacob and Steffi. That very afternoon Pamela cut out a pattern for a new maternity dress, the first of many we would later pass down, which the three of us made by hand in the evenings, when we didn't have rehearsals for *Our Town*.

For days after that picnic I thought about what Pamela had said about Steffi and Jacob. And for a long time afterward I found myself observing couples in a new way. I saw more angles than I would have expected. But we were so young, so many of us newly married. Of course there were angles. Still, I understood what Pamela meant. Some couples had more than others. And a few had none.

Fermi had come and gone all through the spring and summer, but when his wife arrived several weeks later and they settled in, I saw that they were soft, Matisse-like curves. So were History and Herb. And Kate and Lenny Unwin. And Pamela, herself, and Estevan.

What about Peter and me? But there was no way of knowing. Then I thought about my parents, how their bodies seemed to nestle into one another when they talked and walked, even when they disagreed. And then I tried to put it out of my mind. Observing those angles, those nervous edges made me feel, in an uncanny way, like a voyeur.

But I knew why Steffi had been so upset. It was the firebombing of Hamburg. *The New York Times,* which we saw when we could, and the other papers we read regularly—*The Albuquerque Journal, The Denver Post,* and *The Santa Fe New Mexican*—were full of it that August: how there had been a ball of fire so intense it had created winds that spread the fire in waves covering the city, then killing thousands of civilians: the old, the women, the children. The *Feuersturm* showed a new attitude on the part of the Allies. In this summer of 1943 the rules of war seemed to have broken down completely; months earlier the Germans had begun to bomb civilian targets, and there were official reports that they had also started exterminating Jews and other non-Aryans. If Germans could play dirty, so could we. How else to win? This is a war. A war to save the world. A war to make the world safe for democracy. I heard the words over and over in my head. Yet I knew if I mouthed them too often, they would grow bitter on my tongue.

So of course Steffi and Jacob were arguing. I was glad I hadn't heard all of it—her icy voice accusing Jacob, as if he were responsible for killing those poor innocent Germans of Hamburg. But it was more than that. For Dietrich Bonhoeffer had not been released in June, as everyone had expected. In August the Wunderlichs had gotten word from England that Dietrich was still in Tegel, a sure sign that the Nazis had evidence against him.

"But there's no way of knowing, and though there is talk of a trial, it has been postponed more than once. The longer he stays in jail, the harder it will be to get him out—that's one of the laws of life," Jacob said grimly. It was more than Steffi could bear. Dietrich's plight hovered like an unspeakable sadness between them. And when they couldn't stand it anymore, they argued and stood stiffly, their elbows and knees like armor between them. And Pamela and History and I watched them. And judged them. But wasn't the judging its own kind of cruelty?

• • •

We gave three performances of *Our Town;* everyone at Los Alamos came to see us. Even the children were allowed to stay up on those still soft September evenings. When we took our curtain calls, we could see many of them asleep in their parents' arms.

Wilder's play was first performed in New York when I was in college, and several reviewers called it sentimental. When they heard we were doing it, Peter had frowned and Jacob had groaned, "That cliché."

"They're wrong," Kate said when she heard their reaction. "And we'll prove to them how wrong they are."

After working on it, I agreed with Kate. *Our Town* walked a fragile line between sentiment and sentimentality, but so do most really good works of art, and after several rehearsals I realized it was a very tough-minded play, with the true feeling of real life. Noel understood that best of all, perhaps because it was new to him. Or perhaps because he had not had to sit through half-baked amateur performances of it that had played in every small town for the last few summers. Because he and Thea understood what Wilder was after, the play had a pace, a rhythm that made it more compelling than I could have ever believed.

By the time Emily died and then went back to her life on her twelfth birthday, you could feel a tension in the air even at the rehearsals. On the night of the first performance, when Bess as Emily said, her voice tremulous with wonder, "I can't go on! It goes so fast. We don't have time to look at one another. I didn't *realize*. So *all* that was going on and we never noticed." Then "Good-bye, world! Good-bye, Grover's Corners—Mama and Papa—Good-bye to clocks ticking and my butternut tree! and Mama's sunflowers—and food and coffee—and new-ironed dresses and hot baths—and sleeping and waking up!—Oh, earth, you're too wonderful for anyone to realize you! Do any human beings ever realize life while they live it—every minute?" I knew that we had done exactly what Kate predicted.

When people came backstage to congratulate us, their eyes

brimmed with tears. Even Peter and Jacob. And these were two men who didn't easily admit they were wrong.

"It's really Wilder's letter to the world," Noel said later that evening when we were drinking coffee and eating the chocolate cake that Pamela had brought up from Otowi for the cast. "Not to miss any of it, even the hard parts. To wake us up to what is right here, around us. For it is all so terribly beautiful."

Kate's face was triumphant as our eyes met, and she let her glance linger fondly on Noel. I knew what that glance meant, for doing this play had been an experience that changed Kate's life, she confessed to me one evening when we were locking up.

"I've never known anyone who was 'queer,' " she said. Neither had I, I suddenly realized. Certainly no one who was as honest about it as Noel. "And I didn't know how prejudiced I was," Kate added. "But he's a wonderful man. Really a remarkable human being."

9
● ● ● ■

The night air was iron. I stood at my window looking out into the long stretch of blackness. A blackness relieved only by the constellations, which seemed magnified by the vast, dark space across which they moved. Below me were the dying flowers; frost had left the tallest zinnias and dahlias collapsed on their stakes like men shot in the back, and the white nicotiana was a tangle of dew-spangled lace imprisoned in its still-heavy, now almost sour perfume. Straight ahead, shining like the night-light in a child's room, a beacon of safety, was the greenish glow from the hospital where History was about to give birth to her baby, maybe giving birth at this very second.

Fitzgerald's green light, I suddenly thought, yet hardly a metaphor for the wistful, romantic longings of Jay Gatsby. No, more like the eternal light over the ark in the synagogue, always there, a symbol of comfort, of soothing. Yet now a shiver of apprehension rippled down my spine: to wait for so long, and then to have everything happen so quickly. It was not at all as I had expected. Yet I had not really known what to expect.

"Her water broke," Herb had said excitedly over the phone just as Peter and I were finishing dinner. And then we saw them go—History looking immense, her normally small body engulfed by this baby and the clothes she wore to cover it up. Stepping gingerly, as if to avoid puddles (actually to avoid the warm burst of fluid dripping down her legs, I learned later), until they were out of sight and in the labor room that she had proudly showed me only a few days before. Her baby was to be the first official birth here at the Los Alamos hospital; another woman had had a boy, her third child, during the summer, but that baby had been born in Santa Fe. Now, though, the equipment was there, and an obstetrician from Santa Fe on call. He would come to us when he was needed; we had heard that an obstetrician was coming to Los Alamos, but so far no one had seen him. For now the only doctor on this post was a radiologist, Dr. Solomon.

Peter read, and I did a pile of ironing with one ear cocked for the telephone. How lucky we were to have a phone, one of the few on our road. It had been put in by mistake, when the Army thought someone more important was going to live here. We had reported it once, but we didn't persist in reminding them of their mistake after that. The phone was hard to use and full of static, the giveaway that it was monitored, but so convenient, especially now. For as soon as the baby was born, Herb would call, and then we would spread the word. Back and forth the iron went; slowly the wrinkled cotton of our shirts and blouses was transformed into shiny, smooth and sweet-smelling clothes. I kept seeing History's face, for she often sat only a few feet from me when I ironed—her small, regular features beneath her straight blond hair—and I wondered what it must feel like, giving birth. Yet I couldn't imagine History's benign eyes in pain. So I soon gave up and put the ironing board back into the closet. And still no one had called.

Peter looked up from his book. I said, "Shall we walk over to the hospital and see what's happening?"

He shook his head. "He knows where we are, he'll call if he needs us."

When we went to bed, Peter fell asleep almost immediately. I wasn't so lucky. I read for an hour, and now I am standing at the window, waiting for news, for anything that will relieve this tension that has been building since I saw History walk by. Of course I have heard stories of babies taking hours and hours to be born, but until now I didn't understand what that meant at all.

I can smell the acrid odor of the shriveled, dying flowers beneath me, and I pull my robe closer around my shoulders. The beginning of November, and the air is already so sharp. Then I picture a tiny face surrounded by all those warm layers of wool, those doll-like sweaters and hats History's mother knit and sent, those afghans and blankets that are folded so neatly near the crib. Let winter come.

Suddenly the ring of the telephone, crashing into the silence. I check my watch. One-thirty. Five hours. In the end, not bad at all. But instead of a triumphant cry, Herb's low, somber voice, almost unrecognizable at first. "There seems to be a problem. Can you come?" he asks, his words choked with anxiety.

The baby has not been born yet, and History's face is wan as she struggles with the pain and terror. Not the normal terror of having a first child. But terror that something is wrong. It's all there—in History's opaque eyes, in Herb's lips pressed into a fine seam, in the nurse's puckered frown.

"The doctor from Sante Fe was here and said there were hours to go and refused to stay. I just called him to come back. The contractions are much worse, but they're not coming any closer, and she's in too much pain for nothing to be happening," the nurse tells Peter and me. No secrets at least. Everything out in the open.

"Where's Dr. Solomon?" He has monitored History's uneventful pregnancy each month, then, at the end, every three weeks. I know he is supposed to be here, too, and there is no one more reliable than Jack Solomon. But now all they're talking about is this obstetrician from Santa Fe.

No one has answered, so I repeat, "What happened to Dr. Solomon?"

"He has the chicken pox," the nurse replies, then shrugs, as if to say, only at Los Alamos. Now I wonder why another doctor hasn't been hired to be here with History while Solomon is recuperating. But of course I say nothing; besides, History herself may be responsible for that.

"It's no big deal," she kept saying through these last months. "In Chicago the young doctors went into the houses of the poor and those women had their babies on newspapers. They're the best thing to use because the newsprint is sanitary. I saw those babies born myself—we had a friend who was a doctor, and he invited me to come along a few times. There's nothing to be afraid of. After all, we've all been born," she said in that no-nonsense way she had.

But now even she's afraid.

Pamela? But what does Pamela know about having children? Steffi? No. She would get too upset if something is really wrong. Kate. Yes, that's it, Kate Unwin. She has four, she's big and strong, she'll know what to do. "Call Kate Unwin," I tell Peter. But as he goes to the telephone in the hall, I realize that the person we should call is Noel. Of course! Noel is an obstetrician, he will know what to do.

As I rush after Peter, a tall, stocky man passes me, his tie askew and his hair windblown. Most noticeable is his whiskey-soaked breath. I avert my face to avoid another blast of it, wondering what he's doing here. Only when Peter and I return to the door and are motioned out of the room, do I realize that this large, unkempt drunk is the obstetrician. God help us!

The next few hours are like a dream, a surreal dream in which there are voices, sometimes raised, sometimes mumbling, in a steady stream of sound, punctuated by the occasional gasp of a scream that I recognize as History's voice in pain. In which everything I see is through the smoky glass of the door to the labor room, wavy and fuzzy, as it is meant to be. Kate Unwin comes to wait with us, and so does Pamela. And then Noel is there, pants pulled hastily over his pajamas. I see him read History's folder, then confer calmly with the doctor. His gestures are efficient, economical; no time for waste, his body seems to say. I begin to breathe easier. Noel knows what he is doing, Noel will help us. For a quick moment our eyes meet, and I see that he thinks he can help. They are cautious eyes. But hopeful.

After a few minutes Herb comes out. We hear more voices raised, the slurred syllables of the doctor, whose name is McLean, Herb tells us, and then a nurse appears with some operating gowns, and soon we are practically shoved away from that smoky door and asked in firm tones to wait down the hall, away from it all.

"Noel wants to do a cesarean, he thinks that will do it," Herb tells us, but that's all he knows. His eyes are relieved, but he sits with his head in his hands, as if not wanting to subject us to either his hope or his fear. I want to touch him, but the very idea of invading his privacy at this moment seems vulgar.

We sit there, separate, waiting. I think no longer of the baby, but of History. Please, God, don't let anything happen to History, I say over and over in my mind, and then I am sitting next to History and Herb at the short Rosh Hashanah service that was held in Fuller Lodge a few weeks ago. A rabbinical student from Albuquerque had come to do the service, and surprisingly few people showed up then or the following week for the Yom Kippur service. But History and Herb and I were there (Peter never went to any religious service if he could help it), and when we turned to kiss each other at the end of the young rabbi's benediction, History's eyes were shining with expectation. "Only a month more," she whispered to me that day.

It never occurred to either of us that anything could go wrong.

As long as I live, I will never forget the sight of Noel Jenkins standing in the doorway of that room holding History's dying baby in his large, rough-looking hands. It is a beautiful baby, a boy, and much larger than my visions of it—an eight-and-a-half-pound baby, perfectly formed, but born with the umbilical cord wrapped around its neck. By the time Noel got to him, it was too late; the baby had been struggling for hours in History's womb, and the doctor, this drunken Dr. McLean, had not realized that after her water broke he should have been there, ready to perform a cesarean if things didn't move more quickly. Was he drunk when he came the first time? I don't know and never had the nerve to ask. But he was clearly negligent, and the baby drew its last few breaths in Noel's hands. Not even Noel could help us.

I stand there watching the grief in Noel's eyes as he covers the baby with a diaper, and I feel as if we have been catapulted back onto the stage of *Our Town,* that we are in another act of that play, and that the Stage Manager is about to say something about how the thread of life sometimes becomes tangled, turns back on itself, and the normal order of things becomes reversed. That a birth can sometimes become a death.

But we are not in a play, and Noel is not the Stage Manager tonight. No, tonight he wears an old hat, his doctor's hat. "And a damn good doctor, too," the nurses report. "If not for Dr. Jenkins, we might have lost her, too," one says in a clenched voice.

Now History is stirring, and we leave Herb and Noel to tell her what has happened. The doctor has disappeared. I don't know how or when, but he is gone. We never see him again.

In a moment of anger a few months after Trinity, Kate called us all cowboys. The men and the women, the scientists, the machinists, the Army, everyone at Los Alamos. "Cowboys. The ultimate cowboys," she said bitterly. "Ravaging everything that matters on this earth, changing the world, for the worse."

I understood her bitterness, but I never agreed with her. We were all changed from this experience, just as the very earth had been changed. But we were not cowboys, cavalier, self-centered, unthinking. Kate was wrong. The ultimate cowboy was that doctor we never saw again. Who didn't have enough respect for his job to do it properly. Who let History's baby die.

● ● ●

We are sitting around the table in the Lerners' apartment. The day has disappeared in a blur of grief and anger, disagreements, even arguments. Noel has absolutely forbidden History to get out of bed for at least twenty-four hours, and Herb is torn by indecision. His religion commands him to bury the baby as soon as possible, yet he feels that it would be better for History to come to the baby's funeral. Oddly, for I am usually the first to speak up, I don't have an opinion. All I can think is: The baby is dead. Does it matter who is at the funeral?

I feel so detached. So does Bess. I can tell from the way her long body curls in on itself. Her eyes are listless, her usually smiling mouth turns down. And instead of the freshly ironed man-tailored shirts and slacks she usually wears, she's in a dark dress that looks crushed from hanging in the back of the closet too long. We are History's closest friends, yet we have the least to say.

"You can't expect someone who has just had a cesarean to get up and go to a funeral tomorrow," Noel is repeating, again as if he were talking to children who can't understand.

"But you can't have the funeral without her," Steffi interrupts him sharply. From the moment she walked in, I could see her anger, her hostility. She's upset that she wasn't at the birth; though I didn't realize it until this minute, she views herself as the one in charge, and she's hurt that no one called her until it was over. I can tell by the way Jacob looks at her, by the wariness screening his eyes, that he knows how resentful she is.

"It isn't fair. The best way for her to face this is to see the coffin go into the ground." She stares at me with icy eyes, expecting me to agree. But I merely shrug. History can go or not go; nothing will bring back her baby. Besides, I don't really believe much in funerals.

Then Thea asks, "What does History want?" At her question Tom Schweren's head rises sharply. On his lips is the merest hint of a smile; at last someone is talking sense, his eyes say approvingly; he has little patience with agonizing of any kind.

"She doesn't know," Herb replies. "The nurses have encouraged her not to go, whenever it is. They say she should just put it behind her. They say . . ."

"But that's just the point!" Steffi explodes. "The only way she can go on is if she takes part in the burial. What idiots! To think that she can just forget it, that if she doesn't have a memory of a funeral it will be easier—it's so stupid I can hardly stand it." She laces her fingers together as if that would help her control herself.

"Take it easy, darling," Jacob says to her gently, as if they were alone. I am startled by the effect of his low voice and that "darling" on me. He's clearly annoyed with her, yet his voice is filled with love.

I rearrange myself on the sofa. Silence fills the room and is broken finally by the sound of Tom's lighter as he leans toward Thea to light her cigarette. I can't help staring. There is an intimacy about the way their bodies arch toward each other, about the way their heads—his blond, hers a deep brown with gray strands in it—almost meet.

But then Steffi says, "History's feelings *matter*. It's only fair that we do what she wants, she's the mother . . ." her voice fades. I look at Herb. Shouldn't his wishes be respected, too? He's the father, after all, and if the Jewish religion dictates a quick funeral, and he is an observant Jew, then why are we here? He seems to read my mind.

Quickly he says, "One of the best things about religion is that it has rules, ways of proceeding. But sometimes even the best rules seem to be wrong. She was the one who went through the birth, and I want to do the right thing for her."

Now the silence is stiff, starched. Then Steffi's voice, lower now. "Wait until she can come to the funeral. Then it will be real to her. There's so much we have to deal with here that doesn't seem real. Let this, at least, be real." Her gaze sweeps across all of us.

Herb nods abruptly. His voice is a raspy whisper. "We'll wait until Noel says History can get up. However long it takes."

• • •

In the Rosh Hashanah service, the rabbinical student who came to conduct it intoned solemnly, "On Rosh Hashanah it is written, on Yom Kippur it is sealed: How many shall pass on, how many shall come to be; who shall live and who shall die; who shall see ripe age and who shall not; who shall perish by fire and who by water; who by sword and who by hunger; who by earthquake and who by plague; who shall be at ease and who shall be torn; who shall be secure and who shall be driven; who shall be tranquil and who shall be troubled; who shall be humbled and who exalted; who shall be poor and who shall be rich."

I have always been uneasy with those words; they make everything seem so predestined; and free will seems to be erased by them. While I was growing up, several rabbis pointed out the end of that famous prayer: "But repentance, prayer, and charity temper judgment's severe decree," as a way to persuade me that the prayer's harshness is a matter of language and not really of principle, but I have never been convinced.

On the day that we buried the baby, I found myself hating those ancient words.

We are at the Eyed Boulder, on Tunyopin, the Black Mesa. The strange primitive face, eroded into the stone like a blind man gazing upward into the heavens, has full eyes, for it rained last night— full eyes that mirror the movements of the clouds, eyes filled with tears, just as ours are.

We stand here—History and Herb, Noel, Kate, Pamela, Steffi

and Jacob, Bess and Mark, Tom and Thea, Peter and I—to bury Robert Lerner. "The simplest, most common name I can find," History confessed to me before the baby's birth. "If it's a boy, it's Robert, if a girl, Jane."

It was Pamela who suggested that we bury the baby in this long tawny grass where it is always so peaceful and so still. She got permission from the head of the San Ildefonso council, and now she is in charge, she and Estevan, who came to dig the grave in accordance with the Indian rules. He stands quietly next to Pamela. They are both dressed in dark city clothes that seem to drain their faces of their usual color. Pamela's eyes never leave Herb's or History's faces; the rest of us are simply part of the background. If I didn't know better, I could swear that Pamela has been through this herself; she seems to be able to anticipate every move that History makes.

I look around. Like Pamela and Estevan, the rest of us are dressed in city clothes. Finally I am wearing my navy blue suit, and the brim of the hat that I crushed in my hand the day I met History and Thea is over my brow.

Now History stares at the tiny rectangular coffin. Her opaque eyes have that almost blind expression she has worn ever since she awoke with a smile on her face (for once Noel appeared, her hopes rose), and was told, quietly, sadly, that her baby was dead. In these last five days since the baby was born, History seems asleep as she talks to us, as if part of her brain had atrophied. It is the scariest thing I have ever seen, and even Peter's soft whisper, "Give her time, it's all so new," doesn't really comfort me at all.

Quickly and silently Herb and Peter make an indentation in the grave for the small coffin, then they and Jacob and Mark Chanin stand and say the Kaddish together. I am amazed. I did not even know Peter knew the Hebrew words; in all the years we have known each other, in all the times he went to services out of respect for his parents, I have never heard him say a Hebrew prayer.

Herb carries the coffin to the grave, but before he can lower it, History steps forward and kneels down and touches it—caressing it again and again—as if she can't bear to let it go. At last she lifts her hands, the coffin is lowered into the grave, and the traditional handfuls of dirt are thrown upon it.

As I stand there, I hear all the so-called comfort that has been offered: she is young, she will have another, these things happen, doctors can't know everything, this is part of the risk we took coming here. Crazy phrases that mean nothing in the end. So inadequate, this vague language we fall back on to communicate comfort. How can it be the same language that is also so precise? The same language that Peter and Jacob use to describe the elements of science. I shake my head, then look up into the November sky.

For the day is dazzling, the light as brilliant as summer back home. And there are still flowers blooming, though nothing like the frowsy dahlias that remind me of beauties gone to seed in middle age, or even like those final stubborn roses that linger into the cool November days in the Northeast. No, these are of a different order, muted, sturdy desert flowers that will bloom until the snows of winter. Yet today their colors shine like coins flashing beneath a sun that has not yet lost its power to warm and wilt, if not burn.

And then I allow myself to remember that day in History's apartment when she told me about her mother, then whispered that she was pregnant. I see the crib waiting in the sunlight, all those blankets and sweaters her mother has knitted neatly folded in the dresser drawers. What will her mother, who has spent all these months knitting, say? What will she do when she gets Herb's call later this afternoon? For I know that he hasn't called yet. It was too hard. Then I wonder, will History's mother finally acknowledge that this birth and death is one of those accidents of war? Will this tragedy make her see that we on this mesa are also part of the war?

I bow my head in shame. Is this what tragedy does? Make us cruel?

We wait until the coffin disappears, until Estevan makes the ground level with the grassy mound on which the Eyed Boulder sits. He works slowly, methodically, his face impassive as he completes his task. For the first time since I have known him, I wonder what he is thinking. Until today he seemed to melt into the landscape. But today he is one of us, burying a baby whose brief life was so short as to be no life at all.

He does what he has to do patiently. Yet Estevan isn't angry, as I think Noel is, as I know the rest of us are. Estevan has learned to accept whatever comes. Does that come from age or from living here? Or from being an Indian?

Then my glance moves from Estevan's face to that of the Eyed Boulder. A shudder runs through me. For that blessed shrine of the San Ildefonso Indians no longer seems a passive, sacred face. No, now it looks alive: a blind man with full eyes staring upward, beseeching its ancient God as if it, too, wanted to know what on earth has been served by this death.

10

Remember Melville's Loom of Time? Ishmael passing the woof of the marline through the threads of the warp, using his hand as shuttle, while Queequeg slid his sword between the threads. Ishmael dreamily thinking that what they were working on could rightly be called the Loom of Time and he a shuttle "mechanically weaving and weaving away at the Fates." How easily he saw it on that cloudy, sultry afternoon in the few moments before Tashtego sighted a school of whales: in Ishmael's mind the warp had become necessity, his shuttle-hand seemed free will, and Queequeg's sword was chance.

I thought of that Loom of Time a lot during the autumn of 1943. We women were like delicate threads in our own loom, thin silky strands as fragile as those that had fascinated me in that textile factory when I was a child. We knew what the necessity was; we had understood that as soon as we arrived. And we had free will, for no one was here who didn't want to be here. But chance? Had we ever considered the role of chance? Not really. And now chance had sneaked into our lives, and everything was subtly, irreparably changed. Something in that loom of time had unaccountably shifted.

My feelings those first days after History gave birth to her baby reminded me of a time long ago when there was a huge snowstorm on the East Coast in October. I was at my Grandmother Julia's for the weekend. Within hours the temperature dropped thirty degrees, the sky turned a bruised, ominous gray. I must have been about eight or nine, old enough to help my grandmother haul the summer furniture and the potted plants from the patio into the garage. Then we brought in load after load of wood for the fireplace, while the wind became fiercer than I had ever seen it. At last she and I, wrapped in sweaters, stood at the window and watched the freak storm pull down the gorgeous orange and red and yellow leaves.

"It's like a funeral," she said. When it was over, autumn returned, but no leaves, no colors, just those naked trees; and afterward a cloying, too-long Indian summer, surprisingly warm, perhaps because there was no shade.

I remember the light that autumn—an unnatural light that had nothing to filter it. I think it was that extraordinary light that made everyone feel out of sorts. When real winter finally came, around Christmastime, everyone seemed to give a huge sigh of relief. Things were taking their natural course, and now we could forget the ruthless, unexpected storm that had ravaged the trees before their time.

But when would things begin to take their natural course here at Los Alamos?

History went back to work two weeks after the baby was buried, against Noel's wishes. "But perhaps it's better for her to be busy," Steffi said. Her voice was more resigned than I had ever heard it.

Still, as the weeks passed, we realized that History wasn't getting better; if anything, she seemed worse—her paleness approaching that dangerous translucence we had all seen in very sick people.

"She's thinner than she's ever been," Herb confided one evening to Peter, "and so listless. I've never seen her so listless."

When Peter reported the conversation, I burst out, "That's some euphemism, a ridiculous euphemism. She's a ghost. Nothing more than a ghost!"

He stared at me as if he didn't know me, as if he didn't want to know the woman whose voice was so accusing and hard. I hated his staring at me like that, and I looked away. Neither of us had the strength to talk about it. We both knew there was nothing more to say.

One Sunday I tried to talk to History, but I felt as Peter must have felt when he had tried to talk to me. Who was this impatient, brusque creature who brushed away everyone's concern, as if it were simply a spider web she had unwittingly walked into? As if our words, so carefully chosen and rehearsed, were gossamer threads. She had been such a good listener, yet now she was unable to listen. It was frightening. She made us feel like fools, for when words are treated like cobwebs, no one, not even the person who has said them, gives them much weight.

Finally help came from an unexpected quarter. A week before Thanksgiving Herb called me at the office. "You've got to help me, Lily. History's mother has just arrived in Santa Fe. She's at La Fonda del Sol. Someone has to go down and talk to her, tell her how awful History looks. I don't want her to have a heart attack when she sees History. And I can't go. I'm running an experiment that has to be watched."

I knew that was true. Herb was working with Emilio Segrè in his cabin a little way from the mesa; there were only a few of them trying to measure the spontaneous rate of fission, and I knew the work was crucial.

"Besides, Lily, it might be better if it were a woman." His voice sounded so sad, as if he had failed History, had failed us all. I asked Jacob for time off, called Peter, then arranged for a ride from The Hill.

I expected a large-bosomed, tall woman with a commanding voice and a peremptory manner. A kind of latter-day Statue of Liberty who had given birth to Memory, Justice, and History. Who had had what my mother called "the brass" to name her newborn infants those imposing, unforgettable names. The quintessential snob, the opinionated know-it-all. Instead, Amelia Matthews was a pretty, white-haired woman who looked like an older, healthier version of History. Her voice was firm, but so soft that I had to lean toward her to hear what she said. She had come, she began, because she didn't like the sound of History's letters.

"She sounds so tired, so unbelievably tired. And when she described what happened, she made it sound as if it were her fault. As if she could have somehow helped what happened." As I sat there, listening to History's mother, I realized that even if she was all the things History said, she was also much more: She was a woman who loved her child, a woman who was able to put aside everything else and come to her daughter.

I watched her sip her martini in the most delicate, ladylike way imaginable, and I thought of how she had behaved when History told her she wanted to marry Herb, and how far she had come from that day. I could see all the woollies she had knit for the baby, and then I remembered what History had said about her mother's life, how she had never stretched herself.

How wrong History was! For here was a woman who had left her husband and son a week before Thanksgiving and had traveled thousands of miles on trains from Maine to New York and then from New York to Chicago, where she had boarded the *Santa Fe Chief*, finally arriving at Lamy, because she didn't like the way her daughter's letters sounded. She couldn't even tell anyone where she was going, for Box 1663 wasn't supposed to exist.

Therefore, did we exist? It was an old joke among us. "I think, therefore I am. We do not exist, therefore are we?" We had gotten used to it, to almost everything, but then there had been the terrifying death of the baby. And that feeling of anonymity had seemed to engulf us.

Perhaps that was what Amelia Matthews had sensed between the lines of History's letters. She had heard Herb's voice, had listened to his disappointment, his frustration, his anger, which she was too wise to try to allay. And after that she had waited for History's letters. When they arrived she was smart enough to sense that something was terribly wrong. So she had come.

It was as simple as that.

I sat there listening to her soft, educated New England accent, with its broad *a*'s and its soft *d*-like *t*'s, and I could feel myself blush with shame that we had ever laughed at her.

She looked at me thoughtfully, then said, "Things have never been the same between History and me since her marriage. I said some very foolish things when she told me she was going to marry Herb. Things I have regretted." She paused and let her eyes hold mine.

"Herb is a good husband, a good man. He is the right person for her—I knew that as soon as I got to know him. And he's also brilliant. They had to come out here. I understand that. I just want her to understand that she has to get her strength back so she can have another baby. I want her to know that she will have another baby."

That was a long speech for her. She said it almost in a rehearsed monotone, for she was a woman who had trained herself to guard her feelings carefully. As she spoke, I realized how lonely I was, maybe we all were, for that wonderful confidence only a mother can give you. I never really believed it until I heard History's mother say with such conviction that History and Herb would have another child. Even though other people had said the same words, they simply didn't seem possible until Mrs. Matthews said them slowly and firmly, as if she knew I needed to hear them resonate in the air between us. They freed me, and if they freed me to think more optimistically about the future, what would they do to History? At that moment I think I missed my own mother more than I ever had before.

On the way down to Santa Fe only about an hour ago I had wondered why Herb was sending me, why he hadn't sent Bess or Kate, both good Protestants who had so much more in common with Mrs. Matthews. Now it occurred to me that perhaps Herb understood History's mother better than History did, and that it would be better and easier for Amelia Matthews if the cards were put on the table bluntly and quickly, as I was able to do.

She seemed to know what I was about to tell her before I could utter the words. She nodded briefly as I explained how depressed History was, how discouraged she looked, so it seemed useless, even cruel to go into any more detail. I stopped, and we looked at each other for a moment, then she said, "I want to go up there and take care of her."

I frowned. It was such an understandable thing for her to say, almost a reflex. How could I explain to her that it was impossible? If only there were some primer I could refer to, like the Los Alamos Primer. But of course there was no such thing. For who could have predicted what happened to History and Herb? Certainly not Groves or Oppie.

"I'm afraid you can't. Strangers aren't allowed on The Hill."

Her milky-white skin blanched. I'm hardly a stranger, her eyes told me. She was right. And yet in the context of our lives at Los Alamos, that is exactly what she had become. The absurdity of it struck me full force as I sat there watching Amelia Matthews gently lift a faintly scented handkerchief to wipe the tears of frustration filling her eyes.

"Well, isn't there someplace where History can go and just rest, and I can see her every day?" she asked. There has to be a solution, her earnest, troubled eyes urged. I didn't come this far to stay for only a few days and see my child in the artificial setting of a hotel, she explained a few moments later.

Then she looked around the lobby of La Fonda, with almost a sniff of distaste. Ah, here at last was the woman History knew, the woman who couldn't respond to what was strange or new, the woman who thought she didn't like Jews because she had never really known one. Yet I could see her point; this place did look a little like a cluttered stage set to someone unfamiliar with the New Mexican culture.

"There must be someplace, Lily," she said, using my first name for the first time.

Of course there was. As we were speaking, I had considered the Windoms. But Mrs. Windom and Mrs. Matthews would never get along. There was also Thea, who had a house in Santa Fe. But she was so swamped with work; the last thing she needed was houseguests.

Pamela. Of course! Pamela would help us. And even if Groves didn't like it, he would never dare to complain. In Oppie's eyes Pamela could do no wrong.

Within hours Estevan had moved back to San Ildefonso and Amelia Matthews was ensconced in his simple, monklike room. A cot was brought down from The Hill for History, and that evening Herb and History went to Otowi. Jacob went with them, perhaps because Groves wanted to make sure someone high up was a witness, that Amelia Matthews wasn't a spy, or some such nonsense. Who knows? In any case, it was Jacob who told me that when History saw her mother holding out her arms, she finally cried.

"She never expected to see her mother; she thought we were all just going to have dinner at Pamela's. She couldn't have been more surprised," Jacob told me. "It was good for her to cry."

In his voice was the same relief that I felt surging through me. I stared, feeling a strange balm mingle in the space between us, creating an intimacy I had never before felt with Jacob—not even on that day he had been so distraught about Steffi. I knew how upset Peter was over what had happened to History and Herb, but Jacob and I had never discussed it. What was there to say? What was done was done. But now I could see how troubled Jacob was, how responsible he felt for all of us he had convinced to come here.

"It was a tragedy, a real tragedy," he said simply. "It is good that her mother came. You know, my mother used to see her own mother every day when she was a young woman in Berlin," he confided. I thought he was going to say more, but he didn't, just turned on his heel and went back into his office.

Since the *Feuersturm* at Hamburg the tide of the war had been turning. Cologne and Hamburg had been destroyed, the Germans had surrendered in Africa and at Stalingrad, Mussolini had been arrested, and Italy had declared war on Germany. Good news, except, perhaps, to us.

For if the Germans got desperate, would they step up their efforts to complete an atomic weapon? Were they planning to use it soon? There was a huge heavy water plant at Vemork in Norway that had been attacked at the beginning of the year, but might they have built another one somewhere else? And it was rumored that someone in Europe had seen Heisenberg's rendering of a heavy water reactor.

A few days after Amelia Matthews arrived, Peter bounded up the steps. That meant news. But, as always, he waited until we were in bed before he dared to speak. Our touching feet were slabs of ice. The sharp evening cold of late autumn was a shock. Some nights we could hardly get warm. And it wasn't even winter yet. I had pulled our last blanket from the closet and written my mother for another one. Now Peter's feet rubbed mine, absently, as he spoke.

"Schweren's back from Chicago, and they told him that a special mission has just been created in Europe to find out what the Germans are doing about their own gadget. The mission's code name is Alsos, which means Groves in Greek." He looked at me with incredulity in his eyes. "Isn't that ridiculous? Some idiot Army man's idea of a joke. When Groves heard about it, he was furious. Naturally, he wanted to change it but decided against it. That would only draw attention to it." He shook his head. "Boris Pash, a colonel from the Army, is the military head—he's big in intelligence. Someone in Chicago told Tom that he had once investigated Oppie for possible Communist connections. Well, better to have him chasing Germans than making up lies about Oppie. And the best news is that Sam Goudsmit is working with Pash. Goudsmit's terrific. A Dutchman who was working on radar at MIT."

"What does this mean for us?" I asked.

"It'll give us some idea how much time we really have. Maybe take some of the pressure off. Who knows? Some people think they're about two years ahead of us, others think not that much." Peter yawned, then shrugged, and soon we fell asleep.

Strange how some pieces of information imprint themselves in one's mind more sharply than others. From then on, I felt personally connected to Alsos, in the same way that I felt connected to Bonhoeffer through the Wunderlichs and Noel. Those connections became more important as the war went on; perhaps I needed to convince myself that this vacuum in which we had found ourselves was not really an empty anonymous space, but part of a larger whole.

Yet still so many questions. And no answers, except to plunge ahead, to work harder. As the race stepped up, The Hill seemed more like a cage than ever before.

A cage filled with discouragement as well. Arguments about implosion, slowdowns in the search for fissionable materials. I knew fragments here and there because Peter was in on the talks about the plutonium manufacture at Hanford and the uranium separation work at Oak Ridge. He had begun, in all kinds of ways he wasn't even aware of, to warn me that he might have to go with Fermi to one or the other, or perhaps both. Then in August the Quebec agreement between Roosevelt and Churchill, which meant that the English were now coming to Los Alamos to help the Americans. More people, more housing, more personalities. More work for Oppie and Groves, which meant more work for Thea, more responsibility for Jacob.

How different Jacob looked today from the supremely confident man he had been less than a year ago when he and I had argued at Rockefeller Center.

How different we all were. Still, it wasn't all bad. For Jacob was also more approachable, more likable. As I watched him walk into his office and sit down, then pick up the telephone to make yet another urgent call, I realized that I couldn't really remember what life had been like without Jacob. And though I knew lots of things about him—how tentative his stance became when he was worried, how he would roll up his sleeves impatiently when he had a lot to do, how his eyes glazed over when he was angry, how I could make him smile—I also realized that I didn't really know very much about him at all.

When he mentioned his mother, I wondered if she was alive and where she was. And a father? And sisters and brothers? Jacob was so confident he seemed to have come into the world completely full-grown and capable. Yet that was nonsense. He had a family and a childhood, just like the rest of us. And when he mentioned his mother, I sensed that the sight of History in her mother's arms had dredged up feelings he had suppressed for far too long.

Suddenly there was so much I wanted to ask Jacob that morning. But of course I didn't.

• • •

How do people get well? While I was at Los Alamos I learned about the elaborate Indian rituals for healing, but I never saw them, for they were private ceremonies closed to white people.

Only Pamela was allowed to witness some of those rituals. Something about her sense of calm, her mysterious alliance with Estevan, the way she led her life had made them warm to her; she was not merely another white woman. I had even heard a Santa Clara Indian refer to Pamela with awe as a witch. Not some wild woman on a broomstick, or some unhappy, handicapped woman who was burned at Salem. No, a witch in the best sense of the word, someone who could cure the sick. When History moved into Pamela's house, I found myself looking at Pamela in a new way.

For under the care of Pamela and her mother, History's body seemed to grow stronger before our very eyes. "She needs to sleep for at least a week," Noel had said after the funeral, but she never gave herself the opportunity. As soon as her mother arrived, History knew she had no choice. That evening she went to bed and from then on slept long, long nights and rested during the day. The household was quiet; while History was there, no dinners were served. Otowi had become a place of healing, where two older women focused themselves on helping History get well.

Pamela and Amelia looked uncannily alike: lean, small, blue-eyed. Even their gestures had weird similarities. We teased them about it—Bess and Kate and I—and they simply laughed, as if they shared a secret they wouldn't dream of telling us.

While Amelia and Pamela and History lived together at Otowi, time seemed to change. Instead of being our enemy, something we were constantly racing against or wishing would pass, it became our ally, a silky substance that flowed slowly, tenderly, as quietly as the thin stream of the Rio Grande outside the window. A substance with powers we couldn't even guess, enfolding History, healing her.

By the third week in December Amelia made arrangements to leave. It had taken a little more than a month. Now History could look you directly in the eyes when she talked to you. The irises of her eyes, faded to such a pale blue right after the baby's birth, now darkened with hope: the same hope I had seen on the day we unpacked her belongings, the same hope she had had during her pregnancy: the expectant hope of a child.

Clearly, Amelia had done the very thing she had come to do. And probably without words. I was too much a believer in words, I began to realize, and it would come back to haunt me later, when words again became beside the point. It was Amelia's physical presence that History needed, that had helped restore her.

Herb seemed to know that better than anyone else. He came down to Otowi for dinner every night, and instead of being in any way resentful, as some men might have been, he was grateful. He and Amelia seemed to have reached a special understanding. An understanding that the most important thing was to get History well. How this odd arrangement might appear to acquaintances or strangers simply didn't matter. I could imagine Peter and my mother coming to something like this if I was ever sick.

But what I admired most was Amelia's patience and wisdom to stay just a little bit longer than she was needed. By then History had had enough of her mother, so there wasn't a trace of regret when it was time to say good-bye.

● ● ●

While History was getting well, no fewer than three people took her place at the hospital and kept things going; the rest of us arranged a community Thanksgiving dinner and a square dance at the school, where Noel surprised everyone by being a marvelous dancer, and we started rehearsals for Handel's *Messiah,* to be performed on Christmas Eve. This was the first holiday season at Los Alamos, and everyone wanted it to be as festive as possible, especially since the English were to arrive in the midst of it.

You could smell a change in the air as winter approached, a new sharpness making you alert to possible shifts in the weather. At dusk Truchas had a curious purplish cast, an odd iridescence that was more beautiful than those blazing summer sunsets had been. And at night the sky seemed huge, the stars sparkling blossoms in a garden of constellations clearer than we had ever seen them. Yet during the day that same sky could make me feel more alone than ever before.

For when the sun couldn't get through, the winter light had no tact or discrimination; it crept everywhere, like an unwelcome snake, revealing whatever ugliness it found. Some days The Hill looked like the bleakest place on earth. Then I was grateful not to have a child, not to have to stand in a cluster of women watching the children play; grateful that I had an office to which I could retreat. And in the long dark evenings I was glad to go rehearse the *Messiah*.

I had tried to get Peter to come, for he had a lovely voice, but most nights he spent bent over work. After I finished the dishes and read for a while, I would sometimes run my hand along his spine, hoping he would lean back in his chair and smile and rub his eyes clear of those endless equations and talk to me. It happened only once; the other times he didn't even know I had touched him. And on the rare nights when he vowed he wouldn't work, it wasn't much better. He couldn't concentrate on anything else, and I knew that as soon as I left, he would sit at the kitchen table and go through more calculations. So it became easier to go. Besides, just making my voice project seemed to rid me of some of the nervous energy I would have had if I had stayed at home.

There was a six-day work week on The Hill. On Saturday nights we would go out to a party or a movie or sometimes to Santa Fe. And on Sundays there were outings, for until the snow came it was safe to hike or ride.

Oppenheimer and his wife kept horses at their cabin in the mountains and rode on Sunday mornings. Sometimes we saw them and their guests: Tom Schweren, Thea, the Chanins. I'm not crazy about horses, and neither is Peter, so the riders always looked very brave to me. Yet as I watched them, I thought about those angles

Pamela had observed. Some people sat stiffly on their horses, ever so slightly afraid, never entirely comfortable. And others, like Tom, looked as if they had been born to ride.

To get his horse to stop or start, Tom would lean forward and stroke its mane and talk to it; he never carried a crop. Bess told me she had asked him about it. His reply was crisp: "Hitler uses a crop."

It sounded like Tom. For he had a fierce sense of right and wrong, like his cousin Dan, and for him the only place to be was here at Los Alamos, trying to stop Hitler. After he had seen the pile go critical in Chicago, he had never once questioned his decision to come here, and he had no patience with people who agonized over the gadget. "It has to be done—do it as quickly and as efficiently as possible," he would say.

After a while I noticed that Tom wasn't always alone; as the fall turned slowly to winter, he rode more and more with Thea. At first no one thought much about it; after all, Thea was probably ten years older than Tom. But I remembered that moment in the Lerners' living room, and whenever I saw them, I would stare, frankly curious about them. Finally I realized why: there were no angles at all. Then I remembered how pretty Thea had looked at the Wunderlich party, and I tried to recall what I knew about her. Nothing, except that she had a daughter who was off at boarding school. What had happened to her husband? Was he dead? Were they divorced? No one knew, except probably Mrs. Windom, but I didn't want to ask her.

Then one night Thea appeared at a party with her beautiful dark hair down, pinned behind her ears, very different from that rather severe braid that she usually wound around her head. Her hair came almost to her waist: thick dark brown hair that softened her face and made her look years younger than forty, which we guessed was about her age.

When Tom appeared a little later, they stood together having drinks. Nothing wrong with that, I thought as I observed them.

But when I saw her lean toward him again, this time to hear—for Tom had a soft voice—I knew what I had suspected was true. Something was happening to them both.

So I wasn't surprised when Kate told me a few days later that Tom Schweren had tried out for the part of Marchbanks in the production of *Candida* that she was casting for the spring. Thea was to be Candida. "They'll be perfect," Kate said, then added, "They're falling in love and they don't even know it."

• • •

Amelia Matthews left a few days before Erik Traugott arrived. For years I could imagine the headlights of their trains searing the blackness, reflecting against the snow-covered plains, then briefly crossing paths and parting.

In the one going east was a strong-minded, independent woman who had asserted her rights as a mother in a place where such rights seemed to have become beside the point. A middle-aged woman who left The Hill a little bit better than she found it.

In the one coming west was a middle-aged man most of us did not know, a man who would affect us in ways we couldn't suspect, in ways even deeper than Amelia had. For the stranger heading to Los Alamos was not only a brilliant scientist who had been at the very center of prewar atomic research; he was also a man we were going to grow to love and regard as a father for the rest of the war and for years and years afterward.

When I saw him, I could hardly believe my eyes. Peter had talked about Erik Traugott with such awe that I had envisioned a larger-than-life man whose outward appearance would give one a clue to his remarkable integrity and intelligence. But how young I was! Too young to know that the plainest face can shine with intelligence, that conventional beauty doesn't mean a thing.

Erik Traugott was a slightly stooped, stocky man, with blunt features, a balding head surrounded by a fringe of white hair, and a raspy, guttural voice that stuttered when it tried to form certain syllables. How could this be the brilliant scientist whose arrival had been so eagerly anticipated? I could feel my heart plummet with disappointment.

It didn't take long for me to realize how wrong my first impression was. For Erik Traugott seemed to listen with his eyes, and when he spoke, his eyes seemed to speak as well, as if they knew they had to supplement his odd stutter. After you got to know him, the problems with his speech ceased to matter. You simply listened harder.

We met at Otowi. I had come to drop some books off for Pamela. It was a Saturday, the first time I had been there since Amelia and History had left. The house was back to normal, and Estevan was doing the dishes in the kitchen. When I walked in, Oppenheimer was leaving. As usual, he seemed tense, but today he greeted me by name instead of merely nodding brusquely. As Oppie was making his way toward the door, Pamela introduced me to the rumpled man, who was alternately chewing on a pipe and drinking a cup of her coffee.

"Mr. Traugott needed a place to relax for a while," Pamela explained, "and Oppie suggested he stay here until dinner. I was just going to get the chess set."

Then Erik Traugott began to sort the frayed chess problems that had obviously been stuffed in his billfold for some time. Pamela and I talked about History, how well she was doing, how much better she seemed. As we spoke, Erik Traugott seemed completely unaware of what was going on around him. Well, that fit. Peter had mentioned his famous powers of concentration. "He may be the smartest man in the world," Peter had said once, "maybe even smarter than Einstein." And then someone had replied dryly, "Intelligence isn't a tennis game, Peter," and Peter had blushed.

Now the famous Erik Traugott was here. And, it seemed, planning to stay for a while. I had noticed a good-sized valise standing in the corner. Obviously, Oppie had brought him here first and would take him to The Hill after he had had dinner at Pamela's. The same orientation course that Thea had worked out for History and Herb and Peter and me, I realized.

He never lifted his eyes from the chess board, so I was surprised when he looked up as I was leaving and said, "How did your friend History get her name? It's almost as absurd as mine." His eyes were twinkling as he spoke. "The worst part about having a significant name is that people expect you to do significant things. But Traugott is not true God, as many people think, but God in whom we trust. Still a heavy burden, almost as heavy as History."

I told him about History and her mother and her sister and brother. We laughed a little, and soon I left. As I walked home, I realized that I had understood Erik Traugott perfectly. As soon as Oppenheimer had gone and he was alone with Pamela and me, he had stopped stuttering. How odd.

We never figured it out completely. Yet we were all to notice, as time went on, that he never stuttered when Pamela was close by, and we often thought it a pity that Erik didn't take her with him when he paid his momentous visits to Churchill and Roosevelt. If he had, the course of history might well have been very different.

"Why is Erik Traugott here?" I asked Jacob the following Monday.

"Well, the official story is that he is part of the English delegation to Los Alamos," Jacob replied as he shut the outer door to the office.

"And the unofficial story?"

"That he is the only person who can convince the Americans to think about the control of nuclear arms, and the English scientific community feels it is absolutely essential that we begin to do that."

"Isn't that jumping the gun a little?" I could feel myself frown. "Putting the cart before the horse? After all, the gadget isn't even built."

"Some people think so. The old, hard-core diplomats are asking the same question. But some people believe that Erik is right, that the only way to prevent an arms race is to have everything out in the open. Erik says, 'If everyone knows everything, then no one needs to be ahead.' "

"And what do you think?" I asked Jacob.

"Dunno," he answered in his little parody of American speech that he sometimes teased me with.

"Maybe more to the point, what does Groves think?" I suddenly asked.

"Only time will tell," Jacob replied.

• • •

When Erik met Leslie Groves, he was introduced by Oppie as Ethan Thomas. Aliases on The Hill were one of Groves's pet inventions. He had given them to all the famous scientists here: Fermi was Farmer, Wigner was Wagner, Traugott was Thomas. But no one paid much attention to them. Today, however, Oppie didn't want to antagonize Groves.

Everyone, even Erik, had been warned before they came to The Hill how much Groves prized secrecy. What most of the women didn't realize was how vast the Manhattan Project was: a huge octopus with arms reaching to Hanford and Oak Ridge and the Metallurgical Lab in Chicago, to Columbia University and Berkeley and dozens of unidentified college campuses around the country.

Yet they were each supposed to be ignorant of what the others were doing. Another example of how the military managed to make things more complicated for themselves. Another reason that several of the higher-level scientists, Jacob among them, had announced early on that they wouldn't wear Army uniforms and that they would leave if the scientific community on The Hill was forced to become part of the military.

Erik met Groves in Oppie's office. Although he didn't look tall,

Erik was almost as tall as Groves, and at fifty-seven, a decade older. To Groves's credit he treated Erik with the utmost respect, although it was clear to Oppie and Jacob that Groves thought Erik was more than slightly crazy.

"He even asked if Erik thinks he's some kind of spokesman for God, some kind of Messiah," Jacob said, smiling.

"But seriously, Lily, Groves can't understand that Erik is coming directly out of the tradition of physics, which was always so open, so international in its nature. And now that he's here, everyone who knows him—and there are none of us who were born in Europe who don't know him—will want to share our research with him."

Still Leslie Groves was no fool. He knew that he had better listen. For Erik was one of the most respected scientists alive, and the institute in Denmark that bore his name had been the training ground for many of the men here on The Hill.

After the introductions were made and they had sat down, Erik leaned toward Groves and asked, "Do you have a wife, General?"

"Yes." Groves was wary.

"And children?"

"A boy at West Point and a girl in high school."

Erik nodded briskly, as if to say "Good."

"And you, Mr. Thomas?" Groves asked, suddenly more erect.

"Oh, yes, a wife and four daughters and a son, who are all in England." Now it was Groves's turn to nod. He recalled that the Traugotts had left Denmark after the Nazis came.

Then Groves asked, "Why do you ask about my family?"

Erik smiled, his open face almost merry. But his voice was grave. "Because it is your family who will be affected by all sorts of decisions you are making now." Then Erik proceeded to explain to Groves the urgent need for openness, the need to share information not only among the scientists on The Hill, but also with the English when they arrived, and with other countries.

"You know all the physicists working on this in the various

countries know each other. Many of them came to our institute or studied with Ehrenfest in Leyden, or were at Göttingen, or worked with Rutherford in England. Physics was a small community for many years," Erik explained gently to Groves, "and it wouldn't be natural for these men to have secrets from each other."

"But this is war, Professor Thomas, and I am a soldier. My duty is to my country, to this project."

"What an enormous task you have set for yourself," Erik replied. "And do you really think keeping information in little compartments will accomplish that? That is not the scientific way—why, in science, and especially in physics, everyone should know everything."

"Not the Germans?" Groves asked in a startled voice.

"Well, of course not."

"What about the Russians?"

Here Erik looked at him thoughtfully. "If they are really our allies, why not? Better to let them know than have them start an arms race after all this is over."

Here Groves broke in. "You seem so confident that when it is over, it will have gone as planned, Professor."

Then Erik smiled. "I am. You Americans are very clever, and you have, virtually, turned this country into a factory to produce— what is it you call it?" Erik turned to Oppie, who said quietly, "The gadget."

Whenever Erik spoke in his mild, low voice, Groves seemed to be rolling his words around in his head. Now he nodded sharply, pleased that Erik had such confidence in the Americans, in him.

"Later he complained how hard it was to understand Erik. As if he could fudge a little, pretend he hadn't heard. But when the meeting was over, Groves looked totally undone, like someone who had escaped from the loony bin," Jacob reported, laughing a little. "It's hard to argue with someone like Erik, someone who is so convinced he is right. And frustrating."

He looked at me and sighed. "But even if you don't agree with

Erik about international control—and I'm not sure I do—he is certainly right about dispersing information among the various arms of the Manhattan Project. It is simply more efficient. And Groves can't afford to be less than efficient." He got up from his desk, and I thought he was finished, but then he walked toward me and sat on the edge of his desk.

"But Groves doesn't like it, Lily. He doesn't feel that he has enough control. You know, he once told Oppie that he feels surrounded by members of a fraternity he will never be allowed to enter. And he's right. But his job is to get the most out of us, and I don't think he'll throw out the baby with the bathwater."

Jacob was right. So though nothing official was proclaimed, Erik's arrival at Los Alamos in December of 1943 seemed to mark the beginning of a new time, a loosening of some of the bonds that were so constricting.

In my mind The Hill sometimes seemed to transform itself into a world without women, to Captain Ahab's *Pequod:* a group of men focused on a single goal. No, Oppie wasn't as single-minded or as crazy as Ahab, and neither was Groves; neither was anyone else, but they and the men who worked for them were not only highly intelligent, but also extremely dedicated; these were men who knew best how to put their heads down and work. Even their recreation looked like work—the hard hiking and skiing they loved, the horseback riding, the need to pit themselves against this stark ocher landscape. And the Saturday night parties and square dances and musicales had a peculiar fierceness about them.

For they were men at war, and the rigor of their demanding work set them more and more apart. Watching them, I felt what women have always felt during war: a distance, a remoteness, a sense of being in some crucial way superfluous.

Then, into our midst, like a strange, flamboyantly marked bird which has wandered far from its natural habitat, came Erik Traugott. Because of his extraordinary reverence for all human beings, he had an unusual respect for women and particularly those who had come to Los Alamos. Not because we cared for our husbands, cooked for them, made love to them; not because we ran the school or helped out at the hospital or kept the community going or did many things that the Army couldn't or wouldn't ever be able to do. No, Erik never saw us as the necessary evil Groves did, or as the helpmates that Oppie did. He respected and revered us because he genuinely liked women, perhaps more than any other man I have ever known, and also because he envisioned us as part of his plan. Erik believed that every man was an important part of the collective conscience of the world. And so was every woman.

Unlike most men, Erik was absolutely comfortable in the company of women. He liked our talk, he understood our concerns, and he wasn't even above enjoying a bit of gossip now and then. He was happiest, as History and Bess and I were, at Pamela's, and he and Pamela became very good friends.

Erik was also a link to Europe: because of his contacts in British Intelligence he brought Steffi news of Bonhoeffer; he carried greetings from Noel's family; he told Oppie what was known of the German work on the gadget, and he had information about the rebuilding of the heavy water plant at Vemork in Norway. Although only Oppie and Groves and Jacob knew it, Erik had brought Heisenberg's drawing of a heavy water reactor.

Because Erik was absolutely certain that the gadget would become a reality here at Los Alamos, he became a warning system for some of us younger women; like the radar they were developing elsewhere, Erik alerted us to the consequences of this weapon our husbands were trying so urgently to make. And because he had such regard for the way our minds worked, he made us understand that we women were not mere observers.

In some ways, I think, he expected too much of us, too much of everyone. Erik thought we were all capable of his extraordinary love of the world. Yet he underestimated the excitement and the pleasure that would build—indeed had already begun to build—

from the sheer intellectual challenge of making this gadget. And how that would affect all kinds of decisions later.

But who can really comprehend the unpredictability of human emotions, their volatile nature, the randomness of reactions? Especially during a war. Surely it is unfair of me to have expected even Erik to do that. Besides, it is hindsight.

When we were there, within the luminous circle of Erik's unusual intelligence, and he sat on the steps of Pamela's house, rolling the hard New Mexico earth between his fingers, I could almost see him thinking as if in geologic time about our obligations to this earth. And when I talked about him to Peter, I would envision Erik not as the Messiah, but as Atlas holding up the spinning globe with his head and his shoulders: a tricky and difficult task to hold a moving, ever-changing world. But in Erik's case it was not as an agonizing punishment from Zeus, but because it was where he knew he belonged.

1944

1944

11

Indian objects became the rage; wherever you went, you would see rugs made at Chimayo and the black pottery of San Ildefonso and Santa Clara. A few couples had even begun to collect the work of Maria Martinez, who became one of the most famous potters in North America and who was in her prime when we were there. But I wasn't a collector, at least not then, and it seemed a contradiction to decorate our barracklike quarters.

Besides, I mistrusted this sudden interest in the Indians. It reeked of that old missionary odor. You do our dirty work, our menial labor, our housework, we seemed to be saying, and we will buy your beautiful crafts and, most important, show you by our very presence how to be civilized.

I never liked wandering around the plaza in Santa Fe. When the Indians gazed at us, I felt that their eyes were seeing through into our brains, that behind their impassive, correct politeness was a vague contempt for everything we represented.

I kept my feelings to myself, though, and admired whatever our friends bought. But Peter knew. Sometimes it seemed as if Peter knew more about me than I knew myself. Part of me resented it, yet another part of me was grateful for it. And when he pulled me toward him one evening after we left an apartment cluttered with Indian objects, he murmured into my hair, "Promise me you'll never try to become a squaw, like the rest of them."

Then History's son was born and died, and after his burial at the Eyed Boulder, I began to feel a strange, inexplicable tie to these taciturn Pueblos. As Peter got busier and busier investigating the various rates of fission down in the canyon, I began to read more and more about the Indians. By the time Erik arrived, I had become interested in their ceremonial rites, and when Erik wanted to see the dances, I decided to go along.

One of the hardest things for Erik to understand was the simple fact of Spanish oppression of the Pueblos. "How could anyone want to persecute a people who minded its own business?" he would ask. "And how is oppression possible here, where the landscape almost forbids it?" He shook his head, gazing up at that enormous sky in disbelief.

As he spoke, I realized what it was that had bothered me so—for wasn't our coming here a kind of oppression as well? "Just marching in and taking over this whole area? Changing their lives?" I had asked one winter afternoon in Pamela's kitchen. Pamela suddenly stopped kneading the bread and Erik stared at me with a fixed, startled gaze. As if I had spoken the unspeakable.

If Peter were here, he would have said, quickly, "What's done is done, Lily, leave it alone." But Peter wasn't here. And the fact was that Oppie and Groves had enacted a peculiar kind of oppression here, even though no one talked about it.

We all knew how heartbroken Ashley Pond, the headmaster of the Los Alamos School, had been when he realized that the Army was going to take over his school. For Ashley Pond wasn't merely that paltry source of water for The Hill, but a real person, a man with a vision, who had started the Los Alamos School in 1916. A school that had become known for high academic standards and rigorous physical training. A special place that seemed to be loved by everyone involved with it.

Oppie had seen it for the first time in 1922 and had grown to love the Pajarito Plateau and the Sangre de Cristos and the Jemez in the following twenty years. It was he who took Leslie Groves to the Los Alamos School when they were searching for a site for the laboratory. And it was he and Groves and Stimson who rammed through the Army takeover of the school and its land despite vigorous protests by Pond and the school's staff and students and alumni.

And what about the 54,000 acres around the school that the Army took over as well? Some of it was government land, but heretofore it had been open and free. Now it was part of the new installation of the Manhattan Project. How did the Indians feel about that? I had broken the rules and asked.

Neither Pamela nor Erik said a word; we sat there, silent, and then, blessedly, the moment passed.

But we all knew about the subjugation of the Indians, how they were exploited by greedy Spanish governors, that there were the tortures—often with sexual overtones—calculated to break their spirit, and, perhaps most important, how they were forced to give up their gods and shamans and worship the Jesus of the Catholic missionaries.

During the sixteenth and seventeenth centuries the white man never understood the Pueblos, so they, like most oppressors, paved the way for the only really important rebellion against them.

Its leader was Pope, the headquarters was at Taos, the fighting scheduled to begin on August 11, 1680. But on August ninth two messengers carrying strategic information were captured by the Spanish. Rather than give the Spanish too much time to prepare, Pope attacked on August tenth. The mandate was simple: kill all white people.

Because of the intercepted message, about a thousand white settlers escaped to Santa Fe and were besieged by the Indians. With their superior arms and expertise, they expected no real trouble. But they didn't count on the collective rage of the Pueblos. After nine days of battle, the casualties were 21 missionaries, 380 white settlers, and 300 Indians. Another 47 Indians were captured and executed. The Spaniards were defeated, and their governor, Otermin, decided they should leave Santa Fe.

Picture a long string of beleaguered white settlers following Otermin—men, women, children, friars of the Church—moving slowly southward across the parched, open landscape, through the Jornada del Muerto, the Journey of the Dead. What an easy target for a horde of swooping, whooping, scalp-crazy Indians. It could have been a scene from an earlier time, when the warlike Apaches had preyed on the first Spanish conquistadors, who gave the valley its name. Or a scene enacted later, by the same Apaches on the American settlers.

But in 1680 there was no violence. The Pueblos simply watched the Spaniards go. The silence must have been eerie, nerve-racking, yet it was not broken, not even by one angry Pueblo.

For the next fifteen years the Pueblos were left alone, but in 1696 a harsher governor came to Santa Fe, and there was another, smaller uprising. This time the Spaniards were victors, and the Pueblos took their religion underground—practicing it secretly in their kivas, while pretending to be Catholics.

"They have never forgotten the lesson of the Spanish conquest," Pamela told Erik and the rest of us that afternoon. "They despise the Spanish and their descendants even more than the Americans, the people like us, the Anglos. And they will always mistrust anything that is not entirely theirs."

Erik's eyes met mine. Then he looked up, for now we were walking toward Tsankewi, and his eyes seemed to devour the clenched winter landscape that had etched itself as distinctly and sharply as steel under the hard cobalt sky. A landscape that belonged to these Pueblos, I thought, and that we—all of us, begin-

ning with Oppie and Groves—had suddenly descended upon. The nerve of it was staggering.

Yet only Erik wanted to know how the Indians felt. None of the other scientists, not even Peter or Jacob, seemed to care enough to ask questions. They would say they couldn't afford to. They were here to get a job done; they hadn't picked the site, no, Oppie and Groves had done that, and they were merely following orders when they came here. Questions simply complicated things. They were right. Erik would admit that. Still, something in him couldn't leave it alone.

● ● ●

A transparent blue sky that ballooned over the mesa and seemed to stretch forever. It is a Sunday in January 1944—the San Ildefonsan Feast Day. I am going with Pamela and Erik to watch the famous dances. Peter can't come because he must work down in the canyon. Ordinarily Tom would be in the canyon, too, but he has been ordered by Jacob to take a day off because he's been working such long hours.

"I worry about him," Jacob has confided to me. "He doesn't know when to stop." So Tom and Thea are going, and Steffi and Jacob and Noel, and Bess and Mark, and History and Herb. Some of the newly arrived English are supposed to come as well.

We have met a few of the English wives, but they are older and they keep their distance. Just as well. I'm not too interested in them since I heard one call The Hill this "godforsaken desert."

How anyone could call this landscape godforsaken is totally beyond me. For here, if anywhere, you can feel the hand of God. And when you go to San Ildefonso or Taos, you can feel the peculiar pull of the ancient, God-given values continuing into the present day. For those pueblos hark back to another world, a past that is over, yet still oddly alive.

"What an idiot," I muttered to History when I heard that Englishwoman.

History stared at me with laughter in her eyes. "She's just making conversation, Lily, noise really, and you should be able to sympathize. It's exactly what we felt when we first came, you know." History could always put me in my place better than anyone else. Then I realized I was behaving exactly like my mother; she could criticize anything and anyone in our family, but just catch an outsider doing it and he would be withered in a glance.

Now, on our way to Otowi, History says reasonably, "Perhaps the dances will make the English see things they haven't caught on to before." As always, her voice with its broad *a*'s comforts me. She is almost back to her old self; only occasionally do I catch her staring into the distance, a frown furrowing her smooth, pale skin as if her brain must still struggle to absorb what is so clear and painful in her memory.

But most of the time she is our cheerful, efficient History, and sometimes I find myself searching her features, hoping to find some secret sign of a new pregnancy. But of course, it's too early.

"Let her body have a rest, for God's sake, Lily—do you realize what she's been through?" Noel said recently when I dropped a hint about it. His voice had an edge, and I felt like a fool. Slowly I could feel my face reddening with humiliation.

"I'm sorry, Lily. I shouldn't have snapped at you," he said quickly, then came over and lifted my downcast chin with his forefinger. "You must let nature do its work," he said gently, forcing me to meet his glance, "and that always takes more time than we think."

We walk slowly into the plaza at San Ildefonso. When I breathe, the searing cold shoots into my sinuses. Yet it makes everything I see wonderfully clear and vibrant.

Benches are set up on one side of the plaza. Never before have there been such elaborate preparations for visitors, but we heard that this is a special welcome for the people on The Hill. Behind the plaza, to the west, is Tsi'como, and to the north broods the Black Mesa, a frowning sentry that protects this small Tewa town. From where I am sitting the Black Mesa falls between the huge cottonwood tree and the large round kiva, the site of the ceremonial preparations and rituals, forbidden to white men. Its heavenward stair is balanced by that naked cottonwood, more majestic now than when it is cloaked with leaves.

Pamela and Erik and I sit as high as we can. They put me between them. The Lerners are in front of us. As we are getting settled, I see Jacob and Steffi and Noel walk to their seats. Jacob turns around and surveys us thoughtfully. When he catches my eye, he waves. Steffi and Noel are engrossed in conversation, and as they talk, their bodies huddle together. An odd thought flickers across the back of my mind: If you didn't know who belonged to whom, you would think Steffi and Noel were married and Jacob was their bachelor friend.

"How is my darling History?" Mrs. Windom calls to us. She was genuinely concerned about the Lerners after the baby died, and sent a basket of goodies that we all ate for weeks afterward. Now, as she ignores me, I find myself wishing she would stay. For only her kind of idle chatter can keep my mind from wandering down dangerous paths.

My glance wanders across the empty, bleak plaza. A shudder runs through me. Such sharp cold. Bundled up against it, we look like stuffed animals. My breath plumes before me, and my eyes begin to tear. Pamela hands me a handkerchief, and as I am wiping my eyes, I am aware only of a preternatural stillness slowly descending upon us.

Suddenly there is a gasp, and Erik presses my arm.

Emerging from the kiva are long lines of black-painted dancers with huge headdresses; in their powerful arms they hold lances. Not a horse in sight, yet you could swear there is a horde of mounted Indians converging on the plaza. I sit straighter.

"This is the Comanche dance," Pamela whispers. The dance that dramatizes the life of the horse-riding, danger-daring, women-loving Comanches. The aggressive warrior Comanche, the conqueror, the hero—it is all there in the deliberate, confident way the long lines weave across the plaza. This is the way man begins his journey toward war, the gentle Pueblos seem to be saying: thoughtfully, carefully, proudly. The movements of the dancers and their beautiful shadows—like mirror images—make intricate patterns on the hard, frozen earth, transforming the empty plaza into a huge canvas of intricate designs.

On and on the dancers go, faster and faster, the tension building as they come closer and closer to their imaginary enemy. Their songs become less controlled, and the dancer-horsemen move ever more swiftly. My heart pounds with the rhythm of the dance.

Then the strangest thing happens. Almost imperceptibly the taut, disciplined lines of the dance begin to loosen, and before we know it, individual dancers now swagger, no longer part of a tightly knit group.

Suddenly you feel the plans gone awry, the fun begin to disappear, the killing beginning to mount. Pride has no place here; indeed it has been displaced by something larger, something deranged, over which the dancers have no control. The lines of strutting black bodies unravel abruptly, the dancers shifting to and fro. Around me are nervous laughs, people not quite sure how to react. But then the dancers ascend the kiva and wave their banners wildly, as if to ask: How can we take war seriously when it is merely chaos?

A long pause, and the head dancer exchanges his headdress for the female headdress of his partner. I look at Pamela. She says softly, "I've never seen that before." But it is not a mistake. The dancer knows exactly what he is doing as he makes the exchange.

Is his message a special one for those of us on The Hill, or a message to an entire country now at war? He seems to be saying that war is a game which either sex can play. Or that war is merely swagger and noise and role-playing. It's hard to tell, but the uneasiness remains as the dancers shamble back into the robing room.

Between the sets of the Comanche Dance is an animal dance. The dancers representing the buffalo and elk and antelope are also painted black, but wear very large feathered and horned headdresses. As they ascend to the plaza, they give the illusion of a herd, although there are only several dozen of them circling the kiva with the hunters and the buffalo maidens.

Slowly, proudly, the animals begin to cross the plaza as if it were the endless plains. Their pace quickens; the bells on their hips jingle, and their pounding hooves resound through the thin, cold air. Faster and faster. Running, ringing, stamping until they threaten to surround and swallow everything around them. Yet man has killed these powerful, beautiful buffalo and elk, and that hangs over the dance like some kind of unspeakable, sad knowledge.

For me the animal dance seems an unforgettable lament for the old days and ways, for the animals that the white man so wantonly killed, always thinking there would be more and more after that to kill. For now the buffalo and elk are gone, never to return. And if, indeed, they are regarded as gods, then the gods are dead.

The last quieter sets, during which the animals have disappeared and only the maidens and the hunters dance, resemble a dirge, for they are accompanied by a plaintive, haunting melody that seems to be coming from very far away, perhaps from the past: a song mourning the dead gods, the immortal herds who will never be seen on earth again.

The melody floats toward us, lingering through the shadowy dusk. I'm exhausted. Watching these dances has been like nothing I have ever known. As twilight inches around us, I know we should get up and leave, but we can't move. We sit on the benches mesmerized, listening to the chorus that still stands on top of the kiva chanting the strains of the last melody.

Just as we are about to rise, a somewhat shorter line of dancers suddenly appears. Pamela turns to Erik and me and says, "The Snowbird Dance." Today the women are led by Maria Martinez. Confidently they wend their way around the great cottonwood, as if it were the center of the cosmos, and they applaud with their bodies and their voices the hills, the sky, the Black Mesa, the Eyed Boulder, indeed all of nature's gifts.

This is a poignant, peaceful dance which honors the eternal place of woman in a society where marriage is sacred, monogamy the rule, infidelity a crime against the society. Where the birth of a child is a religious sacrament, and child-bearing the greatest good. Flowing with the very rhythms of life itself, the dancers turn again and again as the day darkens, the waves of rosy light deepening to a vibrant lilac. And at the first sight of Venus, that pinprick of light in the now-purple sky, the women slowly, surely, make their way back into the womblike darkness of the kiva.

It is time for us to go. Now, finally, I miss Peter. I look around; Pamela and Erik have gone ahead because we are all going back to Otowi for a meal. But here is Kate, alone as I am. We start to walk. She has remembered a flashlight, and when Noel offers us a ride in his car, we shake our heads silently. We need some time. As we leave the plaza I see Estevan, who was one of the buffalo in the animal dance. He will not go back to Pamela's yet; what we saw in the plaza is part of a rite that lasts several days, and for these ceremonies he returns to the pueblo.

The images from the dances whirl in my brain. We have sat there for almost eight hours without thinking of anything: food, the cold, our physical comfort. And yet neither Kate nor I complain. We move in silence, the only sound our footsteps crunching against the hard, packed earth.

• • •

We are the last to arrive at Pamela's. People are drinking a deep red burgundy (a present from Oppie and his wife, who seem to have a never-ending supply of French wine), and eating some of the famous garlic sticks Pamela makes. A heady recklessness fills the air; it reminds me of those hectic, exhilarated meals of my childhood when my parents would end the twenty-four-hour fast of Yom Kippur—when the past year's sins are atoned for and a new slate begun. And today, like those High Holy Days, it seems as if the outer shell of our personalities has molted so that our true selves can emerge.

We all seem so vulnerable, our faces so naked. Pamela puts a glass of wine into my hand. For a second I feel afraid and wish Peter were here to protect me. But protect me from what? I wonder, then sit down next to Erik. He looks worn out.

"Are you all right?" I ask, suddenly frightened. He is a generation older than I—and the cold, the lack of food, the exhaustion of sitting there and watching—why, he could have had a heart attack after sitting out there all day!

"Are you all right?" I repeat and search his face. Then I feel calmer. His eyes have their usual vibrant light; he isn't sick, just tired and hungry like the rest of us.

"Of course, I'm all right. Just very tired. It was like watching *King Lear*. And I'm always exhausted after that," he replies, then sips his wine and nibbles on a garlic stick, content, as I am, not to talk.

My eyes skim the clusters of people: some of the English couples, several friends of Pamela's, History and Herb, Thea and Tom, Steffi and Noel and Jacob, Bess and Mark and Kate, who is talking to a couple I have never seen before. And some young girls who are here to help with the serving and washing up.

It reminds me of the Wunderlichs' party; there is that same radiance, that same glowing contentment. But today it has nothing to do with the exhilaration of expectation, of not quite knowing what is going to happen; today it has to do with the pleasure of seeing something beautiful, something far more beautiful than any of us had dared to dream. It has left us all distracted; people seem possessed, their eyes rapt, in a witch's spell.

It has the feeling of a slow-motion minuet. I guess everything we do can be called a dance. Still, how different this minuet is from those crude folk dances when we were young—when the boys stood on one side of the room and the girls on the other until one brave young boy took those first tentative steps. And how different both of them are from what we saw today.

I try to explain it to Erik. He laughs, especially at my description of an American high school dance. "The same in Denmark, though they began earlier because we all had to go to dancing school. I was the clumsiest one on the floor. The dancing teacher finally gave up on me and sent me home and told my mother not to waste her money. But then my mother and sisters taught me how to dance, and I'm not bad, especially at the waltz," he confides proudly.

Then his face grows serious, almost somber. "But what we saw today is not dance. No, Lily, it is religion, and it is art. How man makes his home in the world. What physics is about, really, but very different from physics and very different from what you are talking about. This—" Erik gestures toward the room with his stubby hands. "This is a dance, and so were those childhood miseries: a dance that instructs us how to make our way in society, how to cope with other men and women. What we were all learning from the dancing teachers, what we do when we come to a party in any country. And that"—Erik pauses, then shrugs—"why, it's indescribable, really."

We let the wine seep through us, warming our frozen hands and feet. Plates heaped with food are set before us. We eat very slowly, and after we both begin to feel the good effects of the food, I tell Erik about the first day I came to Otowi, with History and Herb and Peter, how we thought we had been taken to fairyland, how naive we were.

He laughs his big, weighty laugh that seems to boom through

the room. People look up and smile. Then Pamela comes over to us with the couple I don't know. She wants to introduce them to Erik. But she doesn't use his real name; she says, "I'd like you to meet Mr. Thomas, Mr. Ethan Thomas."

Soon Pamela ushers her friends away and we are by ourselves again. Erik nods sleepily and refuses a second helping, then lets me take his plate; when I come back he is dozing.

I look around, vaguely searching for Thea and Tom, but they are off in a corner with an English couple. Nearer to me, in front of the fire, are Steffi and Noel. How differently their faces catch the firelight: hers draws the flickering licks of flame to her magnificent, jutting bones; while his round face deflects the fire's glow, spreading it evenly across his features, lightening the surprising swarthiness of his skin.

Although their shoulders are still touching, they have stopped talking. Noel stares into the fire, and I realize that they have been arguing and that the argument is finally over. What about? I wonder, and my glance is drawn again to her face.

How naked it still looks! The rest of us have gathered ourselves together and now wear our public faces. But not Steffi. Her face is bare, almost raw—stripped of its usual pride and wariness, of the stern remoteness that sometimes makes her so forbidding. Utterly bare, and burnished by the firelight, so beautiful. And so young. It takes my breath away. In my head I hear Noel say when he talked about *Our Town*, "For it is all so terribly beautiful." It is as if he were describing Steffi's face at this moment—a face filled with wistfulness and longing. A face in love. Yet that can't be. She is looking at Noel, her old, dear friend, Noel. The brother she never had, she once told someone.

I look down. And that is when I spy her fingers creeping surreptitiously, not quite hidden behind the folds of her skirt. Helpless fingers, creeping into Noel's hand for comfort, for sheer physical contact. And I realize that what I have unconsciously suspected is true: Steffi is hopelessly in love with Noel.

But where is Jacob? Why isn't Jacob with her, why did he let them sit next to each other for a whole day at the dances? How can he allow this? And how did he let it go this far? I am full of accusations and quickly turn my head, expecting to find him watching them. Instead, he is completely absorbed in a conversation with Kate and the Chanins in a far corner of the room.

When I turn to look at Steffi again, I feel Erik's eyes on me. He has not been dozing at all, but watching me. And now he leans forward and covers my hand with his and says, "She is still madly in love with him, I guess she will always be madly in love with him." He stops, as if to give me time to absorb what he is telling me.

"They have known each other since they were children. Noel's mother is from an old Berlin family, and they used to come to Germany for the summers. When they were very young, everyone thought he would get over the homosexuality, that perhaps it was a passing phase, but he didn't. Then we thought that maybe they should marry anyhow and he have discreet affairs with his young men. She could have tolerated that because she was so crazy about him, but he refused. He said he couldn't consign her to a life of such humiliation." Erik pauses again.

"When Jacob appeared on the scene and fell in love with her, we thought it would be all right. After all, he was older, brilliant, stable. Everyone was thrilled. And what a handsome couple they made. People are always fooled by physical beauty, Lily, they think it means more than it does. And Noel is so homely compared to Jacob. But beauty is in the eyes of the beholder. All those clichés have some truth in them, and the marriage was never right. Jacob's mother is a friend of my older sister. Mrs. Wunderlich was never happy with Steffi. She was probably right. Steffi has never gotten over Noel. I guess she never will."

Erik shrugs. "There are some things over which we have no control, Lily. You Americans don't really believe that, but it's true. And this is one of them."

As Erik's voice moves through my brain, I remember Steffi in the Lerners' kitchen, her unhappiness that she wasn't there the night of the birth, and Jacob's patience with her, that low "darling" as he tried to calm her. I thought she was angry at being left out, but now I understand that she was upset because Noel had to face the ordeal of the baby's birth without her. She didn't care so much about History as about Noel. Then I see Steffi and Noel walking in the plaza in Santa Fe—her playful, mischievous smile, and finally sitting on the couch listening to Jacob play the piano that night at the party. Her iridescent dress—that gorgeous green, exactly the color to go with her hair. And such shining, shimmering, happy eyes. Happy because Noel had just arrived at Los Alamos. And miserable, too, because what she wants she can never have.

And I thought it all had to do with having had to come to this high isolated place against her will.

But nothing here is as simple as I would like to make it. I lower my eyes and stare at my hands folded in my lap like a child's. When will I learn to see what is right here, before my eyes? My face begins to redden; I can feel the telltale flush spread across my cheeks to my ears, which feel on fire.

Then I see myself listening to Jacob talk about Steffi, how sorry I felt for him, how puzzled I was by him, how guilty I felt when he accused me and the other women of excluding her. And that day last summer when History and Pamela and I saw them arguing. Then giving him my sympathy, giving her my sympathy, defending her to others, even telling Peter in such detail about it. How could I have not put some of this together?

I turn to Erik and demand, "Does Peter know all this?"

"I don't know, Lily. I doubt it. The Fialkas left Berlin before it became common knowledge. But even if he did know, I doubt he would ever share it, even with you. It's not the sort of thing men talk about. One of those well-kept secrets. Most men feel uncomfortable discussing something like another man's homosexuality. Besides, what is there to discuss? Noel goes his own way, and

Steffi and Jacob are married. People know that they are all old friends. That's all anyone needs to know." Erik pauses and I think he's finished. But then he goes on,

"Most of the time she can keep it in control, I think. But after something like the dances, things like this seem to surface. Against one's will. When I saw you watching them, I decided it was better to tell you than to have you start asking questions, Lily. Asking certain kinds of questions can be very dangerous." Erik's voice is firm, despite its usual hesitant stutter.

Secrets, and more secrets. Walls of secrets as high as the ancient cliff dwellings at Puye and Tsankewi. The Anasazis' secrets, and now ours. But it does no good to dwell on them or to ask Erik to repeat anything he has told me.

Secrets can be told only once.

I sit back in my chair. I am utterly exhausted, far more exhausted than I was after the dances. Then my tiredness felt good, earned. Now I feel stupid, foolish. A chill of fear runs through me. For deep inside me I feel that what Erik has told me tonight has suddenly, inexplicably, set the stage for something larger over which I may have no control, something I can't entirely understand.

Now it is Erik's turn to search my face, to worry. "Lily, are you all right?" His eyes are filled with concern. "Wait here," he says, then goes to get me some coffee. I smile. I couldn't move if I wanted to.

I hold the warm mug of coffee in my hands. When I am able to look around, I see that Jacob has stopped Erik, questioning him; then a few people turn to look at me. From their faces I know that Erik must have told them I felt faint or sick or something because of this very long day. Another lie, a white one and hardly significant, but I'm annoyed at Erik. Still, I haven't time to mull on that. Jacob is making his way toward me, and as he approaches me, I realize that we have both avoided each other this evening.

He sits there quietly. For the second time today, I realize how superfluous words can be. For it is all there in his eyes: his sorrow and what I have called in my head his fondness for me. But now I know that I, too, have been guilty of doctoring the language. I am just as bad as Oppie with his "gadget." For Jacob isn't merely fond of me. He has fallen in love with me.

I think about all the time we have spent together—hours and hours of working, learning more and more about each other. All the little things I know about Jacob he also knows about me: how to make me laugh, how to make me blush, when I am tired or discouraged or angry. We have spared each other nothing about ourselves. I attributed that to my usual openness, my bluntness, my passion for honesty. But the truth is that this has been more than a mere working relationship. And something in me has allowed this closeness, craved it, looked forward to it. I have pretended it was much simpler than it actually was.

Now I merely say, "When?"

"Probably as far back as the ice-skating rink at Rockefeller Center. Maybe before that at Cornell. I once watched you cross the quad; you were in a hurry and gesturing madly at someone, and I remember thinking how alive you were. How gorgeously alive. Everyone was watching you that afternoon, Lily, and you didn't even know it. Or care."

I remember the day. I was furious with a friend who insisted on talking about Melville and Conrad in the same breath, and I was trying to explain that you couldn't lump together books on the same themes, that their visions were different. But I never even saw Jacob.

He goes on. "And that day at Rockefeller Center I was jealous of you and Peter, you looked so marvelous skating together, I think that's why I baited you so." His voice is flat. You asked for the facts, here they are, he seems to say. I don't reply. Then Jacob shrugs, rises. There is a rustling in the room. It's time to go. I see that the young girls are leaving, and so are Pamela's friends. It's past ten, time to go back to The Hill and to sleep so that we can all get to work on time in the morning.

Now Thea stops and puts her hand on my arm. "Feeling a little under the weather, Lily? You scared Erik a little while ago." Then she looks approvingly at Jacob. The attentive boss looking after his secretary.

Before I can answer, she says, "What a pity that Peter couldn't have seen the dances—a splendid day, wasn't it? Say hello to that husband of yours." Her voice lilts with pride that some of her beloved scientists have skipped these remarkable dances in order to do their work.

That husband of yours. Peter. Wonderful, loyal, hardworking Peter. The brilliant Fialka boy. We always knew you would marry, Lily. You were made for each other. He's so calm, so strong, such a good balance for you. And so patient. Waiting all those years for you to grow up. An unbelievable person. You will be happy, Lily, I know it. And mothers know things like that, better than anyone else. My mother's voice is filled with love as it reverberates in my head.

Somehow I end up walking back to The Hill between Erik and Jacob. We walk in silence. The moon is almost full, and bright, the Milky Way a blurry radiant band. The wide ribbon of stars that the Indians believe is the serpent Awanyu—the famed plumed serpent of the Pueblo myths who has thrown himself across the sky—lights our way through the small valley of Otowi and then up the road to The Hill. The dark, usually so diaphanous at this height, seems thick with cold. Cold as thick as fog. As we walk, I feel as if I were pushing my way through it. Too cold to talk, to do anything but plod home. Besides, we have all run out of talk.

The security guards nod at us as we go through the gates, and one says, "Been to the dances?" In unison we nod. Then I think about the dancers, the buffalo and the elk, their heads bent low, as if they were listening to the earth. And we watching, then listening to the recesses of our very selves. That is what those dances did. Opened up the depths of our souls.

How can so much happen in one day? Now all I want is to sleep and sleep. And escape the tangled mass of confusion that is causing such turmoil in my brain.

All day I have longed for Peter, wanted him, yet when I look up at our windows and see them still dark, I am relieved. I will sleep first, then try to sort out all that has happened. Jacob walks up the path with me and waits to see that I have gotten in and put on the light. When I look out the window and wave, he waves back. So does Erik.

You will be happy, Lily, I know it, my mother's voice keeps coming back . . . happy, happy, happy . . . and as I turn down the bed and crawl into it, I feel tears welling in my eyes. But all I can think is: How good it is to be home!

12

As winter closed in, I found myself staying closer and closer to home. Kate was doing *Candida,* and I knew that Thea and Tom were supposed to be wonderful in it, but it was easier to stay home and read. Jacob and I had faltered a little since we decided to read the American writers, but with the coming of winter and the lull after New Year's, we had begun again and were now reading *The Great Gatsby.* I had also resolved to do more reading for my thesis, so at least once a week I would sit in a straight chair at the kitchen table, often across from Peter, who was also working, and jot down notes in a very professional-looking notebook about *Moby Dick.* When I did go out, I preferred to go with History to what was called, for lack of a better name, "The Knitting Club." There we knitted caps, mittens, scarves, and even sweaters for the soldiers in Europe. They were taken down once a month to Thea's office, then given to the Red Cross in Santa Fe.

"The knitting helps," History confessed, "keeps me calm."

I knew she and Herb were trying to have a baby again because one day she said, almost in anger, "I never thought sex would begin to feel like work." And then, "Oh, Lily, life is so strange, isn't it? I never dreamed anything could happen to the baby." I nodded. How often had my mother said, "Man thinks, and God decides."

We went to Pamela's for an occasional meal when she didn't have to serve a dinner. We brought our knitting, and sometimes Erik was there working on chess problems or sewing.

I had never seen a man sew until now, and it fascinated me to watch him mending socks with a big darning egg, or sewing on buttons, or even doing hems for Pamela and the rest of us. Not hurried hems like the ones History and Kate and I made after we had helped each other pin them up. No, Erik didn't approve of our slipshod ways. After he got a hem that was pinned up, he would baste it, and then we would have to try on the dress or skirt again, and if it was crooked, he would baste again until it was straight. Only then would he sew his fine, almost invisible stitches. "It's relaxing work," he would say with a smile. "I came from a family of boys, and we all had to share the chores. One brother is a demon with an iron," he added.

And later, when Erik found out that Arlene Feynman liked bows, beautifully fashioned bows starting arriving with Richard at the hospital in Albuquerque. I can still see Erik's large head bent intently, his capable hands moving gracefully to shape those scraps of fabric: green velvet from an old dress of Steffi's, silk paisley from a frayed tie of Peter's, and cotton prints from remnants he found in Pamela's sewing basket. And, later, pictures of Arlene came back to us—a lovely, pale brunette whose pleasure at our gifts shone in her eyes.

On the Monday morning after the dances neither Jacob nor I spoke about the night at Pamela's. In some ways it was as if it had never happened, yet in one important way it affected us profoundly.

We became afraid of each other.

I, who had never hesitated to say what I thought to anyone, became more introspective, more watchful. And Jacob, too, seemed to curl into himself. Very quickly we established a clear, definable distance between us; our conversation became elaborately polite— stiff and parched.

The worst part was that we no longer laughed together. I understood then that love and laughter are far more intertwined than I had ever realized, and that all those marriages with angles were basically dour, somber relationships. I think that's what Pamela was trying to tell us that day, and now I thought of her eyes meeting Estevan's and the quick chuckle that often erupted from one or both of them. If you can laugh with someone, you must let down your guard—for that is essentially what laughter is—and that can happen between a man and a woman only if there is a capacity for love. Not that that capacity has to be acted upon; no, in most cases it is not. But it has to be there.

The night after the dances when Jacob and I talked at Pamela's had made me see things I had avoided, had made me face how great that capacity was between Jacob and me. So the best thing, the most effective thing was to pretend it wasn't there, had never existed. In the space of a few hours that Monday morning we became, without a word to each other, the paragon scientist and his secretary. I guess we both presumed that this slow ballet could rid us of the feelings that, at least for me, were so frightening. As if our measured movements and cautious phrases could dampen the fierceness of what was happening silently within us.

Our refuge became physics. In the privacy of that tiny office Jacob told me things he never should have told me, never would have told me if he hadn't fallen in love with me. But it seemed less dangerous to talk about the gadget than about each other.

I knew, roughly, how a uranium pile worked, and I knew that what you needed to make a weapon were two masses of matter that would become critical and explode. At first it was thought the two masses had to be uranium. But it turned out that the neutrons that did not collide with U-235 were not lost; instead these neutrons were captured by the more abundant U-238 and could be slowly changed into a new substance, which was called plutonium. It had fission properties similar to U-235, and thus a weapon could be made of masses of either U-235 or plutonium.

I knew that there were two sites that were also part of the Manhattan Project, two newly created cities that were each larger than Site Y, which was the official name for Los Alamos: Hanford on the Columbia River in Washington, where there were plutonium manufacturing piles, and Oak Ridge on the Clinch River in Tennessee, where there were the various plants busy separating Uranium 235 from Uranium 238. Peter had explained to me as simply as he could what they were doing there.

"How much do you need to make a weapon?" I asked Jacob.

He shook his head. "No one knows, but that's what we're trying to figure out—how to take two masses of nuclear material and make them 'critical,' or able to produce an uncontrolled explosion; and then calculate the yield of that explosion. Someone once said it was like building a new car without being able to test the engine."

The materials of an atomic bomb were so unfamiliar that there was a danger that the two spheres of material, the critical masses, would predetonate and dissolve; or that, conversely, a chain reaction might never begin. The times involved were fractions of seconds, sometimes as small as millionths of a second.

"Most of us thought the way to make the bomb was with the gun method. But the gun assembly is unwieldy and uncertain;

besides, it can only be accomplished with U-235. For a while we didn't even know if we'd have enough uranium for the research."

Then Jacob told me the most incredible story. By habit he lowered his voice. "In the fall of '42, when Groves was trying to get this whole thing started, he was unexpectedly told that twelve hundred tons of uranium ore was suddenly available. He was dumbfounded. So was everyone else." Jacob grinned.

I grinned back.

Then he murmured, "Why is it that you're so interested in this, Lily, and Steffi doesn't give a damn?" But he knew better than to wait for an answer.

"Toward the end of 1940 when the Germans were rampaging through Europe, Frédéric Joliot-Curie, the Frenchman married to Irène Curie, and Henry Tizard, an Englishman, had warned the Belgian government that uranium might be needed for German weaponry. Very quietly the director of Belgium's Union Minière du Haut Katanga, which owned the Shinkolobwe uranium mine in the Belgian Congo, decided to ship some high-grade ore to the United States. In October, before the United States had even entered the war, a freighter left Portuguese Angola and landed in New York. The large drums were stored in a warehouse in Staten Island and forgotten for almost two years—until the Belgian government alerted Groves." He shook his head. "Amazing, isn't it?"

I nodded, then asked, "So what's the problem?"

"The danger of a fizzle. And that a uranium bomb may be too big for a plane." I stared. Until now the bomb had been an imaginary thing. Yet suddenly it had become real, something carried to a destination and dropped.

"So what's the alternative?"

"An implosion bomb. Neddermeyer's baby." With his oddly blunt hands that didn't go at all with his slender frame, Jacob tried to show me how an implosion bomb worked, how explosives wrapped around a core would compress a mass of plutonium so that the neutrons that were released would form a critical chain reaction.

"Peter says that's a real possibility," I said.

"Peter's excited about it, but most people aren't as hopeful as Peter. Neddermeyer works slowly, he thinks he's still doing research in a university, and he exasperates Groves. But an implosion bomb would be smaller, and the danger of a fizzle isn't so great." Jacob shrugged, then looked at me a little guiltily. "I always tell you more than I intend," he confessed.

Our conversations were a little like this place, I thought on my way home that night. They got out of hand. When he envisioned Site Y, Oppie had calculated that he would need thirty scientists. When Peter and I arrived, there were hundreds, and with each passing month the population had swelled—by now into the thousands. Though I didn't know it that day, there would eventually be more than five thousand people here: scientists, machinists, technical staff, administrators, Army personnel, the wives and children—all living on the mesa that had once been the perfect site for the tiny Los Alamos School attended by about fifty boys.

• • •

The lab was gray, raw, badly constructed, and more desolate than any other lab they had worked in. "You wouldn't think there'd be that much difference between this lab and the ones we've all known on college campuses. After all, a lab is a lab. But this lab beats everything for scruffiness. And it's so anonymous." Jacob frowned and scratched his head. "As anonymous as we're all supposed to be," he added, then went on to tell me about the meeting.

They had met to welcome George Kistiakowsky, a Russian-born

chemist who was an explosives expert brought in to solve some of Neddermeyer's problems. Besides Kistiakowsky and Seth Neddermeyer, Oppie, Peter, Noel, Richard Feynman, and Captain Parsons, the ordnance expert, were there, too.

The problem? The shock waves produced by the detonators in Neddermeyer's experiments reinforced each other when they collided and produced irregular points of high pressure that spoiled the implosion.

"It won't work," Feynman said. "I said it stank when it was first suggested, and it still stinks."

"Wait a minute, don't be so hasty," Noel intervened. Then he presented the work that had been done by several others on the interactions of the shock waves. "What we need is a workable mathematical model of the continuous motion of these interactions."

"That's just the point," Feynman broke in. "It's very easy to state the problem—what you're talking about is basic hydrodynamics—but then, how do you make the calculations to solve the problem?"

Peter nodded. He had been in on some of the early work done by Stan Ulam and Johnny von Neumann, the Hungarian mathematician who used to drop in on The Hill from time to time, and even they were having problems. "The work can't be done with the machines we have here," Peter agreed, pointing to a desktop calculator. "Even with some of Johnny's simplifying methods."

The air was clotted with discouragement and the wet, penetrating cold that was winter at Los Alamos. Oppie sat slumped in his chair. He was usually so energetic and enthusiastic, but the cold plus Neddermeyer and Parsons were proving too much even for Oppie. And Jacob knew that Oppie had wanted more from this meeting, something positive to show Kistiakowsky. But Neddermeyer and Parsons were at their usual tug-of-war.

"The findings have to be exact, that's the only way you can get results," insisted Neddermeyer in his soft voice.

And Parsons retorted, "When will you get it into your thick head that this isn't a sleepy research project, that this is weapons research, and that we happen to be at war?"

Finally Oppenheimer referred to the computers that IBM was preparing for work on The Hill. Feynman's eyes brightened.

"Okay, now you're talking something real, something possible," he said. "If we can get those machines to do the numerical work, we can have the model we need."

Within seconds Noel started to speak, his thick fingers shaping the images that were slowly filtering through his head. "How about . . ." he began slowly. "How about attacking this from another direction as well?" His voice was thoughtful, tentative. Hardly anyone wanted to listen to someone think aloud, and Oppie had already begun to bait Neddermeyer again about his lack of ambition. But Peter stared at Noel, then moved closer to him and listened.

"I noticed Peter and Noel talking," Jacob continued, "then making some sketches, while Oppie tried to get Parsons and Seth to talk reasonably about what they were doing to brief Kistiakowsky. Then—it was as if wind blew through the lab—Oppie looked up. He raised his eyebrows, almost sneering, like the Oppie I knew at Göttingen, the one you hardly ever see here at Los Alamos." Jacob's voice was quiet.

Jacob was always a little guarded about Oppie. I had thought it was jealousy, but now I realized he had probably been ridiculed by Oppie in the past. Now he shrugged and continued. "But when Peter began to talk about arranging the explosives so that the shock wave would match the shape it needed to implode, or squeeze, Oppie's face changed, and he began to listen." Jacob stopped and looked at me. He could see my confusion.

"What they are trying to do, Lily, is stabilize the explosives.

They call that making lenses because it's similar to optical lenses that focus light. Think of us trying to focus the explosives into the core the way lenses focus light." He began to pace.

"All of a sudden we felt better. Even Kistiakowsky looked interested. I'm glad he's here. He's tough, but fair, and if anyone can get this implosion business going, it's him. But it was Peter who made Oppie listen. I tell you, Lily, he has a natural authority. What an old professor of mine used to call 'an extraordinary capability for wonder,' " Jacob added.

So, according to Jacob, the hero of the day was Peter. Yet Peter credited Noel and, mostly, Oppie. "He's like a magnet, Lily, that pulls the very best out of all of us," he said when we were in bed that night. Although it was warm under the down comforter my mother had sent us, I could see puffs of fog from our breath condensing as we talked. I wanted to show them to Peter, but I knew that he would merely shrug, so I restrained myself. And listened to him talk about Oppie. I guess that was one of the most important pastimes on The Hill. Suddenly I had a vision of all the couples we knew talking in their beds about Oppie.

Although I didn't agree with some of what I heard about Oppenheimer, who had become something of a Pied Piper in the months we were here, I agreed with Peter that night. A magnet was a good description of Oppie, and I had thought of it, too. But it was a unique magnet I imagined: one with the power not only to draw things out of people, but to draw people toward him and somehow give them the enthusiasm that he felt.

• • •

Yet even the imperturbable Oppenheimer suffered strange, unexpected disappointments. As it became obvious that more and more people would be needed for this huge effort, Oppenheimer was always recruiting new scientists. And always with foresight and care; he, better than anyone else, knew what it meant to come to The Hill.

Most of them came and stayed. But a few found the atmosphere intolerable. In some cases it was the working conditions, in others the rules about secrecy, in still others the realization that they had come to work on a weapon whose lethal power would be unprecedented. Whatever the reason, they simply packed up and went home. To Oppenheimer's and Groves's speechless dismay.

Among the ones who stayed there were also disappointments. The biggest one for both Oppie and Groves was Edward Teller. One of the ablest of the theoretical scientists recruited for Site Y and one who had originally hoped to become head of the Theoretical Division—the job given to Hans Bethe—Teller seemed to lose interest in the gadget almost as soon as he arrived at Los Alamos. He wanted to work on The Super: the hydrogen bomb, which was called the weapon of the future, one hundred times more powerful than the gadget itself. When Peter talked about Teller, there was an unaccustomed trace of mockery in his voice. "It's so strange, Lily," he finally confessed. "Here is a brilliant man, one whose brains I admire enormously, but I can't stand him, and I think that of all the people here he's the most paranoid. That's why he can't get along with anyone."

I couldn't help agreeing with Peter. For Teller to come from Chicago not to work on the gadget but on some even more powerful weapon for the future seemed utterly absurd to me. No one who was here could even talk about the future; we were here to try to insure that there *would be* a future. His insistence on The Super seemed a contradiction in terms, a failure of the most elementary logic.

Yet no one seemed able to convince Teller of that. And what was even more bizarre, no one seemed to try. Why Teller stayed on with his family at Los Alamos was a total mystery to me. So was the fact that he went to the weekly Colloquium.

"It has to do with Teller's prickliness," Jacob muttered once when I gathered my courage and asked him about it. He was annoyed. At me or at Teller, I wanted to ask, but didn't. Besides, it didn't seem to matter who was annoyed at Teller. He was there, to stay, turning up like a bad penny whenever you least expected him—ignoring the succession of bells for wake-up, work, lunch, quitting time, sleeping late, then wandering around the mesa, and playing his beautiful renderings of Bach and Beethoven far into the night. His piano playing drove his neighbors crazy. Yet no one could control him. People shook their heads and looked the other way. He offended my sense of justice; while everyone else was killing himself, Teller seemed to lead an almost leisurely existence.

Occasionally people confused Jacob and Teller, because of the piano playing. Then I would retort that my boss was the one who did his work and didn't disturb everyone else with his selfish habits.

Still, maybe Groves and Oppie knew what they were doing. At least here they could keep an eye on Teller, as difficult as he was. If he was elsewhere, who knew what trouble he could cause?

Unlike Teller were some of the younger men who plunged themselves into this research like deep-sea explorers: Feynman, Tom, and Peter. My Peter. The brilliant Fialka boy had become an impressive and imposing scientist. Although he had been trained as a theoretical physicist, Peter was fascinated by the experiments with the nuclear masses; he began to observe them more carefully and then to participate in them. By the time we left Los Alamos, Peter had learned so much from Fermi and the other experimental physicists that he had joined that rare tribe of men who were both theoretical and experimental physicists. *Doppelgangers,* Peter called the few scientists who had that double capacity. "Wizards, magicians," other people referred to them, for they had a crucial role in this project, which was neither entirely theoretical nor entirely experimental, but a strange and unheard-of combination of both.

None of the praise for Peter was any comfort to me. I didn't need to be told how smart he was. Even by people as able or as famous as Jacob or Oppie. No wife needs to be told that about her husband.

Besides, no one who isn't a scientist can grasp completely that kind of unqualified scientific praise. Nor could I totally understand the seductive lure of science: that basic need to become part of a cooperative and cumulative undertaking that had begun generations ago. What each man did depended on what had been done before him and what might be done in his wake. Nothing was unconnected or entirely independent. It was a never-ending search for knowledge, a tightly knit web past comprehension, except for those who were caught in it. For the scientists, their physics became their religion and their art.

Although there were many things that confused me, there were some things I was certain about: that marriage was more than the little ploys women dream up to make themselves desirable to their husbands; that I had to be patient and understanding when Peter had to put in extraordinary amounts of time; that I should feel grateful for being able to be with my husband during this dismal war. And yet, with each month that passed, I knew that I was lonely.

Though Peter sensed my unhappiness, he couldn't seem to tear himself away from the labs where Segrè was measuring the spontaneous rates of fission or where Tom's group was working on what they called critical assembly experiments or from Neddermeyer's implosion work. It was so easy for the men to get flustered or discouraged, especially when experiments had to be performed under pressure, as so many of them seemed to be. Peter's steadiness, his extraordinary patience, and his practical abilities—which had struck me so clearly years before when he put the magnifying lamp together—were all assets that Jacob and Oppie needed.

"Peter is like the ballast here," I once heard Jacob say. His tone resembled my parents' voices—the same awe, the same pride. But although it made me regard my husband in a new way, it didn't really help. Not even when I realized that Peter did for his colleagues what Pamela did for us young wives. At the time I wasn't capable of the generosity, the magnanimity that a young wife would have needed to share her husband with so many others. Perhaps you need more age to acquire that. All I remember feeling was annoyed. Annoyed, and resentful.

As the months stretched into a year, it seemed to me that Peter had to be everywhere—in the canyon labs, in his office, at meetings, and even on trains that traveled hundreds of miles both west and east to Hanford and Oak Ridge and Chicago.

Everywhere but home.

13

A landscape of snows. Melville talks about it in his famous meditation on whiteness. I understood his description of that enormous, bleached, albino blankness only after the first real snow at Los Alamos.

You could feel it coming for days. As the leaves fell and the air tightened, the outlines of buildings and mountains and trees and desert plants suddenly emerged with startling clarity. But as soon as the snow began, all that disappeared, and other things as well: those gentle winter hues—the deep pinks and ashy mauves of the cottonwoods and the faded ambers of the piñon trees, the startled flutter of the migrating birds as they veered—a bannerlike V— into the wintry wind, the sometimes bruised grayish-blues of the swollen, cloudy sky. Gone, totally, suddenly gone beneath an encompassing, muffled, almost frightening whiteness. Thick flakes borne by a slight wind, not enough wind to howl, but enough to cover everything, giving all these now-familiar surroundings a vast and wild anonymity.

Snow fell for two days straight. Such snow left no promise of anything. So white. And yet so unlike that other whiteness we had come to know so well: the white light of physics that holds within it worlds of color, worlds of possibility. For when white light enters a prism, the entire spectrum of the universe is revealed. It is one of the loveliest things in nature, and we have all seen it when we look at the sun and observe, through the prism of a tear, a gorgeous rainbow. We had certainly seen the white light of the New Mexican sunshine all through the summer and fall.

Now, in this invincible white world that beautiful spectrum seemed lost forever. All that was left was this rinsed-out landscape. It reminded me of storms in childhood when my brothers and I would pretend we had to live the rest of our lives in an igloo-like cave of ice. It had the same sense of mystery that scared us then. Yet it was also strangely comforting. While I trudged through the drifts, I felt like a dancer in the Snowbird Dance: suddenly and indelibly connected to this muffled, snowbound earth.

As I take off my coat in the stuffy warmth of the office on the second morning of snow, I am suddenly aware of my body, its peculiar odor, which is a combination of sweat and the cologne I have always used: L'Heure Bleu. When I dab it on my wrists and temples and behind my earlobes and between my breasts each morning, I don't feel so isolated, so far away from the hum of the city that was my home for so long. I sometimes think about all the stores I used to walk through to find this particular scent: the dark correct woods of the main floors of Saks and B. Altman, the sparkling, newer ones of Lord & Taylor and Bonwit Teller. I think of my mother's face as she searches the crowd whenever we meet to go shopping, and how I always stay anonymous just a second more than necessary, because her peering, somewhat shortsighted eyes tell me more than almost anything else how much she loves having a daughter: me, Lily.

"Oh, darling, I thought you'd never get here!" she always sighed happily, as if I had come miles and miles, instead of from high school or, later, the Forty-second Street library, where I used to go to write my papers when I was home on vacation from college.

This morning I thought of my mother as I dressed; in my mind I was describing this tundralike snow to her. And I thought of my grandmother, too, and the Russian snows of her childhood. As I pulled on my boots and flung my coat over the three sweaters I was wearing, my eyes filled with anger that she was gone.

Once out in the falling snow, I couldn't think about anything but negotiating my way to the office. The path made by previous footsteps was obscured every few minutes by the blowing drifts. It was like walking through deep sand; those I passed seemed more like insubstantial shadows than people struggling through the wet, pelting snow.

Yet when I open the door of the office and peel off these heavy clothes, I feel overcome by claustrophobia: the drying wool and boots, the scorched odor of the steam heat that is hissing its way through the offices, and the special fragrance of my own body.

I think about the sponge bath I so painstakingly took this morning. Twice a week I take the shortest shower possible in the narrow stall shower, and the rest of the time I make do, like everyone else, with a sponge bath. Sometimes I miss a bath so much I could cry. I know women at Los Alamos who dream about baths; the thought of a luxurious soak in a tub has attained the guilty tinge of the erotic, because it is so expressly forbidden and because we all long for it so much. Yesterday evening I was standing at the window plotting how to save some of this precious snow. "We could clean out the garbage cans and catch it in those," I said to Peter.

"And then what would you do? Take a bath in the garbage can?" he wanted to know.

Finally I shed my last sweater and stand next to the window with my arms straight out so that my cotton blouse can dry. L'Heure Bleu floats up around me in the dry warmth. But I don't want to think about it, or anything that has to do with New York or the East or home. Instead I concentrate on the window. Snow has stuck to the glass, and there is a lintlike curtain of flakes obscuring the view. On the inside are small patches of frost framed by slashing, jagged lines that resemble the distant sierras. Absently I scrape my fingernail across the lines of frost, then wonder why I bothered. All that is out there is whiteness, and more whiteness.

I hear Jacob come in, then get a whiff of his wet coat as he takes it off and hangs it up on the coat rack near the hall. When I turn around, he is at his desk pulling off his boots. His hair is rumpled because he has worn a cap, a royal blue and white snowflake stocking cap I have seen Steffi knitting. I know exactly when she made it; it was one night about a month ago when she came to the knitting club. She was tired, she announced, of knitting those plain serviceable caps for the soldiers; as a relief she was knitting the most complicated Scandinavian patterned cap she could find for Jacob.

From nothing but a tangle of white and blue wool in his wife's hands to this beautiful cap that has kept his head warm. That cap's birth seems undeniable proof of the solidity of his marriage. Odd, those small things that are testaments to a marriage. Like those clean, ironed shirts that lie so beautifully folded in Peter's drawer and have been transformed from the dirty crumpled piles I pick out of the hamper. Now Jacob's cap sits on the hook over his coat; from where I stand I can see the flakes of snow on the wool becoming droplets of water.

I stare at Jacob's tousled hair. How young he looks. The snow has caught us all by surprise, and for a moment I have a glimpse of what he looked like when he was my age, in his early twenties—not so correct, more carefree. When our eyes meet, he smiles boldly, a natural, spontaneous smile, and I can feel that hard place inside me begin to yield, but then I caution myself not to let down my guard. Given such extraordinary weather, I can understand

how he has forgotten our silent pact. In response to his appealing, almost teasing look, I offer him the narrowest of smiles. He shrugs. Whatever you say, Lily. You're the boss now.

We seem to have entered a cave, that igloo cave of ice from my childhood. This office, which is more spacious than most on the mesa and which has seemed more than adequate for almost a year, suddenly feels like a closet. My head begins to spin and I sit at my desk slowly sorting papers, trying to collect myself.

What has come over me? Whatever it is, I can't let Jacob see. I bend my head over my work, pretending some urgency, and soon Jacob enters my little alcove, looking very serious and businesslike.

He wants me to type a report about the findings in Segrè's secluded log cabin laboratory in the Pajarito Canyon. A really quite logical finding, but one that is so obvious no one thought of it. What Segrè found was that the spontaneous fission rate for natural uranium was the same as it had been at Berkeley, but at the field station in the canyon, it was higher for U-235. Segrè and his men realized that the answer lay in the difference in altitude. The canyon lab is 7300 feet higher than the lab at Berkeley and therefore receives much higher doses of cosmic radiation.

"In practical terms," Jacob says, "it means that the uranium core of the gun bomb would be lighter, the bomb not so large, and predetonation less likely. Amazing what the effects of altitude can reveal."

"And we thought it was only our periods that the altitude affected," I murmur, but that short, offhand sentence suddenly breaks the tension in the room. At first a low, delighted chuckle from the back of Jacob's throat, then a ripple of more robust laughter, and soon we are facing each other as we used to do, laughing almost uncontrollably while our eyes fill with tears of relief. In a few seconds all our carefully constructed barriers have dissolved, as if they were walls of snow that had melted and were now puddled between us on the floor.

I feel myself opening toward him, like some rare and mystifying botanical phenomenon, some odd desert flower that needs extreme cold and then stuffy, hermetic warmth to force open its budding petals. And in spite of myself I remember another warm room at the beginning of 1941, only a few weeks after Peter had told me he loved me.

A lazy but persistent snow drifted slowly down from the bleak Ithaca sky. The gurgling of the radiator was proof that it was getting too hot to study, which I was supposed to be doing, or to mark papers, which Peter was supposed to be doing. Too hot to do anything but nod and finally sleep. I found myself a few hours later on Peter's bachelor bed, a narrow, single bed, hardly wider than a camp cot. A plaid blanket covered me. As I turned, I saw that a gritty twilight was darkening the sky. It had stopped snowing. Peter had pulled up a chair and was marking his papers not more than a foot from me, as if he needed to make sure I was still alive, as if I were sick and he responsible for me.

When I saw him so close through the slit of my not-yet-opened eyes, I pretended to be asleep. I had taken a terrible chance by coming here. I could be expelled from the university if I was found in Peter's apartment, but when I told him that after we took off our coats, he stared at me, then said harshly, "Lily, you can't be serious. Hitler is storming through Europe and the world is falling to pieces and you're telling me that people are reporting Cornell coeds in men's apartments in Ithaca to the Campus Police?" As he said it, it sounded even crazier, so I dropped it. Yet I realized then that he hadn't dated very much. If he had, he would already have known what I told him.

But now he knew I was up, and he was waiting for me. When our glances met, he smiled and put his red pencil behind his ear. I had never seen him do that, and I began to laugh, and soon we were both laughing. I forgot to worry that someone might hear a woman's voice in this bachelor apartment, and then he sat down next to me on the bed and drew me to him, murmuring into my ear. The small, cell-like bedroom with its monk's bed was filling up with the aura of my body, that scent I had worn since my mother gave it to me for my sixteenth birthday. He seemed to read my mind, for he breathed deeply and said, "That's nice, what is it?"

Until now we had not done any more than kiss; it was only a few weeks since that crucial Christmas Eve. But we had known each other for years, and everyone seemed to think it was the most natural thing in the world for us to love each other. I wasn't sure I knew what love was that day we came back from Canal Street, even though I had said yes to Peter's proposal of marriage. I knew I wanted him to touch me, I knew I loved how his mind worked, his earnestness and yet his absolute sense of right and wrong. I liked his sense of humor, his ability to see through everything that was sham. I knew that he would never hurt me. Even when I was a girl he had a surprisingly gentle touch for such a tall, solid person; when he slid his hand into mine while we were skating it was as if he were asking a question, and only after I relaxed did he grip me tightly and sometimes guide me across the ice.

There was nothing to be afraid of, I told myself as I saw Peter's shirt come off, watched him pull off his undershirt, stared at the sinewy muscles of his upper arms. Yet suddenly there seemed so much of him and so little of me. Then I looked into his eyes, those startling, surprising eyes, their familiar dark, almost purplish hue now pierced with desire and that same blazing impatience I had seen a few weeks ago in New York. I began to feel his large hands on my temples and my collarbone and my breasts; slowly I could feel my clothes fall away, and I was aware that I let out a sharp gasp of pleasure; everything was happening so fast; now his mouth was on mine, and my body began to open and open, and the waves of apprehension were replaced by swell after swell of pleasure so like the rocketing of a rough ocean that I was amazed when I opened my eyes to discover we were still on dry land. When I said so, Peter laughed—a hearty laugh still entwined in my mind with the glow of our limbs in the lamplight and the aura of L'Heure Bleu that hung in the air.

Afterward, as we lay there very silent and still, I realized that I had taken a second terrible chance, far more serious than being found in a man's apartment. I could be pregnant. But I didn't say a word. I didn't want to spoil what had happened. Besides, there wasn't time. The second time we made love it was a lot less hurried. And lovely. Really unbelievably lovely. But then I became aware of a hot sensation between my legs and I saw the blood on the thick white cotton sheets. Beautifully clean and ironed sheets. And while I was taking a shower a few minutes later, I wondered about those clean sheets, but again I didn't say a word.

I didn't get pregnant, and I forgot about the sheets. Or thought I had, until a few months after we were married. We were lying in bed not more than few blocks from that small bachelor apartment, and finally I asked Peter if he had changed the sheets for me. He turned and propped himself up on his elbow and traced the line of my eyebrows and my nose and my mouth, and then gave me a long look. For the first time since I'd known him, his glance was sheepish.

"Well, the truth is, I hoped. I knew I would be rushing you a little, but it had been so long for me, Lily. Five years. And I wasn't exactly a baby, you know. When it started to snow, that dark gray snow—it seemed a good omen, somehow. So I changed the sheets and hoped. I even bought some contraceptives and put them in my desk, fully intending to use them." Now the sheepishness had become a kind of amazed remorse.

"But things happened so fast. For weeks I worried that you had become pregnant," he added soberly, then drew back and looked me full in the eye and said, "But you can't hate a man for hoping, can you?"

Oh, where is that man who was so interested in love and sex? I wonder as I stare at Jacob and realize that my feelings now are not for my husband, though they resemble the feelings I have had for him. No, these feelings that I have on the second day of that legendary snow in February 1944 are illicit and adulterous.

But at least our little ballet was over. As if it were inevitable, Jacob leaned toward me, and we kissed. Once more I could feel my body reaching toward his. But then, quickly, we pulled away from each other, as if our feelings were too awful to be acted on.

Still, something had been resolved. After the snowstorm we recognized what was happening between us; instead of avoiding each other, we seemed to reconcile ourselves to the reality. Each day became a threat, a challenge. But we were both strong, I told myself every morning, and our strength would help us not to succumb. Besides, there were Peter and Steffi to think about. Peter and Steffi, whom we loved.

• • •

The snow stopped as abruptly as it had begun. And because there had been no warning of its arrival, some of us were caught short. Noel Jenkins had taken his old car down to Santa Fe to be repaired—the car he had driven from Canada, which he thought would fall apart as soon as he arrived. But it kept going, like some old person who defies all the doctors' predictions, and he nursed it along as carefully as he could. This time, though, when he drove down to Santa Fe and waited for it to be fixed, he was unable to get back up The Hill. So he had spent almost three days holed up in La Fonda, drinking with the Secret Service men who were assigned there (one of them worked as a bartender in the hotel) and reading *Gone With the Wind,* which he had found in the hotel library.

Erik had weathered the snowstorm at Pamela's, mending Pamela's and Estevan's clothes, reading, doing his chess problems, napping.

When History and I finally got to Pamela's one afternoon after the path to Otowi was plowed by the Army, Erik was jubilant at the most recent news from Europe. Not only that the Russians had broken the siege of Leningrad. But also about a report from Norway.

Erik explained that there was a High Concentration Plant at Vemork, Norway, where the Germans had been involved in the production of heavy water, which was needed in a uranium pile. It had been bombed more than once by the Allies, and had finally been shut down in November 1943.

"But in January it was learned from short-wave radio reports that the Germans planned to ship the heavy water remaining there back to Germany," Erik read from the report in an English paper that had been sent to him by a colleague. "Despite the reprisals that would surely occur against the Norwegians if the ferry carrying the heavy water was sunk, the decision was made to go ahead. Elaborate plans were made by the British agents with members of the by-now-famous Norwegian Resistance. A ferry called *The Hydro* was sunk in Lake Tinnsjo on February ninth. Twenty-six of the fifty-three people were killed, and one hundred sixty-two gallons of heavy water sank to the bottom of the shallow lake."

A silence fell as he finished. "They needed that heavy water for their fission research," he said quietly. "Now, the question is, what will they do?"

"Get it somewhere else," History ventured.

Erik shook his head. "That's not so easy. They may simply give up."

"But what would that mean—I mean, for us?" I asked.

"I don't know, Lily." Erik looked thoughtfully at us, then at Pamela, who was chopping onions at the small counter near the stove. "But if the Germans have not made much progress, it's even more imperative that everyone on the Allied side be equal. Because if each country has its own gadget, they will compete with each other after this war is over and be locked into a never-ending arms race."

Certainly History and Bess and I, and of course Pamela, knew that Erik believed the only way to insure world peace was to tell the rest of the world about the gadget and to start thinking about arms control for it after the war. The sinking of the heavy water made him particularly concerned about the Russians; he wanted the United States and England to tell the Russians now. But there were many Americans and Europeans who were afraid of the Russians and didn't want them to know anything about the gadget, even though they were our allies. Erik thought this shortsighted.

History asked, "Don't some people think the Russians are as bad as the Nazis, as barbarous and as ruthless?" She looked at him skeptically, her eyebrows raised. Fine light brows above eyes that shone with intelligence.

"Yes, they do," Erik admitted. "But unlike the Germans, who will be defeated, the Russians will be here after the war, and we will have to deal with them."

He sounded so sure of what he said. I guess that was why he found it so easy to think about the future. Like most Europeans, Erik saw the Germans as the enemy. But what about Japan? We knew almost nothing about Japanese atomic research. But we did know about the Japanese as fighters.

As the news from Europe became better, the news from the Pacific got worse. So many casualties on both sides, and such intense, unremitting fighting—unlike anything reported before anywhere. The more we read, the more terrifying the Japanese became. Whenever we discussed the war in the Pacific, Bess's face would tighten, her breath coming in sharp, almost inaudible gasps; she had a younger brother in the Marines there. How well I understood it. My brother, Ernie, was in Washington translating Russian documents, and Danny was too young. But what would I have been like if either of them were at war? I couldn't imagine.

• • •

The winter dragged on. Kate began rehearsing Chekhov's *The Cherry Orchard*. Some people thought it was too heavy, but I loved the play. This time Steffi played Madame Ranevskaya, and a few of the machinists working with Lenny Unwin decided to have a go at acting. They were wonderful.

"Maybe it's better not to know so much about Chekhov," Kate confided one evening when we were walking home. "I picked *The Cherry Orchard* because it's my favorite Chekhov play. We did it one winter in a community drama group right after Stella was born, and I loved it. Besides, it didn't seem right to do comedy now." You can hear an unfamiliar defensiveness in her voice. "But these men have made it funny in ways I never imagined. And Steffi is just terrific."

I knew that. Jacob and I had seen her rehearse the first act only recently, and even he had been amazed.

"So talented. Everything she tries she does superbly," he told me. Yet he never mentioned the fact that Noel was Lopakhin, a brilliant Lopakhin, almost a seductive one. Jacob seemed to have gotten so used to Noel and Steffi together that he didn't even see them. But I did. And I resented them on Jacob's behalf. I tried not to show it, yet one day History asked, "Why are you angry at Noel?"

"I'm not angry at Noel."

"You look angry every time you see him and Steffi together." She looked at me quizzically. For a second I almost weakened. How I would have loved to confide in History, tell her about Steffi and Noel and how sorry I felt for Jacob, and how confused I was about him and his marriage. But I merely lowered my eyes.

Peter went to Hanford in March for a week, then to Oak Ridge. I escaped to the Lerners', to the Chanins', to Pamela's for dinner.

One evening, unable to sleep, I walked over to the school where I knew they were rehearsing. I had made a thermos of tea in the hope that someone would still be there to share it with me. I packed three extra cups. It was almost ten, and many houses were dark, but here and there lights glowed, testament to people reading, talking, getting undressed for bed. The night was clear, the stars seemed so close. Awanyu, flung across the sky, looked alive, about to spring from the blackness. I shivered and drew my coat closer. I had left the apartment because I was lonely, but now, walking on that frozen earth, hearing my footsteps behind me, I felt lonelier than ever.

When I got to the school, I found Kate about to lock up. She looked exhausted, and her mouth had a peculiar tic I had never noticed before. When she saw the thermos, though, her eyes lit up, and we sat down together inside to share it.

"What's the matter?" I finally asked.

She shrugged.

"Is it the play?"

"No." Her reply was quick. "The play is what's holding me together. And the kids."

I waited. Kate wasn't someone you could prod, and I knew that if she wanted to talk she would. And if she didn't, we would simply finish our tea and walk home together. I concentrated on my teacup.

But when I looked up, I was amazed to see tears sliding down her wholesome round face.

"Oh, Kate, what is it?" I said, unable to imagine what could have shattered Kate's implacable hopefulness.

"It's Lenny. I have the feeling that he's disappearing before my eyes. He's hardly ever home; he's obsessed with that critical assembly lab, and he and Tom are so secretive they're like spies. It's crazy, and I'm worried. I know Lenny, and he has never paid much attention to Groves's rules; when he doesn't talk it's because the work has gotten dangerous."

I stared at her, and her eyes begged me to say something. But there was nothing to say. The work was getting dangerous; that was a fact. A fact that we had not reckoned with until now. But of course it had to be true. As things progressed from theory to more and more experimentation, the work was bound to be riskier. The materials with which they were experimenting were so volatile, so unfamiliar. No one knew what might happen. And some of the machinists, like Lenny, were in the thick of it.

"Listen, Kate, I have an idea," I said. "Why don't I come babysit for the kids this weekend and you and Lenny go down to Santa Fe? Have a little holiday at La Fonda, a nice dinner, a hotel room, a little privacy—how about it?"

Suddenly she laughed, a quick, almost bitter laugh. "Oh, Lily, you're such an innocent sometimes," she said. "But you know, maybe that would help." Now her voice was more the one I knew. I sighed. I couldn't make the work less dangerous, but at least I could do something to break the tension it instilled. And it would make the time pass until Peter returned.

"Are you sure you can take care of the kids? They're good, and Stella is like a little mother, but still, four kids is a lot . . ."

"Of course I can, I've baby-sat cousins for years," I lied.

In the end, I don't know what I would have done without Stella, Kate's seven-year-old. She knew where everything went, what each child needed. The apartment was like a mine field, and we lurched from one near disaster to another. But Saturday passed, and finally they were all bathed and fed. When I looked at the scrubbed, shining faces waiting to be read a bedtime story, I thought: Kate has the right idea. Her life was filled to the brim with these beautiful children; at least she had them when Lenny worked late. Maybe that was what we should all be doing. War or no war. Gadget or no gadget. For here, surrounded by the smells of food cooking and that sweet, ineffable fragrance that young children have when they are absolutely clean, I felt marvelous, better than I had in months.

And even after the kids were fast asleep and it was just Tigger, the cat, and me, it didn't feel lonely or empty. I wandered through the apartment in the almost dark, for the kids insisted on a night-light near the bathroom. A huge bulletin board with photographs of the children was propped in the kitchen. Lenny had built a wire fence around Black Beauty so the children couldn't get too close, and the playpen took up a lot of the living room. How did Kate manage to live in such confusion day after day? But at least there was a sense of life being lived here. That made up for everything that was inconvenient or troublesome. Details, really.

When the Unwins arrived home Sunday afternoon, they both looked better, especially Kate. "It was wonderful, Lily, to have all that time together. I can't thank you enough," she said.

So my simple solution had worked. Yet after I got home, nothing seemed simple. At first I thought it was because I was so tired. I crawled into bed in my underwear and slept for a few hours. When I woke, I tried not to hear the silence around me. I put on the radio. Luckily, there was some live classical music on our own Los Alamos radio station. Oppie and Thea had been pushing for that lately. I listened to a Haydn sonata, and was surprised to hear that it was Otto Frisch playing. He had come as part of the English group, and I heard his mother was a pianist, but I had no idea that he played. Then I wondered if Jacob would ever play. Or Teller.

I made myself some eggs and toast and sat drinking my tea. Then I got out my Melville. I read his letters to Hawthorne, took careful notes, and found myself horrified. That great writer of novels seemed almost despicable when he flattered Hawthorne, needing to be praised. Is pandering the price of artistic integrity? I wondered. Disappointed and exhausted, I closed the book and shut the light. Everything seems to have its price, I concluded later in the night, when I woke, forgetful, and reached across the bed for Peter. My arms groped longingly in the empty space. When I finally realized there was nothing there, I was so disappointed that I began to cry.

14
··· ■

Even at a distance the little house at Otowi radiated excitement. Would such excitement be categorized as "hot," the Los Alamos word for radioactivity? I asked myself as History and I walked through the sparkling air toward Pamela's. But I didn't ask History. It was a Saturday, neither of us had to work, and on rare days like this—getting rarer and rarer as the work stepped up—we had a pact not to talk about anything to do with the research. We were on vacation, if only for the day.

Besides, I wanted nothing to dampen History's spirits, for I suspected that she was pregnant again. I knew she wouldn't tell anyone, not even me; it was much too early. Her natural suspicions wouldn't have allowed it under ordinary circumstances, and after her baby's death she probably wouldn't tell us until she began to show. But I knew: from the soft glow in her eyes and the way she moved just a trifle more gingerly than usual, and from the worry in Herb's eyes. We had seen them last night for dinner before we went to see *Mrs. Miniver* at the post movie theater, and more than once Herb jumped up to do something for History that she could easily have done herself. History was more relaxed than she had been in months, but now Herb was more tense, his eyes clouded with an anxiety he couldn't even begin to name.

"It could be work," Peter said when I mentioned it later. I shook my head. I had seen enough of what I called "work-worry." And this was different.

The aroma of baking bread and chocolate cake and a rich beef stew wafted toward us. Pamela was assembling a huge green salad; tonight was the farewell meal for Erik, who was leaving Los Alamos for no one knew how long and for exactly what. Erik was very discreet, but I believed the rumor that he was trying to see what he called "people in high places."

We weren't invited to tonight's dinner for the brass, and as soon as we entered the house, I wished we hadn't come to say good-bye now. Erik was busy, and we had interrupted him. On the table were *Common Sense* and *The Federalist Papers*. Now he pointed to a passage from Paine I didn't know: " 'Tis not the concern of a day, or a year, or an age; posterity are virtually involved in the contest, and will be more or less affected even to the end of time, by the proceedings now. . . . We have it in our power to begin the world over again." I can still, almost forty years later, see Erik's slightly gnarled forefinger beneath those words.

Erik began to gather his papers. I started to say something when his eyes warned me to be silent. Behind him the door to Pamela's house banged to. Though I could see that it was a San Ildefonsan Indian, a friend of Pamela's and Estevan's, I knew Erik was right. The less anyone else knew of his mission, the better. For everyone.

He closed *Common Sense* and put it back on the shelf. When I glanced at his notes, I could see that they were in English. Quickly he stuffed them into his old briefcase with its faded gold initials, *E.D.T.* I thought perhaps I would divert him by asking what the *D* meant, but he said, "My notes are in English because I must speak in English and I want to think in English. I cannot make any mistakes. Pamela has been helping me prepare." He spoke very slowly, carefully enunciating each syllable. You could almost feel him trying to slow down his brain so that his speech would be absolutely clear. It was then that I realized how very much Erik had undertaken and how very much he wanted to succeed.

Pamela shook her head. "You don't need any help, Erik. You know exactly what you must say and how to say it," she told him, then quickly patted his arm.

He sighed. "I hope so," and then we went on to talk about all the things he must see in New York and Washington, the two places we knew he would visit. His eyes had that deep glow they got when he was excited. He wanted to go to the Statue of Liberty, which he had never seen.

"It's green, you know," I said. History and Pamela stared. "Everyone expects it to be wonderful and shiny, but it's a dull, washed-out green, oxidized copper," I explained to Erik. "I was so disappointed when I saw it for the first time. I was about six years old."

Erik smiled. Suddenly I had a vision of him scrambling up into the Statue's arm to the top, where she held the torch so proudly. Then mingling with schoolchildren and tourists and recent immigrants to experience that huge, oddly ugly symbol of everything that America would like to mean to the world.

Why isn't Erik's wife here with him? I wondered. We had heard that she was a beautiful woman who adored him, and that she was in England. But why wasn't she with him now when he needed as much encouragement as possible? There were probably ten good reasons, not the least of which that people didn't go flying across the Atlantic in the midst of a war unless they had to. Yet I was suddenly, irrationally angry that Erik had to face whomever he was going to face alone. And did he have that thickness of speech, that odd disconcerting stutter when he was with his wife? Or did it disappear only when he was with Pamela?

• • •

Erik told us his first stop in Washington was the Supreme Court. There he was to meet with the small, wiry Supreme Court Justice, Felix Frankfurter. He had met Frankfurter years before, in 1933, when Frankfurter, a Jew, had come to England to arrange jobs in the United States for some of the émigrés who were leaving Germany. And they had met again, briefly, in 1939 in Washington. But they had not really talked until December 1943, when Erik stopped in Washington on his way to Los Alamos for the first time.

"We look like Mutt and Jeff," Frankfurter remarked. But for all their physical differences, the two men got along. So well, indeed, that Frankfurter, with his clipped, sharp speech, was not a bit disconcerted by Erik's low, hesitant mumble. When one of Frankfurter's aides complained, the justice snapped, "You'll just have to listen harder." Frankfurter told President Roosevelt—who complained, too—that he thought Erik's way of speaking was a device to make people think and listen. "Probably unconscious, but that's its purpose, nonetheless." And there was nothing wrong with that, Frankfurter thought, not in these times when it was so easy to go off half-cocked.

Before his appointment with the justice in the spring of 1944 Erik walked along the Mall. When he'd left Lamy, there had been hail and mist, but here azaleas were bursting with the palest pink and white blooms and the air was as soft as summer. When he said so to Frankfurter, the justice smiled and said, "You haven't lived through a Washington summer."

Then they got down to business. They were alone, because this was an off-the-record meeting, but even in the privacy of Frankfurter's office they called the Manhattan Project "X." Frankfurter sat at his desk with a pencil and a yellow legal pad.

"In the six months since we last met, I have seen Site Y and Hanford and Oak Ridge and the Met Lab," Erik began. "Groves has done exactly what he needed to do—he has turned your country into a massive factory."

Frankfurter beamed. He had boundless faith in the American capacity for work and accomplishment.

"And they will build what Oppie calls the gadget, probably by a year or so from this time," Erik continued. "But that is when the difficulties will arise. For if it is used as a surprise weapon and all your Allies don't know about it, there will be not only the end of this war, but the beginning of an arms race that will escalate into something the world has never known. You cannot let that happen. And the only way not to let it happen is to tell everyone— except your enemies—what you are doing so that discussion about international control can begin. *Now,* not when it is too late."

Frankfurter frowned, but Erik was undaunted. Briefly, he outlined the details for an international conference. "This can be the greatest boon to mankind or the greatest disaster. But it must be discussed at once." He waited. What he wanted was for Frankfurter to communicate what he had said to President Roosevelt. Erik had great faith in Roosevelt's desire for peace.

The justice didn't disappoint him. "Knowing President Roosevelt, I have every reason to think he will be responsive to the ideas you have outlined," he said quietly.

Then Erik became bolder. "What I want to do is go to London and tell them what I found here and meet with people from other European countries."

Silently Frankfurter looked over his notes, then looked up. Slowly he nodded. Words weren't necessary. His approval had been given. Then he said, "Your family is well, comfortable in England?"

Erik could feel himself relax. "They have been made very welcome," he replied. "And your wife?"

"Getting along," Frankfurter said. Then, the two men rose, and, as if reluctant to part, they walked very slowly to the entrance of the Court building, where they stood for a few more minutes chatting, and finally shook hands.

• • •

Erik returned to Los Alamos, and Frankfurter went to see Roosevelt late in March. Roosevelt admitted that the whole thing "worried him to death" and said he would like to meet Traugott one of these days, but that until he did, it would be all right with him if the Danish scientist went to London to tell their friends there that he, Roosevelt, was most eager to explore the proper safeguards in relation to international control of the weapons research.

This is like a circle, Erik thought after Frankfurter contacted him. Roosevelt said he wanted him to talk to the English statesmen—Lord Cherwell and Sir John Anderson—yet it was they who had sent him to the United States in the first place to talk to Roosevelt. "What I didn't realize at that time," Erik confessed later, "was that the linchpin in all this was Churchill—and he's not at all convinced that international control of the gadget is the answer."

Early in April Erik went to London and met with Lord Cherwell and Sir John Anderson, who stepped up their previous efforts to brief Churchill. Yet Churchill saw no need to discuss what he called "X" with anyone, including Roosevelt, and certainly not with Traugott.

The prime minister kept inventing excuses not to see Erik. Finally, in the middle of May, his famous stubbornness eroded, he agreed to a meeting.

Lord Cherwell accompanied Erik. Churchill began the interview by berating Lord Cherwell. He would have preferred something more formal when he met Traugott, perhaps a meeting, with other people—vague, slightly unreasonable demands. Cherwell knew better than to respond that this was what they had agreed upon; when Churchill was in this kind of mood, the best thing was silence.

Then Erik started to speak. He had practiced these first few sentences endless times, yet his voice was halting, soft. "You know that the Americans are working on an atomic weapon," he began.

"With English help," Churchill snapped.

"And that this weapon will be unlike anything that has ever been employed in warfare before," Erik continued slowly. But his words seemed to float lazily through the air. After a few minutes Churchill's eyes were wandering. Erik hesitated, then stopped and gathered himself together. When he glanced at Lord Cherwell, the Englishman smiled. But after Erik began to speak again, this time more forcefully, Churchill looked out the window, his puffy face flaccid, bored. He concentrated on bending a paper clip into odd little shapes. Seeing Churchill do that made Erik doubly nervous; he had had a professor in college who did that when he thought his students were unprepared.

At one point Churchill put up his hand to interrupt, but when he spoke, he merely said, "Can you speak up a little? I can hardly hear you." During a pause he glowered at Lord Cherwell, then frowned several times. Erik waited for him to ask for a scientific explanation, but he didn't. He just sat there, never relaxing enough to tilt his head toward Erik or to listen. Just reshaping that paper clip in his pudgy hands.

Fifteen minutes went by, and Erik could hear himself beginning to drone. Twenty minutes. Erik looked at his watch and saw that a half hour had passed. He was wondering how to continue when he heard something tapping on the desk. He looked up. Now Churchill was holding a letter opener in his hand and scowling at him. Embarrassed, Lord Cherwell averted his eyes.

As soon as he saw he had Erik's attention, Churchill snapped again, "I cannot see what you are talking about. After all, this new bomb is just going to be bigger than our present bombs. It involves no difference in the principles of war. And as for any postwar problems, there are none that cannot be amicably settled between me and my friend, President Roosevelt."

Dismissed. "Like a schoolboy," Erik said much later, when it was safe to tell us about the disastrous meeting. "Churchill and I did not speak the same language." His voice was mournful, as if the fault somehow lay with him, as if during those speeches he had so carefully rehearsed with Pamela he had not grasped the essence of spoken English. But of course that wasn't true. Erik had said exactly what he wanted to say. In impeccable, beautiful English. But you had to pay careful attention to what Erik was saying. And that Churchill wasn't able or willing to do. Witnesses reported that Churchill had not wanted to listen, had probably made up his mind how to reply before he ever met Erik Traugott. Years later people said that the only person in the world who had not responded to the unique goodness that Erik Traugott possessed was Winston Churchill.

Before he left England, Erik wrote a more detailed description of the problem and its possible solution and sent it, via Cherwell, to Churchill. While he was waiting for an answer, Erik saw his family. But though they wanted him to stay in England, his wife knew better than to urge him. She had to take care of the children now settled in school in England. But Erik must be free to travel. "You must follow your heart, Erik," she told him. For she knew, perhaps better than anyone else, that Erik was a man possessed.

"Like something out of Dostoyevski," History said bitterly when we knew that Churchill had never even bothered to answer his letter. Erik was overcome with chagrin and remorse. But he had done all a man could.

"And if Churchill didn't respond, that doesn't mean President Roosevelt will follow suit. There's more than one road out of this wood," he confided to his English friends. To see Roosevelt, he had to return to the United States. So once again, he said goodbye to his wife and children.

• • •

After Erik left us in March 1944, the harsh winter turned very quickly to spring. Everyone was outdoors again, and on Sundays the Indian ruins would be swarming with people. If you stood on top of the rock at Puye, you could see one of the most glorious views in the world dotted here and there with clusters of figures hiking in the nearby Jemez Mountains. When we could, we joined them. But more often Peter would be working in the canyon or traveling to Chicago or Oak Ridge. Then Noel would appear in his rattletrap car and spirit me off to Tsankewi or Puye with the Wunderlichs or the Chanins or the Lerners.

Most people preferred the grandeur of Puye, whose long, rectangular courtyard and kiva and great house lie directly under the shadow of Tsi'como. Its drama has been compared in recent years to the magnificent courtyard of pre-Greek Knossos. But for me Tsankewi was more beautiful; here in this ancestral town of the San Ildefonsan Indians you could feel the presence not only of the great Tsi'como, but of the Black Mesa as well. Even the way you come upon Tsankewi is special—through a slit in the mountains that leads to the top of the mesa. And on the left of that pass, a gate, really, to the old ruins, is a charming Anasazi carving of a humpbacked flute player. And then, stretched out before you, are the perfectly proportioned cliff dwellings and terraces and natural rock porches that are still, hundreds of years later, cozy and warm, and that have a splendid view of the old riverbeds where patches of corn once grew.

For a long time it was thought that the Anasazi abandoned the cliff dwellings for the mesa tops, but now we know they lived in both the cliff dwellings and on the mesas simultaneously. For there was no reason at all to leave those serene, comfortable homes cut into the cliffs.

None of us had ever seen anything like those caves cut into the sides of the canyons. Unlike so many ruins around the world, they were built neither for kings nor for noblemen but as homes for the families of ordinary Pueblos. They belonged to everyone, and when we entered their dry, snug spaces, we didn't even feel like trespassers. Would things have happened the way they did if those caves had not been there, within walking distance of Los Alamos?

I don't know, and perhaps I am searching too hard for excuses. Maybe what happened was in its own way inevitable—as inevitable as the events that followed it.

With Erik gone, time speeded up. Instead of his protective influence, there was a peculiar void. With the passing days you could feel people growing irritable, pulling away from each other. When someone murmured at the party for the English, "You can cut the air around here with a knife," no one looked surprised. That old cliché was exactly right. The growing tension was at the very core of this "other war," which is what Jacob called the search for the gadget.

Troubles arose in the Theoretical Division; Teller and Bethe were finding it difficult to work together at all, and finally Teller officially left the Theoretical Division. The German-born Englishman, Rudolf Peierls, took his place. On top of that, Kistiakowsky was locking heads with Neddermeyer.

Steffi appeared to withdraw further and further into her own world as she worked on *The Cherry Orchard*. She had grown her thick chestnut hair very long. I couldn't help wondering how she kept that hair clean in the face of our continual water shortage. When we met on the once-again-dusty roads of Los Alamos, she struck me as completely incongruous, a Madame Ranevskaya who had somehow been dropped onto a strange planet.

History had retreated into a protective solitude. Obviously pregnant, she concentrated almost entirely on the baby within her womb. I had seen other women on The Hill do that, but they weren't close to me; their distractedness and secret smiles didn't affect me. Now I felt abandoned.

Then, early in April, I saw Bess's tall filly-like figure heading for the commissary. On her arm was that Nantucket lightship basket, which I hadn't seen for almost a year. She saw me notice it, and then she put her hand on my arm. When she spoke, her voice was low. "I'm almost at the end of my third month, Lily."

I was so surprised I could only nod. Mark, Bess's Czech husband, had been outspoken in his mockery of the "baby makers," as he dubbed them. He had even said once, quite sharply, "Making a baby doesn't go with making a gadget." And Bess herself had never seemed interested in having a baby, or in the school, or in anything connected with children here. When History and I had appeared in front of the Town Council to beg the Army to build a fence for the pond, Bess hadn't even come. I had been annoyed; we needed as much support as we could get, but it probably hadn't mattered. So far the Army hadn't made a move.

No, Bess seemed totally immersed in her work at the Library and Document section of Los Alamos—tedious, exacting work that required the utmost discretion, for so much of what they handled was classified. We had thought she would be there forever. But maybe the pressure of her brother fighting in the Solomons, or the brave letters her mother sent from Nantucket had gotten Bess to thinking about a child.

For having a child was the most positive thing a wife here at Los Alamos could do, a wife anywhere could do, I suppose. And maybe making a baby had everything to do with making a gadget. For when your husband is working on a weapon capable of unknown and perhaps unprecedented destruction, perhaps the only thing a woman can do to convince herself of a future is to have a child. A kind of balancing act, really. And not, as Groves sometimes said in disgust, that people just didn't have enough to do, which made me begin to hate him. People at Los Alamos were not hibernating animals, groping blindly for each other in the dark, as he would like to have us think.

Pamela agreed with me. "And Oppie understands it, too, Lily.

I know he does. He's far more sensitive about the women here than Groves."

"That's hardly difficult," I wanted to answer, but kept my tongue. Nothing would be accomplished by criticizing Groves.

Yet where did I fit into all this? For although I had clearly begun to think about it, I knew that the last thing I wanted right now was a baby.

I was alone more and more. So I did what most people do when they don't want to go home to an empty house: I delayed getting there. Sometimes, when the weather was good, I walked to Tsankewi. There the long, languorous dusk would flow around me, and I would sit not far from the flute player and watch the dying lilac light wash the ruins. Who I was and where I was and why we were here would cease to matter until it was time to get up and hurry home.

Often it was easier just to stay late at the office. As Jacob left, I would be writing letters to my parents or my brothers or my friends, or reading, or, after an especially busy day, staring off into space. Jacob would usually stop for few moments to chat, but then, as if on cue, he would look at his watch and frown, for those were the nights he was expected to baby-sit for Sam while Steffi and Noel were at rehearsal.

When I finally walked home, I would hear Jacob playing the piano after he had put Sam to bed and Steffi was off rehearsing. Schubert impromptus and Mendelssohn's Songs Without Words and Mozart sonatas would float toward me. Sometimes I would pause at the sound of the music, then daydream: What if I simply appeared in the doorway of his living room while he played? But that was a childish fantasy, and we were no longer children. So I would hurry along, trying to escape the lovely, lilting notes, which would, despite every effort, linger for hours in my head and fill me with a longing I had never before felt. An involuntary longing for Jacob that would be relieved only the next morning when he opened the door to the office. For when I could see him, I was all right. But then the day would fly, and before I knew it, the slow, empty night would begin again.

When Peter was on The Hill and merely working late, we would eat dinner together, and then I would walk him back to the canyon and go home. Anything to take up some time. I always tried to stay awake until he came home. Most of the time I failed. But sometimes I made it and would greet him with a smile of triumph. Then we would lie in bed and talk—somewhat garbled talk because he was always afraid of telling me too much. And sometimes we would make love, but more often than either of us would have liked to admit, it would be a tired, almost mechanical process that left each of us wearier than before.

That will pass, Lily. It's part of marriage. There are ebbs and flows in marriage. Los Alamos is a temporary situation, it will pass, Lily, remember that. I could hear my mother's patient voice in my ears as I imagined a conversation with her.

There were times when I was convinced she was wrong. How can there be ebbs and flows in a desert as dry, as dusty as the moon? Besides, I had begun to feel as if I couldn't even comprehend a word like *temporary*. No, here on The Hill we seemed to be caught in a deadlock where the work would last into eternity.

15

On the day early in May that Peter and Fermi left for a two-week trip to Chicago and after that to Hanford, the weather changed. A pleasant Southwestern spring became, within hours, a tropical summer. The heat pressed down upon us like the heavy hand of a giant, a ubiquitous giant from whom there was no escape. We began to have more than our usual trouble breathing. And although this strange, unexpected weather was in no way like the eerie snow we had had during the winter of 1944, it reminded me of it. If this was only May, what could we look forward to in July? Or would we be roasted to crisps by then?

Catastrophes multiplied, as they always do when something unexpected occurs. A small fire destroyed two stoves in Fuller Lodge, a child was hospitalized from heat exhaustion and dehydration, and Thea came upon another child, a three-year-old, wading unattended deep into Ashley Pond. A soldier who was supposed to be acting as lifeguard was talking to his buddy.

Thea pulled the little boy—who was in seventh heaven and couldn't understand why this pretty lady was shrieking at him—from the pond. She screamed, "You're lucky this kid is alive," at

the startled soldier, then dragged the crying child in his wet overalls into Oppie's office. All she said was, "Now will you fence that pond?" Her low voice was more frightening than her yelling, and reports had it that Oppenheimer blanched, then quietly arranged for the child to be taken home to his mother.

History saw her right afterward. "She was a dragon, madder than I thought she could get." History's voice was solemn. That child had come very close, and we all knew it. I guess that's why Thea chose to go to Oppie rather than Groves. But when Tom heard about it, he just laughed and said, "Now I'm not the only one who knows Thea has a temper."

Then a few days later an Army truck lost its brakes and hurtled down the side of the mountain to Santa Fe; fortunately, the driver had rolled out and watched the truck crash. On the fifth day water was rationed more severely than ever before. A group of angry white-lipped women marched into Colonel Tyler's office demanding to know how the Army planned to fight the fires they felt were inevitable. He had no answer and promised to consult Groves. That satisfied no one. There was an emergency meeting of the Town Council. When I looked around, I could see how frightened people were. And they were right. At midday in this extreme heat you felt as if you were sitting on a tinderbox.

And Noel's car almost burned up on a bridge on the outskirts of Santa Fe. MPs from Thea's office on Palace Avenue reached the car just in time to alert the Santa Fe fire department.

But what was Noel doing on a Tuesday outside Santa Fe? Most people went down there only on weekends. When I mentioned it to Jacob, his head shot up, and in his eyes was a tinge of disdain. His voice was cold when he spoke; I felt as if I had breached some unspoken code of conduct. "He seems to have a lover there," he said, then went back to what he was doing, though he hadn't really answered my question. I didn't pursue it. Besides, as Peter would have been the first to remind me, it was none of my business.

Such strange heat. "It's not like anything I've ever known here,"

Pamela told me, so incredulous it sounded as if she were describing a judgment from God.

Everyone coped in his own way. My escape was Tsankewi, where I could be alone, probably because no one else wanted to use the time or energy it took to get there. But I didn't mind. And it was perfectly safe. In the long dusk that slowly crept upon the mesa, I would put on a hat and a loose dress and meander to the cleft in the mountains, then sit there reading by flashlight in the absolute quiet until the night had crept up around me. Even the birds, which usually wheeled and swooped—the hawks, orioles, swallows, juncos, goldfinches, and blue buntings—seemed to be in hiding.

My only company was a strange cactus that the Indians called Queen of the Night—tall, sparkling, round flowers piercing the dark with their perfectly symmetrical whiteness. The odd, waxy blooms swarmed into the night, from nowhere, really, for during the day their stems were gray, twiggy, dead-looking. But in the dark of late spring these beauties would suddenly appear, catching the moonlight. Such pretty, demure blossoms, the furthest thing from Mozart's noisy Queen of the Night, I thought as I sat there. I wished I could show them to Jacob.

But no Jacob, no anybody when I sat there; still, I was never afraid at Tsankewi. No, when the darkness came, it was a friend, and I would welcome it, inhaling its cooler air, knowing it would give me the succor I needed to return to The Hill.

Then, guided by an oversized flashlight, which was one of the few things Peter had brought with him when he came as a young man from Berlin, I would wend my way home. As I walked, I would wonder what Peter was doing, what he had found at Hanford, how he and Fermi were managing. I worried about Hanford, which was known as a violent town where many of the workers carried guns and lived hard—almost a caricature of the wild West, filled with would-be cowboys and too much liquor and more than its share of loose women.

"Is it the loose women that worry you, Lily?" I could hear Fermi's accented, amused singsong question. Like Jacob, Fermi loved to tease me. No, it's not the loose women, I would answer him in my head. It's the stray bullets. As smart as they both were, neither Peter nor Fermi had much experience with those.

By the time I arrived home from Tsankewi, it was late and most of the windows dark. But I knew from snippets of conversation floating around The Hill that people were still awake, lying quietly in the still-intense heat, praying for the sweet forgetfulness of even a few hours of sleep. After I had gotten myself something to eat, I, too, would lie on our bed until my weariness yielded to a strange, restless sleep. I remember thinking that this might be what old age was like—to lie there night after night tormented, not by weather, but by memories one could neither erase nor change.

On the eighth evening, the winds shifted, as if the giant's hand had swept through the sky. It happened so quickly and sharply that you felt as if something had clicked in your brain. Astonishing. I was at Tsankewi, in the fading pinkish light, when I felt it, and I held my breath, afraid that if I let go, the heat might return. But it didn't, even after I breathed, and my relief was so great that I could hear a surprised laugh echo through the ruins.

Who was it? I turned to see, then realized that it was me, my laugh, a contralto laugh that came from deep within my chest when I was genuinely amazed. I stood up, hugging myself with pleasure that the awful, oppressive heat was gone. In the distance I could hear thunder, but I wasn't afraid. No, I always knew that if this heat was broken by a thunderstorm I would take shelter in one of the ancient caves. I even knew which one and began to walk toward it.

But first I turned to gather my book and flashlight, and it was then that I saw him. He stood in the slit of the mountain, and I knew, without his telling me, that this wasn't the first time he had followed me to Tsankewi. But tonight he hadn't retreated invisibly. No, to-night, as the heat dissolved, he stood there and watched me.

All your life, if you have been brought up as I was, you value reason. For almost twenty-four years, which doesn't sound like a long time, but could be a third of your life if you're lucky and a half if you're not, you live your life as reasonably as possible. You try as a child to be good, to control your temper; as you get old you learn to mask your feelings, to be considerate of other people and their feelings, to do what is expected of you, to honor your responsibilities, your obligations, to have compassion and understanding for the people who are important to you, and to guard and protect—often fiercely—those whom you love. And you live every moment of every day by that code, even when you are not thinking about it. For reason has become a reflex, which isn't so surprising when you remember that it is reason that separates man from other mammals, man from the beasts and the beastliness in the world. At least that is what you can believe if you are still young and have not yet been faced with the terrors of war.

But nothing has prepared you for that moment in your life when reason seems irrelevant, when reason seems to have been swept off the face of the earth by the hand of the same giant who controls the weather. When there is no such thing as reason and all you know is what you want, and the person you want, have wanted for weeks, months, maybe as long as a year, is standing in front of you, is walking toward you, and you can see from his eyes and his smile that right and wrong have nothing to do with what he is feeling— which is what you are feeling—and that what you are about to do is wrong, maybe even the greatest evil of all, and that you are about to do it anyway because the need to do it is stronger than anything you have ever known in your life, stronger than your love for your husband or your duty to family or your capacity to reason.

And that even when you remember it almost forty years later, that person you are talking about is no longer the I, the essence of you, but someone else, someone who is called Lily but who is not at all the Lily you have known or the Lily you will know after this particular time in your life.

• • •

I watch him approach. His face is naked with longing, and that longing has stripped away the years so that the man walking toward me is not the Jacob I know, but a young Jacob, the Jacob I glimpsed the day in the office when he took off his knitted cap. He's wearing a loose shirt and cotton pants and sandals, and his body seems smaller, slighter than it does in his ordinary clothes. How will his body look naked? I wonder, but that will have to wait, for the growing thunder has begun to drum almost unceasingly. When he reaches me, I grab his outstretched hand and guide him carefully along the rocks of the Tsankewi ruins. As we scamper over the rocks, rain begins to fall, at first a few isolated drops, then, suddenly, a sheet of water cascading out of the sky like a piece of paper being formed in a mill from the milky pulp of wood. Translucent sheets of rain that blind us as we run, me leading— really feeling my way to the mouth of the cave.

The entrance is low, and to get inside Jacob must duck a little. We stand in the dry cave, letting the water fall from our drenched clothes. There is so much I thought I would want to say, and yet I can't seem to form the words. So I stand there awkward, embarrassed. Jacob blinks, for it is almost dark, then holds out his arms. In a strange kind of slow motion, as if the memory of what we are about to do had begun with the act itself, we lie down next to each other, and as he begins to caress me, arousing me though my wet clothes are still clinging to my body, I can feel a strange warmth flowing into me.

I frown, and he stops. "I'm not hurting you, am I?" he says, and I shake my head and realize that the warmth comes from the dry stone of the cave. The floor of the cave is still embedded with the warmth of the sun that has been beating down on it for centuries and, most recently, for these last extraordinary days.

We move slowly, more slowly than I could have believed possible, but it is because we must make it last. For who knows when this will happen again? So hanging over our happiness as we caress each other's body is the threat that this is all we will be allowed. We make love over and over again. I am amazed at the power of such desire. It seems to fill me so completely that I imagine myself becoming huge, elephantine, and I'm astonished when I open my eyes and see that I am still inside my small-boned body. But to give and to have such enormous pleasure! I've never felt so powerful, yet also so powerless, as my body leads my mind, then seems to obliterate my mind.

Finally weary, we are silent for what seems a long time. Then we start to talk. Or rather, Jacob talks. We lie there with his arm around my shoulders looking up at the dark ceiling of the cave, and as he speaks what he says is so important, so vivid, that I can almost see pictures of Jacob moving through his life on the dry adobe above our heads, like the hieroglyphics of the ancient cultures that are surely buried somewhere in these walls, untouched by time.

"I left Berlin for several years in the early thirties—to go to Erik's institute, and then to Berkeley to work with Oppie, which wasn't the greatest success because he wasn't all that generous or kind then. He's a different person here, with the patience of a saint. But then he was abrupt and sometimes vicious, and I was disappointed after working with him for a few months, and maybe even a little angry." He stops, but I don't react, even though this confirms my suspicions.

"Anyway, I was seriously thinking about going back when I met this woman at the home of Haakon Chevalier, a friend of Oppie's who teaches French literature and had a kind of literary salon. She's the one I told you about, the colleague who loved Melville.

"She was wonderful, very independent and very smart, a lot like you, aside from the whole Melville business, and we fell in love. But she wasn't interested in marriage, or at least that's what she said, though I suspected afterward that she wasn't interested in being married to a German Jew who might have a hard time making a living as a physicist. And if she knew one thing it was that she had had enough of academia; she hated all its intrigues and conspiracies. But that's where I was planning to make my life. So although we were very much in love, we never talked about the future, and when I told her I was leaving, she didn't really react much. She had a strange way of living her life, or at least it seemed strange to me then, for she didn't try to fight things over which she had no control." He stops and shifts his arm slightly under me.

"For a long time I had no idea what happened to her," he goes on. "And then, just before we came out here, I heard that she had married a philosopher, who was at the University of Chicago, and had a couple of kids. Apparently she decided that a family was more important than an advanced degree. As far as I know, the book on Melville was never published. And I guess when she was really in love academia didn't frighten her anymore." His voice is subdued, resigned.

"Does Steffi know about her?"

"Of course. Steffi and I have no secrets from each other," he says. An involuntary gasp ripples from my throat through the length of the cave. I cough to cover it, but Jacob has heard it, and now he turns to me and holds my eyes with his, then adds, "Except this." His voice is tight. "No one will ever know about this unless you tell them.

"So I went back to Berlin in 1934." His voice is more relaxed now. I can feel my limbs loosen, and suddenly a cool breeze brings out goose bumps on my arms. I pull my dress over me. It has dried just lying on the warm stone floor. As he talks, Jacob reaches for his shirt and arranges it across me. His fingers play like water on my skin, and I long to turn to him again, but he needs to go on.

"When I got there I knew it wasn't going to be for long. The minute you got off the train you could sense something sinister in the air. You could almost smell it. So I didn't even try to live on my own. I went back to my mother's home—she was a widow, my father had died when I was eleven—and wrote letters for jobs to America and England. And played the piano and visited my aunt, who lived in Charlottenburg, and listened to my sisters' problems with their boyfriends. There are three of them, all younger. Now one lives in Chicago with her husband, and the other two went to Memphis, where they live with their families. My mother went to Switzerland to live with her sister. She said she couldn't adjust to living in America."

Now I envision the busy, upper-class European household, the plush rugs, the heavily upholstered furniture, the carved chests and tables, the gold-rimmed dishes, all the paraphernalia of bourgeois happiness in the early part of the century. Even the air is thick with cinnamon from the cake that always seemed to be baking in the ovens of households like Mrs. Wunderlich's. I have heard it described endlessly, by my parents and Peter's parents and by Peter himself. So Jacob had a family, after all. A family of women where he had become the surrogate father when he was still a boy and where he was clearly looked up to, clearly adored.

"My mother wanted us all to be married before we left. 'The world travels in pairs, like Noah's ark,' she used to say. And to her credit, we all got married within the next two years. My youngest sister had known Steffi for years, though they weren't really friends, and my mother had known Steffi's mother a bit, too. When she first met Steffi, my mother was enchanted—because Steffi was so beautiful, I guess. But then something put her off. Maybe she found out about Steffi's feelings for Noel, or maybe it was Steffi's paranoia, which you get to know only after a while, or maybe it was Steffi's friendship with Dietrich Bonhoeffer. My mother couldn't trust anyone who wasn't Jewish in those days, not even Dietrich, who is goodness personified. The thought of his being jailed in Charlottenburg, that sleepy bourgeois suburb where all the well-to-do would go for holidays or had houses . . . it's unbelievable to me . . ." Jacob has to stop.

I turn to him; impulsively I kiss away the salty droplets that are dripping from his eyes. He gathers me into his arms and holds me, and in that moment all the passion we have been repressing for so long seems to flow through us again, but it is enough to lie there, feeling our hearts beat in a syncopated rhythm while I kiss the tears from his face. After a while his voice goes on and with each word gets stronger.

"In any case, by the time I decided I wanted to marry Steffi, my mother didn't approve, and if times had been more normal, she would probably have tried to find someone else for me. But there wasn't time. Even in 1934 you could feel that sense of urgency among the Jews. It governed every aspect of our lives. My mother was a very determined woman, she had to be, and she knew what was coming. The ones who didn't have that urgency—well, that's a whole other story. . . ." Jacob sighs.

"I'm giving you my mother's version of it, Lily, the way she saw it and probably still sees it, but the truth is that I was in love with Steffi, and I knew very early on that we would marry. With or without my mother's approval. The whole business about Noel has never put me off and it still doesn't. Now I regard it as you would some small handicap. Steffi can't help it. But at the beginning it was a challenge and, if anything, made her more desirable. I was convinced I could make her love me more than she could ever care for Noel. I wanted to drown her with love, I used to dream of covering her with kisses, and for a while it was as wonderful as I wanted it to be. And maybe it would have continued that way if I had been able to stay at Cornell and teach the Michelson-Morley experiment and Rutherford's theories and Erik's ideas and Einstein's. But now . . ."

In the silence I understand that there are some things he will never say, some things I will never say, things we simply cannot speak about and will never know about each other.

But it doesn't matter. All that matters is that we're here together in this ancient Pueblo ruin, and that our bodies are shivering once again with desire. We make love one last time, and then, hurriedly, pull on our clothes.

When we leave, the storm has subsided, and now the air is cool and sharp. It is hard to believe it was so hot for the past eight days. We talk quietly—mostly about the weather—as we walk, and I hug the gooseflesh of my arms. But he doesn't come near me or put his arms around me to warm me. I understand why. For if we touch each other again, we'll have to return to the cave, and that we cannot do. It's already past midnight.

How he will account for his absence I don't know and don't ask, nor do I ask what the next step will be. I'm incapable of thinking ahead; I'm overcome by the desire to sleep. My body feels sore, I want my bed. No wonder sensible people make love in beds. But we aren't sensible or reasonable, and our love—if that's what it is—is too fierce for anything as reasonable as a bed. We will make love only once in a bed, and then I will long for the primitive Tsankewi cave with its warm stone floor—the only proper setting for this thing that has happened to us.

We didn't speak of it the next morning. If you had seen us, you would have suspected nothing. Indeed, we did our work as efficiently as possible, perhaps more efficiently than ever before, because we seemed to understand each other better than ever before. Yet we kept very far from each other, as if afraid that even the most casual contact, the brush of a hand or an arm, might ignite the passion we carried within us.

We met several times more during the following two weeks, always in that same cave at Tsankewi, wanting each other desperately when we arrived and perhaps even more desperately when we had to leave. "When normal people would have had enough," I sometimes thought and once said. Jacob didn't even bother to respond. There was nothing normal about what had happened to us, and though he sometimes seemed to feel more responsibility for it—"After all, I'm so much older," he would sometimes say— he knew better than to try to explain it.

Two nights before Peter and Fermi were due to return, Jacob and I went to see *The Cherry Orchard* together. I remember marveling to myself at our duplicity—the proud husband of the star and his secretary making a fuss over Steffi and the rest of the cast. It struck me as I observed Noel and Steffi basking in their well-deserved praise that she was far more honest than Jacob and I. Such a wistful, unfulfilled love as Steffi's had to wear its heart on its sleeve—whereas we who had known such deep pleasure had already become practiced professionals in the art of deception. For what we had could never be shared or even hinted at.

The need to deceive should have made me afraid to be with people. Yet it had the very opposite effect. I became reckless with a compulsion not to leave Jacob until I had to. Instead of excusing myself and going home, where I purposely left some chores to do before Peter's return, I went with the rest of them to the cast party.

Lenny Unwin was as proud as a new father, fielding compliments about his talented wife, darting from person to person with extraordinary energy.

"He's like that when he works, all over the place," Tom said when I found myself standing near him, watching Lenny. "A wonderful craftsman, a wonderful person, a real friend," he added, then looked down at me, his eyes flickering with amusement at Lenny's happiness. Then Lenny was there, clicking beer glasses with Tom, saying hello to me.

"And now I want to toast the most wonderful woman in the world," he announced, and looked lovingly at Kate. Unabashed, she stepped forward, then stood with her husband while someone's flash camera clicked, and they quickly kissed. Such openness about their love—it was wonderful, it seemed to warm the room. Everyone was smiling—Steffi and Noel and Jacob standing together, Tom and Thea, the Lerners, the Chanins, and other couples I didn't know as well.

Except me. I didn't even have to wonder why. All this gaiety, these careless displays of affection only made me feel envious, more of an outsider. Suddenly I wished I hadn't come. I didn't belong here. Jacob did because his wife was the star. But me? Who was I? Peter's wife, and also Jacob's lover. But that no one would ever know. They couldn't know. Yet why did that depress me so?

I should have gone, just slipped away quietly and let them all enjoy themselves. But I couldn't. So I stepped back, watching Kate and Lenny chat with Thea and Tom, and I waited. Then, as the rest of them were gathering their things and starting to leave, I maneuvered myself closer to Jacob and we exchanged a few secret words that meant we would meet at dawn at Tsankewi. We spoke matter-of-factly, in front of whoever cared to listen, like well-trained spies.

And yet we felt no shame. For how could something that brought us both such overwhelming happiness be wrong?

• • •

As I hurry to Tsankewi, I wonder how Jacob and I will survive. For once Peter comes home, this will have to end. I should be filled with guilt, but I feel none—only a sinking feeling of desolation. When Jacob touches me, I feel as if he is peeling off the layers of my skin until he reaches the very core of my existence, perhaps what religious people call the soul. I know there are some people who could dismiss what I feel, impatiently, as "just sex," but this is more than sex. This is an inexorable longing, something over which neither of us has any control.

He is waiting for me. Reading a report from Washington—I can tell by the cover—and I wonder how long he's been here and what excuse he has given to get away. But I don't ask. To ask would be to cross a forbidden boundary. I don't want to know what lies he tells Steffi.

As I enter the cave, Jacob looks up and smiles, then puts his hand over his lips and leads me back to the entrance to the cave. He points into the distance, and I see two figures rummaging in the ruins. When I squint I realize they are carrying pillowcases and searching among the shards, discarding some and putting some into their pillowcases. They are a white women and a young Indian. Something about the woman looks familiar.

"Who are they?"

"Dunno," Jacob answers, then shrugs and adds in his normal voice, "Whoever they are, they're breaking the law. These ruins are protected and everything in them belongs to the government. If they're caught, they'll be charged with felony." I stare at the pair again, and then grope in my pocket for my sunglasses.

Of course the woman is familiar! It's Mrs. Windom. I can feel the laughter surging through me. That proper, compulsively clean and considerate woman, that self-righteous, insufferable bore who seemed absolutely above reproach of any kind, who is the worst snob in the world—anti-Semitic, anti-Indian, anti-Negro—is no more than a common thief. Now I can hear Mrs. Windom's voice reporting her day's progress: "I did the bathrooms this afternoon, they're so clean you can drink out of the toilet bowl," she would tell us, her face filled with rapture and pride. "Virtue is its own reward," was one of her little homilies. And what about stealing? I'd like to ask her now. Or isn't that as bad as a dirty house?

"It's Mrs. Windom," I tell Jacob and explain who Mrs. Windom is. Then I turn to watch them sift through the shards, pick up what they want. At one point Mrs. Windom gives a howl of delight that reverberates through the ruin, then turns around guiltily as if she knows someone may be watching her. I can feel my eyes narrow as I plan how to confront this horrible woman.

But when I catch Jacob's eye, he shakes his head. Of course he's right. I can no more confront Mrs. Windom than I can admit why I'm here and how I caught her stealing. To do that would be a virtual confession. Then I wonder, irrationally, which is worse: adultery or stealing?

I hear myself sigh as I put my sunglasses back into my pocket. I'd like to tell Jacob how helpless, how furious, this makes me feel, but when I look into his gray eyes I know he already knows.

Yet suddenly I'm angry at myself for being here, for being in the wrong, so much in the wrong that I can't speak up for what is right. What I should do is leave, leave now and never come back to this dark, comfortable cave again, never make love with this man who is now waiting so confidently for me to come into his arms, never again walk out of here with the smell of sex so strong on my body that when I get home I sometimes think I'll never get it off. For the smell of illicit sex sometimes seems a stain as tenacious as blood, and even when I have carefully washed myself and removed the diaphragm that I have used so assiduously since that first time, I still feel covered with the evidence of that compelling, almost frightening sex whose smell sometimes lingers for hours, even days, in my nostrils.

But I don't leave. I can't leave, because I have become bound to Jacob in ways I never knew were possible, in ways I don't know how to break.

And, besides, this may be the last time.

When it is time to get back to The Hill and our office, Jacob says, "I have a car and we are going to Santa Fe. I have to drop something off for Thea." About a mile down the road is Noel's car, and we get into it as casually as if we were a married couple setting off to work. Or as if we were what we are—a scientist and his secretary, the wife of his colleague, going to drop something off at Thea's office.

We talk of ordinary things, and anyone listening would find it hard to believe how we have spent the last few hours. There is not a shred of evidence in Jacob's face or bearing of his real self—his tender, needing, passionate, confident, even arrogant self. So I stare at this profile, not really listening to what he's saying, wanting only to touch him to let him know what I'm thinking. But that, too, would be crossing a forbidden boundary.

Thea's eyes light up when we enter her office. Jacob hands her an envelope from Oppie. "Wasn't that a wonderful performance of *The Cherry Orchard*? Really the best play we've had so far," she says with absolute sincerity. But I really can't agree, for watching Tom and her fall in love on stage as poignantly as they have in real life had made *Candida* the unforgettable performance people still talk about. And she doesn't even realize it.

She looks radiant. Her love affair with Tom has transformed her in subtle yet important ways. But perhaps that's what love is supposed to do—transform. Thea carries herself with a pride and confidence she didn't have when we first arrived. Watching her dig something about the housing costs for Jacob from her files, I wonder if my love for Jacob has changed my appearance as well. Sometimes I search the mirror for telltale signs. Our lovemaking is so urgent, so intense, almost violent at times, that I can't believe some evidence of it hasn't been imprinted on me, but I can't find anything. And no one has remarked about any difference, but the real test is yet to come—when Peter comes home. If there is any change, Peter will notice it, and for the first time in all these weeks, my throat constricts with panic.

Then Thea turns to me. "You must be so pleased that Peter's

finally coming home. It's been such a long time for both of you," she says sympathetically, her eyes filled with admiration. Any sacrifice from the women on The Hill gets special kudos from Thea.

I avert my eyes and mumble a vague assent. Then, thank God, we say a quick good-bye.

When we reach the car, a man is eyeing it. A tall man who would be handsome if he weren't so unkempt. His clothes look as if they had been slept in for several nights; in fact he resembles pictures of hoboes I saw as a girl, when the Dust Bowl was always in the news. Now the man has thrust his hand deep into his side pocket for something, but when we approach the car he looks startled. Of course! The man recognized the car and is waiting for Noel. But before Jacob can explain, the man lopes away as noiselessly and quickly as a frightened deer. As he goes, I have an irrepressible urge to follow him and explain. I even start to follow him. But then I stop. I can no more explain to this man than I could berate Mrs. Windom. When our eyes meet, Jacob simply shakes his head and shrugs.

We start to get into the car, but then Jacob puts his hand on my arm. "Not yet. Let's go to the Plaza. I want us to buy something for you, something together, I want you to have something . . ." His voice grows hoarse, and I realize that his throat is filled with tears. Tears of sorrow, anger, frustration? Tears that we must no longer meet, tears that we aren't married and must sneak around like this? "Something we pick out together," he concludes. We shouldn't go, it's foolish to take such a chance, and I start to say something, but when I see the determination in his eyes, I simply nod.

Once after we made love, when he was still inside me and I could feel the steady thrum of his heart next to mine, I wondered how many women he had slept with. Was I just one among many— was it possible that Jacob was a philanderer, a Casanova, a man who couldn't keep his hands off women? But then I dismissed it; I must be crazy; how could I think such a thing? For this wasn't just any man; this was Jacob, brainy, wise, witty, talented, responsible Jacob, the man Oppie trusted as much as anyone else, the one who asked all the right questions about the gadget, whose eye for detail pushed this project along in the exact direction it needed to go, who didn't let personalities and pettiness come into play when he had to make a decision, who had the respect of men younger than he—like Peter—and men older than he—like Erik and Oppie. And yet . . . but weren't there always "and yets" in a situation like this one? I didn't know. I had never been in a situation like this one.

But as soon as I see the uncharacteristic confusion on Jacob's face and hear his fragmentary sentences, as soon as I glimpse those frustrated tears welling up in his eyes, I know that whatever has happened to us is as important to Jacob as it is to me. My heart spills over with relief as I hurry down Palace Avenue after him.

The Plaza hums with activity: tourists eyeing the jewelry and crafts, the Indians gossiping among themselves, their placid, noncommittal faces breaking into occasional smiles or frowns. How different they look to me now, for I've grown used to them, I've learned to understand their silence, their laconic ways. A woman from Santa Clara smiles at me and nods at Jacob, though she knows he is not my husband. I smile back at her. It isn't really all that strange for me to be walking around the Plaza in Santa Fe with the man I work for. No one, not even these monogamous Pueblos, regards it as a crime.

Jacob is heading for the jewelry. "There's a man over there"— he points diagonally across the Plaza—"who makes wonderful things."

As we cut across the Plaza, I feel Jacob's reluctance to touch me, even to guide me with his hand on my elbow, and now my eyes well up with tears. Here we are, going to find a memento of our time together, and we must do it quickly, deviously, so no one will suspect the truth. How blithely people talk about the lure of the forbidden, how casually they remark that illicit love is enhanced by secrecy. They're crazy to think that, and they can only think it because they've never been in our shoes.

I've seen this jeweler's work before. Peter found him soon after we arrived and wanted to buy something for me, but I couldn't decide on anything and he didn't want to pick it out. "Your choice, darling," he said while we gazed at the earrings and bracelets and rings. But it was too confusing. So we never bought anything. I look warily at the Indian standing behind his wares, but he gives no sign of recognition. My heart seems to expand in my chest. Only for a few moments, though.

For suddenly, appearing from nowhere, is Thea. Bright, smiling Thea, holding in her arms a large envelope she had forgotten. "It needs to go back up to The Hill," she explains. Trusting, capable Thea who looks at us fondly, then says, with a twinkle in her eye, "I'm so lucky you had an errand to do—this really saves someone a trip. Picking something out for Steffi's birthday, Jacob?" Such a thoughtful man, Jacob, taking Lily with him to make sure he will get Steffi something a woman would appreciate. It is all there in Thea's eyes as she has joined our little conspiracy.

I'm not sure if I will faint or vomit. I hold my stomach and lean against a column of the Plaza. I want to leave, but of course we can't, so we stand there looking at the jewelry until Thea disappears into the crowd. But when I turn to Jacob, I see he's still determined and refuses to be cowed by Thea's appearance. And that even though I feel awful and look pale, he will not leave this Plaza before I choose something.

The most beautiful thing on the display tray is a bracelet, a free-flowing bracelet, adorned with an interesting combination of onyx and mother-of-pearl. "Awanyu," the Indian tells us. Of course. The plumed serpent of Tsirege, the feathered and horned serpent who is pictured on some of the San Ildefonsan costumes for the dances, the snake that throws himself across the sky, the water serpent who guards rivers and streams, D. H. Lawrence's mysterious, erotic, and ambivalent symbol of the life force.

As Jacob hands it to me, I see that the stones have been arranged to catch the sun like a snakeskin and that if you examine it closely you can see the round snake's eye. But I cannot wear that exquisite, flamboyant bracelet on my arm; I'll never be able to field all the questions and admiration it would cause; I simply don't have the courage for such brazenness.

So I put it down and pick up a simple, carved sterling-silver bracelet. Wide and handsome, it is as conservative and safe as everything else in my jewelry box. The very opposite of the erotic Awanyu piece, which makes me think of Jacob's fingers and lips on my shoulders and breasts and hips, and his tongue deep in my mouth, his sex inside me. I sometimes dream of making love with Jacob and wake up shuddering with bliss, yet unbelievably exhausted, but the exhaustion is nothing compared to my feelings of loss.

It would be a mistake to let Jacob buy the Awanyu bracelet. I'll never wear it and I don't want it in my jewelry box. I can feel his disappointment as I place the Awanyu back on the tray, but I stubbornly press my lips together. I cannot wear a bracelet that would be a daily reminder of this love that has overwhelmed me so completely, this love that makes me feel as if I were living in the midst of battle, in danger of being shot or suffocating to death.

I glance at the Awanyu bracelet one last time and ignore the Indian's shining-eyed pride in his work—how can you resist something so beautifully enticing, Missus? those eyes ask me—then I pick up the wide, safe, elegant bracelet beside it.

What I don't know then is that I will wear the silver bracelet Jacob is now paying for almost every day of my life after that. That it will be the first thing I put on in the morning and the last thing I take off at night, that my arm will become so used to it that it will feel naked without it. And that, even with the passage of years, long after the dreams have stopped, I will regard it not as a memento, but as a warning.

16

● ● ● ▬

Jacob and I didn't know that we had bought that bracelet on D day until later that night, after we returned to The Hill. All through May Hitler had been warning his generals, with uncanny clairvoyance, "Watch Normandy!" But they thought he was wrong, so the German high command was very surprised on June sixth when the Allies made the greatest amphibious assault ever attempted, in the words of its commander, Dwight Eisenhower. More than 150,000 Allied soldiers and 1,200 warships, 1,500 tanks and 12,000 aircraft were initially involved in the attack that finally penetrated the defensive Western wall that Hitler and his generals had so carefully created.

When the news that Hitler and his cronies had been caught short started to come over the radio, the excitement was palpable; the air was buoyant with joy, really glee. And even when the reports of the casualties, which were heavy, came in, spirits refused to be dampened. For here, finally, was the turning point in the war.

A few hours later I could feel a tingling in my hands when I heard Peter bounding up the steps to our apartment. They had been delayed, the train was late, and now it was past midnight. Nervously I glanced in the mirror near the front door, but all I saw was Lily—me, Lily, ordinary, dark-haired, dark-eyed Lily, Peter's wife, Lily. "You know, the small, thin girl with those enormous chocolate eyes, who works for Jacob Wunderlich," someone once described me a few weeks after we arrived. In the mirror there she was, same old Lily, nothing new or different. Whenever I caught a glimpse of myself, I was glad that my parents had named me for a beloved aunt with the simplest of names. "Lily of the valley," my father used to call me when I was a little girl. The flower that heralds spring and is as profuse as a weed. Nothing rare or exotic about it, or me.

"Oh, darling, you look wonderful, absolutely wonderful," he murmured again and again as he gathered me into his arms.

I had not even tried to predict how I would feel, and now I was dumbfounded: Jacob seemed to belong to a different life, a different me, and all that had happened while Peter was gone had receded to a place as far removed as the moon, a place reserved for the wildest fantasies or the most forbidden memories. But certainly no place as real as Peter was now.

Surely this was the weirdest feeling I had ever known, but just as surely this was the mind's protection, the mind's way of not forcing me to face what had happened too soon. As the weeks passed I wouldn't continue to be so lucky, but at the moment of Peter's return from this long trip, on the night of D day, I still felt like two people: the Lily I had known all my life, who belonged to Peter, and that strange volcanic creature who had fallen in love with Jacob. I lived from moment to moment. What might happen to me was something my mind did not—perhaps could not—grasp.

Peter and I talked and ate and slept together and made love, just as we always had since our marriage. Strangely good love, I realized, certainly better than what we had had in the months before this trip. Did he wonder about it? Or notice that I was taking more initiative? I didn't know. If he did, he kept it to himself.

"I don't trust talk about love," he once told me. The only time I ever heard him mention love publicly was during a discussion with Herb and Mark. He said he had believed when he was a student that there were mysteries in physics that would never be solved—like the mysteries of love—but that now, it seemed, he might be wrong. Those mysteries in physics were coming clear. And the mysteries of love?

So no talk about love. Or about anything different. That wasn't Peter's style. Nor had he noticed the bracelet until several days later when I told him—without a tinge of guilt—that I had bought it from the jeweler whose work he had liked.

And yet I knew Peter loved me more than ever before, and there were times when we sat across from each other eating our dinner and I could feel his purplish eyes devouring my features, my gestures, the way my clothes hung on my body. Such protective, trusting love. Love that allowed no suspicion. Not even a suspicion that there might be another kind of love.

When I caught Peter looking at me like that, I felt utterly safe and happy. Jacob might have been some apparition, the product of a feverish imagination. But then I would go to work and feel Jacob's eyes on me, piercing my clothes, my skin—seeing through me, almost. I could feel my heartbeat quicken with what surely must be lust. But I did nothing to change the situation. And although there were days when I felt I was about to choke with unhappiness, I continued to work for Jacob, to long for Jacob, and to be a wife to Peter. Those were the days when I would have liked to ask Peter: Oh, my darling, do you know how mysterious love really is?

The dirt and dust at Hanford in Washington State were legendary, worse than anything at Los Alamos, people said, though we never believed it. Yet when Peter came home, I was convinced. I could feel it on his arms and face when we greeted each other; it had crept beneath the beard he had begun to grow, it formed a film on his clothes that I thought I could never remove. Even after he had shaved and showered a few times (guiltily exceeding our ration for water), he complained about the grit in his eyes and ears, and when I made our bed those first few days I would sweep out stray clusters of sand.

As annoying as they were, the inconveniences of life at Hanford were relegated to a minor place when compared to the amazing engineering feats that were being accomplished there. "It's a rough town, Lily," was all he would say when I questioned him that first night, probably because he knew he would have to go back. Yet I could see that beneath the tiredness there was a profound sense of excitement and relief. What Peter had found this time at Hanford had lived up to, perhaps even exceeded his expectations.

"What they have done is monumental, Lily, more complete than anything we could have imagined." For he and Fermi had found a second gigantic factory where they were making the ingredients that might lead to the completion of the gadget.

At Oak Ridge they were extracting the fissionable and rare Uranium 235 from the more plentiful, nonfissionable Uranium 238. At Hanford they were working to extract the new transuranic element, plutonium, from Uranium 238.

Plutonium was discovered by Emilio Segrè, Glenn Seaborg, and Joseph Kennedy at Berkeley in 1940 when they bombarded uranyl nitrate hexahydrate, a solid uranium compound, in the cyclotron with the hope of transmuting some of it into neptunium. Instead they discovered a second transuranic element, a byproduct of neptunium, which they called 94 239, since it was the ninety-fourth element. What made 94 239 so valuable was its ability to undergo fission when bombarded with slow neutrons. Two years later it was officially named plutonium. For the ninth planet away from the sun, Pluto, and also for the Greek god of the underworld and death.

A few days after his trip to Hanford, Peter admitted that all the rumors about the place—the violence, the prostitution, the bleak-ness—were true. "People say it's the closest thing to Hell. Or maybe . . ." He rubbed the side of his cheek with his palm, a sign that he wasn't quite happy with the analogy. "Or perhaps more like limbo, Lily." But absolutely and totally necessary. Of that we were all convinced. For now, more than ever before, this was a race.

What was amazing, if you thought about it, was that thousands of people were working in those two huge factories at Oak Ridge and Hanford to produce critical masses that would weigh about a pound each. When the war was over, everyone understood what the critical masses were and exactly how they worked. By then we had not only seen the films of Hiroshima and Nagasaki, but had also suffered our own devastating loss here at Los Alamos. Still, while we were at Los Alamos—as well as for the rest of my life— whenever I thought about the gadget I would always be flabber-gasted by the destructive possibilities of those two masses: each no bigger than a bunch of grapes.

• • •

The weekend after D day several of us met at Pamela's. By now the implications of D day had begun to sink in. While we gloried in the Allied victory, which grew more decisive with each passing day, we also worried. Would these repeated defeats through France force Hitler to press for the completion of a German atomic bomb? The mood that night was more somber than I had expected.

Tom, especially, seemed upset. Usually so unflappable, he kept turning his wine glass in his hands or running his hands through his blond hair. I edged my way over to him and Thea while Peter was talking to Noel and Herb. "You have no idea what a maniac he is," Tom was saying. "I saw him when he visited Kassel. I was a small boy. He looked like a monster, and his voice sent chills down your spine. He went through the town on a horse, whipping it for the least hesitation. The horse was more human than he was. If he gets desperate, who knows what will happen? He'll push every physicist in the Reich to create a weapon."

Then he looked meaningfully at Steffi. Tom knew she didn't think Hahn and the other German physicists wanted to be responsible for creating a weapon. He thought she was dead wrong. Thea looked around nervously. She hated to hear us argue; it didn't go with her vision of what should be happening on her Hill. And, luckily for Thea, Steffi refused to rise to Tom's bait; she merely looked away while someone poured more wine.

But at least there was news from Erik. After that catastrophic encounter with Churchill, he had spent some time with his family in the English Lake District and now was back in Washington. His son, Axel, was with him. In his early twenties, Axel was also a physicist and was going to Princeton in September to do graduate work.

When Erik arrived in Washington, he immediately reported the dismal outcome of his meeting with Churchill to Felix Frankfurter. Like Erik, Frankfurter wasn't easily fazed. He had great faith in Roosevelt's ability to be fair, to listen. He also understood what Erik believed so completely: that the development of an atomic weapon would put the world in a completely new situation, one that could not be resolved by war. When they talked, Erik was emphatic: "This weapon is a far deeper interference with the natural course of events than anything ever before attempted. It will completely change all future conditions of warfare."

"Why don't you write a memorandum to FDR saying just that?" Frankfurter said.

Erik holed up in a Washington hotel with Axel. The streets were like a sauna; so was their room. Now Erik knew about the Washington summer. How could anyone think in this sultry air? Erik mused out loud; his son recorded his thoughts. They talked endlessly while Erik mended their clothes. Early in July they delivered the completed memorandum to Frankfurter.

Then they went to Princeton, where Erik saw Einstein and other old friends and got Axel settled for the academic year. A few weeks after Frankfurter submitted the memo to Roosevelt, Erik was on his way back to Los Alamos. When he arrived, one of the first things he said to Pamela was, "I hope Roosevelt will realize that openness, not secrecy, is required. An unprecedented openness, which needs the vision not only of statesmen, but of scientists as well."

"That's why he had to return to the States," Pamela admitted to History and me a few days later. We were picking wildflowers near Otowi. She told us only the bare outlines of what had happened. For these were secrets too momentous to be revealed in any detail even to friends. Observing Pamela's caution, I realized how lonely Erik must be—having to leave his family to accomplish his unique mission, yet not being able to share it with others.

Still, I knew that if I were to question him, he would reply, "It's not all that bad, Lily, for at least I can come back here where there are people who have sympathy for what I believe."

Sympathy. It seemed a key word when Erik said it. But time would reveal that there wasn't as much sympathy as he thought.

When we saw him at Pamela's house the next Sunday, Erik looked older, wearier. Still, his eyes lit up at the sight of us. Approvingly he took in History's maternity clothes, then narrowed his eyes when he observed me.

"Have you changed your hair, Lily? You look different." He stared at me thoughtfully. "No, it's not your hair. Still, something's different. I can't put my finger on it. But I'm glad to see you both looking so wonderful. You two are—how do you Americans say it?" He looked at us quizzically, then his eyes twinkled in triumph, as they always did when he had mastered one of our idioms. "You two are a sight for sore eyes." We all laughed, and slowly the tiredness in Erik's face began to dissolve. We sat there in congenial silence, eating lemon cake from a new recipe Pamela had tried, and sipping that strong, espresso-like coffee that was unlike any coffee we had ever tasted.

How shrewd, how observant Erik was. He had sensed a change, and Peter had not. But I couldn't even think about it. For at this point Jacob seemed to have happened to someone else, someone I didn't know or even want to know.

So instead of thinking about what Erik had said, I began to conjure up a vision of Erik talking to Eleanor Roosevelt. If he could get to her, she would surely listen. In my mind I could see them talking, her beloved, homely face leaning toward Erik's to hear him better, her famous high voice answering his low one. If only they could talk, perhaps she could somehow soften the blow Erik had suffered at Churchill's hands, and make Franklin see.

For hadn't women been crucial on the road we were now traveling? Madame Curie, Lise Meitner, and the few women physicists who worked here on The Hill? I knew only one, Leona Wood, but she had gone out to Hanford soon after we arrived. Why not a woman to help make policy as well?

When we walked home, I mentioned it to History. Slowly she shook her head, but her voice was gentle. "No, Lily, I don't think so. The days of Queen Elizabeth are over. Women don't make policy in the twentieth century."

● ● ●

After Dietrich Bonhoeffer had been in the prison at Tegel for a year, he sensed a change in his situation. The first few months in Tegel had been spent in interrogation. Then in July 1943 a charge had been pronounced against him: "subversion of armed forces." He waited hopefully for a trial, for he believed that there was no real evidence against him. Yet nothing definitive happened. Dates for trials were set and canceled.

At the end of a year at Tegel, Bonhoeffer wrote a report on prison life that, like many of his letters, was smuggled out to his family and friends through the kindness of some sympathetic guards. He described the poor conditions, and his discomfort after almost two weeks when the authorities became aware of his family connections. His mother's brother, Paul von Hase, was the City Commandant of Berlin. After that he was placed in a large cell, offered more rations, which he always refused, and the luxury of a daily walk. "The little man with no connections, etc., has to submit to everything," Bonhoeffer wrote, and then described the lack of food, space, privacy, lights (the warders were too lazy to turn them on), occupation (there was no work or religious services or games, and only three books a week were allowed each prisoner from a "mediocre library"). Casual violence from the warders was also something that the little man had to endure.

Yet there was nothing desperate in the tone of this report, for at this time Bonhoeffer knew, from the letters in code he received from his family, of a plot to overthrow Hitler and his government, and he had every hope that soon not only his jail term but those of his fellow prisoners would be at an end.

In May 1944 he wrote his thoughts on the day of the baptism of his grandnephew, Dietrich Wilhelm Rudiger Bethge, the son of his niece Renate Schleicher and Eberhard Bethge. It gave comfort not only to Bonhoeffer's fiancée, a young woman named Maria von Wedemeyer, but also to his old parents and brothers and sisters.

We have grown up with the experience of our parents and grandparents that a man can and must plan, develop, and shape his own life, and that life has a purpose, about which man must make up his mind, and which he must then pursue with all his strength. But we have learnt by experience that we cannot plan even for the coming day, that what we have built up is being destroyed overnight, and that our life, in contrast to that of our parents, has become formless or even fragmentary. In spite of that, I can only say that I have no wish to live in any other time than our own. . . .

We thought we could make our way in life with reason and justice, and when both failed, we felt that we were at the end of our tether. We have constantly exaggerated the importance of reason and justice in the course of history. You, who are growing up in a world war which ninety percent of mankind did not want . . . are learning from childhood that the world is controlled by forces against which reason can do nothing; and so you will be able to cope with those forces more successfully. . . . We may have to face events and changes that take no account of our wishes and our rights. But if so, we shall not give way to embittered and barren pride, but consciously submit to divine judgment, and so prove ourselves worthy to survive by identifying ourselves generously and unselfishly with the life of the community and the sufferings of our fellowmen.

And then, among the quotations he included was this from Psalm 30: "Weeping may tarry for the night, but joy comes with the morning."

Dietrich's letters home and to his nephew-in-law, Eberhard Bethge, were cheerful, hopeful, and, as always, filled with energy and intelligence. On June thirtieth he wrote to Bethge about a visit from his Uncle Paul von Hase and said, "I hope we shall be together again early in the autumn." Like his brother-in-law, Hans von Dohnanyi, who was also imprisoned, Dietrich was banking on the forthcoming putsch to release him.

The putsch was masterminded by Klaus von Stauffenberg, a member of the German aristocracy, a brilliant, handsome young man who had become a professional soldier. When the war began, he fought enthusiastically in Poland and France. But when he was sent to Russia, Stauffenberg became disillusioned with the brutality of the SS and the increasing cruelty toward the Jews, Russians, and prisoners of war. Then in April 1943 he was severely wounded when his car drove over a mine field. He lost his left eye, his right hand, and two fingers of his left hand, and also suffered injuries to his left ear and knee.

Most men would have retired from Army service after such an ordeal, but when he knew that he would live and see, Stauffenberg became determined to overthrow Hitler and his Nazi government. He convinced many highly placed German officers of the rightness of his cause—among them Paul von Hase and Admiral Canaris, who was head of the Abwehr, the German bureau of Military Intelligence. A plan was developed that would involve not only the assassination of Hitler, but the takeover of the government by the conspirators. They called their mission Valkyrie, after the maidens in Norse mythology who were supposed to have hovered over the battlefields deciding who would be slain.

Thursday, July twentieth was hot and sultry. Stauffenberg, now a colonel, flew to Hitler's "Wolf's Lair" at Rastenburg. In his briefcase were papers concerning new Volksgrenadier divisions on which he was to report to Hitler, and, wrapped in a shirt, a time bomb made in England. It could be set off by breaking a glass capsule whose acid then ate away some wire, which released the firing pin. The whole process would take ten minutes, but how could a man with only one hand that was missing two fingers do what needed to be done? Stauffenberg solved the problem with a tong he held in his three fingers, and with which he could break the capsule.

He went to the meeting with General Keitel, Hitler's loyal Chief of the Armed Forces, but just before they started out, Stauffenberg pretended he had left his cap and belt in the anteroom of the general's office. When he went back to it, he opened his briefcase, broke the capsule, then closed his briefcase.

"We're late," Keitel shouted as he approached, and they hurried into the conference room. Hitler was listening to a report and playing with a magnifying glass, which he needed to read the maps before him.

"Colonel Count Stauffenberg," Keitel said.

Hitler gave the younger man a curt nod. He would get his chance to speak shortly.

Stauffenberg sat down and put his briefcase inside the heavy support of the large table at which Hitler sat, six feet from Hitler's legs. There were five minutes to go. While Hitler and his aides bent over the map, Stauffenberg slipped out of the room.

No one noticed, but after Stauffenberg left, a General Brandt tried to get closer to the map and discovered that the briefcase was in his way. He shoved at it with his foot, but it was too heavy, so he picked it up and set it down so that now the heavy support of the table was between the briefcase and Hitler.

The reader of the report droned on. The room seemed to grow hotter with each word. By now Stauffenberg was with another conspirator a few hundred yards away. At precisely 12:42, to the second, the bomb went off. There was no doubt in Stauffenberg's mind that everyone in the conference room had been killed.

But Stauffenberg was wrong. Although several men were killed, several badly wounded, Hitler had only been slightly hurt, his hair singed, his right arm bruised, and his back injured by a falling beam. And Keitel was not even hurt.

When Stauffenberg returned to Berlin, still believing that Hitler had been killed, he discovered that none of the mechanisms for the government takeover had begun. Confusion reigned. And though Stauffenberg began to give orders, it was too late. Generals who were straddling the fence refused to throw in their lot with the conspirators once they learned that the Fuehrer was still alive. Keitel realized that Stauffenberg was the culprit, and the SS moved quickly. At one o'clock the following morning Hitler addressed the German people over the air. "If I speak to you today it is first in order that you should hear my voice and should know that I am unhurt and well, and secondly, that you should know of a crime unparalleled in German history." He then went on to name Stauffenberg as the planter of the bomb and to denounce the conspirators as a "gang of criminal elements which will be destroyed without mercy."

• • •

Most Americans had very little interest in the July twentieth plot. By now the idea of any "good Germans" seemed an oxymoron. But to someone like Steffi the news of the failure of the conspiracy was something else. For the putsch was the Bonhoeffer family's last hope: Dietrich's older brother, Klaus, had participated in planning it, and they all hoped that it would free Dietrich, Hans von Dohnanyi, and Rudiger Schleicher.

When news of the putsch's failure appeared in *The New York Times* Steffi rushed to our office. The newspaper hung from her trembling hands. "Where's Jacob? I must see Jacob." Her voice was harsh, frightened, yet commanding.

We had all heard the news on the radio, but here in the newspaper were the details of Hitler's rage and determination to kill not only each person connected with the plot on his life but also their families and every other individual who had conspired against him. That, of course would mean Dietrich Bonhoeffer. "No mercy!" Hitler's venomous voice had proclaimed.

Over my lunch I had read whatever I could find in the newspapers about the conspiracy, and Jacob and I had discussed it before he went to a meeting with the head of the Theoretical Division, Hans Bethe, and Oppie. Yet here was Steffi, as if she were the only person in the world who knew this terrible news.

She reminded me of a wounded bird. Her natural grace had disappeared; her movements were spasmodic, sick. The newspaper hung from her hands as she stood there, staring at me.

"Do you know what this means?" she began, but didn't wait for an answer. "This means that that maniac has won, that he will kill everyone in Germany who has ever conspired against him. Dietrich and Hans von Dohnanyi and the others, all the ones who could create a new Germany. And that all who will be left will be the old people and women and the Nazis, Nazi scum who don't understand anything about Germany and its history." She stopped, and I thought she was waiting for me to say something, but then she went on.

"How can you understand? You're an American, you were born here, and you have no notion of what I am talking about. It's ridiculous to try to make you see; the only person who understands this is Jacob. Jacob knows—and he knew what I was talking about then, but he wouldn't listen. No, he thought Dietrich was a dreamer, a philosopher, and he wouldn't listen or go back. But if we had gone back, we and the other people who believed as we did, there wouldn't have been these Nazis and the SS and the concentration camps—or any of it!" The walls of the small office seemed to quake as her voice rose, higher and higher. I lifted my head in the hope of stopping her, but she became more and more frantic— a wounded bird caught in a house, flailing from wall to wall in an effort to escape.

"We would have been able to stop it—I know we would have. There were Germans who would have listened to reason, they just needed more people in that conspiracy, better leaders. Instead we were cowards, we fled like mice, and now we're here in this vile place, when we should have been there . . ."

Her voice trailed off into a wail, and, exhausted, she almost fell into Jacob's chair. Her eyes were filled with such rage and desolation I could hardly look at her. Then she began to read randomly from the paper, scraps and snippets about how determined Hitler was, how merciless his plans were. Her voice came from some strange nether world; it quivered with tears and anger, and I suddenly realized that I had to stop her, that I couldn't let her go on and on, like a madwoman.

I stood up and snatched the paper from her hands. "You can't believe that Hitler will win. He's lost already. The Allies are moving across France, and the Russians are coming from the east." My voice was cold. "And you had no choice but to come, otherwise you would have died." Utterly cold and reasonable. Facts. They were cruel, and so was I.

I expected her to argue, but at the sound of my voice her whole being seemed to click into place, and the Steffi now rising abruptly was the Steffi I knew: a tall, statuesque woman in control. She took the newspaper from me and walked quickly out of the office. If she said good-bye, I didn't hear it.

If Jacob had been here, I would never have seen what I did that summer afternoon. And now I knew what no one needed to know: that this was not a marriage between equals, that he lived in a place worse than Hanford or Los Alamos or Limbo, that he was consigned not only to a crazy triangle of Noel, Steffi, and him, but also to a marriage filled with paranoia and bitterness.

I wished I hadn't seen it; there are some things no one needs to see, things too private to be revealed. I felt violated by what I had seen, as if I had watched them make love.

Yet now I knew why Steffi flung herself so fiercely into those theatrical performances, and the book list Jacob and I had been reading. Or why she had taken on more hours of teaching. She needed to be too busy to think about Dietrich or about Germany. Until, maybe, her firmly held hopes would come true. But now those hopes had been dashed; she was broken by reality and would never be the same again.

Jacob returned a few minutes later—fifteen minutes that might have made all the difference, I thought as I told him Steffi was looking for him. Something about my face must have alerted him; he didn't even reply, just hurried out.

The next day he came to the office looking years and years older than the man who had met me at Tsankewi or had bought the bracelet for me in the Plaza or had baited me in Rockefeller Center. A man at war with himself. My heart turned over when I saw him.

Each day grew harder and harder for us. I yearned to touch him, nothing more. Such a simple thing, touch. Yet so powerful. Everyone talks so much about sex, but is that so important? Some days all I wanted was to put my hand on Jacob's arm to comfort him. And there were times when I wished I hadn't seen Steffi that day, for then I might not feel so sorry for him, for them both.

But then I thought: wasn't it better that I knew? And in some way, didn't this new knowledge absolve me a little?

17

. . . ■

When Peter returned from Hanford, he learned that the implosion experiments were going poorly. Like a patient who refuses to recover.

Kistiakowsky had been hired by Oppie to get implosion moving. Instead, Kistiakowsky felt he had become an arbitrator. "On one side is Parsons, a Navy Ordnance man, who never had any faith in implosion, and is as conservative as the Daughters of the American Revolution." Kistiakowsky's voice held a trace of snideness. "On the other side is Seth Neddermeyer, brilliant and thorough, but he putters around in the lab as if he had a lifetime to figure this out. I can't work under these conditions. I think I should resign," he told Oppie. "Or," he added, "maybe Neddermeyer can pursue the scientific and technical aspects more vigorously but dissociate himself from all administrative and personnel matters. He's a fine physicist, you know."

Oppie knew. But he valued Kistiakowsky too much to let him go. In mid-June Oppie presented *his* solution to the problem: Kistiakowsky would be fully in charge of the implosion work under

273

Deke Parsons. Neddermeyer would become a senior technical adviser to the group.

Neddermeyer was angry and left the meeting before it was over. "I wish he had gotten screaming-yelling mad," Peter told me later. "But he doesn't seem able to allow himself that luxury."

I listened. Everyone talked about Neddermeyer with great respect. They all knew he understood implosion better than anyone else—it had been his idea after all—yet now they had taken it away from him. I couldn't understand it. And although I didn't know him well, I hated to see Seth retreat into a silent and enduring bitterness.

Still, Oppie's decision was probably the best one, and in light of events soon to come, it seemed prescient. Because of the properties of plutonium and the way it responded to neutrons, they concluded that there was no feasible way to use plutonium in a gun assembly. A plutonium bullet and target would melt down and fizzle before the two parts had time to join, even if they approached each other at something like 3000 feet per second.

"No go on a plutonium gun," Oppie told Groves on the telephone. His voice was weary. "And the uranium gun is very unwieldy. Now we've got to figure out implosion, it's the only hope we have, the only way we can go ahead."

Groves sighed in disappointment. Fortifying himself with some chocolate-covered mints, he called Washington. "Bad news," he began.

Oppenheimer became visibly depressed. His weight, which was never high, began to fall. Pamela sent chocolate cake, lemon pie, coffee cake, up to The Hill with Estevan's nephew almost daily. Jacob used every spare minute he had to get Oppie out to walk and talk. You could see them at dawn or dusk taking a few steps, then stopping, gesturing, and going on. All the way to the nursery school, then to the laundry, and then on the outer road that led to the icehouse, around Ashley Pond and past the firehouse to the administration building. At a distance you might have thought they were men walking for exercise, as you sometimes see them today, almost forty years later. But when you got up close, there was no tinge of relaxation in their faces or their bodies. These were men under pressure, incredible pressure.

Jacob looked exhausted. Oppie wanted to resign. "He can't resign, Lily, there's no one else who can possibly do this job," Jacob said to me, his voice rising more in frustration than anger. I was amazed. Oppie, who looked more sure of himself than anyone else in the world, needed to be reassured. So people took turns, walking and listening and reassuring. I wished Erik were back from Washington. Patiently Jacob and several others, including Peter, met with Oppenheimer, and finally he agreed to stay.

He called a meeting of all the group heads. He announced that he was creating two divisions from Parsons's Ordnance Division. One was to be called G (for gadget) under Robert Bacher to investigate the physics of implosion, and the other was X (for explosives) under Kistiakowsky to perfect explosive lenses, which were necessary to successful implosion methods, the ones Peter and Jacob had explained so carefully to me.

Parsons was furious. He never forgave Oppenheimer or Kistiakowsky. Not only for being relieved of his command, but for the fact that they, as civilians, could do what they pleased, without his military approval.

"But Parsons has plenty to do without implosion," Peter told me. "And Bacher's good." Peter's interest in plutonium had placed him on the periphery of the implosion experiments. "Besides, Deke is also in charge of designing the uranium gun assembly." And I knew that Deke Parsons was more and more important in the life of The Hill. He and his wife, Martha, had slowly taken over many of the social responsibilities at Los Alamos. Kitty Oppenheimer wasn't really interested. A complicated, high-strung woman who drank too much, Kitty was hardly one's idea of a Hill hostess. But Martha was.

"So Deke will have to content himself with that, and the uranium gun," Jacob said when he gave me his version. His voice was so reasonable. As if responsibility at Los Alamos were not a political scramble, but a large pie, with a piece for everyone.

● ● ●

At the end of the day we were required to burn the carbons of anything we had typed. Each office was equipped with a little wire basket to do the job, and the smell of burning carbon signaled the end of the day around The Hill. Jacob usually waited for me to do it—I suspect there was some directive from General Groves on that—and then we locked the files and could leave. Simple, straightforward, safe. Until one afternoon in the middle of August.

The heat parched our bodies, as if our blood, saliva, sweat had dried, and we were, like the Tin Man, in need of oil. I longed for a sponge bath, then saw myself stretched out on our bed, wet and naked and cool. I glanced at my watch. In fifteen minutes I would have my wish.

Quickly I stuffed the paper into the basket, then lit a match. As I looked at it, the wall behind seemed to quiver, part of a mirage. Then sudden, intense heat on my neck. I looked down. The paper leaped into flames higher than the basket. I stared, unable to move, at the tongues of flame in my hands. Then I cried, "Jacob!" not daring to let go of the basket, for I knew that if I did the dry wood of this office and all the ones adjoining it would soon be crackling with the sound of a spreading fire. Everyone's nightmare.

Jacob wheeled around to face me. Without thinking, he simply hurled himself at me, stemming the flames with the sheer bulk of his body. In his hurry he knocked me down, and now we sat on the floor, the basket smoldering between us.

As soon as I saw the fire was no longer threatening us, I lifted his shirt, ragged with burns, to examine his chest. My hands moved slowly, gingerly, in the silence. I could feel his eyes studying me as I concentrated on my task, yet I couldn't bring my eyes to meet his. The hairs on his chest were slightly singed—so were his eyebrows, I realized when I looked briefly at his face—but nothing more than one small burn that was now beginning to blister on his rib cage.

"It's a miracle you aren't hurt," I said as I removed the rest of his shirt. By now we were standing; we had allowed ourselves to take a breath, and in the silence I could hear the last gasp of flame shudder to blackness in the basket. I walked around him, fingering his chest and back and shoulders as if I were blind.

He stood there patiently, then asked playfully, "Are you satisfied, Florence?"

But I didn't think it was funny. "It's a miracle," I whispered, staring at his naked torso, avoiding his amused eyes. "An absolute miracle."

At that point I should have fled. That would have been the wisest, safest thing to do. He didn't need me. He had an extra shirt in the bottom drawer of his desk—which he kept in case he was called to a meeting with the big boys—and all he had to do was put that on and stop at the hospital for some burn ointment, and the incident would be over. Another close call at Los Alamos.

But neither of us wanted the incident to be over. If I had, I would never have touched him so thoroughly, nor would he have stood there so patiently. And now when we finally looked at each other, I saw a younger Jacob, my Jacob, whose eyes were bold, taunting me, daring me.

"I'll meet you in the Loretto Chapel in an hour," he said. It was half-question, half-command, another point at which I could have simply left.

I frowned, then nodded. In a split second I seemed to have stopped thinking. I felt like a robot.

"You can get a ride if you go to the gate. With Noel." Of course. It was Tuesday—Noel's night out.

I called Peter and said I had to go to Santa Fe to do a special errand with Jacob and I didn't know when I'd be home. "But don't wait up," I added awkwardly.

"I'm not making any promises. See you later, Lily." Peter's voice had a cheerful ring to it.

I didn't speak very much on the ride down to Santa Fe, and Noel didn't press me. That was one of the nicest things about Noel. You never had to apologize for anything with him, and if you preferred to look at the sun sliding through the sky spreading its deep umber tones across the Espanola Valley, you didn't have to explain.

The Loretto Chapel, the Chapel of Our Lady of Light, is a small Gothic chapel built by the Sisters of Loretto, the first religious women to come to New Mexico. I first saw it with History when we were exploring Santa Fe during our stay with the Windoms, and a few weeks later I dragged Peter to see it.

According to legend, the chapel was started in 1873, and only when it was finished did the Sisters realize they had neglected to build a staircase to the choir loft. They prayed to Saint Joseph for help. Soon after that a stranger arrived in Santa Fe. He said he was a carpenter and offered to build the Sisters their staircase. They gave Saint Joseph their thanks as they watched the carpenter fashion a remarkable spiral staircase made entirely of wood, without any screws or nails, yet with two complete 360-degree turns to the loft above. And utterly sturdy and safe.

The Sisters of Loretto and the citizens of Santa Fe were astonished by this feat of engineering, yet before anyone could question him, or even pay him, the carpenter disappeared. The staircase became as much of a puzzle to structural engineers as the sudden appearance of the carpenter was to the Sisters of Loretto. For both of these reasons, it was known as The Miraculous Staircase.

Today the chapel was almost empty. The ten or so people in it were singing the last few notes of evensong. But what a good choice

Jacob had made: the rubbed wood surfaces of the chapel had a soft, soothing effect. I looked around, taking in not only the remarkable staircase but the strong lines of the Gothic arches and the white altar and the pearly lights around it. Slowly that inner tumult I had been feeling since the flames licked up the wire basket quieted. I stood there thinking of nothing.

But then there was Jacob's swift step across the floor, and his arm on my elbow. We hurried down the Santa Fe Trail to a taxi Jacob had kept waiting. The neighborhood began to change. Well-cared-for adobe houses with well-planned and carefully watered gardens gave way to a genteel shabbiness, disrepair, and a wild profusion of weeds. I had wondered where the poor of Santa Fe lived; when the cab pulled up in front of what looked like a down-at-the-heels adobe rooming house, I knew.

Still, this was no time to be fussy. What we needed was here: four walls where we could be alone, away from prying eyes. We turned to each other, the aura of our desire already filling the small grubby space; I felt faint with relief that now, finally, we could make love again. Then I thought about that fine distinction I had made only a few weeks ago between touch and sex. Of course I had been lying to myself. Touching was nothing compared to this.

We fell asleep as if drugged, our bodies wet with sex and sweat. When I woke up, I let my eyes take in the cobwebs and dust and filmy mirror, the lumpy bed and the rough, maybe even dirty sheets. This was no rooming house; this was a whorehouse.

I could feel an irrational anger surging through me. And indignation as well. How could he do this to me? But he had done nothing to me; I had done it to myself as soon as I agreed to meet him. He had done the best he could, had found a place where no one would know us or even care who we were.

My eyes found the window. On the hard floor at Tsankewi I would sometimes daydream about making love with Jacob in a room, a freshly washed white curtain billowing toward us as the breeze touched our temples and throats. That puffy curtain, like a sail luffing at sea, seemed the height of luxury. But this window was covered by a flapping, tattered shade, so browned by sunlight it looked burned in spots.

Now Jacob stirred as my fingers grazed his forearm. His eyes widened as if in a dream. Then he, too, looked around the room, but he merely shrugged, as if to say, it's not wonderful, but it will have to do. As usual, he refused to waste energy on what he couldn't change. I sighed and stared at the peeling ceiling. But when he turned toward me, gathering me again into his arms, I knew that, given the chance, I would come here again.

I got home around ten. Very official, in an Army car, and then Jacob walked me to our apartment. We had gone to La Fonda for something to eat. That was part of what I was to tell Peter, part of my alibi, I thought grimly as I walked up the steps. Jacob had had to meet someone at La Fonda and I had had to take notes.

Peter was sitting at the kitchen table. His eyes were tired, but they filled with pleasure when I walked through the door. On the counter he had rigged for me near the sink was a sandwich. I could see its outline under a damp dish towel. One of the tricks Pamela had taught us for keeping things fresh in this heat.

I don't know why, but it was the sandwich that somehow did me in. As I stood there, then sat down and answered his questions, which were discreet, for he had as much respect for my job as I did for his, I went over in my mind the picture of him slicing the bread and making the filling and putting together that sandwich. It was an act of love and trust. Absolute, ingenuous trust. I stared at it, yet all I could think about was how to get into a shower before Peter came too close to me.

But I knew I should eat the sandwich. I knew I should stay here and listen to him talk about his day. Sheets of calculations covered the table: equation upon equation slashing the pages in his bold, sure hand. I used to tease Peter that if physicists ever wrote love letters they would be in the form of mysterious, coded equations.

And now, as I looked down, I knew that those calculations were a love letter to me, for he had sat there doing them in order to be up and waiting when I returned.

Still, how could I sit there and pretend? That seemed worst of all, so I heard myself say, "I'm too exhausted to eat, darling. I'm sorry, it looks like a wonderful sandwich, but I'll take it for lunch tomorrow." Then I pleaded a headache and avoided his arms when he held them out toward me. Quickly I retreated to the bathroom, where I turned on the shower, washing all evidence of Jacob from my body, grateful that if Peter should come in and wave to me while he brushed his teeth, as he sometimes did when we were getting ready for bed, the water running down my face would mask the tears of shame that were welling up in my eyes.

$$\bullet \ \bullet \ \bullet$$

Frédéric Joliot-Curie, Marie Curie's son-in-law, had remained in France after the Germans invaded. Many people—at Los Alamos, in England, in France—believed he was a collaborator with Marshal Petain's Vichy government and that he had surrendered his laboratory to the Germans. Yet it was he and an Englishman who had made sure the United States got twelve hundred tons of uranium in 1940. It didn't fit. And whenever his name came up, Erik was quick to say, "We don't know the whole story."

The Allies entered Paris on August 23, 1944. Two days later, on the twenty-fifth, Samuel Goudsmit and the Alsos mission went to see Joliot-Curie, certain that they would get some badly needed information on the progress of a German atomic bomb.

To their surprise, they discovered that he had had very little contact with the Germans, who had virtually left him alone, and that his laboratory was a front for the French Resistance. Amazing. Here was this soft-spoken scientist who knew people were accusing him of treason, yet he had never bent to the temptation to tell the truth. This was a unique kind of courage, they wrote to Groves.

By now General Groves was irritable with impatience. What were the Germans up to? How he'd love to know! He had pinned his hopes on Alsos. But nothing. He was so disappointed that he got angry when he reported the news to Oppie.

"How can you be angry at a man like Joliot-Curie? A man so audaciously brave?" Oppie asked. Groves shrugged. "That's crazy, General," Oppie added. Looking sheepish, Groves finally agreed.

Alsos also reported that they had located thirty-one tons of uranium at an arsenal in Toulouse. But that was only a small part of the thousand-plus tons of uranium the Germans had confiscated when they invaded Belgium. What had happened to the rest? That was another part of the puzzle of the German atomic bomb. A puzzle not yet solved.

A day later, the twenty-sixth of August, Erik Traugott had his long-awaited meeting with Franklin Roosevelt in Washington. They were alone. Unlike Frankfurter, Roosevelt did not jot down notes on a pad. He depended on his memory.

He sat somewhat listlessly in his wheelchair, but he leaned toward Erik and listened to his hesitant voice. He told Erik he didn't need a short course in physics. He knew about fission and Hahn and Meitner and Frisch. He also knew about Hahn and the two younger, brilliant German physicists, Heisenberg and Weizsächer.

When Erik said, "The knowledge being explored at Site Y is by no means exclusive," Roosevelt nodded. His mouth flattened into a grim line. So far no one seemed to know how far the Germans had progressed in making their own weapon.

Then Erik paused. He straightened a little, and suddenly Roosevelt realized what an impressive-looking man he was, what extraordinary eyes he had, and what a large, well-shaped head. "The most important and pressing fact is, Mr. President"—Erik now spoke more surely—"that a weapon of unparalleled power is being created that will completely change all future conditions of warfare." Almost verbatim from the memo Traugott had sent FDR.

"Churchill says it's just a more powerful bomb," Roosevelt replied softly, his voice almost hopeful.

Erik shook his head. His eyes were beginning to blaze with anger and frustration. Why did Churchill pretend to know more than he did? "No, Mr. President, if you'll forgive me for saying so, the Prime Minister is wrong. This is a weapon of completely new materials, it is totally unlike conventional forms of warfare, and far more dangerous. Quite apart from the question of how soon the weapon will be ready for use and what role it may play in the present war, this situation raises a number of problems that call for most urgent attention. We must reach some agreement about the control of the use of such weapons."

Roosevelt sighed. Churchill wasn't having any of this kind of talk. But he could hardly share that with Traugott. He gestured him to go on.

"Any temporary advantage gained by being the first to develop this gadget, as Oppenheimer calls it, will be outweighed by the dangers this weapon presents to the human race. Dangers that we have never before known."

"They said that about gunpowder," Roosevelt said, a vague weariness creeping into his voice.

Erik shook his head. "This is far more lethal and dangerous than gunpowder." Then he went on to describe an open world for atomic research.

"You know scientists, and especially atomic scientists, have enjoyed very good international relations before the war, because of Rutherford's Cavendish lab and Ehrenfest's mathematical training center at Leiden and the work that was done at Göttingen and at our institute in Denmark," Erik added. "These same scientists could forge this new openness between nations, but they must begin now, while the discoveries are still being made, when it is all new and we are all fighting for the same cause. Later it will be too late."

"So you think we will win, Professor Traugott?"

"I know it. And I also think Oppenheimer and Groves will develop the gadget before the year is out. They are doing unbelievable work. Oppenheimer is remarkable. So, in his way, is Groves. That is why I am here. You must act now, because when the war is over each country will be interested only in its own future."

Roosevelt smiled.

"You think I am naive, Mr. President?" Erik asked.

Roosevelt nodded. "Yes, but there's nothing wrong with that. Naiveté sometimes goes further than cynicism." His voice was quiet, but its tone was respectful. It was that tone of respect that gave Erik some hope. As he walked from the White House into the muggy Washington afternoon, his heart lifted a little.

Soon after his meeting with Erik, Roosevelt spoke to his advisers and they incorporated some of Erik's ideas in a report they issued a few weeks later. When Erik returned to Los Alamos from that mission to Washington in late summer, he seemed more content. He told Oppie that he thought Roosevelt might even consider sending him on a mission to Russia. But even if that didn't happen so soon, he had been allowed to speak his mind. Plainly. Truthfully. The right people would surely listen.

Now he would simply have to wait.

• • •

Peter went back to Hanford with Fermi and a few other scientists from The Hill a few days before Rosh Hashanah. I went to services with Herb and History. There were more people here than last year. It comforted me to be here, to see Herb praying with the same kind of enthusiasm my father had for these ancient phrases and melodies. Despite the war and the gadget and their baby's death, despite everything, Herb believed fervently in the existence of God, and here, at this makeshift service in what amounted to little more than a shack in the desert, he, too, was comforted.

For me the holiday was a chance to think. I had come to a crossroads. No longer could I separate the Lily who was Jacob's lover and the Lily who was Peter's wife. There was only one Lily and the time had come for her—for me—to face the consequences of what I had been doing.

A few days before this I had imagined telling History everything; I had the feeling that if I could say the words out loud, then perhaps I could think a little more clearly about what they meant. But when I was standing there, next to History, who was pregnant again, I knew that I wouldn't tell her or anyone else. This was one thing I would have to figure out by myself.

I knew—quite simply and clearly—that I had to end my affair with Jacob. For that was what it was. An affair.

But when I met Jacob the following Friday afternoon, for we had quit work early, it was not so easy. As soon as I entered the cliff dwelling at Tsankewi, my brain seemed to fly out of my head, and all I was left with was my senses. As soon as he touched me, I felt totally helpless, wax in his capable, knowing, loving hands. The last rational thought I had, as we were shedding our clothes, was that perhaps I wouldn't feel anything, that somehow a part of my brain would not succumb. But by now Jacob knew very well how to arouse me, and our lovemaking was as it had always been. Afterward I fell asleep, a strange sleep, a numb sleep too deep even for dreams.

The next thing I knew he was shaking me. I was astonished to see that I was lying naked, under the blanket Jacob had brought. I had never slept here before, just dozed now and again, and I couldn't believe I had slept so soundly.

"It's time to go, darling," he told me, then held out my clothes. He was already dressed. "I hated to wake you, but it's getting late, and cold."

I nodded and pulled on my clothes. He folded the blanket and tucked it under his arm. When we left, I turned for one last look at the cliff dwelling; my flashlight revealed its undulations and shadows and the few faint cave paintings that were still visible. Probably done by Pueblo children, people said. And then I slipped out of the mouth of the cave into the amber dusk. Jacob was right. The dark came more quickly now; soon the shadowy path would be black.

I went slowly. Jacob was several yards ahead of me. Without his hand to guide me, I clicked on the flashlight. Suddenly I had the sensation of being watched, and when I turned, I met the impassive gaze of Estevan, who was standing near the highest point of the ruin with a pair of binoculars in his hand. I knew that the Indians had gotten wind of the pilfering of the ruins and that they had established a vigilante system. But if I had not used the flashlight, I would probably not have been seen, for our cave was off to the side and tucked under the main part of the ruin, out of the sight line of the watch guards.

I was too astonished to avert my eyes. I had never dreamed that anyone would find us out, especially here. But now in the autumn twilight our gazes—mine and Estevan's—were locked together. It must have been only for several seconds; it felt like minutes. Not a word or a nod was exchanged, but I could feel the utter contempt in the Indian's dark eyes. Then, slowly, he turned away.

I hurried to catch up to Jacob, who didn't seem to have any idea what had happened. My throat was choked with humiliation. I put my hand to my neck, as if that might help me swallow, for I had the sensation that I might never swallow again. A strange, debilitating vertigo swept over me, but it passed as quickly as it had come, and I got through the slit from Tsankewi, hugging the wall to keep my balance.

That night I dreamed of Tsankewi. I was in our cave and next to me was a bucket and a scrub brush. I looked at Estevan and he gestured toward the bucket. I got down on my knees and began to scrub the floor. Estevan stood over me as I scrubbed, inch by inch, the floor of the cliff dwelling where Jacob and I used to meet. I could hear voices of people I knew—Jacob, Steffi, Mrs. Windom, Pamela, History—but I couldn't make out what they were saying or where, exactly, they were. Estevan was silent, and so was I. A crushing silence that seemed to cover us as I moved slowly on my hands and knees, scrubbing that floor, until I reached the mouth of the cave.

18

The next day, a Saturday, dawned bright and clear. Such an innocent swath of blue sky, it seemed to stretch to infinity. I dressed and ate breakfast and tidied up the apartment. I was supposed to go to Otowi for lunch, but now that was out of the question. Though I knew Estevan would not betray me, I also knew I couldn't bear his knowing silence.

Still, I couldn't stay here. The emptiness pressed against me. As odd as it might look, I had to get out of this apartment until Peter returned. If I didn't leave here, I might be tempted—again—to meet Jacob, and that I could not do.

Where could I go? My friends were all expecting babies: History, Bess, and now Kate, quite far into her pregnancy with her fifth child. The last thing any of them needed was me. And I knew I could never convince Housing to let me move into the women's dormitory. "Why on earth would you want to live in one of those cells when you have that whole apartment to yourself?" an incredulous voice would ask. "Are you crazy?" Besides, it was hardly practical. Peter was due home in ten days.

But I was determined not to stay. So I went down to Palace

Avenue to see Thea. I didn't know how much I would have to tell Thea, but I knew that somehow she would help me.

What would it take to unsettle Thea? She knew something was wrong the moment she saw me. I told her some of the truth—that I was desperately lonely and having trouble managing without Peter. She didn't blink an eye, but merely nodded and said, "I was wondering when it would get you down. The other women who have been left alone for stretches of time have children. I'm not surprised, and it's nothing to worry about. Pack some things and come down to my place for a while." As if it were the easiest thing in the world.

Thea's house was a rambling adobe house on the edge of the main section of Santa Fe. The guest room was austere but comfortable, and in it I felt as if I had left my life behind and had only to take care of myself. I slept better there than I had for weeks, maybe months. Each evening an Army truck would wait for me and take me down to Thea's, and in the morning another truck would wait for me at Thea's office on Palace Avenue and take me to The Hill. Most evenings Thea and I had dinner together; sometimes Tom would join us.

Even when I was in my room at the back of the house, I would know when he arrived; his amazing whistle reverberated through the rooms. Usually some great choral work: the *Messiah*, the Mozart Requiem, a Verdi aria, or his favorite, the "Ode to Joy" from Beethoven's Ninth. Since he and Thea had fallen in love, his tireless energy had intensified, so that the air around Tom seemed to crackle like sheet lightning. Sometimes he stayed for a meal, sometimes only for a drink, though I knew that he often returned and spent the night.

He never discussed what was going on in the canyon lab, but his eyes would shine with excitement when Thea asked him how his day had gone. And then they would joke and chat, like a married couple. No angles at all, just beautiful interlocking curves. It was a pleasure to watch them, and when I was in the kitchen with them, I thought about Peter and our marriage, about marriage in general. After a week or so, I asked Thea if they had considered getting married.

She lit a cigarette and smiled at me through the smoke. "You always get to the heart of the matter, don't you, Lily?"

I shrugged. It didn't seem such a strange question to me. And yet she wasn't offended. Just amused. "We've never discussed it, if you can believe it, Lily. I'm so different from you, I never push my luck. It seems such a miracle that . . ." Her voice dwindled; she couldn't really say it; she was afraid that if she uttered the word *love* something disastrous might happen. It was like asking for the evil eye; my mother acted like that all the time.

"You don't have to explain, Thea, I understand. Why, my mother—"

"No, you don't, Lily," she broke in. "You couldn't possibly understand at your age what it means to someone like me who thought that part of her life was over forever, to have Tom— young, intelligent, handsome Tom—fall in love with you. It's beyond comprehension. Which is why I can hardly talk about it." She shook her head. Then, "For years I never thought about this sort of thing. My first marriage had been a disaster, and we never divorced—I didn't press for one because that part of my life seemed over. But my husband died soon after Oppie gave me this job, and then I met Tom, and suddenly everything was different. Maybe when all this is over, maybe then we can think about it. . . ." She shrugged, still afraid to mouth the words.

When Jacob asked me why I was staying with Thea, I explained that I was tired and needed a change of scenery. Nothing more, even though we had planned to meet during Peter's trip to Hanford, and I knew he had to be disappointed. But I couldn't tell another lie. I was done with lying.

Jacob didn't question me further. It was clear that he thought all I needed was time, which we had. I never knew if he'd seen

Estevan watching me at Tsankewi, and I never asked. For Estevan wasn't the problem. Estevan merely helped me see the problem.

• • •

More than a hundred miles east of Mount Rainier, at just about the point where the immense Columbia River bends westward to form the boundary between Washington and Oregon, were the Hanford Engineer Works, which was one of the largest installations in the Manhattan Project. Peter had been there in June with Fermi, then the two men went again early in September.

Although Peter hated Hanford itself, he loved the opportunity to spend time with Fermi, who was one of the most exciting men here at Los Alamos. Cool and calm on the outside, Fermi had a mind that seethed with ideas the way a volcano churns lava; you never knew what he would come up with next. When they got to Hanford that September, he immediately wanted to see the salmon, and on their first afternoon there they went to a nearby dam installation to see the famous Pacific Chinook salmon swimming madly over the ladders, up the man-made falls, to return to their birthplaces far to the north. For that is where the salmon must do their spawning.

And even at the end of their trip, dejected and upset, Fermi was still game for something new. They spent their last day at Hanford watching an amateur rodeo, complete with bucking broncos, cursing riders, and scantily clad rodeo girls.

I heard all about it later. But when Peter returned to Los Alamos and hurried along the path to my office, the last thing on his mind was Hanford. Someone he met at the gate had told him I was staying with Thea, and he was worried, sure that something had happened to me. That, added to his exhaustion, made him look terrible. When he opened the door, I was so frightened by his appearance that all I could say was, "What's wrong?"

"That's what I'd like to know," he replied. "Why are you staying at Thea's? What's happened?" There wasn't time to answer. For as soon as he saw that I was all right, he vaulted over my desk and pulled me from my chair into his arms. I was astonished. Proper Peter, behaving like a cowboy. But, then, he hardly looked like himself. He hadn't shaved since he'd left Hanford, and the stubble on his face made him look tired, but younger, reckless, rough, almost. Like those characters who were supposed to be at Hanford. I buried my head in his shoulder. He smelled of dust and travel. But how good to feel his arms around me.

"You're all right?" he kept asking.

"Fine, fine," I replied, startled that I had frightened him so much. Then I whispered, "Just a little lonely, and it seemed better to go to Thea's."

I wasn't quite sure how to respond to his searching gaze. Did he suspect something? But before he could ask another question, Jacob came out of his office.

"Why Peter, how are you?" His voice was guarded, but his smile was warm.

"Fine, fine, but the question is, how is Lily? They gave me a fright at the gate when they said she was staying with Thea."

"I just needed to get away," I murmured, my eyes lowered.

Jacob wasn't rattled at all. "Did her good to go to Thea's. It can get lonely on The Hill, you know," he said, his eyes resting fondly on Peter and me. The older teacher, the father figure.

How can he have such aplomb? I wondered. I averted my eyes from them both, ashamed.

"Good trip?" Jacob asked Peter.

"Okay," Peter said tentatively, and I thought they might talk. Instead, Peter took my hand and said, playfully, without his usual reserve, "You don't mind if I spirit this girl off before quitting time?"

"Of course not," Jacob said, then stood there and watched us from the door of the office. His gray eyes were steady, as usual, but sad. That strange, ineffable sadness that had drawn me to him in the first place.

As Peter and I walked, I could feel Jacob's eyes on my back, but that hardly mattered. Nothing mattered now. Peter and I were going home. Where I belonged.

Our apartment had the air of an abandoned friend. While Peter showered, I went through it with a dust rag, but there was no way I could get a meal together. The food I had left in the refrigerator had spoiled, and the commissary was about to close. Quickly I wrapped up the moldy food in newspaper, chagrined that I had been so wasteful.

"We'll have to eat out," I said sheepishly when Peter appeared with a towel around him. "I guess I get failing marks for house-keeping this trip."

"Of course we'll eat out," Peter said. "We'll even sleep out," he said, his eyes glowing. "It's time for a celebration."

We ate a leisurely dinner in the dining room of La Fonda, talking mostly about the mail that had come while Peter was gone. Peter ate heartily and smiled a lot, but without the stubble on his face, I could see how tired he was. Sooty circles under his eyes, and an occasional, almost imperceptible twitching of his left shoulder. He was exhausted. When we got into the room, it was his turn to be sheepish. "All my big plans," he said as we undressed. "I'm wiped out," he explained, and was asleep before I came out of the bathroom.

He looked so vulnerable. I touched his shoulder—just to touch him, to reassure myself that, yes, he was there—and he stirred a little and reached for me. We slept with our arms around each other.

At dawn we were awakened by noises drifting from the kitchen. Then, finally, Peter told me, in a whisper, what had happened at Hanford. His voice was flat, as if he were lecturing his colleagues at a Colloquium.

The enormous pile, the largest pile on earth as far as we knew, went critical just as they'd hoped, producing the predicted chain reactions, which would, in turn, produce the badly needed plutonium. But then it died.

"Absolutely fizzled, with not a trace of warning. Zap. Nothing. Imagine, Lily, the first plutonium-producing reactor in the world. Hundreds of uranium rods and fifteen hundred aluminum tubes with the rushing waters of the Columbia River flowing through them to cool them and everything working, and then—kaput. Nothing. Dead."

He stopped, remembering. "And then the next day it started up again, no reason, just started spontaneously, which was really strange, but everyone went nuts with excitement. They said the failure was a fluke, that this time it was really working. Fermi was beside himself with joy. But within twelve hours it began to die again. As if it had a mind of its own. It was horrible. Like watching someone you love fade away. You could smell the disappointment as you stood there." He shook his head; it was still unbelievable even here, hundreds of miles away.

"It was crazy, and frustrating, but I'm glad I was there. I had heard about Fermi at work under pressure but had never believed it. He's amazing. I've never seen such powers of concentration. He sat there with a yellow pad and made calculation after calculation, as if the rest of us didn't exist. Finally he looked up and began to ask questions. Then we realized what had happened.

"There are poisonous byproducts of uranium in a pile, and Fermi realized that they were absorbing neutrons, which meant the chain reaction couldn't continue and the pile would die. That explained the first fizzle. Then when the poisons decayed to a point where they couldn't absorb neutrons anymore, the pile started up again, but only for a limited time. Then the absorption process started again, which caused the second fizzle. It's a vicious circle. But once Fermi had sorted it out, we knew we were on the way." For the first time in this explanation Peter smiled.

"We thought the poisons were Xenon, and after Fermi and John

Wheeler did some calculations, they called the Argonne lab and checked it out. Sure enough, they were right." Peter's voice sounded as if he were describing a bad detective novel.

"They called Los Alamos, and Groves went nuts, screaming into the phone, 'What the hell is Xenon?' Over and over. Like a crazy man. Like one of those people who think everything you do in science is infallible. Finally Fermi cut it short and said he'd call him back.

"Then we realized that we were saved. Wheeler had worried about poisons when they were building the pile, and had been able to convince Du Pont, who built the pile, to increase the number of uranium channels for a margin of safety. So they have essentially what they need to prevent the poisons from building up, and now all they have to do is hook up the extra channels to the water supply, and they'll be able to get it running again.

"It wasn't only what Fermi calls details. Some detail! Over forty thousand people working there, and the pile goes dead. Still, that wasn't what was so scary. It was the tension and the anger when they thought it wouldn't work. Watching and listening to them, I realized more than I ever had here on The Hill, how high the stakes are in this game we're playing, and how uncertain the outcome is. Not the weapon. No, I think a weapon will be made." He stopped and looked deeply into my eyes, as if to assure himself I had heard every word.

"But here on The Hill we think we have some control over what will happen to it, and the fact is that we're only a small part of this operation. And not nearly as powerful as we think. When you see how many other people, how many other powerful people there are running this show—well, it's pretty scary . . ."

He turned to me, a frown between his brows, his eyes as worried as I had ever seen them. "I can't explain why, but it frightened me. Yet it made me understand Erik's passion. If you're not relentless in pursuing what you believe, like Erik is, the whole thing can run away from you."

Hosea, my father had said, "What will you do with the whirl-wind?" But I didn't say anything. Peter had said it already.

Then, quickly, he sat up and looked at me from beneath troubled brows. "It's like standing on quicksand—you never know what's coming next. If it's scientific, we can deal with it, but if it's political"—he hesitated—"that's when it gets dangerous. None of us are politicians. Just because we met other physicists at international conferences and there was some rapport—well, that's not politics, and besides, that was before the war. Now it's different. And I'm not sure people here really understand that." Peter shook his head.

"You know, Lily"—now he grinned, his eyes deepening with the pleasure of coming to a satisfactory conclusion—"it's a little like Heisenberg's uncertainty principle. The minute you know one kind of measurement, another becomes uncertain. The closer we get to the weapon, the more unsure the other elements in the picture become."

Then he leaned back into the pillows and shrugged, as if to say, the lecture's over. I replied, quietly, "But you did what you went to do. You figured out how to get the pile going."

He nodded. "Yes, but it will take months. Months we don't have. That's why Groves went so crazy." Then he looked at the pale adobe-colored walls, the imitation Navaho rug hanging in the corner, the patterned drapes, as if seeing them for the first time. He frowned. "I can't believe we're finally away from everything and everybody and haven't made love," he confessed.

I started to put my hand on his mouth to stop him; he didn't need to apologize. But he grabbed my wrist and held it; he seemed to need to say it all. "I had such big ideas when I suggested we come here. All I could think of on the trip home was making fabulous love with you, like a boy, but then it seemed more important to talk, and now I can't believe how tired I still am. . . ." His voice faded helplessly, and he smiled and gathered me close to him. We slept again.

When I awoke it was after nine. I knew I should wake him so

we could both go to work. But I couldn't move. I had to let him sleep as long as he wished, for I had never seen him like this.

I dozed a little, and thought, and dozed again. That restlessness that had plagued me even when I was asleep during these last months was gone. I thought about what Peter had said about the uncertainty principle. I knew what it was, both Peter and Jacob had explained it, but I didn't really understand it. I doubted that I would ever understand it the way they did. But now I was thinking of it because I had reached a moment in my life that seemed, even then, to sparkle with the brightest light. A moment when the uncertainties I had been living with for too long fell away and everything was suddenly clear.

Then I slept. As I opened my eyes, Peter was staring into them. For the first time since he had returned from Hanford, he looked entirely like himself. I could feel myself grow limp with relief. He started to bend forward to kiss me, but I stopped him and held his face in my hands. Then I said, too bluntly, as if I were making an announcement, "I think it's time to have a child." He didn't need to speak. Surprise and joy spilled from his eyes.

• • •

Over the weekend, for I didn't go back to work that Friday, I made a plan. In my mind I rehearsed what I was going to say to Jacob. I even wrote some of it down while Peter slept, then burned it in Black Beauty. When I walked to the office the following Monday, my palms were sweaty. I glanced at my watch, then told myself, in an hour this will be over. It will be finished, and I won't have to think about Jacob again.

When I got to the office, Jacob was reviewing some calculations. His glance was polite. He started to rise, then sat down again, when he saw me turn the lock in the door. A smile played upon his lips, and his eyes were alight with amusement. If I had let him speak, he might have said, "Have you come to seduce me, Lily?"

But I didn't let him speak.

"This has got to end, Jacob."

His eyebrows arched inquisitively, and he stood to face me. "It's wrong, and it's got to end," I repeated.

"Why? Why should something that gives us both such pleasure have to end?" His voice was smooth, confident.

"Because I love Peter, and this is wrong."

"I love Steffi, too, but this feels absolutely right to me. And to you, too, Lily." I didn't answer. "Besides, you don't love only Peter, you love me, too. And I love you, Lily." Now his voice was rougher, lower.

My head shot up.

"Yes, you heard me."

"You've never said it, never, not once," I said.

"Well, I'm saying it now."

There was a time when I would have felt pure joy on hearing those words. Yet not now. I was suddenly so weary that I wanted to sit down, but I knew I could not. If I sat down and he stood over me, I had the feeling that I might lose whatever resolve I had. I grasped the back of the chair across from him and said obstinately, "No, Jacob, it's over."

He frowned and his eyes grew soft. I felt as if he were caressing me when he looked at me. "I can't believe you want to give up something that is so right, so beautiful," he said. Then he sat down.

"Because it's wrong, utterly, totally wrong. And there's a difference between right and wrong. And you know it, and so do I." My voice was flat. I felt overwhelmed by a fatigue I had never before known. Still I didn't sit down.

"No, I don't. All I know is that we love each other, we're good for each other. Isn't that enough? Most people in the world would give a lot for that, Lily."

"But it's wrong. It's adultery, and wrong!" I lashed out, my voice shriller than I intended.

"Oh, Lily, you still believe in all that Old Testament nonsense, don't you?" His eyes sparkled, challenging me.

"I don't know what I believe in, I just know that it can't go on." Silence. His eyes grew serious, concerned. But when he spoke, his voice was its most persuasive. It reminded me of that day at Rockefeller Center.

"Look, Lily, be sensible. We care very much about each other, and for different reasons, we are both locked into marriages that don't satisfy us. But does that mean I must give up the best thing that has ever happened to me?"

I stared at him. How dare he compare my feelings for Peter to that hell he lived in? We had never discussed my marriage, and his marriage and its problems had nothing to do with mine. Did it?

I was so exhausted I dropped into the chair. Silently I stared at Jacob, but the more I turned his words around in my mind, the more I realized that his conclusion was perfectly logical. I had gone of my own free will to the cave where we had made love until we were drained, until we were covered with sex and sweat and could hardly move. Not once, but many times. And never a word until now of shame, or guilt, or any such thing. Just pure happiness.

So, of course, he thought what he did. What reasonable man wouldn't?

Yet he was absolutely, utterly wrong. Dead wrong. I loved Peter and would always love Peter. I couldn't imagine living without Peter. I had realized that when I stayed with Thea, and I had felt it when Peter returned. I could hardly manage when he was away. Which may have been why I got myself into this mess.

Yet, surely it wasn't so simple. For since I had come to this place I had had an odd, reckless need to play with danger, to assert my independence, to be something besides Peter Fialka's wife. And here, working every day with me, was Jacob—who needed to be loved. So I had loved him, as well as I could.

But to blame my marriage? No. It was I and no one else who was to blame.

I looked at Jacob. His eyes were a deep slate. He held out his arms. "Lily, darling Lily, how young you are. Don't you know that what we have is so precious . . ." He stopped. "You're so young, don't you realize that this is what people dream about? Why, we'd be the biggest fools on earth—this is something we could have all our lives. . . ."

I put my hands over my ears, exactly like the child he thought I was. Anything not to hear the rising desperation in his voice. Jacob was not a man used to pleading, yet here he was, doing just that. He had thought this would go on forever. Why not, Lily? I could hear History's reasonable voice say in my head, why would he want to give up such a good thing?

I shook my head, refusing to listen, and when he stopped, I said, "Don't cheapen it, Jacob—for God's sake, don't cheapen it." My eyes were brimming with tears of anger. And his? What did his tears mean?

I didn't stay long enough to find out.

• • •

When I was young, I imagined God as a stocky Uncle Sam or a bearded rabbi. When I was older, He was an amorphous, cloudlike figure with the features of Franklin Roosevelt. When I got to college, God seemed part of the curriculum, intangible, but rational and intelligent, perhaps present in that marvelous picture that hung in a classroom at Cornell of Hawthorne and Melville walking briskly through the Berkshire fields. By the time I married Peter, God no longer seemed to have a human form, but it was just possible that God was nature, or justice.

As one grows older one learns that there is no such thing as justice, or one logical punishment for each unforgivable sin. Some sins go unpunished and sometimes good people seem to suffer inordinately. Then what you once thought of as justice becomes luck, or chance. Or chaos.

At twenty-four, it is still possible to have a concept of order; thus, I was completely unprepared for the astonishing turn of events after Peter returned from Hanford in September.

When the nausea began, I went to the clinic, convinced I had caught the flu. The doctor could find nothing and smiled a mysterious little smile, then asked if I might be pregnant. Impatiently I shook my head. I knew my body.

Yet the queasiness persisted. A queasiness beyond anything I had ever felt. For at least a day and a half I was convinced I had gotten some terrible disease, maybe something Peter had brought back with the dust and grit from Hanford. Something no one had ever seen before. My mind became clotted with one dramatic anxiety after another.

Then, just as I was about to return to the doctor with some outlandish suggestion, I discovered that if I didn't let myself get hungry it wasn't so bad. I knew that was a sign of pregnancy, and I had certainly heard enough about pregnancy here on The Hill. I was also a little late with my period, but that had happened before. Besides, how can your body react so soon to an infinitesimal egg? It seemed impossible to me, but I felt a bit better, so I tried to ignore what was happening.

Only when History stared thoughtfully at me while we were having lunch and said, "You look so green around the gills—are you sure you're not pregnant?" did I suddenly realize what an idiot I had been.

I walked back to the hospital with her after lunch and had a test. A few days later she called, laughing. "The rabbits died. You have to come back for another test." The next time she called, her voice was high, excited.

"An Independence Day baby," the doctor announced. I stared, shaking my head. From the moment I had talked about having a child I had expected to have trouble conceiving. Wouldn't that be the logical punishment for loving Jacob? I had asked myself dozens of times. But no. I must have conceived about two weeks after Peter returned.

I couldn't believe my luck.

After Jacob and I parted—for that was what I called it in my mind—I was prepared to leave his office and go to work for someone else. I couldn't imagine working with him day after day. But he didn't agree.

"You'd be right if we were anyplace else. But we're here, and for you to leave this office now would create all kinds of problems, Lily, and draw attention to us in ways that we both don't want," he said. His voice was sensible, his manner businesslike. For after he realized that I could not be persuaded to change my mind about us, he had simply withdrawn.

What problems? I wanted to ask. Changing jobs or trying to explain why I could no longer work for him? But I didn't say a word and accepted his decision. Such a paltry thing as a love affair had no importance at Los Alamos, except maybe to me, I decided. Adjust, Lily.

One day a few weeks later Jacob looked at me and murmured, more to himself than me, "I don't know what I would do if I couldn't see you every day." His gaze held mine. Those steady, reasonable gray eyes. Eyes that people sometimes thought were cold. But what did they know? What did anyone know about another? I wondered in the silence. And then we went back to work, as if nothing had happened.

After that there were occasional awkward moments, times when one of us would leave to get a breath of air or take a short walk, times when it was difficult for us to be in the same small space. But we had made up our minds to manage, and there was really no choice.

Thus I learned that the human spirit is more resilient than I had ever suspected. In my mind I sometimes saw it as the leathery skin of a crocodile, toughened by a searing sun.

Besides, once I realized I was pregnant, my connection to Jacob began to diminish. It was strange, but as the weeks passed, I became mysteriously detached from everyone and everything except the baby that was growing inside me. Even Peter seemed to recede into the background. Finally I understood that sense of separateness I had observed in other women when they were pregnant. I felt totally alone, yet now my solitude was chosen, and necessary.

At first it frightened me. "It will go away after you begin to feel the baby moving," History reassured me. So I didn't fight it and merely focused on myself, my small household, and getting enough food and sleep. I wasn't interested in the new play, *Arsenic and Old Lace,* and although I could still feel a catch of worry in my breast when I saw History growing bigger, I wasn't as concerned as I had been when I first heard she was pregnant again.

Finally I understood the optimism History had felt the first time. Nothing, it seemed, could go wrong when you were in this state. I didn't even worry about the time I squandered—the daydreaming, the slow-moving reverie that sometimes overtook me. In some strange way I felt like a child again. A child with an incredible secret. For no one but Peter and History and the doctor knew.

My childlike contentment was disrupted early in November. One morning Jacob's eyes rested on the silver bracelet I had continued to wear. He was dictating a letter and hesitated midsentence, then stopped. When I looked up, his eyes were curious, his voice light. "Why do you still wear it?"

"I don't know," I replied. "I've tried not wearing it, but I can't. I feel naked without it." My voice was defiant.

Then, with no warning at all, he got up and turned to look out the window and said, "Steffi is expecting a baby in April. I wanted you to know before she started wearing maternity clothes."

I felt as if he had slapped me. Although I knew it was completely irrational, I felt betrayed. And hurt, and angry. Of course I knew he had been making love to her while he was meeting me; that was part of the bargain I had made, and I was guilty of no less myself. But to plan a child in the midst of our love affair—why, it seemed obscene.

When he turned to face me, he saw everything I was feeling. No longer were his gray eyes shielded by correctness. No, now we were going to be completely honest with each other.

"She felt me pulling away from her, and she decided she wanted another child. We'd been talking about another child before we left Ithaca, but after we came here, she refused even to discuss it. I was the one who kept pressing. I never wanted to have just one child. Then, at the beginning of the summer, she told me she'd changed her mind. As I said before, I think she felt the change in me. I don't know . . . I couldn't help it, Lily. It's what she wanted, and in a strange way it made it easier, she was so distracted, so turned in on herself, she didn't notice so much . . ." His voice trailed off.

Of course! Now that I was pregnant, I knew exactly what he meant. But still it was obscene. Or at least it felt that way to me.

Yet as I sat there watching Jacob's discomfort, I was again reminded that there is no morality and there are no rights when you are in the wrong. So, as horrified as I was, I knew I had no right to point out that there was something profoundly wrong about deciding to have another child with his wife while we were lovers, that my own decision to get pregnant had come only later, once the relationship with Jacob was over. No, that would only sound self-righteous. And besides, who cared? No one but me.

And now Steffi and I were expecting babies within months of each other. The irony of it should have been able to make me laugh. But I couldn't laugh or smile or congratulate him.

I couldn't even speak. I rose and put down my things and left. I walked quickly, pulling the cool November air as hard as I could into my lungs. Don't think, I instructed myself. Just concentrate on getting home. When I opened the door to the apartment, I surveyed the living room and then the kitchen and bedroom as if I were a stranger. From its neat appearance, the well-watered plants, the scrubbed-clean kitchen and bathroom, the fluffed pillows at either end of the sofa, you would assume that the people who lived here led orderly lives, exemplary existences. What a joke.

I threw myself on the bed and took the nap I would have liked to take every day. When I woke up about two, I was ravenous. I ate, then wrote Peter a note explaining that I had to work late; as I wrote, my handwriting sure and firm, I realized how easy it is to write quickly when one is telling the truth. And how much better I felt. Lucky, really, that I had had the instinct to get out before now. I could not imagine what it might feel like to have heard Jacob's news when we were still lovers. The thought chilled me.

When I went back to the office, Jacob had gone for the day. The next morning I went into his small office and stood over his desk and said, "I'm pregnant, too."

"I know," he told me calmly. His face was impassive.

"How?" Surely History hadn't betrayed me. Had Peter, in his excitement, said something? Jacob didn't answer.

"Who told you?" My voice was harsh.

"You did. In a dozen different ways you weren't even aware of." His voice was cold, matter-of-fact.

I sighed. And I had thought that in this atmosphere where secrecy was so prized, I would learn to be more guarded. But no, I was still the same old Lily. I want to ask, Tell me what I said, Jacob, tell me how you knew. But I also knew that there was no way he would answer me.

Though I knew it was an illusion, the office seemed to grow bigger in the ensuing months. And as the weeks began to pass, Jacob's shell of coldness, as stiff as armor, softened. We had been in love, after all, and it's hard for people who have loved each other ever to be strangers again. So we adopted a strangely formal attitude—something between a minuet and a waltz.

And when we met in public, it was as if nothing had ever happened. I was Lily, Peter's wife and a capable secretary, and Jacob was my avuncular boss who was sure he couldn't manage a day without me.

19

Peter sometimes talked about physics to the uninitiated, which meant me during the first few years of our marriage. He would put his head down, rub his palms together, then begin. "You understand, of course, that physics is a description of nature." That always made people listen, and once he had their attention, he would explain that in its simplest form nature is what you can see. But physics in the twentieth century is almost entirely focused on what is too small to see: atoms, and their fascinating, complicated properties. Tiny bits of matter that come together in the most astonishing ways. Unable to be comprehended, really, yet capable of what someone once called distant harmonies. "Beautiful, really. Mysterious and beguiling and beautiful, like music," Peter would conclude.

One of the most interesting things in physics is the apparent paradox between the way certain phenomena—like light—behave under different circumstances. The dis-harmonies, if you will. In many frequencies light appears to behave like a wave; in the higher frequencies it behaves more like separate pieces of matter, like particles.

Events have similarities to light. At some points in a life events seem to be a wave, with a beginning, middle, and end. Like falling in love with Jacob. At other points what happens seems more like particles, discontinuous and random. Like the fall of 1944.

Less than a month after Erik met with Roosevelt, Roosevelt and Churchill met at Hyde Park. Churchill expressed deep reservations about Dr. Traugott. He worried about his ties to other scientists, his friendship with Frankfurter, his desire for openness regarding the atomic weapon, particularly with Russia.

That made Roosevelt worry, too. Were Traugott and Frankfurter violating the security that was at the very heart of the Manhattan Project? Roosevelt didn't know for sure, but the whole thing made him nervous.

A few days later Churchill wrote Lord Cherwell: "How did Traugott come into this business? . . . What is this all about? It seems to me Traugott ought to be confined or at any rate made to see that he is very near the edge of mortal crimes. . . . I do not like it at all." Then: "The suggestion that the world should be informed . . . is not accepted. The matter should continue to be regarded as of the utmost secrecy."

Lord Cherwell was devastated. He and Sir John Anderson had sent Erik to the United States to convince the Americans that openness was the only course, and Erik had done his job superbly at Los Alamos and other installations of the Manhattan Project. They had even hoped that Churchill and Roosevelt would agree to send Erik on an exploratory mission to Russia.

And now Churchill was sabotaging their efforts. Worst of all, he was subtly persuading Roosevelt to side with him—to the disappointment of several of Roosevelt's aides. In their hearts, they knew that international control was the only sensible solution, and a treaty to maintain secrecy about the bomb between the United States and Britain, which excluded the other Allies, was utter folly.

Letters about Erik's ideas were exchanged between London and

Washington, but they merely made things worse. Neither Churchill nor Roosevelt wanted to listen to the views of Erik Traugott or anyone who agreed with him.

So Erik was dismissed. Again.

I heard the news at Pamela's. I had come to borrow *The House of Mirth*. Erik sat with Lord Cherwell's airmail letter in his hand for a few moments, as if afraid to read it. Then he scanned Cherwell's words. His hand trembled as he looked at us, then he began to read parts of the letter aloud, too upset to care that I was there. "Churchill says there is no need for Professor Traugott to concern himself further in this matter." Cherwell concluded, "There seems no hope of approaching the Russians now."

It was terrible to see Erik's disappointment. His face seemed to crumple before my eyes. I could hardly look at him. I fled.

After he had rested for a few days, he looked almost like himself again. In fact, he looked quite fine: a somber, thickset man, with mild, compassionate eyes. An ordinary man with the only clue to his intelligence a larger-than-average head. But if you knew what we knew, you could see that he had aged.

There was more bad news—a rumor filtering through official channels that Churchill and Roosevelt had also decided the United States and Britain would collaborate on the bomb indefinitely after the defeat of Germany. For the first time, Erik told us, there was talk of using the atomic bomb against the Japanese.

The bomb that had not yet been built.

• • •

The push across Europe intensified during November 1944, and on the fifteenth General Patton captured Strasbourg. Right behind Patton was Sam Goudsmit and the Alsos mission, still trying to uncover work on a German atomic bomb. Strasbourg was a key city, because Weizsächer had recently come there to teach. And Weizsächer and Heisenberg were the two German physicists who *had* to be at the center of any German atomic weapons research.

When Goudsmit and his aides hurried to the university, they were told, "Weizsächer left months ago."

"But we were told he was here," Goudsmit protested.

"Look for him if you wish," the university official said with a shrug. You are the conquerors, do what you want.

From the state of Weizsächer's office, Goudsmit concluded that the German physicist had left recently, and in a hurry. In too much of a hurry to take all his files. That night, by candlelight, Goudsmit and an aide went through Weizsächer's letters and documents in the hope of finding, at last, some clues to how far the Germans had progressed on an atomic bomb. Shells rocketed past the windows: German shells from across the river, Allied shells from this side. Outside, the whine of airplanes and air-raid sirens was deafening. Inside wasn't much better. A few feet away, some exhausted American soldiers were playing poker as if their lives depended on it.

"Not exactly an ideal setting," Goudsmit remarked, but he was a determined man. After combing Weizsächer's papers for two long days and nights, in that noisy, smoky candlelight, he concluded that there was absolutely no evidence of the existence of a German atomic bomb. Nor any evidence that one was being made.

"What if this is a ploy on the part of the Germans to divert the Americans?" Groves prodded. For that Goudsmit had no answer. Goudsmit knew what the Germans were capable of. His parents had been dragged from their home in Amsterdam and killed by them.

Yet Goudsmit's instincts told him that there was no German weapon. Still, Goudsmit wasn't responsible for this Manhattan Project. "We don't know anything until we find Weizsächer or Heisenberg or Hahn," Groves wired Goudsmit. And to Oppenheimer he said, "As far as Alsos can tell, there's no sign of any plutonium research. But that doesn't mean a goddamn thing. It could be a colossal trick to divert us, so we relax. No one knows what that bastard Hitler has up his sleeve."

Groves couldn't trust anyone. Not even Goudsmit. What he wanted was proof. And until Goudsmit and Alsos could give him cold, hard proof that there was no German atomic weapon, work on the gadget would continue at Los Alamos with fierce and unflagging effort.

The same day that Patton rode into Strasbourg, History took herself, calmly and quietly, to Dr. Stanton, the obstetrician who was now stationed permanently at Los Alamos. Her contractions had begun. The doctor called Herb. "Of course we'll have to do another cesarean," he said. Herb nodded. And later that day History gave birth to a beautiful little girl whom they named Jane.

That night we all went to the hospital, and with wine that must have come from Oppenheimer, we toasted History, Jane, Herb, and even Los Alamos for bringing us all together. Nearly everyone who mattered to me on The Hill made an appearance that night, including Oppie, and on each face was a profound sense of relief. And joy.

In the midst of the celebration, Herb touched my shoulder and asked me to follow him. We went to Dr. Stanton's office, and he handed me the phone. He smiled and said, "After all, Lily, you were the one who did the dirty work the last time." His face was lined with tiredness, but in his eyes were triumph.

I patted his arm. "We were all in this together, and if anyone did the dirty work, it was Noel."

He nodded. "But I want you to tell Amelia all the things a woman wants to know." So after he gave her the good news and hurried back to History, I told Amelia everything I could about History and the baby, down to the shape of the baby's fingernails and toes.

"Oh, Lily, what wonderful news!" Her voice rippled with exhilaration. It was so good to hear her that I surprised myself. There, in that small office, all alone, except for Amelia breathing at the end of the line, I said, "I have more good news."

She waited expectantly. I hesitated. I hadn't yet told my parents, but the words formed themselves. "I'm expecting a baby, too. In July." Saying them made my pregnancy real. I could feel my free hand moving absently across my abdomen, looking for a sign. But of course it was still too early.

"Oh, Lily, how happy I am for you," she said. I sighed with relief. Had I been so secretive because I was waiting for some kind of punishment, because I didn't really believe I would ever have this baby? But now, as I heard Amelia's voice, those fears dissolved—as suddenly and as irrationally as they had come.

A few weeks later I received a letter from Amelia.

I was so happy to hear about your pregnancy, Lily, as happy as I was to hear of Jane's birth, and I hope all goes well. It is strange how, out of every sadness, there comes something good. For now I can place History and Herb and the rest of you in that beautiful landscape. Do you know this poem by Dickinson, Lily? I've been reading her a lot since I came home. Odd that the Southwest should send me back to her—I always thought she was the quintessential New England poet, yet she seems to know the roughhewn look of New Mexico and the sky and that amazing sense of space better than anyone else.

Here it is: "This is my letter to the world/ That never wrote to me/ The simple news that Nature told/ With tender majesty." I think it's my favorite because of that phrase, "tender majesty." That's what I felt there, with you and History and Pamela at Otowi.

Amelia's letter sent me back to my collected Dickinson, which was one of the few books, besides Melville, that I had dragged here with me. The poem went on, "Her message is committed/ To

Hands I cannot see/ For love of Her—sweet—countrymen/ Judge tenderly of me."

Judge tenderly of me. Oh, how I needed those words then.

Less than a month later, on the third anniversary of Pearl Harbor, Kitty Oppenheimer gave birth to a baby girl named Katherine, but soon called Toni, to distinguish her from her mother. When the telephone call came, I was at Pamela's. Pamela listened calmly. Suddenly a flash of relief crossed her features. I watched her, startled by how old she looked. In the course of our daily life, Pamela was so open, so warm, so much one of us, that it was easy to forget she was a generation older. But now, when her careful serenity had been disturbed, I could see her age. It was like suddenly finding the first inevitable crack in a beloved piece of porcelain.

When she hung up the telephone, she gazed somberly at me, for by now she knew I was pregnant. I looked at her curiously.

"Oppie was so worried," she said finally. "His mother was born without a right hand. She always wore a glove over a rather primitive prosthetic device, and no one ever talked about that puzzling glove or why she wore it. People thought she had been badly burned or something like that. But the truth was simpler. It usually is." She smiled. "Oppie said he scarcely thought about it until he married. Strange, how you could know something like that all your life and not realize how important it might someday become." Pamela stopped and shook her head.

"One day only a few weeks ago he confessed how fearful he was. Which is perfectly understandable." Now she pushed a lock of hair away from her face, then searched my eyes. I could feel them widen with surprise. I hardly ever thought of Oppie as a husband or a father. And now he had two children. Peter, who was three years old. And Toni.

"He has so much to think about with the work here"—she gestured toward The Hill—"that people forget he's human, too." I never forgot Oppie was human. To remind yourself, all you had to do was look into his eyes. But a lot of people, especially the women, were so awed by him they couldn't do that.

• • •

Bits and pieces kept floating around me: how hot the Omega canyon labs were, how worried Thea was, "the dragon," "the guillotine," Frisch's bravery, Noel, Tom, "most dangerous experiment of all," "crazy," "foolhardy," "crucial," "necessary," "simulation of an atomic explosion," "scary." What did those phrases mean? I didn't know, but after Thanksgiving I decided to find out. "Nothing is as bad as you can imagine," my mother always said.

All I knew was that a dangerous experiment was being conducted in Omega Canyon under the leadership of Otto Frisch, who sometimes played the piano on our local radio station, and who had helped his aunt, Lise Meitner, understand Hahn's fission experiment.

I went to a rehearsal of *Arsenic and Old Lace* with Thea, hoping she'd tell me something. Yet all she said was, "Tom's working twelve, sixteen hours a day." Her face turned gray as she spoke. And her features, usually so robust, looked pinched.

A few nights later I went to Kate's. The children were fed and bathed and I helped her get them ready for bed. We worked quietly, in tandem, putting arms and legs into pajamas. Smooth, beautiful limbs, faces flushed with the heat in the kitchen, eyes wide as they listened to Kate's clear voice reading them their bedtime stories. Stella lingered with me, and we talked about school and the new baby that Kate was expecting. Such a wise little person for only eight, I thought, for she looked at me a bit more carefully, almost as though she knew I was pregnant, too. But I didn't say anything, as we watched a few of Tigger's tricks.

Tigger was the Unwins' cat. I had seen him the weekend I took care of the children, but then he had stayed outside, shy of a stranger. Now he knew me, and I agreed with Lenny and Kate that Tigger was really quite remarkable, with a sixth sense about the children's whereabouts and an uncanny devotion to Lenny. He often went with Lenny to the canyon and waited until quitting time. "As if he knew how tired Lenny is, and how much he likes the company," Kate remarked. Now I thought, If only Tigger could talk, maybe we would know what's going on in that lab.

Finally the kids were bedded down. Kate and I sat quietly at the kitchen table, talking about the play, the gifts she was scraping together for Christmas. But she wasn't her usual ebullient self, and she wasn't really surprised when I whispered, "What's going on? What's the 'dragon'?"

Reflexively, her head shot up. Fear sharpened her features as she looked over the doorway to the kitchen. That's where someone had told us there was a listening apparatus installed in each apartment. I didn't believe it, and neither did Kate. Yet rumors were powerful.

She rose and went to their bedroom and came out with some sheets of paper. On one was a rough sketch. So even Kate was worried. "I found these in Lenny's pocket a few weeks ago, and when I asked him about it, he told me."

What Kate told me was this: A few weeks ago the U-235 that was needed for the experiments had begun arriving from Oak Ridge. U-235 was responsive to slow neutrons, which was why you needed the heavy water of a pile to create criticality. But down in the canyon, where Tom and Noel were working, researchers had been searching for ways to make the U-235 responsive to fast neutrons as well. They mixed the enriched uranium metal with hydrogen-rich plastic, to reflect back neutrons; the trick was to lower the hydrogen content of the substance in order to get faster and faster reactions. If that could be accomplished, the "final package" would be small enough to fit into an airplane. Now Frisch had to construct an actual critical assembly in order to verify their theoretical calculations.

But when you attempt to create an instantaneous criticality, there's always the possibility that the assembly will simply run away with itself, killing whoever monitors it with radiation. Frisch had already had a very close call. Now he wanted to go even further. He proposed that the U-235 that was finally arriving should be assembled by stacking bars of it into a hollow box without its central part; that way no chain reaction could occur. But the missing piece was then to be mounted above the hollow space on aluminum guides, ready to be dropped into the assembly so that for a split second there would be the condition for an atomic explosion, although only barely so. Of course, Lenny would construct the machine.

"They call it the guillotine." Her voice was grim. She shrugged. "But at least it's honest. Richard Feynman calls it 'tickling the tail of a sleeping dragon.'" I nodded.

"To stir the dragon requires incredible precision. But everyone working on it is exhausted. And they've got only so much time—because the uranium they are using has to be returned in a few weeks to Oak Ridge. They need it for the final package."

For months the final package had seemed so far away, something in the distant future. Yet now it had a new reality. An inevitable and frightening reality.

When I left Kate's apartment, it was late. The air was cool, though not yet deadly cold. I could see Orion's belt, and his dog at his feet as I walked. And then my eyes found Draco—the dragon.

Now I knew that the experiment *was* crucial, for it would help determine the amount of metal needed for the gadget. Not the theoretical amount but the actual amount. The bravery required to obtain such valuable information was staggering. And it was our friends—Tom, Frisch, and sometimes Noel—who were risking their lives.

When I told Peter about seeing Kate, he stared at me with a worried frown. "If you know this much you might as well know it all." So later we sat up in bed, with my oversized copy of *Moby Dick* as a desk, and he drew some pictures and wrote some new words and explained in more detail what they were doing in the Omega lab.

"We don't know how much energy will be released when the core of moving U-235 drops through the hollow space," Peter explained. "Frisch has devised monitoring equipment that will function during that split second when the chain reaction occurs as a sort of stifled explosion. What we're afraid of is that we may get too much radiation even from this short burst." Nothing more.

I looked at Peter's sketches and notes. Were these, like those endless calculations, another kind of love letter for a physicist's wife? I asked myself. No wonder Thea's face was gray. Silently I thanked God Peter wasn't involved in this experiment. But then I realized I couldn't be sure he wasn't working on something equally dangerous.

• • •

I was sitting in the kitchen as close as I could get to Black Beauty. There was trouble with the heat in our row of apartments. I was reading parts from *Moby Dick* and listening to the radio. Suddenly the music was interrupted by a United Press report of an unexpected German offensive in the Ardennes Forest in France. For months Eisenhower, Montgomery, and Patton had been pushing farther and farther into Europe; yet now Hitler had taken the offensive. Worry filled my small smoky kitchen. You could hear it in the announcers' voices. My heart began to pound.

Then the bang of the door, Peter's step, his excitement radiating toward me as he approached, home from his third trip to Hanford. Too intent even to notice the raw cold, he pulled me to him and murmured, "The pile at Hanford has gone critical. They solved the Xenon problem and ran it for a few days without telling anyone." I could feel his heart beating as he held me. So they had turned it all around; they could begin to produce the plutonium they so badly needed.

It was wonderful news. Because even if the Germans lagged far behind our atomic research, what might happen if Hitler had more surprises in his pocket? What if this new battle, called the Battle of the Bulge because of the shape of the battleground, was the beginning of a huge German offensive to split the Allied armies? From the way the newscasters were talking, the war in Europe, about which we had been so confident these last months, was far from over.

In the days that followed, that battle plodded on. We went to see *Arsenic and Old Lace*. I didn't know most of the actors, except Oppie, who played the corpse. "Of course," someone said later, "he's the skinniest one here."

Steffi was happy and relaxed that night; she smiled a lot. As always, she stood between Noel and Jacob, but that wistfulness of last year was gone. Instead she had that expectant glow that most women have toward the end of their pregnancies.

I stood there thinking. Each person lives in his or her own world, and the only certainties are the earth beneath our feet, the air we breathe, and our perceptions of what is happening around us.

When, as everyone hoped, Hitler was defeated, the rest of the country would be jubilant. But what would it mean to us? Hitler had brought us here. Now, how could we justify staying? I didn't dare to ask.

At the very end of 1944 I emerged from that protected, euphoric state of early pregnancy. I read the newspapers as if I were learning English; each word seemed freighted with hidden, scary meaning. Some evenings I would stand in our bedroom waiting for Peter and watch Truchas darken in the evening light. The black horned sentinel. A devil in disguise? I wondered. No, there was nothing to fear. Here we were safe. No planes droning overhead, no air-raid shelters, no concentration camps.

"This is another kind of war," Jacob had said so firmly. Yet how was it possible we would be spared? I remembered the frown on Kate's face, the way she fiddled with Lenny's sketch. And Peter's sigh when I came home that night. Beguiling and mysterious, he called this science. But where was it taking us?

1945

20

••• ■

An arctic wind blew down across the Rockies, turning the mesa into a barren plain. No snow, but intense cold, and that fierce wind blowing all night long. Sleep was often troubled, restless, our dreams filled with noises as harsh and as unremitting as loose shutters banging against the side of a house. We would awake reluctantly to a landscape whitened by hoarfrost, to frozen cacti thrusting upward in weird, surreal shapes, to needled grasses piercing the January dawn.

But such light! Never have I seen such sharp, glittering light. It glinted off the icy surfaces in the strangest ways; when we walked to work, we were angels with splintered halos around our heads; and after garish, gaudy sunsets its eerie luminescence streaked from one clump of frozen vegetation to another.

The intensity of the light seemed to match our moods. Strange, when you thought about it. If anything, the pressure should have lessened, now that we were almost certain the Germans didn't have a bomb.

"They're at least two years behind us. Goudsmit is convinced that Heisenberg and Weizsäcker have done only the most rudimentary research into a weapon, and that the Germans have no idea how to make plutonium," Peter told me. If Goudsmit was right, the Germans were certainly not going to catch up now, when Hitler's big offensive at the Battle of the Bulge had at last been broken.

But where did that leave those scientists who had come to Los Alamos motivated by their hatred of Nazi Germany, their fear that the Germans would develop a bomb? Now logic might have dictated that they stop. But logic had nothing to do with it, and work at Los Alamos was more frantic than ever. I think it was that built-in need to see this experiment to the end. To go as far as they could go.

They looked like men in love. But a love beyond its first throes, a love that was not merely passion—no, far more than passion, more like obsession. In *Doktor Faustus* Thomas Mann says that a kind of demonism is built into genius. Here was demonic genius at work before our eyes. Now, at last, they were incredibly, enticingly close to the answers they had been seeking, some said, for three hundred years.

A breathless exhilaration lit their faces, hurried their steps. All the necessities of life—the eating, the dressing, even the few hours of sleep they allowed themselves each night before returning to their labs—were done as quickly as possible, with the least expenditure of energy. What they saved themselves for was their work. Work that was fulfilling every expectation they had ever had and that engaged them more than anything had ever engaged them before. For they were rearranging nature to create energy in ways that had never been done before.

Men in love. Yet I soon realized that they were also men at war with themselves, plagued with worry—the same worry I had glimpsed when Peter returned from that second trip to Hanford.

That worry was an extension of Erik's worry. It began like the roll of thunder that sometimes started over Tsi'como, in the shape of a black cloud curling and uncurling, slowly muffling and compressing the sound of the thunder, so that you had to strain to hear it.

Peter brought home the stack of fliers on a freezing day. The sheets of paper were as stiff as laundry on a winter clothesline. He thrust one under my eyes and I read: "The Impact of the Gadget on Civilization," with the details of a meeting to discuss it. Quickly he left to meet Herb, armed with flashlights and hammers and thumbtacks. They planned to spend the evening putting up the fliers. "We have to do something," Peter told me.

I wasn't surprised. No one had listened more eagerly to Erik during all those discussions at Pamela's than Peter and Herb. But who else would stand with them?

Of our friends, only Noel and Mark Chanin. Noel had come from a long line of pacifists, and Mark, a Czech, understood the war in Eastern Europe better than any of us. He knew that Stalin was not really the benign Uncle Joe presented to the American people and Russia was not an ally the way Britain and France were. Our alliance with Russia was mere pragmatism: we needed Russian manpower to win the war.

"Stalin is a ruthless, cruel man," Mark had said more than once. He often reminded us that the Russians had been as brutal as the Germans, for he had known people killed in the famous Stalin trials, yet he also knew how smart the Russians were. "If we're working on a gadget, so are they. That's why the only practical, logical course is openness. We must share everything we're doing with them; if we don't, they will simply see it as a race that they must win."

Fifty men showed up at the meeting, including Oppie. There was talk of the gadget's tremendous capacity for destruction, of the need for the United States and Britain to share their knowledge with the Russians, and questions about what the new organization that was just being formed, the United Nations, would do regarding the gadget.

"Oppie even got up and said that the people at the preliminary meetings of the United Nations would certainly consider a demonstration of the gadget, so that everyone, even our enemies, can be warned of its terrible power," Peter told me when he came home. "He was trying to make us feel better, but it was just talk, Lily. And it's hard to gauge the implications of a weapon that doesn't even exist yet." His voice was tired; he was disappointed. Several people he had expected to come had stayed away.

Many of the younger men believed, as Tom did, that there was no point in meetings or talk. Talk was bullshit, they didn't have time for talk, they had a job to do. "If you were worried about the moral implications of this thing, you should have stayed home, like my cousin Dan," Tom snapped when Peter asked him to come to the meeting. And Jacob didn't agree with Peter either.

"You can't come to a country that welcomes you and gives you work and position and then presume to tell it what to do. It's not only bad manners, it's ridiculous to think that you will succeed. Erik should know better. So should Peter," Jacob said to me the morning after the meeting. I knew that voice. I simply turned away. I knew then that this worry about the gadget would creep into our lives in small, subtle ways. What I didn't suspect was how acutely it would affect our friendships, or that it would leave at least one marriage in its wake.

• • •

After the war I met a woman who had gone to Washington in 1944, when Winston Churchill was there, to show her small daughter the great man. I listened to her tell a group of us at a dinner party in the late sixties how they had gotten close enough to Churchill to brush his coat, and how that daughter had been so inspired by his greatness that she had gone on to become a member of the Foreign Service. How she was now married to the second in command in the embassy in Rome and had a job in the embassy herself. I listened carefully to the woman's smug yet starry-eyed account, but I couldn't share everyone else's admiration and awe. I looked directly into the woman's eyes and said, "Winston Churchill was not a great man. He was a clever and canny politician who fooled the world into thinking he was a great man. No one who engineered the atrocity of Dresden can be considered a great man."

There was an awkward silence, in which Peter gave me a warning look. For I had more than once made a fool of myself trying to explain to people who had no understanding of Los Alamos or Erik Traugott how Churchill had been the greatest obstacle to international control of nuclear arms. But I was finished that evening, and while the hostess chirped for a few minutes about Kurt Vonnegut's new book about Dresden, I merely looked at my hands and waited until people began to talk about something else. We were never invited there again, nor did that wide-eyed Churchill lover speak to me when we passed each other a few months later in the Boston Public Gardens. But I didn't care.

I knew I was right. Dresden would always loom in my mind— with Nagasaki—as one of the worst actions taken by the Allies during the war. Because both were absolutely gratuitous. And for that reason, utterly unforgivable.

Kate had used the first weeks after giving birth to her fifth child— a boy—to start a quilting club. We all came with the squares we had prepared at home. It was a change from knitting, and the idea was to finish a large patchwork quilt and display it in Fuller Lodge. Each of us had made a square picturing a building or some other scene on The Hill. Mine was of Ashley Pond, which looked a lot bluer than the real thing. I saw what Kate was after: a record of our time here. It would be a beautiful quilt, an idealized version of Box 1663—there was even one square of the post office with the box number cross-stitched on it—and the loveliest square of all was Kate's: of Otowi and, standing next to the house, a thin faceless figure that exactly captured Pamela's stance.

It was easy work and suited all of us who were pregnant. Around us were the schoolchildren's valentine decorations; only yards from me was that red mailbox, the inevitable mailbox that was part of every valentine celebration, and feared by children everywhere who worried that they would be forgotten. Above us hung the glittery silver paper and pristine white doilies against which were pressed deep red, perfectly shaped hearts. Just getting the paper to make them was a feat, and I wondered who had gone to Santa Fe and hoarded these supplies so that the children could have a normal St. Valentine's Day. And how many women all over the country had done the same? For the first time in weeks I felt connected to the America that surrounded us, yet seemed so far away.

Then suddenly Jacob appeared, and I knew that something terrible had happened. His face was taut, his chin sharp-edged, his usually erect posture almost sloppy from weariness. He whispered something to Steffi and they left without a word. Something told us not to ask any questions. A valentine above me fluttered when they slammed the door.

We searched for a radio, and as soon as we heard the newscast from Albuquerque, we knew why he had come. He wanted to tell Steffi about Dresden himself, so she could cry and rail at the Americans and British to her heart's content at home, not embarrass him and the rest of us with her uncontrollable anger. Strangely, I wished she were here, because we all felt as one on hearing about the firebombing: why Dresden, why that magnificent city, that place epitomized by those delicate figures displayed proudly in all the houses of our childhood? Why Dresden now, when the war in Europe was practically over?

In my mind the firebombing of Dresden was inextricably mixed with those elaborate, lovingly made valentines, those deep-red hearts against the silver-and-white backgrounds that hung above us that night.

• • •

But then, as if to remind us that there was a real enemy, the news came about Iwo Jima. My throat tightened. Bess. Where was Bess? For her brother was stationed right near there.

That evening when I finished preparing supper, I left a note for Peter, then walked toward the Chanins' apartment. They lived a few blocks from us but had no phone. Slicks of ice covered the roads, so I walked slowly. I could see women standing in their kitchens, cooking, talking to their children, helping them with homework, passing that last hour or so before most of the men got home.

When I reached the Chanins', the door was open, but no one was there. On the kitchen counter was a pile of string beans and some hamburger meat. Two potatoes were in the sink with a vegetable brush. In my mind's eye I could almost see an MP coming to the door to get her. A telephone call could only have meant bad news.

I found a piece of paper and wrote Bess a note, then left. I heard them before I saw them. A faint throbbing cry, like a child's sobbing, coming toward me in the cold dark. As I turned the corner, I could see Bess and Mark huddled together, his body cradling hers as he pulled her along. I wanted to disappear. But I couldn't, and there was no way they would pass me without seeing me.

I hurried back to their apartment and found some brandy and poured it into two water glasses. When they came in, they didn't seem surprised to find me. Their eyes were listless, their movements slow, as if they were in a trance. Before Bess sat down at the kitchen table, she pushed the chair back to make room for her very pregnant body. Then she looked at Mark and me, and said, in the most resigned voice I had ever heard, "I knew from the beginning he wouldn't make it. I don't know how I knew, but I knew." She took a sip of brandy. I sat there remembering how her eyes would dart whenever the war in the Pacific was mentioned, and those sharp gusty breaths she always seemed to need to take.

There was nothing I could do for them. Soon I kissed them both and slipped out the door.

A few nights later, when I had finished a letter to my brother Ernie, and was beginning one to my other brother, Danny, our telephone rang. Peter was working late, and I let it ring a few times, expecting to hear his voice. But it was Mark.

"Bess has had a baby girl." His voice was jubilant. "Small, only four nine, but fine." I nodded, dumbly, counting in my head. She was almost two months early.

"Lily, did you hear me?" he shouted into the phone.

"Oh, Mark, that's wonderful, I was just so surprised, it's still so early." My voice came in a rush.

He laughed heartily, laughter of relief. "Yes, it's amazing. Dr. Stanton says that if she had carried to term she would have had a ten-pounder. She was a big baby and so was her brother—they say it's hereditary, birth weight, I mean. You'll tell History and Herb and the others?"

"Of course. You know me. I'll tell the whole world."

"I knew I could count on you, Lily," he said, then he was gone.

Bess's baby, Barbara, was put immediately into an incubator and placed in a darkened room, "as much like the womb as possible," Dr. Stanton explained. He had learned that from the Pueblos, among whom he had been practicing obstetrics for years. Within a week the baby was taken out of the incubator and began to thrive.

Yet instead of being happy that her baby was well, Bess could only talk about what had surely precipitated her premature arrival—Bess's brother's unbearable death. "They're not human beings, they're animals," she said over and over. In only a few days she seemed to have absorbed every cliché about the Japanese; her irrational fear had been replaced by an irrational prejudice.

At first Mark tried to shush her, to make her see that she wasn't being fair, that she couldn't take this so personally, that this was war, after all, and people get killed in war. But when he did, she would turn on him and say coldly, "Don't you dare talk to me like that. You can't hope to understand what I'm feeling."

Bess, who had never said a mean or angry word to anyone in all these months on The Hill! Bess, well-adjusted, unobtrusive Bess, the envy of anyone who had felt even a tinge of *Weltschmerz*; our all-American Bess from Nantucket who seemed to be blessed with a special brand of American optimism. "That's why I married her," Mark used to joke. "She's the perfect foil for my Eastern European cynicism."

But now Bess had been touched by an unnameable affliction. Anything that would stop the Japanese was more than all right with Bess. She had no patience with Erik's ideas or anything that smacked of moralizing about the gadget. The Japanese had become her deadliest enemy; in her anguish, she wanted an eye for an eye. What her husband thought meant nothing to her; indeed, she seemed to need to attack him as well.

"It may be postpartum depression," Pamela suggested, and went to see Dr. Stanton. They took Bess to see a healer at San Ildefonso. Bess seemed to calm down, at least outwardly, and she did take beautiful care of the baby. "She'll be fine," everyone told Mark, who was astonished at the terrible change in his wife. But I wasn't so sure. Something told me what had happened to Bess had very little to do with the birth; I suspected that it was death that changed people. Watching her, I could feel my hands and feet grow numb with dread.

And Steffi? Does anyone know what happened to Steffi? She was like a woman turning to stone in the first few months of 1945.

Each bit of news seemed to harden her. She hated Churchill, Stalin, Roosevelt, Hitler, and the Japanese equally. No one dared to mention world events to her, though I think she and Jacob discussed them endlessly at home; to the rest of us she pretended to be totally absorbed in her child and her home, for she had stopped teaching and was just waiting for her baby to be born. Like Bess, she had no patience with Erik or Peter or Herb. She became almost rabid about finishing the gadget. Anything that would end this terrifying war was fine with Steffi; what she didn't seem to understand was that using the gadget might be the worst terror of all.

When Steffi's daughter was born, a few weeks after Bess's, I went to see her at the hospital, praying as I walked to the large white building that this birth would make her happy.

Jacob was there when I arrived. As I entered the room, I was once again struck by Steffi's beauty. She was thinner now than she had been when we first arrived at The Hill, and her features were more exquisite in their sharpness. She held her head high, even in bed, and although she looked at her baby with pride and love, she remained ineffably remote.

I tried to talk to Jacob about it a week or so later. But when I began to speak, he stared at me as if he had no idea what I was talking about. Quickly I changed the subject. From his cold, wary eyes I knew I had overstepped some forbidden, unspoken boundary.

This time even Noel couldn't reach Steffi. When she was well enough to go out again, I would see them walking and talking sometimes, his large hands gesturing amply as if the width of those movements would somehow convince her that her bitterness didn't help anyone, least of all Jacob and the children.

By then she didn't care. She seemed to accept her lassitude as an old person might; she walked slowly, picking her way like someone blind. How I longed to see her old proud stride! But no. Now her body resembled an overstarched piece of clothing, stiff and hard and unwearable. She seemed to be dragging it around behind her.

After the firebombing of Tokyo she didn't even seem to care whether Noel was there or not, and when he was one of the people chosen around this time to go south and help set up the testing site for the gadget, she hardly reacted. Do what you want, she would say when asked her opinion. What she didn't say was, what does it matter? What does anything matter?

I sometimes wondered how Steffi could nurse the baby in the state she was in—wouldn't such bitterness turn her milk sour? But Andrea was as round as a Buddha, with fair pink skin and almost black hair and those wonderful no-color eyes that newborns have. And she was as alert as any baby on The Hill.

Like everyone else, I watched Steffi and felt helpless. Jacob was extraordinary in his loyalty. Even to me, he talked only about what a good mother she was, what a capable woman, what a fine cook and gardener she was becoming. And then one day in the middle of March he told me how last summer she had found and cultivated this absolutely gorgeous wildflower, a wildflower that Estevan and Pamela called Queen of the Night, which she had planted in a corner of her garden. She had never before seen a flower that blossomed so profusely in the dark, he said; she was planning to gather seeds from it this spring, and try to interest some nurseryman she knew back in upstate New York in selling them.

What an amazing instrument the human brain is! He told me about all this as if he had never heard of the Queen of the Night, as if I had never pointed it out to him, as if I had never met him in the cave at Tsankewi. As if the most important thing in the world was his wife's discovery of this gypsy of a night-bloomer.

After work that day I headed for Otowi. I needed Pamela's sanity, her serenity. And I needed Estevan, too, if only to acknowledge that he knew my secret, that I hadn't dreamed Jacob. I imagined telling them everything. Sitting in that friendly room, in front of that glowing piñon fire and confessing it all. Even my horror that Jacob had simply erased our love affair from his brain.

As I walked, feeling the baby stirring inside me, I suddenly realized what it was that Steffi reminded me of. A figurehead on a ship. A figurehead that waits motionlessly, stoically, for what must come. A face and body of painted wood that, with time, is honed to its barest essentials by the weather and the sea.

But when I got there, Pamela and Estevan were gone. The little house was as inviting as ever, but empty.

Of course I never told them. And later, much later, I realized that Jacob had been talking to me in a code of his own. Like Richard and Arlene Feynman's codes that had no key. What Jacob was telling me that day and what I was still too young to realize was that nothing between us would ever be revealed, not even a small detail like the Queen of the Night.

• • •

Ten days after the failure of the conspiracy against Hitler, Dietrich's mother, Frau Bonhoeffer, had written to her grandson-in-law, Eberhard Bethge: ". . . Everything was already going well, but now . . . prospects have become much more difficult, if not impossible. . . . Man thinks and God directs. That now seems so clear to one, and yet we go on thinking and thinking how we can do everything in the best and wisest way . . ."

At first the Bonhoeffers thought that Dietrich and their son-in-law, Hans von Dohnanyi, might be saved, for the Nazis could prove no connection between them and the July twentieth plot. But at the end of September newly discovered Abwehr files revealed their participation in an earlier conspiracy. Hans and Dietrich considered trying to escape, but then Dietrich's older brother, Klaus, and Rudiger Schleicher, another son-in-law, were arrested. Surely there would be reprisals if anyone connected to them was to escape. The Bonhoeffer parents now had two sons and two sons-in-law in jail.

Early in October Dietrich was moved from Tegel to the higher security prison at Prinz Albrecht-Strasse. Conditions were worse there, yet he still received his Wednesday packages from the family, and there was no news about a trial.

By February 1945, though, things began to deteriorate. Klaus Bonhoeffer and Rudiger Schleicher were given the death sentence for conspiracy by the People's Court. Hans von Dohnanyi infected himself with diphtheria to make himself unfit for trial and gain more time. On February third Dietrich's parents were delayed in an underground station because of a heavy daylight Allied air attack on Berlin. They were bringing Dietrich a present for his thirty-ninth birthday: food, a copy of Plutarch Dietrich had requested, and some letters. And miraculously, although there was a direct hit on the prison, no one was hurt, and his parents left the parcel on the following Wednesday, February seventh.

In the letter to his son Dr. Bonhoeffer wrote: "We are looking forward to being allowed to see you soon. There are many things to be sorted out at our age, things that have to be discussed with one's children. . ." That afternoon Dietrich was taken from Berlin. The next Wednesday his parents and his fiancée, Maria von Wedemeyer, were told there was no one there to receive their packages. What they weren't told, although they feared the worst, was that Dietrich had been moved to Buchenwald.

21

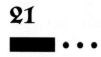

Spring came unannounced to the mesa. Suddenly the light was silkier, the dusks longer. My body swelled, and I was grateful for the softer air, the less slippery roads. When my heels sank into the mud, I didn't even mind. "You're going to have a big baby, Mrs. Fialka," Dr. Stanton told me each time I saw him, and that seemed, somehow, good news.

Peter was much more involved with this pregnancy than I had expected. The scientist in him made him acutely aware of each phase, and he was curious, then amazed, as I was, by the incredible resilience of my body. By the way the skin could stretch and stretch. Or by the active churning movements of our baby as it shifted its position under our palms.

As my pregnancy progressed, time raced as never before. The only way I could stop it was when I worked on the quilt. Then time meandered comfortably while we chatted over our squares, as women had done for generations before us. Sometimes we met at Pamela's, other times in one of the schoolrooms. I was one of the few women who was still working, the rest were home with their families. For all of us the quilting was a welcome respite from the grinding routine. For the men on The Hill now worked around the clock—seven days a week and most evenings. Kate had given up trying to plan another play. Erik had returned and was staying at Pamela's, and people from Chicago, Hanford, and Oak Ridge floated in and out as well. For now, we were all concentrating on one thing: When would the gadget be tested?

I had learned in the two years at Los Alamos that it's a lot easier than most people think to find out things. You just listen very hard and put little scraps of information together, like stringing differently shaped shells on a necklace, shells that look as if they would never fit together, and then, surprisingly, they do. I had learned how to do that in those years I spent at the beach with my grandmother, and it fascinated me more now than it did then.

Once when I let something slip about a test in the desert south of us, Jacob said, "Maybe it would be better if you didn't know so much, Lily."

"That may be true. But once a person knows something you can't take it away from him," I replied, my voice defiant. Jacob's eyes flickered with amusement, and, I think, a kind of admiration at my refusal to agree with him.

It was astonishing to me that Groves could believe we women were in the fog he pretended we were. And yet, though several of my friends and I knew that there was a testing site designated, that it was called Base Camp, and that it was roughly two hundred miles to the south of us, there were plenty of women on The Hill who had no idea what was going on. But that wasn't my way. There was no way I could live in Groves's fog. For what I imagined was far more frightening than what I knew.

• • •

One Thursday I asked Jacob if I could leave a bit early. The quilters were meeting at Pamela's that night, Peter had worked late for three nights in a row, and I needed some time to shop and cook for the weekend. I also wanted to stop by and see History. Jacob and I worked through lunch, and I got to the commissary around four.

It was crowded. Soon Steffi came in and stood behind me; she had Sam with her, and when he recognized me, he gave me a broad smile. Steffi and I talked over Sam's head. She looked a little better today, not as listless as she had. But she was still distracted, obviously jumpy. We soon ran out of conversation.

Then Steffi said, "Say, Lily, can you watch Sam for a minute? I want to call home. Andrea was fussy when I left." As she put Sam's hand into mine, she murmured, "Oh, Lily, I wish I could be more like you, so down-to-earth. It's a curse to be so anxious." She paused, then straightened, as if deciding she could trust me. "But I have this feeling that something awful has happened. For the last few nights I keep waking up and seeing Dietrich's face on the ceiling."

I stared; she had never mentioned Dietrich to me after that day in Jacob's office when she brought news of the July twentieth plot. To divert Sam I suggested we play Twenty Questions. He wanted me to go first.

"Animal." I smiled mysteriously at him. He was a beautiful, easygoing child. People wondered how such a nervous woman had brought up such a placid child, but one thing didn't seem to have much to do with the other. Or perhaps it did. Perhaps she was happier at home with her children, and perhaps the children felt cherished because they sensed that.

"A man?" Sam asked.

I nodded.

"Someone I know?"

"I don't think so." I laughed.

"Someone in the newspapers?" I nodded again. He was five and could read a little, but I couldn't exactly imagine him reading a newspaper.

"In pictures, I mean, in the newspaper?" he asked, then looked stricken. "Does that count as another question?" I shook my head. Relieved, he waved to Steffi, who was walking toward us.

"Everything's fine," she said, looking embarrassed. We both concentrated on Sam. He was getting close, and his mother listened to his questions with a smile playing about her lips. As I watched them enjoying each other, I thought: His world is as solid as the rock of this mesa, and that's the way it should be.

"FDR!" he shouted triumphantly after the fourteenth question. "I knew it, I knew it way back on the tenth," he told me, "but I wanted to make sure."

I smiled at his pleasure; then, to reward him, Steffi and I took his hands and swung him a little when the line moved. Sam's hand was still in mine when the MP stood at the door and clapped his hands to get our attention. You could tell just by looking at him that he had planned to do this differently, but that all he wanted at this moment was to get the next few moments over quickly. He leaned against the doorjamb for support, then said loudly, "Ladies, I have very bad news." My grip tightened around Sam's hand. Had something happened in the canyon or Base Camp? Peter? Where was Peter? My mind clicked away, but then stopped as I heard the words, "President Roosevelt has had a cerebral hemorrhage." A pause, then the words as flat as stones landing on concrete, "And died."

No one moved; all I could hear was "And died, and died, and died" reverberating in the large, ugly space. I don't know how long it took for anyone to react, but soon there were whispers, voices, coughs, cries. I felt a lump in my throat as large as an egg; no matter how many times I swallowed, it wouldn't go away. Then Steffi turned to me. "I told you something terrible had happened," she said. As I listened to her, the lump dissolved.

Suddenly Steffi crumpled to the floor. I never knew if she fainted or if her legs simply gave out from under her, but as she fell, I lifted Sam into my arms and held him tightly while he screamed, "Mama, Mama!" until the MP could get Steffi into a chair and she began to blink her eyes. Sam struggled, wanting to go to her, but she didn't yet seem to know where she was, so I held on to him while the tears streamed down his face, and mine.

Once he saw that his mother was all right, Sam looked at me. FDR was like the moon or the sun; hadn't he just been the answer to Twenty Questions? How could he be dead? For dead is gone, and how can the moon or sun be gone? It was all there in Sam's eyes, the same gray eyes as his father's, but I had no answer. I simply hugged him tighter until Steffi held out her arms. But even with Sam in her arms waiting to be comforted, Steffi looked gaunt and spent, lashed once more by life's unpredictable sea.

Not everyone was as sympathetic. As I walked heavily from the commissary, I heard someone whisper, contemptuously, "So dramatic. Why is she always so dramatic? She's not even American, for God's sake." I didn't even turn to see who'd said it. Better not to know.

I hurried home and didn't seem to breathe until I saw History coming toward me. All I remembered for a long time about that afternoon was the salty taste of Sam's tears as they streamed down his face and mingled with mine.

At first no one wanted to be alone; I remember eating meals with the Lerners and other friends, all of us huddling together like children until it was time to go to bed. Numb, sleepwalking through the daylight hours. The only one who seemed to have any energy was Richard Feynman. As soon as he heard about Roosevelt's death, he jumped up, ran to his room for some clothes, and cajoled an Army driver going to Santa Fe to drive him to Albuquerque. "I want to be with my wife," he said simply, and the driver couldn't refuse. Everyone knew, though no one talked about it, that Arlene Feynman was very ill. The code letters had stopped a few months ago; now she had hardly any strength left, and Richard was often torn between seeing her and staying on

The Hill. Today, though, there was no hesitation. I called good-bye to him as he dashed toward the gate.

We were all stunned. Although pictures of Roosevelt in the last months had shown him looking more and more frail, no one had seemed able to realize that he might die, that he *could* die. And from what we heard on the radio or read in the papers, the whole country was as dazed as we were.

But what did Roosevelt's death mean? Would the work being done here have to end? Those first few days no one seemed to know. By Saturday night, though, that initial need to share the grief had passed; now we had to come to terms with a world without Roosevelt.

That evening the air was tense at Pamela's. Only weeks ago, Herb, Peter, Mark, Noel, and Erik had all signed a letter requesting a meeting with Roosevelt to discuss the implications of the gadget. Now that Roosevelt was dead, would their letter be read—would the meeting be granted? By whom. No one knew.

Mark turned a glass of deep red wine around in his bony hands. The candlelight from the table was reflected in the glass and onto his face as he spoke. "Roosevelt understood what a terrible weapon this is. He was a man who could grasp moral subtleties, he would have listened to talk about an international demonstration. But now . . ." His voice faltered, and he looked at Bess, who was sitting next to him.

She refused to meet his eyes and bent over her sewing. We were working on our squares. Kate had decided to ask Erik to make a square—"he's one of us," she had said—and now he was stitching the white roof of the hospital onto a pale blue sky.

"But what if it's a dud? Won't we look like asses if we insist on a demonstration and nothing happens?" Peter asked. I knew he was playing devil's advocate, that he didn't really believe that. I looked up at Erik's face. His face was impassive as he continued to make his neat, tiny stitches. He didn't want to lead this discussion; he wanted the others to talk.

"So it's a dud. Sure, we'll look like idiots, but at least we will have tried to warn them." Noel's voice was practical. "That's what's important."

"It's not going to be a dud. If we have something it won't be a dud." Herb's voice was firm. With good reason. For at almost the very moment when Franklin Roosevelt was drawing his last breath in Warm Springs, Georgia, Frisch and Tom and Noel had just completed a successful experiment with Lenny's guillotine. They now knew the size of the critical mass of U-235 that would be needed for the gadget. A wave of relief had swept through the top offices at Los Alamos that afternoon, as palpable as the grief that accompanied it.

There was a pause. Pamela put out some coffee cake and a large pot of coffee. As she handled the black pottery plates made at Santa Clara, I thought: Why are we doing this to her, why have we made her serene home a battleground? Yet I knew that if I asked her, she would reply, sensibly, "Where else, Lily? At least at Otowi people aren't afraid to say what they feel."

Now Jacob was frowning and shaking his head. He was here without Steffi, "to try to knock some sense into people's heads," he had told me. He thought all these protests and plans to try to influence the government were fruitless.

"Don't you understand that this government has to justify the expense? Almost two billion dollars has been spent on this thing—that's why Groves is in such a panic. As far as he's concerned it's got to be used, and believe me, they are not going to waste it on a demonstration. No matter what Oppie says, or the United Nations' organizers want. We are in the midst of a war, and until Japan surrenders, she's our enemy, and if she is still our enemy when the weapon is finished, they will use it against her."

There was an awkward silence. Everyone looked down, as if ashamed. Then Bess said, "But Japan started it. Why does everyone seem to forget that the Japanese started it?" Her voice was high, strident, as if she knew she was breaking an unwritten rule.

Mark stared at her, incredulous. Then he murmured, "Bess, you're beginning to sound like Johnny-One-Note."

Her head shot up, her eyes angry. But she didn't reply, just stood up, gathered her square and her sewing things, and went out into the night.

I looked at Mark, expecting him to follow her. But he didn't move, and when our eyes met, his were hard, angry.

"Aren't you going to go after her?" I asked, as if we were alone. I could feel Peter's hand on my arm to restrain me. But it was too late; the words were out.

"No, Lily, she doesn't want me. I don't know who she wants, but it isn't me." He looked around the table; we were all staring at him, speechless. All I could think of was how he cradled Bess's pregnant body that night they learned her brother was dead. But now that strong, almost primitive instinct to protect his wife was gone. How had it happened? I wondered silently, as History and Thea and I helped Pamela clear the table.

On the way home Peter and I stopped at the Unwins'. Kate had called earlier in the day and left a message with Peter. Something about the cat, Tigger. Everyone's favorite cat. Even the soldiers in the canyon knew Tigger.

Now he was sick. He lay on the floor like a blob of orange marmalade. "He has no energy, no appetite, can't seem to hold food down," Kate told us. Stella was still up, and her soulful brown eyes stared at Peter as he picked the cat up. There were ugly sores on the cat's stomach. Oozing, suppurating sores.

"I've tried every salve I can think of. And everything my neighbors can think of, too," Kate said.

Peter looked troubled. "I'd take him in to see Jack Solomon," he suggested.

"But tomorrow's Sunday and the memorial for FDR," Kate replied.

"I know, but you want to make sure he's not contagious, not infecting everyone with what he's got," Peter cautioned.

Kate shook her head. "This has been going on for days and the kids have been passing him back and forth. No one is in the least bit sick."

When we left the Unwins', I said, "What do you think it is?"

"I don't know. But those sores looked peculiar. I'd hate to see the kids get some obscure thing carried only by cats," Peter replied.

All I could do was shrug in reply. I was exhausted. My mind kept returning to Mark and Bess. Were they arguing, or icily silent? How would it feel to be so estranged from your husband? I hated to think about it.

Suddenly it began to snow. Always such a surprise—spring snow. And it was sticking—soft, blanketing fairyland snow. I stuck out my tongue to taste its wet freshness. By the time we reached home, our hair and eyelashes were covered with a fine, white veil.

In the morning winter had returned. A sapphire sky and that sharp light rocketing off the mounds of snow-covered cactus and mesquite. A deep blue silence stretched over the mesa, muting the noises of ordinary living as we made our way to the memorial service at the theater.

Footsteps were heavy, discouraged. Dressed once more in winter clothes, slowed down by grief and fear, everyone moved at a snail's pace, especially bulky me. Even Oppenheimer spoke more slowly than usual: "When, three days ago, the world had word of the death of President Roosevelt, many wept who are unaccustomed to tears, many men and women, little enough accustomed to prayer, prayed to God. Many of us looked with deep trouble to the future; many of us felt less certain that our works would be to a good end; all of us were reminded how precious a thing human greatness is.

"We have been living through years of great evil and of great terror . . . All over the world men have looked to him for guidance, and have seen symbolized in him their hope that the evils of this time would not be repeated, that the terrible sacrifices which have been made and those that are still to be made would lead to a world more fit for human habitation. It is in such times of evil that men recognize their helplessness and their profound dependence. . . ."

I stood there next to Peter, listening to Oppie's cultured voice, looking at the tears streaming down the faces around me. Even the men were crying unashamedly. Through my own tears, I thought: The evils of this time are Hitler and the camps and the Japanese and their fierce call to battle. But what about the gadget? Where did it fall in the spectrum between good and evil? We wanted to believe that the gadget was going to accomplish some marvelous stroke against all the evil that still existed in the world. Yet how could we be sure?

When it was over, Peter took my arm and guided me outside. Suddenly Kate was standing in front of us, blocking our way. Her face was grim. "Jack Solomon says there's nothing that can be done with Tigger," she blurted. "Those sores are burns—from radiation. He says we should put him out of his misery, put him to sleep." Her voice was shaking, her eyes brimmed. I reached out to touch her. But she had already turned on her heel and was hurrying away.

• • •

The snow melted quickly, and soon the desert earth began to gush forth the radiant, sun-resistant flowers we had grown to love, those startling colors that were a testament to the secret life that had slept all winter beneath the hard desert floor. Without warning, the snakes and jackrabbits and lizards appeared, and it was not an uncommon sight to come upon a group of children huddled around the tormented movements of a snake they were planning to capture.

Into that atmosphere of burgeoning lushness came one of the greatest understatements of the war: "The mission of this Allied

force was fulfilled at 0241, local time, May 7, 1945," wrote Dwight
D. Eisenhower to his superiors. The long, terrible war in Europe
was finally over. And the despised Hitler was dead, too. He had
committed suicide on April thirtieth, just a week before.

I celebrated V-E day with Stella and Kate and Pamela in Santa
Fe. We were looking for another cat for the Unwin children. Pamela said she knew exactly where we would find a sturdy tomcat,
whom the Unwins planned to name Ike.

Kate had borrowed Noel's car, and when we rumbled down the
hill to Santa Fe, we felt as if our teeth were rattling in our heads.
The town looked like New Year's Eve. Confetti flew along the
breezy streets, and clusters of people were singing and laughing,
beckoning to us from doorways or front yards to join them. We
waved back, enjoying the excitement, which seemed contagious.
On The Hill, the news had been welcomed, but the reaction had
been curiously subdued. No time or energy to celebrate, too much
to do. It was almost as if they were afraid to stop and think about
what this victory really meant. They seemed to have lost their
ability to react, I had thought as I watched them return to work
after the announcement. So, for me anyway, it was a relief to be
here in Santa Fe.

Quietly Pamela gave Kate directions, and soon she was driving
to the seedy neighborhood Jacob and I had visited that desperate
night. I tried not to look out the window, and I concentrated on
what Stella was telling me about the swimming test she was taking
next week. The streets got scruffier and more familiar. I could feel
a telltale blush creep over my face. I bent my head.

"We're going to a Spanish restaurant I know. The owners are
friends of mine, and their cat just had kittens," Pamela said, then
pointed to a small awning. Kate stopped. While the others went
into the restaurant, I lingered. My memory had made the hotel
more tawdry than it was, I realized, then hurried after Pamela.
The last thing I needed was to be recognized.

One of the kittens was orange, and, of course, Stella wanted that one. She snuggled into its warm furriness. "Hello, Ike," she purred.

When we got back into the car, Pamela chuckled and murmured, "Well, we got our kitty, and you ladies have now seen Santa Fe's red-light district. Just one place, but only the locals know that. The Chamber of Commerce lists it with all the other hotels and inns in the brochure. I wonder how many people have ended up there and been horrified," Pamela explained with a hearty laugh. I bent my head lower and wished I could apologize to Jacob. But of course I never would.

• • •

Just before V-E day Sam Goudsmit and his Alsos mission found 1100 tons of uranium ore and eight tons of uranium oxide in the German town of Stassfurt. And then, in the small village of Haigerloch, they found a cave on the side of an eighty-foot cliff towering above the town. Inside the cave was a concrete pit about ten feet in diameter, and inside the pit was what the Nazis called the uranium machine. It was really an atomic pile, cubes of uranium moderated by heavy water, cleverly constructed, but quite primitive compared to what the Americans had done. They were not even near where Fermi had been with his Chicago pile in 1942. A few days later Alsos found Weizsächer, Otto Hahn, and Heisenberg scattered in nearby villages—to the great relief of those who feared that the Russians would capture these German physicists.

All of Sam Goudsmit's hunches proved true: The Germans were years behind the Americans and had not even reached the point where they knew they could use plutonium to make an atomic weapon. Finally even Groves was convinced. And still no one said "Stop" to the Manhattan Project.

You could feel them getting closer and closer. You didn't have to be down in the canyons. As the days grew longer and warmer, as the men worked harder and harder, as Oppie's gaunt figure hurried among us, you knew that it was only a matter of time.

Enough time? That was the question. For although there was no German atomic bomb and the war in Europe was over, there was still Japan. A country of enigmatic, fierce fighters whose strength was still incalculable.

The fighting on Okinawa, which had begun on April first, was terrible; losses on both sides were enormous, and the Japanese fought as hard and as aggressively as ever. Was there nothing that could break them?

"The gadget," Jacob said quietly one day in the office. "No one wants to hear about international controls, Lily. American soldiers are being killed by the thousands, the Japanese started this damned thing, and no one is going to let them get away with it. You're dreaming, Lily, you and Peter and Erik and Noel and the rest of them, if you think we won't use it."

I was so disappointed in Jacob. And in Bess, and Steffi, and the rest of them who only wanted to see the gadget finished. Sometimes I found myself staring at Jacob in wonder: I had slept with this man, I had been in love with him, I might still be a little bit in love with him, yet we were absolutely divided on this. I could hardly believe that a person of such intelligence could refuse to see what was so clear to me.

And it wasn't just a matter of pride or principle. If Jacob had understood, he might have helped us. For he had been invited to attend an important meeting in the middle of May in Oppie's office. I tried one last time.

"Even if you don't agree with Erik, won't you present his case? That the world will never be the same if this weapon is used— that everyone should be warned about it?"

He shook his head. "I love Erik, but I don't agree with him," he said stubbornly. "And presenting his view isn't my job." So convinced he was right. I knew that arrogance, and once I had loved it. I also knew there was no persuading him.

All he would tell me when he returned was that Oppie had put a new quotation on his wall. "Or if it was there before, I never noticed it. It's a paraphrase of Lincoln," he told me. "'This world cannot endure half slave and half free.'"

Jacob added softly, "The gadget will make everyone free." At that moment, as he stood there while I sat in the chair opposite him, I think I hated him. What he didn't even seem to want to understand was that none of us, least of all Erik, denied that the completion of the gadget was a great achievement. But what Erik and the rest of us were talking about was something much, much larger.

An international demonstration was what Erik had urged on Churchill and Roosevelt; now it seemed imperative. For if the Japanese were invited to witness the terrible, destructive power of this weapon, then, maybe, they would surrender. And someone had to convince Truman and Secretary of War Stimson that Erik was right.

But not Erik. "You know I am regarded in Washington as a suspicious character," Erik had told us. The idea was so ludicrous it never failed to elicit a smile. But as silly as it was, it was true. The younger men on The Hill had to find someone else to put forth their ideas. Someone they could trust.

The solution was obvious. Oppie. The man they all admired, perhaps even adored. The man who had the widest-ranging mind they had ever encountered. The man who was as interested in literature as in science. The frail man with a will of iron who had the ear of everyone who was making the important decisions. The American-born director of Site Y who spoke a beautifully inflected English and had moved the research on The Hill faster than anyone had a right to expect. Surely he could make them see, if anyone could.

It looked like a brilliant choice. In reality, it was the worst one they could have made.

22

What we couldn't know but what was obvious to everyone on the higher levels was that Harry Truman, the new president, was overwhelmed by his duties. He was particularly confounded by the scientific material in a report Secretary of War Stimson had prepared about the Manhattan Project. It was long, dense, full of incomprehensible details—so Truman decided the best way to handle it was to form a committee. An S-1 Interim Committee with Stimson as chairman and Oppenheimer, Fermi, Ernest Lawrence of Berkeley, and Arthur Compton of the Chicago Metlab as scientific advisers. There was also a Target Committee that would determine which Japanese cities would be the best targets for the bomb.

Erik Traugott was fundamentally excluded, but he waited patiently in his hotel, always anxious to hear what had been decided. The first meeting with the scientists was on May thirty-first and was Oppie's first opportunity to present the moral objections of the men on The Hill.

Yet he didn't take it. Although he advocated telling the Russians about the bomb and said, "If we were to offer to exchange information before the bomb was actually used, our moral position would be greatly strengthened," he did not go on from there to tell the committee of the agonizing doubts plaguing some of the scientists. Nor did he raise the issue of the bomb's radioactive potential; he didn't even distinguish between the atomic weapon and conventional fire raids, muddying the issue by saying only that the number of people killed would be about the same. And neither did he push for a demonstration. Instead he agreed with Groves that the only way to have "a demonstration would be to attack a real target."

When Stimson expressed his regret at the mass murder of civilians in Hamburg, Dresden, and Tokyo—which would have given Oppenheimer a perfect opening to oppose using the gadget— Oppie was curiously silent. And when General Marshall wanted to know how to approach the Russians, Oppie suggested that we try to feel the Russians out in a tentative and very general way, without giving them any specifics about our efforts. When Marshall later surprised everyone by suggesting that we invite two Russian scientists to observe the test at Base Camp, Oppie said nothing. Again.

When Oppie returned to The Hill, his report on the meetings was exasperatingly vague. Peter and Herb had to wait for Erik to return to Los Alamos, for Erik had talked to the other committee members and learned the truth. When Erik told them, they were stunned. How could Oppie have let them down?

"He must have a reason, he must know things we can't possibly know," History said staunchly, but her voice was filled with disappointment.

Early in June Peter and Herb drew up a petition warning that in a nuclear war the geographical makeup of the United States—with its concentrated industrial centers—would be at a disadvantage compared to countries whose populations and industry were more diffused. The petition denounced a surprise attack against Japan, claiming that such an attack would cause world public opinion to turn against the United States and lead to an inevitable arms race. Instead, they requested a demonstration of the new weapon in a remote part of the world. Such a demonstration would make it possible for many nations to make the decision to use such a weapon against Japan. That way the United States would not be solely responsible.

They sent the petition to Stimson, who was impressed with it. He wanted it carefully assessed at a meeting of the Interim Committee on June sixteenth at Los Alamos.

Peter made a special request to speak at that meeting. It was our last hope, and a good one, we thought. For perhaps here, in his own office, Oppie would be more forceful in expressing the concerns of his troubled men—concerns that grew daily, for now Frisch and Noel and Tom had successfully tested two plutonium masses for criticality. At last, a plutonium bomb promised to work.

Although it was still early, just past dawn, you could already feel the heat. It was going to be a scorcher. I hadn't slept well and had a vague backache, but I dragged myself out of bed to eat breakfast with Peter. He had gotten a deep tan down at Base Camp; his blue eyes flashed against his darkened skin. He needed to be available all day, waiting for Oppie's call to come whenever they could fit him in. Now I could see how nervous he was—nervous and excited. Too excited for me to mention my backache. After he left I dressed slowly, then walked to work.

Dust flew around my thickened ankles. I felt like a lumbering animal. But the baby was still moving around, and I had at least three weeks to go. "They quiet down before they're born," History had told me.

Just before I reached the office I heard the pounding of feet behind me. I stepped aside as Richard Feynman streaked by. Ordinarily he would have stopped, greeted me, made some good-hearted pun about my bulk, but today he simply kept running.

Only one thing could make Richard that distracted. Arlene. Something had happened to Arlene.

When I got to the office Jacob was on the telephone. A few minutes later he stood over my desk. "That was Thea. Arlene Feynman died last night. Noel wanted to go with Richard, but he preferred to be by himself. An MP is driving him to Albuquerque." His voice was bleak.

We had never even seen Arlene—Albuquerque was too far away for visiting—but she had become part of our lives. I could see all those bows we had made for her and the pictures of her wearing them. Although I never heard her voice, I knew in my mind what it sounded like. I had never thought about it before, but she was undoubtedly the bravest wife here, passing the days as best she could, waiting patiently in that hospital for Richard's visits, waiting patiently to die.

Soon Jacob left for the meeting in Oppie's office, and I plodded through the reports he had left until lunchtime. The bell rang for lunch, and I became aware of a vague sensation in my lower abdomen. Before I could get used to that, I was suddenly standing in a puddle that had gushed without warning out of me. I sat down with my hand on the phone. Peter. I wanted Peter. But what if this was a false alarm? I still had almost a month to go. No. I couldn't call him until I knew for sure.

I tried the office next to ours, but there was no answer. They had gone to lunch. History? No, there was no way I could get to History; she had no phone. But I had to call someone. Thea was too far away in Santa Fe. Pamela. Quickly I got through to Otowi and Pamela answered. Her voice was high, expectant. "Any word about the meeting, Lily?"

"Not so far, but I'm having pains, and I'm standing in a puddle of water. I didn't know who to call—" I said foolishly; she must have thought I was an idiot.

"Your water's broke," she interrupted. "Stay put, and I'll call an MP."

Within minutes I went from panic to calm. A strange calm in which I felt utterly safe. I was aware only of the pain and the baby. The world seemed to have closed around me.

Then the MPs arrived and wanted to put me on a stretcher. "That's ridiculous," I said and began to walk to the car. They kept watching me nervously; the last thing they wanted was to deliver a baby. When we got to the hospital, I could feel the baby pushing down. I could hardly believe it; the doctor had said the baby was big and had warned me of a long and arduous labor, yet here I was, walking to the labor room three weeks early with water pouring down my legs and my baby wanting out.

While I was being wheeled into the delivery room, I heard Dr. Stanton and Jack Solomon, then Pamela's voice, and Noel's. I smiled. They had taken every precaution they could. And how lucky I was that Noel wasn't at Base Camp. But what about Peter? Another pain, deep and hard; it made me gasp, but then it receded, and I could breathe once more. Pamela's face was bending over me. Suddenly I was overwhelmed with the need to see Peter. A sweaty fear washed over me. As if without Peter, we would be doomed. But then there was more pain engulfing me and I could hear myself calling for Peter, my voice coming at me from a long distance, and then the baby moving within the pain, a great movement, and I felt as if I were being buffeted by a wave. How I longed for Peter's voice! My heart sank in disappointment, and then a deep blackness engulfed me. I struggled to see something, anything. But nothing. Had I died? I wondered. The blackness came over me again.

A nurse bent over me. "You have a beautiful eight-pound boy, Lily, the best-looking baby we've had in a long time." And in my room, waiting for me, were Pamela and Erik, their faces shining with relief. At that moment they both looked years younger than they were. Pride poured from their eyes, as if I had actually done something, as if this weren't a matter of colossal luck.

I tried to say so, but my speech was thick and sounded peculiar. "They gave you some gas," Pamela explained. "Just a little gas, at the end. He was such a big baby, Lily."

When Larry Stanton came in with Noel, they were both smiling broadly. "A huge baby, Lily, healthy as a horse and wonderfully alert. He looks three months old already," Noel told me. "A boy . . ." I nodded and stared behind him. Where was Peter? Why hadn't they called Peter? And then he was there, bursting into the room, his purplish eyes gleaming.

"I got here just in time, Lily—Erik called. I arrived just after they put you out. I saw the baby born," he said triumphantly. The others slipped out of the room as Peter approached. He had a towel streaked with blood in his hand. "I helped wipe him off," Peter told me. "He's beautiful, Lily, absolutely beautiful." He kissed my hairline, my temples, then pulled out a handkerchief and wiped my face. I could feel the sweat dripping onto my neck. "And so fast—you're a demon, Lily, a positive demon. I told them 'Anton,'" he added. I nodded. That was the name we had decided on, Anton, after Peter's grandfather. Anton Fialka, born at Box 1663.

The nurse brought the baby in and placed him in my arms. He looked so small to me, yet he was heavier than I had expected. I traced his features with my forefinger. Then, silently, Peter and I inspected the baby's torso, limbs. We looked into his dark, still no-color eyes. Felt the fineness of the black fuzz on his scalp, the incredible softness of his skin. Our baby. Anton. Tony. He reminded me of History's little boy, but he was moving, scrunching his fingers together, crying. Helplessly, I looked at Peter, who smiled, and then the nurse came and took the baby away. I felt as lightheaded as if in a dream.

Peter sat on the edge of the bed, pulling the blanket a little so that it tightened uncomfortably around me. But I didn't care. At least he was here. I had felt so lost when he wasn't.

"I have to go back now, Lily. The meeting—they're still having the meeting," Peter explained. I shrugged. No strength even to wish him good luck. No, now I just wanted to sleep.

When I woke up, I felt guilty. And a little embarrassed. It had been so much easier than I'd expected. It seemed vulgar to have had a baby so fast and with so little pain.

But Pamela and Erik were delighted; their beaming eyes greeted me when I woke up from dozing. They looked as if they had settled in for the duration. Finally it dawned on me: They had made a pact with Peter to stay with me if he couldn't. They had planned it all without me.

"Don't you have to go home to cook?" I asked Pamela. "You know, I'm fine."

She smiled and shook her head. "The only thing I have to do is be here," she told me.

• • •

Peter was bitterly disappointed by the meeting in Oppie's office on the day of Tony's birth. His voice broke several times as he told me about it, and his eyes were dull with misery.

"Oppie said no one knew beans about the situation in Japan, and then confessed that he didn't feel comfortable about making policy. What a joke. The director of Site Y doesn't feel comfortable making policy, but making a bomb is fine." Peter shook his head as if he still couldn't believe it.

"He mentioned the possibility that it might not go off, 'the awful possibility' he called it, and the committee went on and on about that, until Oppie finally said their conclusion was: 'We can propose no technical demonstration likely to bring an end to the war; we see no acceptable alternative to direct military use.' They didn't even address the issues in our petition; they were polite, but I might as well have been invisible. I can't understand it, Lily, all Oppie had to do was open his mouth and they would have listened. But he didn't."

What was going on that we didn't know? Or understand? Were the Japanese gaining ground that we didn't know about? Or was it simply, as Jacob had so coldly pointed out, that no one wanted to see the expenditure of two billion dollars go into a mere demonstration? Secrets, and more secrets. The fact that not only Groves but Oppie might be seduced by the promise of fame and power that a war-winning gadget would bring had, simply, not occurred to us.

The men went back to work, exacting, exhausting work that now involved constant travel back and forth to Base Camp at Alamogordo. Their route was the Jornada del Muerto, the Journey of the Dead that had been traveled by the refugees of the 1680 Pueblo rebellion.

While the men were working, their wives visited me because I had the newest baby. One morning, when I was putting Tony down for his morning nap, Bess came up the path with her baby, Barbara. On her arm was her lightship basket, which she had taken to wearing all the time. When I remarked on it, she said, "No use saving it, Lily," but I knew it was more than that. Today she had a present in it for Tony.

Then, within minutes, History arrived with Jane, and Steffi with Andrea. I made coffee and we chatted while the babies gurgled at the ceiling or slept. We sat contentedly, sipping the coffee, eating the coffee cake that Pamela had sent up when I came home, talking babies and laundry and what I called "commissary talk." The kind of benign purring that is undoubtedly good for babies, which is probably why women have been talking that way over babies' heads for centuries.

But suddenly the conversation shifted to Arlene Feynman and Richard, who had been as stoic as everyone might have expected and had refused any comfort when he returned from Albuquerque.

"I don't understand it, you'd think we might have had something, a memorial service, a prayer, something," Steffi said.

"He didn't want anything. Richard is a very private man," History said quietly.

"I don't think it's hit him yet," Bess offered. "He's so exhausted, I don't think he really knows what has happened."

I nodded. They were all exhausted. But then I asked myself: Did they need to be exhausted so they wouldn't think? So they couldn't think about what they were doing and what the consequences would be? I made the mistake of saying it out loud.

"What consequences? That this horrible war will finally be over? That those animals in Japan will surrender?" Bess's voice was harsh, even though she spoke in a whisper.

"They're not animals, Bess. They're people, like you and me. Like all of us." History's voice was patient, resigned.

"But they're different from us, History—they're yellow. Do you think Truman and Stimson would be thinking so seriously of using the gadget against Europe, against people who are white and have the same culture that we do?" My voice was angry.

There it was. I had said the unspeakable. Of course it was you, Lily, their silent eyes said to me. No one else has the nerve to say such things. But it was out, and now they were staring at me, speechless, shocked.

Finally Steffi asked, "Oh, what's the difference, Lily? Could anything be worse than Hamburg or Dresden? It's all horrible, and the sooner it's over, the better." Get it done, her eyes said. Just get it done and let me out of here.

But Bess couldn't let it alone. "It isn't the same. The Japs are vile, disgusting and vile, and deserve whatever we can think up to destroy them." Her eyes filled with frustrated tears.

No one replied. The air around us had darkened with tension, and one by one they gathered their babies up. I tried to thank them for coming; they scarcely answered me. All they wanted was to leave and get home.

● ● ●

A few days after that Erik went back to Washington, and Peter went to Base Camp. I had thought I would find it strange not to go to work, but I was so busy with the baby and getting my strength back that I hardly thought about work. Jacob had visited me in the hospital and was very pleased to see such a beautiful, healthy boy. More than that would have been not only unnecessary, but also inappropriate, so I was surprised one morning about a week later to pick up the telephone and hear his voice. It was hoarse, low. My heart sank.

"Can I stop by, Lily?" he asked.

"Of course," I replied, then nervously tried to decide which to straighten first, the house or myself, and eventually did neither because Tony wanted to nurse.

But as soon as Jacob pushed open the door to the apartment and I saw the letter in his hand, I knew what had happened. I still don't know quite how I knew, but I did. Steffi's face on the day of Roosevelt's death came back to me, as it would over and over again, long after we had left this place.

The letter was written on airmail paper and addressed to Jacob. It was from Sabine Leibholz, Dietrich Bonhoeffer's twin sister, who was living in England. It began with an explanation that she thought it best to write to Jacob, so he could break the terrible news to Steffi.

Then, translating from the German, he read to me:

On the morning of 31st May, Pastor Rieger telephoned to us from London and asked whether we were at home because he had something to say to us. . . . Soon from the window I saw our friend arriving at the house. The moment I opened the door to him I felt fear. The expression of his face was so pale and drawn that I knew that something serious had happened . . . then Pastor Rieger said with deep sadness, "It's Dietrich. He is no more—and Klaus too . . ."

Somehow I had been living wholly for the moment when I

could be reunited with Dietrich in a new and better Germany
. . . Now I felt as though all the lights had been put out.

Then there were details: Dietrich had been moved to Buchenwald, then taken to Flossenburg and shot by a Nazi firing squad
on April ninth. Klaus Bonhoeffer and Rudiger Schleicher had been
shot in Berlin, and Hans von Dohnanyi had been moved back to
Sachsenhausen and killed there.

Four young vital men in one family. I didn't know how parents
could live through that. My arms enfolded Tony and held him
tighter.

I looked at Jacob. For the first time since I had known him, he
looked completely bewildered. "I didn't think it would end like
this, Lily. I kept thinking that no news was good news, and we
hadn't heard anything, and then when Hitler killed himself—well,
I thought it was only a matter of time till they rounded everyone
up and sent them home." He paused, then paced a little.

"It wasn't so farfetched. He made it almost up until the end.
That's what's so awful. He almost made it." Then Jacob shuddered
involuntarily. "I can't really imagine a world without Dietrich,"
he added softly, "but we have been living in it for almost three
months. And we haven't died. So I guess we'll survive." He
sounded old and sad. Sadder than I had ever heard him.

He stood up. "I'm sorry I did this to you. But I needed a place
to gather myself together, to get some strength . . ."

We went into the kitchen, and I heated some coffee. He accepted
it gratefully. We drank it in silence, and then he rose again. He
had to go.

"I think she knows, Jacob. I think she's known for months," I
told him, remembering Steffi's face the day Roosevelt died.

"I'm not sure, Lily. Hope is a powerful thing. Sabine is right.
Now all the lights have been put out. I don't know how she'll take
it. I'm worried for her." But I knew he would take care of her, no
matter what.

Then he took my hands and slowly rubbed his thumb along my knuckles. Flesh against flesh. It never failed to comfort. Our eyes met briefly, but we said nothing.

Then he leaned forward and his lips grazed my cheek. "Goodbye, Lily," he whispered, then hurried out.

23

Almost unbearable heat. We had had heat like this before—that pressing heat of last summer that no one seemed to remember but me—but this was different, this was heat compounded by anxiety. Anxiety and loneliness. For almost every one of the scientists had gone to Base Camp or was planning to go to Compania Hill to witness what they hoped would be Trinity, Oppie's name for the test of the gadget. Only the scientists and Groves's men would be there to witness the greatest triumph of research ever achieved, or what might be the most dismal failure of the war.

"It's just a test, Lily. It may be nothing; the whole thing may not go off. A dud, they're calling it, on the basis of some measurements. Maybe they were right not to have a demonstration. If it's a dud, at least only we will know." Peter shrugged.

I looked up *test* in the dictionary. The word came from *testum* in Latin, a particular kind of earthen pot used by alchemists in the Middle Ages to examine metals they wanted to turn into gold. When I told Peter, he said, "I'll tell Oppie. He'll like that." Then he was off again.

He came home for a day, Friday night to Saturday night, went over some calculations with Bethe and others in the Theoretical Division, and took off again for Base Camp at about eleven o'clock that night. I wanted him to stay until morning, but he said it would be better if he left that night. He didn't want to go down to Base Camp tomorrow in the group of buses that were scheduled to go. "I can't bear being in a group right now," he explained, then we kissed and stood over Tony's crib and watched the baby sleep.

Before I could say anything more, he was gone. "No good-byes, Lily," he had warned me a few weeks ago. And no talk of what might be: that they might all be killed down there, or burned by radiation. That I certainly understood; no point in talking about anything you couldn't control. And he had to be at Base Camp, just as he had had to be in the canyon or at Hanford or anywhere else. That seemed part of the bargain we had made when we came.

But I wondered why he couldn't have refused to go to Trinity. Stan Ulam did. And no one seemed to think twice about it. Like Bartleby. I would prefer not. So simple, why didn't we think of it? For the first time in months I thought of Sophie and Dan Schweren. We would prefer not, they said. She's a mild-mannered, vague-looking girl, very blond and green-eyed, a pushover, someone once called her when we were back in Ithaca. Some pushover. It had taken a lot of strength to buck the tide, and they had done it. And now I thought about Dan's face, his black piercing eyes, his strong chin—very like his cousin Tom's—and his seamed mouth when he was determined. "It's against every principle I hold dear," he had told us, curiously formal because he felt pressed to the wall. "Atomic energy or power, a replacement for gas or coal or water power, is one thing. That I would work on, but weapons, no, that's where I draw the line. You will open a Pandora's box of evil." That is a fact, and I cannot come. No excuses or apologies. I am a free man in a free country, and this is my decision.

The pessimist and the optimist, he and his cousin. One with an absolute abhorrence of weapons, the other who seemed fascinated by the process, who couldn't stay away from the most dangerous experiment.

Now I envied Sophie Schweren, taking care of the new baby girl they had had last fall, pushing the stroller up and down those hills, seeking relief from the muggy Ithaca summer at the shores of Cayuga. How calm and safe her life sounded to me these days!

Or why couldn't Peter go to Compania Hill where Teller and Bethe and Lawrence and that reporter from *The New York Times* were going? That was twenty miles away from Ground Zero; surely it must be safe if they were taking the reporter there, mustn't it?

I have a clear picture of what is called the Trinity site because I drew myself a map based on what Peter has told me: Ground Zero, with the tower on which the gadget will be placed, south of that Base Camp, where Noel and Sir John Anderson from England and Kenneth Bainbridge and the others have created their headquarters, and between those two places—roughly 10,000 yards south of Ground Zero—the South Shelter, which is a bunker beneath the earth, like a bomb shelter, with a concrete slab for a roof. This will be the control center for the test, and another bunker 10,000 yards north of Ground Zero, called North Shelter, will house recording instruments and searchlights. The only building that was there before the Army arrived in the late winter was a ranch belonging to David McDonald, which was being used as a field laboratory and headquarters for the MPs. It's about 3500 yards southeast of the tower at Ground Zero. The only markings on official maps of this area are Oscura Peak and the Jornada del Muerto to the west. Peak of Darkness and Journey of the Dead. What is in between, on the map I have made does not officially exist, and if it's totally destroyed there will never be any cartographer's proof that it ever existed.

In my mind I see Peter in all the places on my map at once: on the tower, in the shelters, at the McDonald ranch, though, of course, that is impossible. Just as impossible as it is to know what the range of the gadget will be. Or as impossible as knowing for sure that Peter will come home safely to me.

All the men in our immediate group of friends are there: Jacob and Herb and Mark went down in the last group of buses, and Tom and Lenny and Noel have been down there for days, Noel for weeks. Even Erik is there. He arrived from Washington two days ago. Rumor has it that he was called by people close to Oppenheimer and asked to come, "so he could calm Oppie down."

But the one thing that didn't fly out of Pandora's box was hope. "A powerful thing," Jacob called it ten days ago. And what we must live on for the next twenty-four hours.

When the hailstorm came this afternoon, we thought the heat would break, but if anything it got worse: a thick haze of heat, more like New York or Washington. I walked over to Otowi after the hailstorm, carrying Tony in my arms, because Pamela told me I must bring the baby and be there by three o'clock. "So there will be time," she said, her voice unusually authoritative. I had no idea what she was planning; all I knew was that when Peter left the last thing he asked me was, "You will see Pamela tomorrow afternoon?" What was she talking about? Time for what?

She isn't here. Only Estevan is here. When I push open the door, he gestures me to sit down. The baby stirs in my arms, and Estevan looks at him briefly, then smiles. Nervously I pluck at my skirt. I have avoided Estevan since that evening last summer when he spied me at Tsankewi. Since then his eyes have been either neutral or inquiring, as if to say, Oh, hello, Lily, that's you, isn't it?

"Where's Pamela? Isn't she coming?" I ask.

He nods. "She'll be here. She went out for a walk. She needed to pray," he says matter-of-factly. I feel so close to Pamela, yet how little I know about her. I have never imagined her praying. But it makes sense. And God knows we need some prayers today. "She needs to be outside," he explains. That I certainly understand.

Then he frowns and looks at Tony and me. He walks across the room and picks up a shawl-like weaving that has graced the back of the couch since I have been coming here. It is from Chimayo, green with a blue and cinnamon and yellow design. He runs his fingers across it, then looks at me. His voice is slow, deliberate.

"You know, Lily, that the Navahos always include some small mistake in their weavings, for they believe that if a weaver creates an absolutely perfect weaving, he is ready for death?"

I nod. Yes, I know that. Perfection has no place on this earth for the Navahos; it portends mortality.

"Well, the Pueblo weavers at Chimayo, and probably everywhere else, believe that, too." He rubs his finger across a half inch of the weaving and comes closer to me. Then he points to the faintest imperfection in the weave. "There it is. To be perfect is not really human," he adds.

Nothing more, but when he looks at me again, his eyes do not have that distant, questioning expression. No, now they resemble the eyes I knew when we arrived. Eyes as enigmatic as wells. But kind and sympathetic.

I can feel my body relax. I knew he would never betray me, but I never expected him to forgive me.

He tilts his head and looks at me holding the baby, then beckons me to sit. He takes the weaving and pulls a scissors from his pocket and begins to cut into it.

"What are you doing?" My voice rises in alarm.

"She told me to use this one, and you need something to carry the baby in," he tells me. "When we go up the mountain."

Finally I understand. Now I know why Peter was so insistent that I see Pamela today.

"Do you think we'll be able to see anything?" I ask. He shrugs, and bends his head to the cutting, and then the sewing. But why that weaving, why the one that Pamela has used every day that I have known her, and probably for years and years before?

When she returns a few minutes later, I turn to her with embarrassment, and, maybe, a little anger in my eyes. I feel so foolish, like a child being led through a maze by adults. But I cannot argue with her. Pamela's face is stretched with tiredness; its skin fits over her bones like a mask. Though it is summer when she is usually brown and healthy, her face looks chalky.

"It's the softest weaving we have," she explains, "and we didn't want to wrap Tony up in something scratchy. Besides, Estevan insists that this design is lucky. He says it brought his mother luck a generation ago, and that now it will bring you luck, too. That's hardly a proposition we can turn down, Lily."

• • •

The baby carrier fits perfectly: a wide band at the back of my neck and shoulders that goes under my right arm and then the actual pouch and another wide band that extends across my left shoulder. The baby's weight is distributed so that I can walk easily and have my hands free. A lucky thing, too. For we are picking our way quickly up the mountain path, and occasionally I need my hands for balance. We started around midnight, climbed for two hours, rested for a bit, and are now almost at the top. We are climbing as high as we can to get as good a view of the south as possible. Trinity is almost two hundred miles away.

It's almost five A.M., cooler now; a soft breeze blows from the north. History, Kate, Pamela, and Estevan are ahead; Bess and I hang a little behind. Thea is still back on the The Hill with Steffi, who couldn't seem to get herself to come. I am the only one who has brought her baby, because I am still nursing Tony. No one says a word.

Maybe Steffi is right. Why are we punishing ourselves? Wouldn't it be easier to hear the news in our apartments or at Otowi, where we are surrounded by what we know? But there is no way I would have missed this. And Peter knew it, and so did Estevan and Pamela; they planned for me to be able to bring Tony in this Indian baby carrier as soon as he was born.

As we walk, stopping now and then to catch our breath, I wonder if they are thinking, as I am, of all these crazy things—of helpless bodies strewn around that tower at Ground Zero and beyond, the blackened dead bodies of our husbands, or moaning near-corpses, still alive but suffering the agony of radiation burns. I remember the sores all over Tigger's body, Kate's face when she told me that nothing could be done to save him. Are we going to be left with husbands who have to be put to sleep?

I feel myself begin to tremble. Kate notices, and we slow down, find a place to sit.

"Maybe I should have stayed home with Steffi," I say.

"What good would it do? What's going to happen will happen. It's out of our hands."

"But how are we going to get through it?" I ask, feeling like a child. Help me, Kate, is what I'm really saying.

Her voice gets warm, nostalgic. "Try to think about how pleased Peter was to come here. I'm thinking about how pleased Lenny was to be asked to come here, about how honored he was that the great Fermi had come to Cleveland to see him personally," she says simply. "That was a very important day in his life. And one of the reasons we came was that they seemed to *have* to succeed. That was the premise on which we all based the decision to come here. Don't abandon it now." Her voice is firm, more confident. As if by convincing me she is also convincing herself.

"They're very smart, Lily, some of the smartest men in the world—why, you should know that better than anyone else. Give them the benefit of the doubt." Her quiet faith makes me feel disloyal, and when we walk again, a little faster now so we can catch up with the others, I think of Peter's face on the bus back to my parents' apartment that night after we went to Rockefeller

Center and saw Jacob and Steffi. A face full of pride and wonder. Can it be done? That was what he most wanted to know.

Why can't I see his face now? It has disappeared; no matter how hard I try, I can't see it before me. But I can hear his voice. Thank God, I can still hear his voice. So I walk to the overlook that Estevan has scouted for us, with Peter's voice murmuring into my ear—not even real sentences or words that make any sense, just the timbre of his voice in my ear.

The last communiqué from Base Camp said dawn, and now you can see a faint line of light breaking slowly over the distant hills, though most of the sky is still sheathed in darkness. A few of the women are wearing sunglasses, but no one thinks they are necessary at this distance. For days there has been talk about sunglasses, welder's glasses, suntan lotion, and all sorts of other precautions; when I asked Peter what he was going to do, he assured me that he would be careful. But how? He didn't offer any explanation, and I didn't ask.

Slowly we become like mutes, and finally all the mindless talk about baby food and diaper rash and gardens and the yellowing mesquite, which means a hot summer, stops altogether. In the early light the mountains glow with the gold of the aspens. The sky is a pinkish-gray. I can smell the aura of pine that comes so unexpectedly from the clumps of trees gathered together here and there, like soldiers at the ready.

I suddenly wonder about all the wildlife that throbs in the Jornada. What about the rattlesnakes and the tarantulas and the frogs and the Joshua trees and the mesquite and cactus and yucca? What will happen to them? The frogs that made the loudest honking love, the snakes and lizards that Peter told me they shook out of their blankets and boots in the mornings? The spiny cactus that goosed them if they weren't careful? Would the animals simply dive into the sand for shelter? Would the flowers figure out some way to hide their seeds so they could propagate again? Crazy questions, but at least they pull my mind away from thoughts of Peter and the others.

The baby moves; the motion of our walking has kept him asleep, but now the stillness wakes him. It is almost three hours since he last nursed, and he may be hungry. I move away from the others and open my blouse. His fist gropes in the air and his mouth opens; out of it floats an ordinary baby cry, a hungry cry that tears the silence. Everyone laughs, grateful for such a human sound. Kate motions me toward a rock that leans against another, so I will have a backrest, and slowly the baby's blossom of a mouth closes around my nipple and he begins to suck. A deep, primitive shudder of contentment surges through me as it always does, each time, no matter how tired I am or how preoccupied, that my body and the baby indefinably become one.

I breathe deeply, letting that involuntary ease overcome me, and suddenly, with no warning at all, there is a flush of yellow light filling the sky, as if the curtains of darkness were being swept away by a mammoth hand and the brightest sunlight were spilling through the universe. A garish yellow light that seems to splinter the sky and then rise a little, as if it were lifting the earth, as if everything we are and know were going to break apart in the lifting. I bend over the baby, whose mouth is still cupped at my breast, but he is not afraid. And besides, there is nowhere to go, no protection but my own body, and as my head comes closer to his, I see his dark, oddly greenish-brown eyes blink at the furious light, and I gather him closer, as calm as I have ever been in my life, though I am convinced that in a matter of minutes we will both be lifted from the rock and be thrown into the roiling con-catenation of light and blackness, wherever that blackness still exists.

Light pushing itself into the sky, shining madly, like some crazy person's idea of light, like the light a blind person might yearn to see—they told us, those who were closer—yet now turning a lurid greenish-yellow, and then a strange purplish-violet gush within that wide span of light, like a wave rising higher than the rest of the ocean. Even at this distance I sense that rising wave, and my body strains for sound, any sound, for mustn't thunder come after such wild slivers of garish yellow silvery-white light? But this is like nothing I have known before, not like the beginning of a distant thunderstorm or the northern lights. No, this is something different, something the world has never seen before—but what if the light never stops, what if it lasts forever? So now I clench my body onto this seat of rock in the wilderness, my hands grabbing the ledge on which I sit, barely conscious of Tony's rhythmic sucking, and I lower my head so that it touches the shawl and rests on my baby's body, for if we are going to be lifted into space and flung into eternity, at least we will be together.

How smooth the shawl is against my cheek. I am conscious of only one thing: this being that is the two of us, and I bend over him, filling my mind with the sound of his sucking, but soon Tony senses my fright and stops. His eyes stare into mine, and I pull him closer to me, and his sweet baby's breath engulfs me, and neither of us moves, for we are waiting soundlessly through time, although we haven't yet moved at all, although it is ridiculous really to talk about time, for time has been eclipsed by something larger, something over which I have no control.

At last, after who knows how long, I hear a long, low growl, like the most distant thunder I can imagine, and then I know that we are not going to be blown apart. The sound has resolved something, and soon I feel the touch of a hand on my shoulder, and a soft, "It's all right, Lily, you can lift your head now," and there is History standing next to me. When I raise my eyes, I see that the light in the sky is being pulled away by some invisible force and is much fainter now, and the rocks are gray and black and pink and white, and the aspen still glow their eerie shining gold, like light on the most beautiful hair, and nothing has been bleached white and dry, and all the color in the world has not disappeared;

it is there, every bit of it, in its tender majesty, and our faces are still the same faces they were when we scrambled up this mountain. Then I feel myself breathe, and I put my hand on my heart and can feel it beating. And soon I feel that familiar tug on my breast as Tony goes back, totally unconcerned, to his nursing.

My knees tremble, but I don't want to sit down, I want to walk and talk and even shout. But when I open my mouth nothing comes out, as if I were in a dream pursued by something frightening and cannot scream. I make an effort to swallow again and again.

"Well, it worked." Kate is the first to recover. I look at my watch—about twenty minutes have passed since the immense flash of light began. Silently we hurry down the mountain.

As I put one foot in front of the other, I realize that Pamela and Estevan are hanging back, and then I stop and look behind me. They are talking, Pamela has her hand on his forearm, and Estevan's shoulders slump as if he had been shot. I am glad I cannot see his onyx eyes. For I think I know what I would find. And as I turn and make my way down the mountain with the rest, all I can think of are Estevan's triumphant eyes on the day of the dances—when he wore his buffalo headdress and bent his great head and danced across the plaza that seemed to have been transformed into the endless plains and listened to the earth. That day belongs to another time, another earth, another planet.

On The Hill the news comes through an MP who cannot relax his hold on the rules even for this historic moment. It seems, we are told by his matter-of-fact voice, that there was a message from Oppie sometime between 6 and 6:30 A.M. to his secretary. A message that she was to relay to his wife—he shakes his head, then delivers it—"that she can change the sheets." And then, in the most discreet breach of security, the narrowest of smiles.

I am faintly aware of sharp gasps all around me. It seems that now, finally, we can really breathe. A chorus of breaths. Relief. Trembling. Even tears.

They are alive.

24

$\bullet \ \bullet \ \bullet \ \blacksquare$

They came back looking like men who have fought in battle. No wounds or blood or even blackened faces or tattered clothes, but like fatigued soldiers whose features are stamped forever by combat. Some were jubilant and relieved; some looked dazed with awe; others shell-shocked; still others grim and pensive. They were all exhausted, but whatever their mouths said, their eyes were the giveaway. Eyes scorched not merely with the weariness and anxiety and the light and the heat on their faces and the overwhelming sound of the blast, but also with the knowledge of what they had done.

Oppenheimer had quoted the *Bhagavad Gita*, "Now I am death, destroyer of worlds." But Peter said he preferred what Bainbridge had said to Oppenheimer, within earshot: "Now we are all sons of bitches . . ."

"It worked, Lily," he said before he got ready for bed. He shook his head. Then he added, in a voice I had never heard, "When I saw it start to rise, I couldn't believe its power, and I felt utterly forsaken, like the last man on earth."

What struck me most was Peter's amazement. His eyes were still

374 • Roberta Silman

wide from all that he had witnessed. When I heard him speak, I realized that, for all its exactness, this scientific endeavor—the most monumental organized scientific endeavor in the history of mankind—had been a mystery, even to them. Had the gadget worked far better than they had dreamed or even intended?

"I am death, destroyer of worlds." So dramatic. Peter was right, I much preferred "Now we are all sons of bitches . . ." Yet what about "Judge tenderly of me"? I wondered while Peter showered and I changed Tony. But I said nothing. Then, in the full light of afternoon, we went to bed, exhausted beyond belief.

Peter woke up only two hours later, too tired to sleep (it would take him weeks to be able to sleep through the night again). When I was awakened by Tony's cry, he was reading next to me from a folder he had labeled "Pros and Cons" last spring. His face was worn and troubled.

I brought Tony back to bed to nurse him; Peter kept on reading. When he was finished, he put the pages back into the folder and said, "It will be like burning them alive, Lily, worse than the firebombs, and God knows they're bad enough. We must try to stop them. Maybe now they'll listen. There's been talk of a demonstration in the Tokyo harbor. I hope they'll go for it."

Hope, that last gasp.

It sounded so right, so reasonable that morning, which would become known as the day of Trinity. I imagined physicists and statesmen—everyone who had seen it—having similar conversations with their loved ones. But for all I had learned here on this mesa, I was still an innocent in the ways of war.

• • •

At the party at the Oppenheimers' that began after dinner that evening, I remember shining, flushed faces filled with relief and the effects of too much liquor—or tired, worried eyes. Nothing in between.

As I stood there watching, I thought about that party at the Wunderlichs' two years ago. That sense of expectation, of embarking on a great adventure was nowhere evident now. Nor were there pretty dresses and gorgeous food and wonderful music. No, tonight we were down to essentials, in pants and light shirts, our faces reamed with tiredness, yet also with triumph. Our husbands had done what many had said could not be done. And no longer would we have to ask that crucial question: What would happen to us? It had happened, they were successful, and tonight, at least, we were home free.

Yet the triumph was tempered by an almost palpable sense of dejection. These men who had been afraid of nothing, who had plunged ahead with great energy and pride in what they were doing, these men in love suddenly had the one luxury that had been denied them all these months: time to think. And now some of them were clearly worried.

Noel, Steffi, Jacob, Erik, History, Herb, Bess, Mark, Kate, Lenny, Thea, Tom, and the rest—everyone—even Pamela was here. But not Estevan. As a friend of Pamela's, of ours, he had clambered with us up the mountain. Yet I doubted that Estevan would ever come to a party with us again. I heard that he was at a meeting of the San Ildefonsan Council. We had come and bulldozed their land and turned their gorgeous canyons into a mysterious factory. And then we had unleashed the gadget on their beloved desert. I could hear Erik pressing us, "What do they think of all this?" he wanted to know. And now? What would they do now with the legacy we had left them? Of course Estevan was at a meeting, and there would be dozens and dozens of meetings after this one.

Trinity had taken place without their consent. And there wasn't a damned thing they could do about it. What would happen now was really out of our hands, too, for we were as helpless in our way as the Indians were in theirs. The scientists were a cog, an important cog, but just a cog in a huge machine.

Now I looked around for Peter. I had told him when we came not to worry about me, I would make my way, and he had been talking to Erik since we arrived. But I was too tired to make conversation; it was better to stand here in the shadows and let the excellent scotch flow into my toes and fingertips and create a pleasant blurry haze in my brain. We could leave soon, I knew; Peter had promised we would stay only long enough to show our faces.

I looked up. The sky was clear, that deep purplish-black speckled with stars. Not even twenty-four hours had passed since the gadget had unleashed all its power into this place and into this air and sky, yet the universe showed no trace of it. Here was the blackness in its usual place again. As I shook my head, I felt someone touch my elbow. History.

"How fast the earth has recovered. It's like a miracle," I said, thinking of the last words of *Moby Dick*. The New Mexico sky had become a shroud, like that great shroud of sea that covered everything—the whales and the men and the blood and the murderous impulses and the meanness, and also the honesty and the nobility and the innocence.

"But will it ever be the same again?" she said. "We can't see anything as we look out, but what is really out there? What have they really done?"

I could always count on History to ask the right question.

• • •

Two days later a top-secret cable from George Harrison, Stimson's aide, reached Stimson in Potsdam where he was with Truman. In it was coded news of Trinity. "Doctor has just returned most enthusiastic and confident that the Little Boy is as husky as his big brother. The light in his eyes discernible from here to Highhold, and I could have heard his screams from here to my farm."

What it meant was that the Little Boy, the bomb earmarked for Japan, would undoubtedly do the job as well or better than the bomb exploded at Trinity; it also told Stimson and Truman that the flash at Trinity had been visible for a range of 250 miles, and the actual blast had been heard for 50 miles.

Truman was in a tight spot: the Japanese were the canniest enemy the Allies had encountered. The last island campaign had been Okinawa, a bitter eighty-two-day battle during which 12,500 Americans and more than 100,000 Japanese were killed or missing. Russia still had not declared war against Japan, which Truman wasn't even sure he wanted. If he was beholden to Stalin for putting down Japanese troops in Manchuria, what would that mean regarding Poland? And even George Marshall, who had favored a demonstration of the bomb for the Japanese and Russians, was now worried that continued conventional bombing of the Japanese might not be enough.

Not everyone agreed with Marshall. Admiral Leahy felt that using an atom bomb was morally wrong, and Eisenhower hated the idea of the United States being the first country to use such a terrible weapon, especially when Japan seemed close to surrender. LeMay wanted to use more conventional bombs against Japan.

But strangest of all was Stalin's reaction. When Truman told him about the Trinity test, he said, "I am glad to hear it and I hope you will make good use of it against the Japanese." Truman couldn't fathom such a casual response. That Stalin might have already known about an atomic weapon being developed in the United States didn't even occur to Truman.

And then there were the estimates of how many lives would be lost if the war continued. They ranged from hundreds of thousands to almost a million in Churchill's view. Time was crucial—the important thing was to act and save American lives. Everyone was tired of this war.

What we did know were the reactions to Trinity at Los Alamos. In a desperate eleventh-hour measure, Peter and Herb drew up another petition calling for a public demonstration and for the government to consider international control of the bomb. But

Groves quickly took care of that. He decided the petition came under the heading of "Secret" and insisted that it be filed away.

Erik was indefatigable. "Now that you have seen it," he said at Otowi, in the labs, wherever he could assemble a few people, "you must get something down on paper to urge international control of such a shattering, awesome weapon. Now that you've seen it, you know that whatever comes after this will be more powerful."

But the mechanism of war is relentless, even more relentless than Erik's superhuman persistence. While we were recovering from Trinity, the wheels of war were turning in their inexorable way. Trinity had been a plutonium bomb; now the first uranium bomb, Little Boy, was being transported from Los Alamos to Tinian, a small island in the Pacific near Guam. There preparations were being made by the crew of the *Enola Gay*, the B-29 named for its pilot's mother, to fly toward the Japanese mainland. Not for Tokyo again, for there was scarcely anything left of Tokyo after the firebombing except the Imperial Palace.

No, this time the target was the one designated by the Target Committee. A city that had suffered no damage so far in this war, a city that had been spared because it was important to see exactly what the destruction would be if an atomic bomb were to be used. A city that was the 2nd Army headquarters for Japan, with 50,000 soldiers, but that also had 290,000 civilians. A city built on a delta, surrounded on three sides by mountains, and divided by seven rivers. A beautiful city that meant "wide island," revered because in ancient Japanese tradition water meant sustenance, life. A city that no one had really heard much about before. It was called Hiroshima.

● ● ●

The tower at Ground Zero had, literally, evaporated into thin air. Where it had stood was a crater 1200 feet in diameter and 25 feet deep at the center. And where there had been dull ocher desert sand was now a jagged circle of green, a huge flower of "trinitite." A green ceramic substance resembling jade that glittered like jewels in the sun. The pearls of Trinity, it would also be called, the process that produced it unique. The heat of the atomic fireball had scooped up the ashen grains of sand and hardened them into this glassy matter. Why green? Something to do with the temperature at which such a process takes place. A beautiful, iridescent green.

So beautiful that a local artist wanted to be the first to use it for a collage. She called Groves's office and got no response, then Oppenheimer's office. She made such a pest of herself that finally an MP was ordered to see her. She greeted him in a negligee. "I could see everything," he reported ruefully. She wasn't young, but she wasn't old either, and she was prepared to make any sacrifice to get a piece of that beautiful new substance. But he was a good soldier, kept his distance, and informed her that no one could have one of the "pearls of Trinity," because it could contain dangerous, even lethal, substances. Then, reluctantly, he left.

No trinitite for art, not yet, at least.

All that was left of the snakes and lizards and frogs was an occasional fossil, a carbon shadow embedded in the trinitite. About a half mile away from the tower some eviscerated bodies of jackrabbits were found. Apart from that there were no signs of life or vegetation within a mile of the crater. And all the grasses and yuccas and Joshua trees and mesquite and cactus, every bit of sturdy desert vegetation seemed to have been carried away by the heat of the fireball. The sensation of the very earth lifting, which I had felt so many miles away, seemed to have been a real force near Ground Zero.

A blind girl on her way to Albuquerque with a relative had sensed the incredible light of the explosion, even at a distance of a hundred miles, and had asked, when the flash suffused the sky, "What's that?"

Because the gadget had been detonated only 100 feet up in the air there was less blast than expected and more radiation. If there was to be an atomic bomb used in warfare, the scientists concluded that it should be exploded at a much higher altitude. That would insure more blast and less radiation.

When radioactivity from Trinity was measured by monitors in the desert, it was shown to have occurred in a swath at least a hundred miles long and thirty miles wide. The radioactive dust was white; cattle were rumored to have lost their hair; angry farmers greeted the soldiers monitoring the test with shotguns; and lawsuits began against the Army within a month after the test.

The McDonald ranch still stood, but the doors had been pulled away from hinges bent like overused coat hangers. The window glass had exploded and lay in shards on the floor and the sandy ground outside.

Oddly, there was no smell in areas affected by radioactivity. But right near the crater a peculiar odor hung around for weeks, an odor of singed hair or fur combined with something metallic that attacked the nostrils and made those who stumbled on it hold their breath. Anything to avoid inhaling the putrid stench.

● ● ●

Because of our phone I was the first in our row of apartments to hear. "They did it. Hiroshima has been destroyed," Peter's voice said when I picked it up on the afternoon of August sixth. Oppenheimer had called a meeting and had stood there with his hands clasped over his head to make the announcement, he told me. My mother had always said she never trusted anyone who lifted his hands over his head when he had to tell a crowd something. Strangely, that was the first thing I thought of as I waited with

History for Peter and Herb to come home. And then—relief. Newscasters were predicting that the war would be over in a few days. Finally our parents and friends back East would know what we had been doing and why we had been sequestered on this mesa for so long.

History and I played with the children and spoke as little as possible. There was nothing to say, so we listened to the radio and heard the atomic bomb that had exploded over Hiroshima described as "the greatest achievement of organized science in history." We heard reports of jubilation in Europe and in the Pacific, where young men now knew they might live instead of die.

Bess called a little later, wanting to know if we were going to La Fonda to celebrate. Her voice was excited, happy. "Isn't it wonderful, Lily? Isn't it wonderful that the war will finally be over?" she asked.

But the war wasn't over yet, the Japanese had not surrendered, and we had no desire to celebrate. No, that we couldn't do.

"Celebrate what?" I asked.

"Celebrate the end—which is in sight! Come on, Lily, everyone's going," she said. That was a lie. I could hardly imagine Mark going, but Bess and Mark were rarely together these days.

"I'm afraid not, Bess."

Then she hissed into the phone, "Spoilsport! You and Mark and the rest of them, you make me so angry . . ." she began, then hung up. Spoilsport. It was a word my brothers had used. But this was no game.

The next day the scientists gathered in the theater and saw the photographs that had been taken of Hiroshima. The burning sky, the blackened ash of buildings, the dead in what had once been streets, and the living floating down the rivers, where they hoped to find relief from the fire that was engulfing them. But the rivers themselves became fire. Rivers of fire. About 100,000 killed, and God knew how many more had suffered radiation burns. "It was a hell on earth, and this is just the beginning," Peter said when he came home. Then we sat there silently, watching Truchas fade in the dying light.

And still the Japanese didn't surrender. The Russians declared war on them on August ninth, and the next day Fat Man, the first plutonium implosion bomb ever used against an enemy nation, was dropped on Nagasaki, a city surrounded by steep hills. This time the blast was not as great as at Hiroshima, and 70,000 people were killed. By the time the Japanese surrendered on August fourteenth, we were numb.

When he realized there was no way he could stop the inevitable, Erik had returned to England. He had failed, and there was no reason to stay at Los Alamos any longer. "It was terrible," he wrote when he got news of Hiroshima, "especially because no one here really understands what this means, they can't even conceive of the radiation and the misery that has only begun." He also reported on some of the German scientists who were being held on a country estate not far from London.

"Otto Hahn was so upset by the news of Hiroshima that his fellow prisoners feared he might try to take his own life. Max von Laue and the others stayed with Hahn and talked to him for hours. He became more and more agitated, but finally, near dawn, he fell asleep, utterly exhausted."

Then the letter went on, "I don't think Hahn will ever get over this." Erik was right. Hahn never recovered from the shattering news of Hiroshima and was filled with despair and self-reproach until he died.

● ● ●

A week after the Japanese surrender, when we were beginning to realize what this would mean in our lives—that we could begin to think about the future, what we would do, where we would live, who might stay here and who might go—Tom went off to the Omega lab whistling, as usual.

Today it was Mozart. "The Mozart Requiem," Tom replied when Lenny asked him what it was. "It's beautiful and full of life." Then, with a shake of his head, "Doesn't really sound like a requiem to me."

Once again Tom was working with two spheres of plutonium. This experiment was similar to the dragon, but it was done by hand. Since the Trinity bomb had been such a success, the research had continued. The end of the war did not mean the end of atomic weapons research. Now they were trying to verify theoretical calculations about the behavior of the plutonium spheres. As usual, Tom was prodding the spheres along an aluminum rod with two screwdrivers. Seven of his colleagues stood there watching him. Slowly Tom moved the spheres toward each other. Closer and closer. His control was amazing. But then, it always was. He was the coolest experimenter any of them had ever seen.

Suddenly a dazzling cobalt light filled the room. It took the others a second to realize what was happening. This weird, blinding glare meant the spheres had become critical, releasing lethal radiation. A scrape of feet moving backward. Then dead quiet as they watched Tom tear the spheres apart with his bare hands, interrupting the chain reaction.

The men were transfixed. Only seconds had passed. Yet they had seen Tom save their lives. And now they heard his calm voice instructing them: "Stand where you were when you saw the glare." In the eerie silence the men went to their places. Tom went to the blackboard and drew a diagram of where everyone had been standing as the spheres became critical. "This is so the doctors will know how much radiation each man has absorbed," Tom explained. As if nothing had happened. It was unbelievable.

In awe they heard Tom call to Lenny, who was working in the

next room, "We need a car to take us to the hospital. I think Noel's car is nearby."

"They'll be all right," Tom told Lenny as Noel started the car. "But I don't have a chance." And then he did a calculation on the back of an envelope as to how much radiation he had absorbed.

I was in the kitchen making dinner when Kate burst into the apartment. Her face was distorted, as if she had had a stroke, and as soon as she saw me, she fell into my arms and started to sob.

Here it was. What we had all feared, what I had unconsciously been waiting for. Would we be spared? How many times had I asked myself that question? Well, I knew now that we would not.

Tom knew exactly what he had done. He gave himself ten days. His voice was flat, resigned. "There's no hope, so don't waste your energy needlessly," he told Lenny.

Kate looked at the telephone. Thea. We would have to call Thea, for the doctors had their hands full.

"I'll do it," she said, then added, "I'm older." She was as direct as possible. "Thea, this is Kate. . . . There's been an accident. . . . Tom. At the hospital." The simplest of words. Yet it wasn't the words that told Thea what had happened. It was the silences between them.

We met her at the hospital. History came with us. We had wiped our tears and daubed our faces with powder. When Thea got out of the car, her face was hopeful, her head high. He must live, he has to live, we have too much to live for, her eyes seemed to say. But when she saw us, she knew. A film flitted across her eyes. She had been waiting, too, I suddenly realized, remembering her reluctance to discuss their love affair. She had never believed they might live happily ever after.

The treatment for Tom was ice. By the time Thea got to him his hands were plunged into buckets of ice. For the first few days Thea sat at his bedside, and no one except the doctors and nurses invaded their privacy. They talked and she read aloud to him, and when she needed to catch a few hours' sleep, Tom read to himself because Lenny had rigged a reading device that turned pages whenever Tom pushed a button with his toe.

"It's beautiful, Lenny," Tom said when Lenny brought it to him on the second day. "As beautiful as your guillotine." Only Tom could talk like that. Only he could still think the guillotine, or any piece of equipment connected with this place, was still beautiful.

I knew without hearing it what he would say. "I took a risk by doing that experiment, Lily, and my hands slipped. That was part of the risk."

The rest of us weren't so philosophical. We took refuge in silence. A strange, spectral silence descended over our lives while Tom lay there in the hospital. A silence as pervasive as that sirocco-like wind that sometimes blew uneasily across the mesa.

On the second day, as if he had been aroused from a deep sleep, Jacob suddenly realized he had to call Dan Schweren. Peter was with him when he made the call. And then we waited for Dan's arrival.

The doctors pumped Tom full of penicillin, he had a dozen blood transfusions, but by the sixth day his speech was becoming blurred and his mind fuzzy. Jack Solomon insisted that Thea go to bed in a nearby room, and while she slept, the rest of us took turns sitting at Tom's bedside. The pain must have been excruciating. Yet never once did Tom cry out or complain. This is my fate, his eyes said, and I must accept it.

On the fifth day Peter and I went to Lamy to collect Dan and his wife, Sophie, and they stayed with us.

They were stunned. "We were so sure that everyone here was safe. After we heard about Trinity, how no one had even been hurt, we were so relieved. It never occurred to us . . ." Sophie began, but she couldn't finish. And Dan couldn't speak. Not even when Oppie came to see him. He listened to Oppie explain about the dangerous experiment, how brave Tom was, how sorry we all were. Dan listened, his mouth pressed into a deep line, then nodded, and turned on his heel.

In my head I heard Peter say, "Now we are all sons of bitches." That was what Dan thought, I knew. And I didn't blame him.

But while the rest of us buried ourselves in a sad silence, Thea was unbelievably brave. She watched the doctors try everything as Tom's hands ballooned to several times their normal size, as his body became covered with radiation burns, as he faded into a never-never land where he had no idea who we were or who he was. Yet she never gave up. Each day I would see her tall figure walking to the hospital, and I marveled at her dignity, her grace. She was convinced after he fell into a coma that he could hear her, and she continued to read to him. I was astonished to learn that one of the books she read from was *Moby Dick*. "He had always loved it," she told me.

Sometimes I wondered if they had ever talked about this happening. Odd. They never talked about marriage, Thea had told me, yet I could see them talking about this. And during those two weeks, Thea retained a good deal of the radiance she had had before. At least I have known great happiness, her body and her eyes seemed to say, and it gave the rest of us the courage we needed to face what was coming.

Tom Schweren died twelve days after the accident in the canyon lab. Hundreds of people came to the short funeral conducted near Tunyopin by his cousin, Dan. Tom was buried near History's baby, Robert, and after the burial, his close friends went to Pamela's for a meal. After that we sat there quietly drinking wine and listened to a scratched recording of Beethoven's Ninth on Pamela's victrola.

Yet there was never a news report from Los Alamos of the radiation accident or Tom's eventual death. The government and the rest of the world weren't ready for that yet. So, although everything else was out in the open now, this remained concealed.

What should have been a dignified death became, at Box 1663, a shameful secret. And even that didn't destroy Thea. She wore that radiance of their love like a badge of honor.

She wears it still.

1982

25

Life never goes in that straight line that you think it will when you're young. Ahab doesn't always end up harpooned to the whale, their destinies linked into eternity. Mysterious twists and knots sometimes tangle the line of life in unexpected ways.

After Tom died, Noel and Mark left Los Alamos in Noel's rackety car. I watched it go through the gate in astonishment. They had come to say good-bye, brief, almost formal good-byes, no explanations, no regrets, nothing, and then they were off. We heard they spent six months hiking and camping mostly in the Northwest and Canada, and then Noel returned to England and Mark went back to MIT. At the time of the Klaus Fuchs trial, Noel was investigated because he was part of the English mission, as Fuchs was, but, of course, they didn't find anything linking him to Fuchs. I never knew David Greenglass, Ethel Rosenberg's brother, who had been a technician at Los Alamos, but even those who did know him were surprised to learn of his spying.

Mark and Bess were divorced, and Mark married a small, dark, intense woman named Eva. They have four children; Mark seems happy, almost gay, compared to the man we knew at Los Alamos.

Over the years he saw his and Bess's daughter only when she came East. He refused from the beginning to return to Los Alamos, where Bess still lives and works as a librarian and archivist. People who have seen her there tell me she lives a quiet life, taking pleasure in her job and her spacious office, where the patchwork quilt, finally finished, now hangs.

General Groves and Oppie left Site Y triumphantly locked in an odd symbiosis we didn't understand until almost a decade later when Oppie was investigated by the Atomic Energy Commission for his opposition to the hydrogen bomb. His early ties to the Communist movement before he came to Los Alamos were denounced, he was humiliated and betrayed by some of his former friends, and he was denied further access to secret, classified material. Only then did we realize how complex the relationship between Oppie and Groves was at Los Alamos, and why it was so hard for Oppie to buck the general and speak out against military use of the gadget.

Thea stayed in Santa Fe, which was her home, after all, and continued to work for the Army at Los Alamos. She and Bess still go to Pamela's for dinner once a week. Pamela, still active in her eighties, and Estevan live at Otowi, and once every few months either History or I hear from Pamela or Thea. Steffi was probably as close to a nervous breakdown as anyone could get when she and Jacob returned to Cornell, but slowly she recovered. She raised Sam and Andrea and teaches German at Cornell. Although we live in different cities, History and Herb and Kate and Lenny and Peter and I have remained friends, and we see each other as often as we can.

And Jacob? Peter and I saw Jacob and Steffi occasionally after we left Los Alamos: at the memorial service for Fermi in 1954 when everyone was overcome with sadness—for how could that vibrant, confident man be gone forever?—and when there were reunions, or at conferences, and once, absolutely by chance, at the

Metropolitan Opera on a snowy night in January when we stumbled on them during the first intermission of *Der Rosenkavalier*. Jacob was always happy to see us and would usually make some comment about my appearance—that my hair was longer or shorter, or that I had a tan, or that I was still as thin as ever: the kind of remark no one found odd from an old friend but that never failed to make me blush slightly. And that would only prove to him what an easy mark I still was.

Yet I can't honestly say that I felt very much on seeing Jacob. I noticed his hair growing white, then thinning, I saw that the lines in his face had grown deeper, I would observe his gray eyes darting around crowded rooms—searching, always searching, for what? I wondered—and more often than not I would feel those enigmatic gray eyes finally rest on me. I was guilty of turning my better profile toward him more than once. But that was only vanity, to tell him that I had managed, as he'd known I would, very well without him.

As the years passed, I would sometimes almost gasp as I remembered some intimate detail of our time together, how his hands or lips felt on my skin. But those are visceral reactions, helpless reflexes of the flesh, and as I got older, they became rarer and rarer. There were often months, then years when I scarcely thought about Jacob, and when I did, I was so detached that I was another person, another Lily—"Lily Bart, Lily Briscoe, Joyce's Lily in 'The Dead,' Lily of the Field?" I could hear Jacob's low voice asking me. All those Lilys I had told him about. No, none of those, but someone still within me whom I scarcely knew anymore.

Until one day in 1974, a gray March day when the wind lashed at the house and the sky was a thick, soupy gray. A package arrived at my office at Brandeis, where I taught two courses in American literature, addressed in Jacob's hand. I knew I would want to open it at home, where I couldn't be disturbed, and I was relieved when I got there that Peter was still at work.

Slowly I went upstairs to my study, Anne's old room. I opened the package warily. I felt, if anything, an odd weariness. Would this never be over? I wanted to ask.

It was a notebook, a black marbled notebook that was sewn together, like the ones I had had as a child, the kind my children had also had but that you hardly ever saw anymore. Frayed at the edges with a faint, scorched smell.

The covering letter was short, to the point:

Dear Lily,

I have stomach cancer and they are going to operate next week. I don't know what the outcome will be, but whatever it is, I think it's time I gave you this. It has really belonged to you all these years, and each time I knew we were going to meet, I brought it with me, but somehow there never seemed to be a right time. Now it seems right.

J.

Here was his legacy to me.

JULY 13, 1945 *This is another kind of war, a war without combat, without foxholes or artillery or unremitting noise or mines or seared flesh or blood leaking from mutilated bodies, though we may have some of that soon enough if we fail. None of the scientists talks about the possibility of failure, but it is here like a faint odor that you cannot identify. Not enough really to smell, only something you get a whiff of now and then. The machinists and technicians are more open about it. More practical about everything, even the possibility of death. Only last night I overheard one of them say, "There's really nothing to worry about, mate, if it happens you won't know what hit you anyway. Not a bad way to die. No blood and guts. Clean. A big explosion, then you're gone." I didn't have the heart to contradict him, for surely it won't be that easy. Madame Curie taught us that. Yet there's still so much we don't know about this gadget, what's the use of speculating?*

Better not even to admit the possibility of failure and concentrate on all the careful specifications that have to be met as we do all that needs to be done for this test.

As you know, it's called Trinity. God. His Son. And the Holy Spirit. Isn't that what it means? No one even thinks of it; we're not exactly the most religious bunch out here. I remember my mother when she tried to explain to me the difference between Jews and Christians. She was very firm and clear when she said she didn't believe Jesus was God or even the son of God, but it was quite possible, even probable that he was a fine teacher and a prophet. But no, she couldn't believe in the Trinity, the Holy Spirit, or the Virgin Mary, and there was no such thing as an immaculate conception. It was simply an impossibility and the people in this world who believed it did not have a proper grasp of reality. I never forgot her using that phrase.

Sometimes I think that our nerve in thinking we could create this gadget is just as bizarre and unbelievable as that Trinity or the immaculate conception, and that we, too, do not have a proper grasp of reality. I'm sure that's not what Oppie had in mind when he named it. He said he was reading Donne. A sermon, someone said it came from, or something religious. But it couldn't be a sermon, the rhythm isn't sermonlike, it's a poem, I think one of the Holy Sonnets, though I haven't had a chance to look it up yet, and I know it only in German, so this is probably a poor translation, but I think it goes something like this: "Batter my heart, three person'd God, for you/ As yet but knock, breathe, glow, and look to mend/ That I may rise and stand. Throw me over and bend/ Your strength, to break, blow, burn and make me new . . ." It's the "make me new" that I remember, and a professor in some survey of literature telling us how wonderful Donne was in English, a good reason, along with Shakespeare, to learn English. Little did I know when I was eighteen and sitting in a class that I really didn't like that I would spend most of my life speaking and thinking in English, or, wonder of wonders, writing to you about that poem.

Make me new. Well, we have done that, and now we shall see how it goes.

Such a completely different kind of war out here, our secret war that has been fought in this New Mexico desert, our private war in which intelligence and precision matter in ways never before known, where things are not as chancy most of the time as on the battlefield, but at other times more chancy, and just as tense, just as scary. Death seems to have settled in here, but is that so surprising, Lily? After all, this is the end of the Jornada del Muerto, the Indians' famous Journey of the Dead.

This desert is the bleakest place on earth, not even the Sahara could be so bleak, it seems to me, but of course I don't really know. The sand and dust are those neutral buff and gray colors of deserts everywhere, and they are like a premonition of death—in our eyes, ears, mouths, noses, everywhere; our bodies have become repositories for this blowing heat and dust and grains of sand, nothing more. We are ghosts covered with it, learning to feel as little as possible so that our brains can work as quickly, as efficiently as possible, in isolation from our bodies.

A fitting end to our labors, I sometimes think.

Death's work in this land of death.

JULY 14. *In the tents at night people read; I share a tent with Segrè and Fermi and Herb Lerner. Segrè is reading* The Counterfeiters, *Fermi has a bunch of scientific journals he is catching up on, and Herb is reading Ovid's* Metamorphoses. *He says it's how the world started and he's never read it, and he wants to be able to tell those stories—those wonderful stories of Phaëthon and Icarus and the rest to his children. History knows them all by heart, she read them in Latin when she was a girl still in high school, and it's time he knew them, too. The irony amuses me, and Fermi too, for he smiled broadly when he saw it, but it seems to have escaped Herb, or if he's aware of it, he's not talking. No* one seems to have much talk, and all I can hear as I write to you, Lily, is the turning of pages and the almost constant clearing of our throats that has become as much of a reflex as breathing in this place. And the scrape of my pen along the pages of this notebook.

You are the only thing that seems real to me, Lily, the only thing that has seemed real in these past months while I have walked through my life like a robot. Oh, I think of Steffi and Sam and Andrea, and I know that I want to see them again and hear their voices and feel the children's soft, sweet skin against mine. I know that once this is over—if we get out of here alive—Steffi and I will make a decent life with each other—for the children, if nothing else.

But it is you, Lily, your incredibly alive face and eyes that are like a spark in this valley of death. It is because of you, Lily, that I want this test to succeed, that I do not want to die an ignominious statistic: one of the "geniuses" who thought they could overwhelm nature and perished in the horrible conflagration they invented and engineered themselves. What a news report that would be. Or would they keep that secret, too? And simply let all you widows and children return to your lives without even an explanation?

I can see your stern glance, Lily, your silent admonition to me not to make jokes about such serious, important things. Yet if I can't joke, and to you, then surely this life isn't worth living. I bought this notebook intending to keep a diary of our time here at Trinity, Lily, but what I wanted to write, I realized when I began last night, was a letter to you. A long uninterrupted letter that you will not have to type, one that will tell you now, at this time when our lives are on the line as they never have been before, how much you mean to me.

I could never even say "I love you" when we lay there in that cave that had been warmed so beautifully by the sun, or that one time when we had the luxury of a bed. A shabby bed in a place that could hardly even be called a hotel, but for us it was the only *bed we had, and it meant a lot to me that we were able to have it when we did. You wanted me to tell you how much I loved you there and in the cave, and I think you began to distrust me when I couldn't say the words, when I couldn't admit to you that saying those words made me feel like a cheap adulterer. That in some crazy, perhaps warped way, I believed that if I withheld those words I wouldn't be so unfaithful to Steffi, or that I wouldn't loathe myself quite so much. It is so hard to explain; but it was important to me that I never say it; I guess I was like someone who might refuse to perform some small physical act with a lover, something that might be special to a wife or husband. I could see you wondering—after we made love or even sometimes in the office when you would look at me with a bewildered look on your face—if I was just a cad, some evil cad who always took a lover (isn't that how those smart English novels put it? Michael Arlen and the rest?) because his marriage had not turned out the way he hoped.*

I couldn't say "I love you," Lily, until I knew I would lose you that day in my office. But by then it was too late. I guess I was afraid that if I talked about it while we were still together, I would tell you more than you needed to know, more than anyone needs to know about my marriage to Steffi, and that that would be its own kind of evil. So I chose the lesser kind and made up my mind that I wouldn't mention the word love, *that I would never say it but simply let my body express as well as it could what I felt, what I know I never felt before, what I know I shall never feel again.*

You were a gift of light, Lily, in a life that had grown increasingly dark, and it is that gift that makes me want to live as long as I can. You made me feel alive, Lily, more alive than I have ever felt in my life, and now I know I can stay in my marriage and do what I have to do professionally and still be an honorable man. A man who lives a decent, upright existence and hurts no one in the bargain. As long as I have the memory of you.

———

JULY 15. *I know I have disappointed you in these last weeks. I didn't fight the military bureaucracy and Groves hard enough for you, and some small part of me—and of all of us, I think, though of course I cannot know—wants this test to fail, so that we won't be responsible for all that this bomb will bring to the world. Yes, you and Pamela and History are right, this weapon will change the world forever, in ways that none of us can predict, and probably not for the better, but surely the world will be changed after this war. So much of what happens in war goes on in back rooms among politicians. We aren't as powerful as you would like to believe. You and some of the other women, and Erik and the rest of them.*

Yet part of me also wants it to succeed. It is, as Fermi is so fond of saying, "Superb physics," and no physicist, even the ones who are so worried about the future, like Erik and Peter, can deny what an accomplishment this weapon will be if it works.

You can feel the exhilaration and the excitement mixed in with the fear. Like those gods in Herb's Ovid who thought they were invulnerable, and who became powerful and strong and, yes, arrogant. For something in each of us knows it will not fail. We are too smart for it to fail. So we walk around in the dark, wondering what it will be like, for sleep is out of the question; now the test is just hours away.

A little later I am overcome with doubt. There is no assurance that we will succeed, and the proof of that seems to be Oppie. He looks like a ghost, worse—if you can believe it—than he did as the corpse in Arsenic. *A walking ghost, and when I see his worn features, his exhaustion, I am reminded that all this strutting is just show, and that we can fail as well as succeed, and he knows it, too. But people keep moving and talking and walking, some playing poker, others placing their bets on all the odds Fermi has cooked up as to how well the gadget will perform, and the air is so thick with dust and anticipation that we can scarcely breathe.*

Oh, how I wish you were here, Lily, so I could see your beautiful face at least one more time. Yes, beautiful. You don't know it because, like most women, you confuse physical features with beauty, but beauty comes from inside, it is an inexplicable radiance. No one can describe it, but everyone can recognize it. Except, perhaps, the person who has it, because beauty never appears in its full glory in a mirror. That's just one of those laws of life, maybe even a secondary law of physics.

Do you know one of the things I regret most of all, Lily? It's such a small thing that I am almost embarrassed to say it, but I must. I think I regret most of all having to keep our love secret, not being able to walk into a room with you and have your beauty declare that I was the person who was making you happy.

But even if the world couldn't know, we knew. And we made each other happy, and now that you have taught me a little better how to live, I don't want to die.

That was it. I read it over and over again. His handwriting was firm, clear, and a little larger than usual. As if he were still a child practicing penmanship in this child's notebook. And the ink meant he had brought his fountain pen with him—and a bottle of ink— and that he wanted it to last.

I think he believed these words when he wrote them, and I was glad he sent the notebook. It is never too late to receive a letter like that one. As I sat there holding it, I was engulfed by memories—sharp, intense memories of being with Jacob. Maybe it was better that I hadn't known then how much he loved me.

But even as I sat there with this beautiful love letter in my hands, I knew that Jacob and I did not believe in the same things. His world was more gray than mine. Good and evil were not so clear to Jacob as they were to me. I knew that when we were at Los Alamos; it was why I knew that we must part. And somehow I knew even then that Jacob would live his life very differently from Peter. For more than anyone else, except maybe Oppie and Teller,

Jacob was seduced by the lure of the gadget and the power he thought it would bring. He became rich doing research for the military, and he worked for years on the hydrogen bomb. He seemed to need that edge of danger to make life interesting. And whenever I saw someone from The Hill after we all left Los Alamos, they would never fail to tell me about Jacob's love affairs. But maybe he was simply more resigned, more of a realist, than I could ever be—either then, or now.

And yet. There are always "and yets," I had learned. As I stood there with his notebook in my hand, I couldn't really say I was sorry. I had loved this man who, just before Trinity, could make promises about how he would live when he thought he was facing death, and who could talk about love when he was consumed by fear.

Knowing him—and loving him—had informed my life in ways I couldn't have ever suspected when I was young. Perhaps that means that I am not a good woman, just as Jacob is not a good man. But there it is.

Jacob was seventy when he had the cancer operation. What the doctors found was a malignancy but nothing as bad as he had been led to expect. He and Steffi still live in Ithaca, and Peter and I see them occasionally when we go back for a visit. Jacob has grown more introspective and has clearly slowed down since his surgery. That teasing expression in his eyes is hardly ever there anymore. He has become, as many older people do, less interesting than the stories that are told about him.

But he is always a subject of conversation when a group of us meet. What a provocative teacher he was. How he filled up every room he entered. How he became a great reader of American novels and English poets and was occasionally invited to give a lecture combining physics and literature. Now the stories come more and more frequently: that he no longer works for the military, that he adores his grandchildren (there are seven), that he doesn't have a mistress anymore, that instead he has taken up gardening. He and Steffi work together for hours in their garden, which is known for its Japanese section and which has been photographed in many national magazines. "But he still plays the piano every day," the reporter inevitably concludes, as if that were a virtue that could balance out the flaws.

Maybe it is. But playing the piano beautifully is not proof of a man's goodness. That much I have surely learned. Still, he brought all the tenderness that I had loved so much to the music when he played. That's why people loved to hear him. I sometimes thought when I listened to him play that he might have become a concert pianist if the war had not occurred. So I'm happy for him now, especially when I heard someone say, with a mixture of admiration and envy only a month or so ago, "Do you know that Jacob gave a small Schubert recital at Cornell, and several famous musicians and a critic from *The New York Times* were there?"

"No, I didn't," Peter answered. "But I'm not surprised. He always loved Schubert—why, one summer he must have played everything Schubert wrote for the piano. And when he played those pieces, they were like a prayer."

I stared at my husband, wondering if he was trying to tell me something, but his eyes were as clear as I have ever seen them.

26

• • • ▬

After our unexpected visit with Tony at the Trapp Family Lodge, we didn't see him again until Passover. He and Jo came down from Maine with the children, and Anne and her family came up from New York. We read out of our Reformed Haggadah the story of Moses, the parting of the Red Sea, the Four Questions. We sang *Dayenu*. At the end of the seder Tony and Jo showed Peter a different Haggadah. *A Haggadah for the Nuclear Age.* All the ancient events had parallel references to modern times. Peter leafed through it, shrugged and smiled. The arms of that octopus we called the Manhattan Project were spreading further and further, into places we could not have dreamed of.

"What can I say?" Peter asked his children, his usual defensiveness gone. But in his eyes I saw something new, something that frightened me. I am too old to justify myself endlessly, his eyes said; I want to be left alone to do my work and enjoy my family. I am not even willing to argue, as an intellectual exercise, the pros and cons of the issue any longer. I cannot keep defending the past.

I thought Tony was going to push his father further, but he simply closed the Haggadah. Then Stephen, Tony's oldest child, said, "It's interesting, though, isn't it, Grandpa?" Peter nodded, and for a moment their eyes met. My brain reeled backward, and I could almost hear a strange grind of the clock's hands. It seemed as though someone were in this very room turning them backward.

Suddenly, before me is Erik, talking about peace and openness on the day Tony is born. Erik's eyes are excited and smiling; he's amazed to see the baby, my baby, an almost nine-pound boy born in less than an hour. "Marvelous," he says over and over again in his low mumble. "So quick, never have I seen a baby born so quickly. You are a magician, Lily." His voice grows stronger, clearer. But the admiration isn't only for me and this beautiful baby who is lying so peacefully in the basket next to my bed; the admiration is also for this baby's father who has gone back to Oppie's office to speak for the views that Erik believes in so fiercely. And so while Peter speaks for Erik, Erik becomes a stand-in for Peter, and etched forever in my memory of that day are the sweetness of Erik's expression and the awe in his voice. He has forgotten the problems of the world for this short time, to witness the miraculous birth of a child.

And now, thirty-seven years later, Tony's child, the eldest boy whose middle name is Erik because Tony loved Erik when he came to visit us, was talking to his grandfather about the nuclear age. I stared at him, speechless with the eeriness of it. The child spoke as if Erik were inside of him. Is the passage of time measurable by clocks and calendars, or by people who seem to reappear in other people? Who continue to live through succeeding generations? Who reach from their graves to fight for their beliefs?

When I last saw History, she shook her head a little and said, "I don't understand time." And then we laughed. A woman named History should be able, if anyone could, to understand time. But she doesn't. Neither does anyone else, I suppose. At this very minute, I felt as if I were back at Los Alamos, on the breathless hot June day of Tony's birth, or even years later, when Tony was a little older than his son, and we were sitting around this same table at Passover or Thanksgiving, and he, too, was beginning to talk about the atomic age.

I turned to watch Stephen. His almost black eyes were gazing at his grandfather, his famous grandfather whose name is in the encyclopedia and in the history books and can even be called up on a computer, they tell us.

Will it ever stop? I wondered.

The scene came back to haunt me through the spring, and when Anne called to say that Tony would be speaking at the disarmament march in New York in June, I told Peter I planned to go.

"Would you like to come along?" I asked him.

He shook his head. "I'm not a marcher, Lily, you know that. But you go. It will be an interesting experience, and you'll have a chance to see History." We smiled at each other. That was something I could never resist.

• • •

I step off the train at Rye, and there is History waiting for me. I feel her arms encircle me, the soft fragrance of her cologne floating into the air between us. Briefly her lips touch my cheek. Two women in their sixties, old women to the teenagers observing us from their bicycles, but still young in our minds. It is a gorgeous day, and when we drive back to her house, the New York suburbs are festooned with the soft pastel blossoms of June: the peonies and rhododendron and laurel and even a few of the late long-lasting azaleas, barely moving in the verdant air.

So sane and peaceful, these New York suburbs. So far removed from anything dirty or unpleasant. Miles and miles of beautifully cared-for houses and radiant green lawns and glowing, healthy bushes. Not even a clothesline visible to spoil the view. To the uninitiated who have not read novel after novel of the pain in those houses, these neighborhoods must look like the modern version of paradise.

They remind me of the gardenlike campuses around Boston: those idyllic, enclosed, protected quadrangles where only the highest forms of learning occur. But Boston doesn't have such tidy outskirts as this part of Westchester; even the old white elephants of Brookline look shabby and more interesting than these manicured, smug, winding lanes near New York.

History reads my mind. "I thought when the kids grew up we would move back to the city, near Columbia, where it's really like a neighborhood, more like the real world. But when the time came, I couldn't bring myself to give up this boring serenity. I have to tell you, Lily, that once I finally got used to it, I have actually learned to like it. The temple and the library and the garden club and all the things we thought were so stupid back then. I've become a stereotype of the suburban matron."

As usual, she's too modest. She has brought up four successful children and run a busy household for her famous physicist-husband, she has gotten her Ph.D. in history, and she teaches courses in the Renaissance part-time at a local college. In many ways she is the most successful of all of us. Of course there's Kate, with six kids, but no degrees; and Steffi and I with two children apiece. But none of us has had great careers, and compared to women ten, fifteen years younger, we aren't very impressive.

I wonder if anyone has ever done a statistical study on the energy it takes to be married to a brilliant, well-known scientist? Yet isn't that what all this noise these last years has been about? No more brilliant, famous men in traditional marriages; now there will be brilliant, famous women!

When we pull into the driveway, I begin to feel a sense of suppressed excitement. I glance quickly at History, but she only smiles. Maybe one of the children is here. Maybe Jane has come to join us. She lives in Minnesota and is a doctor with a husband and two children, but maybe she has decided to come to New York for the march.

Although I can feel myself getting more and more curious, I know better than to spoil History's surprise, so I pretend I don't suspect a thing. But even I am astounded to see Thea walking out of the side door toward the car. A regal Thea of almost eighty. As straight as a girl, lovelier than ever with her crown of white hair braided around her head.

"I came for the march. When I read about it, it seemed the right thing to do. And anything for a trip East," she explains as she gathers me into her still-strong arms.

We stay up much too late that night, much later than Herb, who smiles when he comes in to say good night around one A.M. Of all of us he has aged the least; his small wiry body is fit, and his hair is abundant and brown with only a few flecks of gray. He is going to join us tomorrow even though it is Saturday; he says his Judaism, which he observes more than he did on The Hill, has dispensations for peace marches. "You ladies better get to bed. I don't want to hear how tired you are when we're walking tomorrow," he says. But History just waves him affectionately away.

As we are walking out of Grand Central the next morning, two small, gray-haired women in our sixties, a brown-haired man also in his sixties, and one tall white-haired woman of eighty, all wearing sneakers, we pass a young woman in her twenties with long brown hair and gorgeous skin. She is obviously the leader of a group of women. On her left breast is a large round pin that says "Jane Wyman was right."

I am tempted to stop and ask her where she got it, but we go on, heading toward Fifth Avenue. The writers and teachers are supposed to meet near the Forty-second Street library. No one seems to know where the scientists are, and Herb wants to walk with History and me. And when we reach Fifth Avenue, there are people as far as the eye can see—up into the Fifties and Sixties and down into Greenwich Village. A sight as beautiful as an Italian piazza in midafternoon.

I look around and feel History press my hand. In front of us is Donald Barthelme and his wife. Next to him, a tall woman, wearing a hand-embroidered blouse. I have a feeling I know her, but it is probably from a book jacket.

Then I see Hope Eliason. Dressed in a terrific flowing silk outfit, she greets people as if she were the hostess at this party. But I hang back, behind Thea. History realizes what I'm doing, and though she's clearly puzzled, she joins me. Soon Hope disappears into the crowd.

"Who is she?" History wants to know.

"A physics teacher we met in Vermont in February." History tucks her arm in mine, and I tell her about meeting Hope and Ted Eliason in Vermont and the town meeting and seeing Tony.

A peculiar, expectant quiet stretches over the streets—so different from the usual relentless noise of this city. Walking down the middle of such a silent Fifth Avenue reminds me of those deep snowstorms I knew as a child when the upper part, above 59th Street, would be closed to all but pedestrians. "This was 'the country' at the turn of the century," my mother would tell us. "Cows and sheep grazed up here and all over Central Park in Henry James's and Edith Wharton's time. That's why it's called the Sheep Meadow." Where we are headed today. Where there is a platform and chairs and microphones and speakers—one of them my son—who will address this crowd.

For now, though, no cows and sheep, but people. Everywhere. People marching and people standing at the windows of their apartments and on the sidewalks and at the entrances to the stores and hotels; people watching us, smiling, even some old diehards giving Churchill's victory sign. I see faces I think I know, younger versions of faces I knew once. History meets her son and daughter-in-law, and from a distance I spy the Wunderlich children with their families.

Soon after we pass Scribner's bookstore, then Atlas holding up the world at Rockefeller Center, I feel Anne's arms close around me.

"Hey, Ma, it's so good to see you. I wasn't sure you'd make it," she says, her voice jubilant with pride. "Tony will be so pleased." She kisses the others, then takes in our clothes and our footwear, murmuring lightly, "The sneaker brigade from Los Alamos." History's head shoots up, a startled look flitting across her thin features, but no one else has heard.

Anne is wearing jeans and a light sweater and looks younger than she did when we last saw her. Her husband, Jon, and Lisa, their older child, are with her.

"Where's Natalie?" I ask, as I hug Jon and Lisa. Anne's second child is named for my mother, who died just before she was born.

"With Jon's parents."

Anne is proud of us, and her father, and the accomplishments of all the scientists she has known since she was a child. How many times have we talked together, she and I, about the Nazi threat, and then the men fighting in the Pacific, and the Japanese intransigence, and the political games Churchill was playing with Russia, especially after Roosevelt died. Like Tony, Anne knew Erik and loved him till he died almost ten years ago. Whenever he came to the States after the war, he would stay with us, and we visited him and his family in Denmark more than once. He was Uncle Erik to both our children, but while Tony sees Erik's life as a tragedy, his struggles and defeats symbolic of everything that is wrong with the world, Anne understands that Erik's life was a triumph and that his ideas have blossomed now—many years later—in this march, in Tony's work, in that chalked face asking *Wir Wollen Kein Euroshima* in *The New York Times Magazine*.

Yet not everyone feels as Anne does. Better not to identify us here, History's eyes warned. I know how she feels; I have felt it many times, in the most unexpected places, and each time I do I hear Oppie's voice in my head on the day he gave up the directorship.

That sparkling October day, a sky as deep as lapis, his voice resonant, low: ". . . If atomic bombs are to be added as new weapons of a warring world or to the arsenals of nations preparing for war, then the time will come when mankind will curse the names of Los Alamos and of Hiroshima. The people of this world must unite, or they will perish . . ."

The words are still planted so firmly in my mind. Perhaps because he spoke them so convincingly. Perhaps because the path seemed so clear. But it didn't happen. And we haven't perished. Still, Hiroshima has become a curse, as Oppie predicted. And Los Alamos?

As we near the Sheep Meadow, I see rows of Japanese women on the fringes of the march holding out brightly colored objects. I beckon Anne to follow me, and when we get closer, I see that the strings of color are necklaces made up of dozens of varicolored origami cranes. According to Japanese legend, the crane lives for a thousand years, and the folding of a thousand paper cranes is said to cure any illness. After Hiroshima and Nagasaki, the folded cranes became the symbol of those who were dying of radiation sickness. But now they have become another symbol, a symbol of peace, like our dove, and those crane necklaces are being offered to us by Japanese women as a gesture of peace and unity. And forgiveness.

"Oh, Grandma, look!" five-year-old Lisa cries as she takes one, examines it, then lets the Japanese woman put it gently around her neck. The woman is about my age, maybe a bit younger. Hard to tell, because their hair doesn't ever seem to grow gray. But she has lived through the war: You can see it in her eyes and the way she hands the crane necklaces to the marchers; you can sense it in her very presence here. I have something urgent to tell you, her whole body seems to say. You must listen.

Her English is impeccable but very slow. The words push their way out. "My family lived in Nagasaki, but I was away for the summer at an aunt's in Kyoto." She stops. I can feel my limbs grow rigid with fear for what she is about to tell us. But she says nothing more about her personal life. Only goes on to say how there is a huge movement for peace among the women of Japan, and the young people as well, and that this must never happen again. Then she hands Anne and me our necklaces and turns to someone behind us.

Batter my heart, three person'd God; for you
As yet but knocke, breathe, shine, and seeke to mend;
That I may rise, and stand, o'erthrow mee,' and bend
Your force, to breake, blowe, burn and make me new . . .

Jacob had it almost right. Batter my heart. Well, it did that at Trinity—then, and afterward, at Hiroshima and Nagasaki. And here, around us, on this mild June day, on Fifth Avenue in the city where I was born and grew up, are the remnants of those battered hearts as well. But not broken.

For a second I want to go back, to tell that woman about Trinity, how we saw that garish yellow light lift the sky so that for an instant the very world seemed about to fly apart, and how we knew, even at that distance, that it was evil, that it had no place in a world of our making, and how we were helpless to do anything about it, for by then it was too late, and besides, there was a war to win . . . But even if she would listen—a big if, indeed—what good would it do? What earthly good would it do?

Farther along there is a group of older women who have photographs of Hiroshima and Nagasaki, but that is all. No blame on their faces, no accusations; no, simply, this is the way it was. Here no one has trotted out the young women maimed by Hiroshima and who were shown, like freaks in a sideshow, in the fifties. The Hiroshima Maidens. Now they must be middle-aged. But they aren't here. No, here there is restraint and dignity and forgiveness. And grief.

We meant so well. But every beginning has an end. What will

you do with the whirlwind, my father asked. Did he know that the whirlwind would always end up in my head, bringing uncontrollable tears to my eyes? I gesture to Anne to go ahead with Lisa, for I don't want the child to see her grandma cry.

Now I am walking next to History and Herb and Thea again. All over the Sheep Meadow are people, lying and sitting and listening, for the speeches have begun. It's hard to hear, but every now and again there is the roar of applause.

I concentrate on the slow, careful articulation of syllables that is now coming through the microphone. If I listen very hard, I can hear words, I realize, and then in the next second it comes to me: Here are inflections I know. My son's. That slightly nasal *n* and *r*, the brief hesitation before the *s*. Now Tony is speaking, not at a town meeting in Vermont, but here in New York, before thousands of people. He is giving facts about nuclear arsenals. The very thing we hoped would never happen. His voice is calm, matter-of-fact. No fervor here, just facts, and reasonable conclusions, nothing like the breathless intensity that comes during war.

It was so exciting, so exhilarating to think that what you were doing would change the world, would really matter. I used to think that was what war was. But I was wrong. Wars before our war weren't like that, or wars afterward. No, there was never a time on earth like that, and there was never a place like that mesa. But that kind of urgency and—yes, I'll admit it—happiness and love and madness and push weren't because of war. They had to do with discovery. Of knowing that you have created something entirely new, something never before known, and of believing that what you have discovered can end the insanity that is war.

Make me new. Begin the world again.

That was what we thought we were doing, or wanted to think.

Then, this is the way it was. This is the reality. *Wir Wollen Kein Euroshima.* Judge tenderly of me.

I stand there looking at the sea of faces around me and hear again the thread of my son's voice. Our son, the baby who was born on the mesa and who watched Trinity at my breast. The helpless blinking of his eyes as I shielded him with my body from that silvery, splintered light. My limbs shaking with relief and fear and pride.

Through my tears I look at Thea and History and Herb. I cannot read their faces. Besides, they cannot help me. This is not between them and me. This is between me and my son. So I stand there quietly and listen to Tony's voice rise to stir this enormous crowd. I want to meet him with a dry and smiling face.

"Ma, you came, you really came," he will say, astonishment spilling from his eyes. He didn't believe me when I promised.

I must try to be calm. And try to see through the nauseous lurid light of Trinity that keeps blocking my vision of this sunny June day and the women carrying their babies in contraptions like the one Estevan made for me, that beautiful Chimayo weaving he cut and folded and sewed, then fitted across my chest so I could carry Tony up the mountain, and which I still have, wrapped in tissue paper, because it was too lovely to throw away.

But most of all I see the expectant, hopeful eyes of everyone who is here. And I listen: to the words of the speaker, who was the baby at my breast and is now my son. My son whom I love, and the son of his father, whom I also love.

I learned a long time ago that there is no sin of love, that the sins are of betrayal, ignorance, passion, adultery, pride. But they remain, along with the love. And there is nothing you can do.

Slowly my glance scans the crowd and I spot Anne. She's waving madly to attract my attention. Now a deafening applause washes over us as Herb and History and Thea and I make our way toward my children. The sneaker brigade from Los Alamos.

We move more slowly than we did then. How impatient we were! Always rushing from one task to another. War is like that. Exhausting, acute, then over. Surely that is part of its appeal. I must remember that to tell Tony.

But peace? Ah, that is another story entirely. Peace is so tame

compared to war. Peace has a sweet languor about it, a forgetfulness, almost a laziness. Yet that is all the more reason why Tony
is right, why we must be vigilant. For unlike war, peace has no
drama and no end. In peacetime you need more than faith and
brains; you need the strength of Atlas, of all the gods on Mount
Olympus, all the gods in every religion, everywhere. That's what
Erik tried so hard to teach us, and what each of us must learn so
painfully for ourselves. Patience and superhuman strength and a
tenacious vigilance that must never cease, is never over, but must
go on and on. Like that New Mexico sky that stretches into eternity, forever.